D0419145

JACQUOT AND THE ANGEL

Martin O'Brien

headline

First published in 2005
by HEADLINE BOOK PUBLISHING

1

Cataloguing in Publication Data is available
from the British Library

ISBN 0 7553 2285 1 (hardback)
ISBN 0 7553 2289 4 (trade paperback)

Typeset in New Caledonia by Palimpsest Book Production Limited,
Polmont, Stirlingshire

Printed and bound in Great Britain by
Clays Ltd, St Ives plc

Headline's policy is to use papers that are natural, renewable and
recyclable products and made from wood grown in sustainable forests.
The logging and manufacturing processes are expected to conform
to the environmental regulations of the country of origin.

HEADLINE BOOK PUBLISHING
A division of Hodder Headline
338 Euston Road
London NW1 3BH

www.headline.co.uk
www.hodderheadline.com

For Fiona,
with my thanks and my love

Part One

Église St-Jean, Cavaillon, Provence: June 1944

*I*t was a cart, clattering over the cobbles in the street below, that
woke Sandrine. She came to with a start, wincing at the tightness in her neck, the stiffness of her shoulders. She took in the dusty
boards, the panels of slatted wood and knew immediately where she
was, registering with a jolt of annoyance the soft grey light where
before there'd been only chill, inky darkness.

She'd fallen asleep. How many times had she stayed awake before,
waiting and watching? Yet some time in the night, in the belfry of
Église St-Jean, she'd let her cheek rest against her sleeve, closed her
eyes. Later, she would think how fortunate she'd been to pass those
last, lonely hours in sleep.

Slowly, stiffly, Sandrine eased herself into a sitting position and
peered through the belfry slats into the courtyard of the
Kommandantur *across the street. The single caged bulb above the
passageway still shone, but the puddle of gold that it threw on
the shiny black cobbles had faded with the light. She pulled back the
cuff of her coat and looked at the watch he had given her, its circle
of fat green numerals glowing with luminescence. A little past five.
Not long now. Soon they would come, up from the cells and out
through that passage, beneath the caged bulb, and she would watch,
and see him one last time.

3

There had been six of them left alive and four taken by the bridge on the road to Brieuc. Somehow she and Bonaire had been missed in the sudden, sweeping beams of torchlight, in all the barking and the shouts, the crashing through undergrowth, the pop of sidearms and the crackle of machine-gun fire. Side by side when the ambush came, they had managed to sink back down the bank and follow the river's tangled course until they were far enough away to stop and catch their breath. Downstream they heard two more isolated shots, and then, to their right, along the road from Brieuc, the sound of trucks passing, the juddering of brakes and the clatter of tailgates swinging down.

Both had the same thought. How had it happened? The Germans had been waiting for them. They were prepared. They knew.

Then the young Bonaire cursed and began to sob and Sandrine, woollen trousers wet and cold and heavy against her legs, felt the first great wring of loss, as though some part of her had been wrenched away and left there by the bridge.

He was alive, that was all she knew. But taken.

High in the belfry Sandrine shivered, drew up her knees and hugged the coat round her. It had been a long night but now, she knew, it was almost over. She'd come to the church the previous evening, attended Benediction and, according to plan, as she made to leave, she'd slipped through the curtain near the font and climbed the winding stone steps that led to this look-out. She'd made herself as comfortable as possible, eaten her bread and cheese and, as she sipped the Cognac in her flask, she'd thought of all the other nests she'd waited in, hunkered down, sometimes too stiff or too scared to move. In the hills outside Céreste, in the woods above Pertuis, peering into the darkness, heartblood pulsing in her ears, waiting.

Always waiting.

And listening.

Listening for the sound of an approaching train, supply convoy or enemy patrol, the snap of a twig or a muffled cough, or for the hollow, signal hoot of a nightjar that told them to prepare. But now, with so little time left, cold and alone, Sandrine thought only of him. So close: just across the street. If she shouted his name, he'd hear her. That close.

And then the steps came, distantly, the soft scuffing of boots on stone. She turned and pressed her forehead against the panel of slats, finding the best angle as the first soldiers stepped from the passageway and into the courtyard, rifles slung from their shoulders.

She counted them, as she'd been trained to do.

Nine . . . ten men, dressed in shadowy feldgrau uniforms, gathering together near the centre of the courtyard. Cigarettes were dug for and a match flared in cupped hands, darting like a firefly as it was offered round. For a moment Sandrine fancied she could hear them speak, but she knew she was too far away for that.

Then one of them laughed, the rough ring of it reaching up to her, and she wondered at it with a worn hatred. How could they laugh on a morning like this? How could they? But Sandrine knew their kind, knew they didn't care. They'd done this many times before, in this same courtyard, at this same hour. Just another way to start the day.

Before she could think any more about it, an officer strode out into the courtyard. Sandrine could make out the peaked hat set at a jaunty angle, the too-short field jacket and the sagging seat of his jodhpurs. She didn't need to see the twin shafts of lightning on the man's collar to know he was Schutzstoffel – SS. The soldiers flicked away their cigarettes, snapped themselves upright, then gathered around him.

The minutes ticked by. Another laugh, a shared joke.

And then they were there, the men she'd been waiting for, stepping out from the passageway, one by one, attended by armed guards.

Grion the Corsican was first, stooped and limping. He, too, had tried to run like Sandrine and Bonaire but he'd left it too late, chosen the open road and been brought down easily, the two shots they'd heard from the deep, damp shadows of the riverbank. The right leg of his trousers had been ripped away and a length of bandage ran from knee to thigh. He used a crutch to walk and his left arm was cradled in a sling.

Holding her breath, Sandrine waited for the next man. It was Jean-Pierre, tall and lanky, the electrician from Barjas who rigged *their explosives, and behind him, the boy Druout from Chant-le-Neuf.*

Then, last in line, pausing a moment beneath the light to gaze up at a sky he wouldn't have seen for the last three weeks – and would never see again – came Albert.

Albert . . . Albert . . . Albert. She wanted to run to him, take him away from that terrible place and hold on to him for ever.

Instead she watched him take a breath, roll his shoulders in that way of his, then start forward after his comrades, casting around with his single eye as though weighing up the odds on some last-minute dash for freedom.

But there was no chance of that. Not this time. Not in this place.

In a slow, straggling line, Grion first, followed by Jean-Pierre, Druout and Albert, the four men crossed the yard of the Kommandantur. All were bearded save Druout, and all four bare-foot, dressed only in the shirts and trousers they had worn beneath their jackets and coats on the night of the attack. Apart from Grion, each man's hands were tied behind his back.

One by one they filed past the officer and soldiers, and one after another they disappeared below the parapet that cut off from Sandrine's view the bullet-pocked wall and the wooden stakes where they would be tied.

Unslinging their rifles and working the bolts to check their load, the men in the firing squad lined up as the guards who'd escorted the prisoners reappeared. The last of them carried Grion's crutch and Sandrine gasped as he turned, swept it up to hip level and pretended to machine-gun the men tied at the posts. Then he shoul-dered the crutch like a rifle and, with a clowning swagger, joined his comrades behind the line of guns.

The officer shouted something, loud enough for Sandrine to hear his voice but not make out the words, then stepped to one side as the soldiers lifted their Mausers, put a foot forward, braced the stocks against their shoulders, took aim and fired.

Silent puffs of smoke, muzzle flashes, a second's silence. And then the sound, a short, sharp clapping of shots that ricocheted off the walls of the Kommandantur *and erupted over the rooftops.*

Above her, pigeons rattled off the belfry roof, wings flapping, whirling away into the morning sky, beady black eyes already searching out another perch.

And in her wooden nest, forehead pressed against the slats, Sandrine let the tears slide silently down her cheeks.

1

February 1998

As Madame Ramier would tell anyone who asked, it was not a
morning she would likely ever forget.

It was a Wednesday, the last in February, a bleak, beleaguered
time in the country around St Bédard-le-Chapitre when the ground
is as hard as iron and the vines are as bare and brown as a beetle's
legs. It's a time when clouds can gather in a moment and press
down with such malign intent that people forget the shape and
substance of shadows and start to believe the sun has gone for ever.

That was how it had been for the last few days, the widow Ramier
would tell you, low clouds screwed down tight as a lid over the
rooftops of St Bédard and the slopes of the Brieuc valley. But some
time in the early hours, under cover of darkness, those same clouds
had slipped away just as quickly as they had arrived. Now, at a little
after eight o'clock, a pale sun peered into a sky as blue as cobalt
and brittle as butterscotch.

That was how it was – bright and sharp, chill and crisp – the
morning Odile Ramier found the first body.

For Madame Ramier the day had begun like any other, sitting
alone at the kitchen table in the house that she shared with her
sister Adéline. Listening to the boards creak above her head as
Adéline moved around her bedroom, absently dipping the last of

8

Tuesday's Doriane baguette into the camomile and ginger infusion, which Adéline prepared for her every night, Madame Ramier had no idea – no idea at *all*, she would say later – what that winter morning held in store. Just the usual round of chores at the Martners' place, she'd supposed – polishing, vacuuming and dusting her way through their old farmhouse.

As she fetched out her Solex from the store-cupboard under the stairs, the only thing on Odile Ramier's mind was whether Madame Martner had remembered the beeswax polish for the oak dresser in the salon, or whether she should take her own. As she wheeled the moped down the hallway, Odile decided she'd trust to Madame Martner's memory and, reaching for her coat and scarf and calling out *'adieu'* to her sister, she manoeuvred herself and her bike through the front door.

Outside on the pavement – scarfed, gloved and snugly buttoned up – she tugged on a helmet and goggles, mounted up, tipped the bike off its stand, and started to pedal as it picked up speed down the slope. When the two-stroke engine caught, she stopped pedalling, sank her chin into her collar and turned left at the bottom of the *place*, leaving St Bédard along the Chant-le-Neuf road.

Twenty-three minutes later, red-cheeked and breathless, Odile Ramier returned to St Bédard, shoulders bent over the handlebars as though this position might provide some small measure of extra speed. Coming to an abrupt halt at the town's *gendarmerie*, she let the Solex drop to the ground, back wheel spinning, and hurried up the steps to report her discovery.

2

It was, everyone in St Bédard agreed, just the most dreadful thing. Certainly no one had seen its like since the last days of the Occupation. By the end of that Wednesday morning four bodies had been found but, as later reported in the national press with something approaching gruesome relish, there were five deaths in all.

Dr Josef Martner and his wife, Jutta, had lived on the lower slopes of the Brieuc valley for ten years, four miles north of St Bédard along the 'new' road to Chant-le-Neuf, which the Americans had put down at the end of the war. The couple, both German nationals, had bought an old farmhouse and twenty hectares of land, renovated and refurbished the property, then added a considerable extension to its eastern flanks. Built in the same stone as the original, it enclosed a prettily gravelled courtyard set with blooming terracotta pots, a small fountain and pond. Part of this extension, comprising one entire side of the courtyard, was a lofty, temperature-controlled hot-house in which the doctor raised and nurtured a celebrated collection of orchids.

It was in this farmhouse, in their first-floor bedroom with its wide stone terrace and breathtaking views down the valley, that the couple had died in their bed, killed by a volley of shotgun blasts that shredded the Provençal quilt covering them and rendered unrecognisable their feather-stuck remains beneath.

Downstairs, in the doctor's hot-house, sprawled among his highly prized specimen flora, lay their daughter Ilse, also despatched with a fusillade of close-range shots, those few patches of her cotton nightdress not drenched in blood sprinkled with a dusting of powdery gold pollen from the stand of scarlet *cymbidiums* into which she was hurled by the blast.

Unlike the others, the fourth body, that of Ilse's seventeen-year-old daughter Kippi, was found outside the house, lying spread-eagled half-way along the driveway leading to the road. Judging by her left shoe, a rope-soled yellow espadrille found some twenty metres behind the body, and given the ejected shell casings found midway between body and shoe, it appeared that the killer had chased after Kippi from the house, caught up with her when she lost the shoe, stopped, aimed and fired. Having brought her down, the killer had walked up, stood between the young girl's ankles and finished the job at close range.

As for the fifth death, that was only revealed later, during autopsy, and apparently leaked to the press by someone in the pathologist's office. According to this source the blonde-haired youngster had been three months' pregnant.

In the initial crime report filled out later that day by Sergeant Lanclos, sixty-eight-year-old Odile Ramier stated that she had found Kippi's body at approximately eight fifty-five in the morning. Madame Ramier also said that she had seen nothing unusual when she turned off the road to the Martner place. It was only as she rounded the curve in the driveway, she said, puttering along between the vines which surrounded the house, that she came upon the body, skidding to avoid it but managing to keep herself in the saddle.

Madame Ramier had not dismounted ('I did not need to: it was clear there was nothing I could do,' she had told Lanclos, with considerable composure), simply turned the bike round and sped back to St Bédard.

When Lanclos asked why she'd come back to town, rather than go on to the Martners' home and phone from there, Odile Ramier had given the old sergeant a withering look and replied: 'Do I look crazy? Miss Kippi had been shot. Maybe her killer was still in the house.'

11

3

Some forty minutes after Odile Ramier bustled through the doors of the St Bédard *gendarmerie* to report her find, Sergeant Lanclos, accompanied by his corporal, Frenot, arrived at the Martner property. They found the first body exactly where Madame Ramier had told them they would. As she had said, a glance was enough to establish there was nothing they could do for the girl, arms flung out, lying belly down in the dirt.

The two policemen left their car between the body and the road, then walked on down to the house, taking the precaution of drawing their guns just in case Madame Ramier's fear about the killer still being in the house should prove correct.

The front door of the farmhouse was half open, a strongly planked door studded with blackened nail-heads and set with exposed spear-tip hinges. Lanclos pushed it with his boot and stepped cautiously inside, followed by Frenot who, for reasons best known to himself, saw fit to shout, 'Police,' earning a glare from Lanclos.

It was at that very moment, standing just inside the Martners' front door, that Lanclos noticed a large crater, pitted with a halo of tiny holes, that decorated the wall above Frenot's head. It was clear that a heavy-calibre shell had done the damage, littering the tiled floor with chips of masonry and plaster. At their feet a fringed Oriental rug, also covered with plaster and stone, was rumpled and askew, as though someone had slipped on it.

Stepping around the rug, the two policemen made their way along the hallway, checking the salon, dining room and the doctor's study as they went. So far as they could tell, nothing had been disturbed, nothing appeared to be out of place.

In the kitchen, beyond the dining room at the back of the house, it was a different story. Here Lanclos and Frenot found an upturned chair and a stone-flagged floor dusted with plaster and scattered with the shredded remains of onions, garlic and dried herbs. On the kitchen table in the centre of the room, these were mixed with larger scabs of plaster and greying splinters of lath brought down from the ceiling by a shotgun blast that had punched a hole in it the size of a serving dish.

Lanclos and Frenot stepped cautiously round the debris.

'Jesus, what a mess,' said Frenot, looking up to marvel at the ceiling, while Lanclos tiptoed over to the sink, plaster and onion skins crunching beneath his boots. He leaned forward and peered through the window. Outside, the gravelled courtyard was still in shade, the surface of the pond covered with a thin white sheet of ice, unbroken save the lead spigot of a fountain in its centre.

It was the first time that Lanclos had visited the house since the farmer Taillard had lived there, and he marvelled at the changes that had been made: the old farmyard where chickens had once clucked around a long-armed water-pump was now enclosed by the three wings the Martners had added – a utility room and sun-lounge to the left, guest quarters directly opposite the kitchen and, to the right, the wall of the doctor's hot-house, its glass roof and side panels thickly whitewashed to protect the interior from direct sunlight.

It was there, with water from the sprinkler system dripping off the leaves, that Lanclos and Frenot found the second body, that of Kippi's mother.

At this point, the two men parted company. While Frenot hurried back to their car to call up Regional Crime in Cavaillon, as Lanclos had requested, the older officer holstered his Beretta and continued his search of the property.

Brushing drops of sprinkler water from his tunic, he left the hot-house and prowled through the adjoining guest wing. Both ground and first floors were empty, though each showed signs of recent occupation: a curled paperback face down on the arm of a sofa, a copy of German *Vogue* on the floor beside a Sony Walkman and a scatter of CDs, a supper tray on the coffee-table in front of the television, warm ashes in the fireplace and, in the two guest bedrooms, double beds with winter quilts pushed back, pillows crumpled into comfortable shapes and, in the shared bathroom, all manner of female toiletries. It was the same story in the sun-lounge, empty but clearly lived in.

Back in the main house, somehow certain there were more bodies to find, Lanclos returned to the entrance hall and climbed the main stairs to a long, galleried landing with three doors leading off it. He opened the first and looked inside, a walk-in airing cupboard shelved from floor to ceiling and filled with neatly folded linen. The second door, also closed, gave on to a marble-floored bathroom furnished with a free-standing, roll-top tub, a glass shower stall and twin wash-basins set beneath a wall-length mirror. Beyond the basins, in the far corner of the bathroom, was another door. Lanclos guessed that this would lead to the master bedroom, but he kept to the landing, making his way along it until he reached the last of the three doors. Noting the shell-casings on the floor, he paused a moment and sniffed. The smell of cordite was strong here, hot and coppery, but laced with another, more sinuous, sinister scent.

Only once before had Sergeant Lanclos smelt anything like it, as a young boy standing by the bridge at the Brieuc turning, its stony verge lined with a row of crumpled, lifeless bodies, a dozen resist-ance fighters and six Germans. The uniformed corpses of the soldiers had been separated from the *résistants*, but their blood puddled together in the space between them, a drying scarlet pool reeking of the butcher's slab and busy with flies.

And here it was again. That same thick, throat-tightening smell. The only things missing, this chill February morning, were the flies. Lanclos shuddered as he reached forward and pushed open the door, taking a deep breath as it picked up its own momentum and swung into the room.

There was only one thing that Lanclos saw. Blood. Splashed across the rough, stuccoed walls at the head of the bed, pooling darkly on to the stone floor, and soaked into the matted mess of quilt and down feathers that only partially concealed the ruptured remains of the good doctor and his wife.

Blood. Everywhere.

Lanclos was sick on his way back to the car, spattering his boots as he heaved up his breakfast beside the stunted vines lining the drive. A few steps further on he saw that Frenot had done the same. By the time he reached the car, Sergeant Lanclos was sweating heavily despite the cold and gulping in the sharp morning air as though it would somehow rid him of the acid coating of vomit in his throat. As for Frenot, he was leaning against the car, on the other side from the body, his usual ruddy complexion drained of colour.

The two men looked at each other without a word.

Down in the valley, along the Brieuc road, beyond the bridge and the St Bédard turning, they could hear the first, distant wail of police sirens.

4

Chief Inspector Daniel Jacquot of the Cavaillon Regional Crime Squad was four blocks from his office when Frenot's call from St Bédard reached the switchboard at police headquarters.

Eleven minutes later, as he turned into the car park at the back of the town's *gendarmerie*, the first person Jacquot saw was his assistant Jean Brunet. Pulling on a coat, the breath clouding from his mouth, Brunet was briefing a group of gendarmes gathered round him. A black police van, its twin blue lights revolving, smoke billowing from its exhaust, stood nearby. A moment later, the men dispersed, climbed into the van and Brunet, spotting Jacquot's car, hurried over.

Jacquot leaned across the passenger seat and opened the door. 'So? What's up?'

As Jacquot turned and followed the police van through the court-yard's stone-pillared gates, Brunet briefed his superior. A message had come through from St Bédard-le-Chapitre, out on the Brieuc road: two bodies so far, maybe more, found in the old Taillard farm-house. The place was owned by a German couple, Brunet continued. Name of Martner, Josef and Jutta. Retired. Resident not visiting. According to the St Bédard gendarme who'd called in the incident, the two bodies, both female, were the Martners' daughter and granddaughter.

'Cause of death?' asked Jacquot, following the police van as it swung out to pass a line of cars waiting at a stop light on Cours Renan. The two vehicles slowed only briefly before accelerating over the crossroads.

'Looks like gunshot,' replied Brunet, pulling his coat round him and settling into his seat with a 'brrrrrr'.

Jacquot, catching up with the police van and overtaking it, frowned. This was not how he'd planned his day. Claudine's daughter, Midou, had been staying with them and he'd promised her a farewell lunch at Chez Gaillard. With two bodies, maybe more, there seemed little chance he'd make the date. As they left town, heading east on the Brieuc road, Jacquot called Claudine and left a message warning her he'd likely be held up, and that she and Midou should go on without him. He'd get there if he could.

Twenty minutes later they lurched off the road and turned into the Martner driveway with the police van close behind. In the rear-view mirror, Jacquot saw the van stop and two gendarmes clamber out to secure the entrance with a roll of blue and yellow scene-of-crime tape. Fifty metres further on, round a curve in the drive, he pulled up beside an old police Peugeot.

Standing beside it were two gendarmes, a sergeant and corporal. Despite the chill, both men had taken off their kepis, the sergeant's hair cut tight to the scalp, the corporal's curling over his collar. As Jacquot got out of the car, he decided they looked like they could use a stiff drink.

The sergeant snapped off a salute when he saw Jacquot. Buttoning the collar of his jacket and taking up his kepi from the bonnet of the Peugeot, he led them round the car to Kippi's body, now covered in Frenot's police cape.

Jacquot knelt and lifted a corner. There was little left to see above the girl's shoulders, just thin, outstretched arms, turned wrists and the ragged stump of a neck, the cratered ground splashed with blood-matted, hair-tangled shards of scalp.

'Is this how you found her?' asked Jacquot, dropping the cape and getting to his feet.

'Yes, Chief,' replied Lanclos. 'Just covered the body, you know. It looks like the granddaughter. Kippi, she's called.'

'How many more?'

'Three, Chief. Grandparents and Kippi's mother, Ilse. In the house.'

'Show me. How you found them. Exactly what you did. Each step of the way.' And then, turning to Brunet: 'Have the boys spread out and check the vines – fifty metres either side of the drive to start with.'

'Yes, boss,' said Brunet, and hurried away, back up the drive to the posse of gendarmes gathered at the van, rubbing their hands and stamping their feet.

Jacquot said nothing as Lanclos led him down to the house, the old sergeant pointing out the ejected shell casings and lone espadrille, laces coiled round it. A chill breeze had started up from the valley, and despite the blue sky and sharp sunshine Jacquot pulled up his collar as Lanclos filled him in on the discovery: the cleaning woman, Odile Ramier; her reporting back to the *gendarmerie* in St Bédard; their initial search of the premises.

The house, Jacquot noted, was like many converted *mas* in the region, the same golden, blistered stone patched with *crépi*, the same small, shuttered windows and low-pitched roof of bleached rose tiles. But appearances were deceptive. It might still look like the farm it once had been, but Jacquot had seen enough of these conversions – indeed, lived in one – to know that its renovated interior would be large and spacious, with beamed salons, flagstoned terraces and sensitively added extensions. The old farmer who had once lived here, with family above and livestock below, would never have recognised the place.

Parked outside the house on a circle of gravel was a green BMW estate.

'The Martners'?' asked Jacquot.

'That's right,' replied Lanclos.

Jacquot looked through the driver's window. All four door locks were down.

'Does the daughter have a car?'

Lanclos looked uncertain. 'A Volkswagen, I think. Probably in the garage.' Lanclos pointed to a pair of barn doors at the end of the building.

'You checked?'

Lanclos frowned, shook his head.

Jacquot walked over, tried the doors then peered through a gap in the planking. In the gloom he could make out the grille and headlights of a black Golf saloon, and a German registration.

Gravel crunching underfoot, he rejoined Lanclos at the front door.

'The door was open?' Jacquot asked. 'Like this?'

'Just as you see it, Chief.'

Jacquot sucked his top lip and nodded. Just an old thumb-latch door-handle and two locks – one old, one new. No keys visible. Inside or out. No sign of forced entry. Either the door had been left unlocked and the killer had just walked in. Or he had had his own set of keys. Or maybe the Martners had let him in.

Inside the house, as Jacquot had requested, Lanclos retraced his steps, albeit less cautiously. Pointing out the rug and damage to the wall, he led Jacquot along the hallway, showed him the salon, the dining room and the doctor's study, then stepped through into the kitchen.

Pausing just inside the doorway, with Lanclos beside him. Jacquot looked around. Despite the hole in the ceiling, the upturned chair and the plaster, lath, garlic and onions that littered the table and the floor around it, the Martners' kitchen was the homeliest, the most lived-in of all the rooms he had seen so far. For all the mess of violence, it was a grand-looking space, the heart of the house. The old farm fireplace was filled with a massive cast-iron woodburner, the stone mantel above it ranged with books, and the chimney-breast hung with clip-framed family photos, the blue of sea and sky, the white of snow in these holiday snaps standing out in vibrant contrast against the smoke-blackened plaster.

Set round the hearth, in creased and faded chintz covers, were a pair of old armchairs and a sagging sofa. They looked well used and deeply comfortable, just the spot to put up your feet on a chill February evening. Just as the Martners had probably done only a few hours earlier, Jacquot decided, noting the newspaper on the arm of one armchair and, in the other, set down in the seat, a bundle of blue wool stuck with knitting needles. Time for bed, the newspaper and needles said, both wearily put aside. Even without Brunet telling him on the drive out to St Bédard that the Martners were retired, there'd have been no doubt in Jacquot's mind that this was a house where old people lived – snug, orderly, dated.

But for all its cottage cosiness the kitchen was also a working room. If appearances were anything to go by, and they usually were in Jacquot's line of work, it was clear the Martners liked their food as much as their comfort.

With its high, beamed ceiling the kitchen was larger than any of the preceding rooms and, so far as Jacquot could see, equipped to near professional standards: the double oven, eye-level grill and ceramic hob were state-of-the-art, the fridge-freezer of almost industrial dimensions, the butcher's rack above the sink crowded with a veritable *batterie de cuisine* – saucepans, frying-pans and enough kitchen implements to answer any culinary requirement – while the beams were hung with dried wild flowers and herbs, strings of garlic and onions, and smoke-blackened sausages.

At last Jacquot stepped into the room and, like Lanclos, made for the window.

'We found the light on,' said Lanclos, 'but the cooker was off. Looks like someone was getting themselves some breakfast.'

On the work surface beside the sink stood a butter-dish, a mound of grated cheese, a box of eggs, pepper and salt, and a glass mixing bowl. Two eggs had been broken into the bowl, unwhisked, their cracked shells cupped and tossed into the sink. A wide metal frying-pan with a pat of butter dropped into it had been placed on the hob, waiting for heat that would never come.

Omelette au fromage. Claudine had cooked him the very same that morning.

Leaving the sink, Jacquot turned back to the table. Among the debris was a brown-paper bag dusted with plaster. He leaned forward, opened the twist of paper and looked inside. A tin of beeswax polish. For the kitchen table, he thought, or the oak dresser he'd seen in the salon. No furniture spray for the Martners.

As he moved round the table, Jacquot came to the upturned chair. He pushed it aside with his boot. Beneath, darkening the tiled floor, was a long smear of what looked like oil. He bent down. Put a finger to it. Sniffed. Tasted. Olive oil. Just as he'd thought.

Jacquot stood up and looked across at Lanclos. 'Where are the bodies?'

Lanclos pointed to the hot-house door.

'Through there, Chief.'

The door Lanclos indicated was half open and Jacquot stepped through into a narrow tiled vestibule and then, unexpectedly, through a second open door into what he could only have described as a miniature rainforest. He stood stock still, astonished at the difference between the two rooms. In only a few steps.

Behind him Lanclos whispered, as though in church: 'Quite something, eh?'

Quite something indeed, thought Jacquot, gazing up into a canopy of branches that pressed against a whitewashed glass roof maybe twelve metres above their heads, coils of creeper trailing down and loaded with blooms. And at ground level the undergrowth was as dense and dark as the foliage above, a jungle landscape pillared with palms and giant ferns. Indeed, so thick was this ground cover and so convoluted the path they now followed that it was difficult to estimate the size of the hot-house, its furthest reaches lost in a green, shadowy gloom.

And the heat. Incredible. A hundred degrees, had to be, thought Jacquot, feeling the sweat creep in like a warm, wet tide beneath his clothes. Walking beside him, Lanclos tipped up the peak of his kepi and wiped a sleeve across his brow.

Somewhere near the middle of the doctor's hot-house, the sergeant stopped at a tiny glade set with stand after stand of gorgeously coloured blooms. They reminded Jacquot of exotic butterflies which, at a clap of his hands, would flutter up and away before resettling somewhere else.

'Orchids,' said Lanclos. 'My nephew did a school trip here, told me all about it. "The German's Jungle", they call it. Apparently the doctor was a real prof about orchids. Nothing he didn't know.'

Jacquot nodded again, still trying to get his bearings.

'And the bodies?'

'This was the second we found, Chief. Right here,' replied Lanclos, squatting on his heels and pushing aside a screen of patterned, pointed leaves that formed the glade's border. 'Far as we can tell, it's the girl's mother, Ilse.'

Jacquot was startled. He could have walked right past and never seen it, the body thrown off the path by the power of that first shotgun blast to land face down among the blossoms, the bloodied nightdress with its flower-like fragments of white cotton and dusting of gold pollen an effective camouflage against the russet topsoil, the red tapestried slippers colourful enough to pass for some exotic bloom. He hadn't even noticed the ejected shell casings lying on the gravel path like long red petals tipped with gold.

Following the sergeant's example, Jacquot knelt down, reached out a hand and clasped the woman's bare ankle. Thanks to the heat and humidity, the body was surprisingly warm. Shifting his position, Jacquot leaned forward to inspect it more closely. Like the daughter in the driveway there seemed little left of anything above the shoulders.

'Watch that pollen, Chief,' warned Lanclos, pointing out a spray of fat, bulbous flowers hanging perilously close to the shoulder of his coat. 'The devil to get out,' he continued, brushing at a smear of gold on his own sleeve. 'Stains something dreadful, it does.'

Jacquot edged away from them, their stamens loaded with dusty yellow pollen, then looked back at the body and frowned.

'She's wet,' he said, fingering the hem of the nightdress. Between the bloodstains and pollen splashes, he could see the brown of her bare legs, buttocks and back where the material stuck to the skin.

'Sprinklers, Chief. Some kind of watering system.' Lanclos nodded to the roof. 'It was doing it when we got here.'

Above them, through the branches, Jacquot could just make out a gridwork of pipes running the length of the hot-house ceiling.

'Any of the windows broken by the shots?' asked Jacquot, leaning back from the body, careful not to brush against the flowers.

'No, Chief. Nothing we've found. Not a one.'

'And were the doors to the hot-house open or closed when you arrived?'

'Open, Chief.'

'Well, let's keep them closed for now. We don't want the plants dying as well, do we?'

Leaving through a second set of double doors at the far end of the hot-house, Lanclos led Jacquot into the doctor's laboratory, its workbench furnished with a computer, a microscope, boxes of slides, an angled magnifying lamp and a wooden trug of dirty, tuberish roots. Set against the wall a half-dozen shelves were filled with books, files and an assortment of beakers, bottles and flasks. There was no chair that Jacquot could see, but the bench looked high enough to lean against comfortably. He wondered if the good doctor had a bad back. He certainly liked his cigars: between the computer and the microscope was a heavy glass ashtray with a stub tilted into the bowl. Jacquot turned it with a fingernail till the label showed – a whiskery face, a uniform jacket with high military collar and the legend 'Bolivar Numero Dos'. It was as though the good doctor had just put it down, stepped out and would be back at any moment.

He also liked his music, Jacquot noted. A rack of CDs was set beside a compact Sony hi-fi. He slid out one of the disks. Mozart Meisterwerke: the *Haffner-Serenade*, *Flötensonate*, the *Prager* and *Pariser* symphonies, performed by the Mozarteum Orchester Salzburg. He put the disk back and switched on the hi-fi. A gentle, floating violin concerto rose from two speakers at either end of the workbench. Stepping past Lanclos, Jacquot went back into the hot-house. From unseen speakers, the same concerto played through the branches and foliage. Maybe not his choice of soundtrack, Jacquot would have been the first to admit, but exquisite nonetheless, particularly in these surroundings.

Back in the lab, he switched off the hi-fi and followed Lanclos through another set of doors into the guest wing, noting the supper tray on the coffee-table in front of the TV, the Walkman, CDs and magazine that the sergeant pointed out.

'Did they live here?' asked Jacquot, as they climbed the stairs to the bedrooms, remembering the German numberplate on the Volkswagen in the garage. 'The daughter and granddaughter? Or just visiting?'

'Just visiting, Madame Ramier said.'

'And how long had they been here?' asked Jacquot, coming out of the second bedroom and glancing into the bathroom.

'According to Madame Ramier, just a few days,' replied Lanclos. 'The end of last week, I think.'

Back in the salon, Jacquot pulled a handkerchief from his coat pocket and tried the french windows to the central courtyard. They were locked. 'Any other doors this side of the house? To the outside?' he asked.

'Four, Chief. These here, one in the guest kitchen back there. The other two in the sun-lounge. But they're all locked. Bolted too.'

'Keys?'

Lanclos shrugged.

From the guest salon, following the circuit of the courtyard, they stepped down into the sun-lounge. Appropriately furnished with cushioned rattan sofas and chairs, it was well named. Even on this bleak February morning it was a bright, airy room, its two outside walls made up almost entirely of glass. One of these windows gave on to ranks of wizened vines trooping up the hillside and the other on to the gravelled central courtyard. Above them, supported by a half-dozen exposed A-frame beams, was the bare underside of the building's tiled roof.

Set behind one of the sofas, on spread legs, stood an empty easel and a trestle table loaded with brushes, paint pots and tubes. A line of canvases, stacked according to size, was ranged along the wall behind it.

Jacquot bent over and fingered his way through one of the stacks, floral studies mostly, a mix of watercolours set on board and unframed oils, all of them minutely and expertly detailed. Jacquot let the paintings fall back into place, noting as he did so the signature 'JM'. He wondered which of the Martners was the artist. Husband or wife? Josef or Jutta? He looked round the room. Two of the larger studies – a spray of flowers lying on a table, and a faience vase filled with exotic blooms – had been framed and hung on the whitewashed stone walls. They had a delicate, feminine touch. The wife, he decided. Jutta.

Leaving the sun-lounge, Jacquot followed Lanclos down a narrow passageway, through a utility room fitted with washing-machine, tumble-dryer and sink, and into the kitchen once more. Stepping around the mess of plaster and shredded vegetables, they made their way back down the hallway to the front door.

'The other bodies?' asked Jacquot.

'This way, Chief. Up here,' said Lanclos, making for the stairs.

'A moment, please,' said Jacquot, putting out a hand to hold him back. 'When you first went up, did you go by the wall or the banister?'

Lanclos frowned. He couldn't quite recall. 'The banister, Chief,' he replied. And then: 'But I didn't touch it,' he added hastily. 'No, sir.' Which had been a lucky break, he said to himself, thinking about fingerprints for the first time that morning.

'So go on up, just as you did. Show me.'

As instructed, Lanclos climbed the stairs.

Up on the gallery landing, the old sergeant stood aside as Jacquot opened the first two doors, just as he had done himself. Only Jacquot did it with a fingernail against their edges rather than grasp their handles.

'Were these doors open like this, or closed, when you arrived?' asked Jacquot without looking round.

Lanclos felt a flush of dismay. 'I think they may have been closed, Chief.' Jesus, he thought, how stupid could I have been?

But Jacquot said nothing, just moved along the landing, stepping round the shell casings, pushing open the last door with the toe of his boot. 'And this door?'

'Not closed,' replied Lanclos. 'Just a little open, you know. Like it is now.'

As he'd done in the kitchen, Jacquot paused in the doorway, taking it all in: the built-in wardrobes; the shuttered windows; the connecting door to the bathroom; the scatter of shell casings on the floor; the bloodied bedclothes; and the lumpy, silent shapes beneath.

When, finally, Jacquot went in, Lanclos stayed where he was, saying nothing, watching the man's every move. Under his kepi, his bristle-cut scalp prickled with excitement.

So this is Ponytail, he thought, as Jacquot paused in the middle of the room, turned slowly, running his fingers through the curve of black hair that had earned him the nickname, the ponytail that was definitely not regulation but that no one 'upstairs' had ever managed to do anything about. Lanclos had recognised Jacquot the moment he pulled himself from the car – the jeans, the cowboy boots, the five-thousand-franc topcoat. And the ponytail, of course. Frenot too. There was no mistaking him.

Ponytail. *Dieu!*

Like everyone on the Force, Lanclos had heard of Ponytail. Who hadn't? The stories from Marseilles, the busts, the action, pictures in the papers, rumours of dubious practices and a quiet transfer to the country. And that try, all those years ago. That run. Beating those *anglais* on their own turf. A legend on and off the pitch, he was. But they'd never met. No reason to, until this. And even when he'd had Frenot go and call it in, Lanclos had never imagined, not for a moment, that Ponytail would be the man to come.

'You didn't say anything about dogs,' said Jacquot, standing by a wicker basket beside the bed.

'Dachshunds,' replied Lanclos, looking at the bloody remains half in, half out of the basket, the blood darkening the blanket, spattered against the shredded weave, vibrantly red against the dogs' smooth, shiny black coats. 'They had a pair of them. I didn't think . . .'

Abruptly Jacquot turned on his heel and strode back out of the bedroom, Lanclos tripping over his feet in his haste to move out of the way.

On the landing, Jacquot paused and the sergeant saw the younger man's eyes light on the banister. Without saying a word, he walked over to it, bent down and sighted along it to the front door. Straightening up, he ran a finger along the top, and then beneath it, between the posts. He nodded to himself, then took a couple of steps back and looked again, eyes squinting, down into the hall.

Lanclos watched intently, though he hadn't for the life of him the vaguest idea what Jacquot was doing.

Jacquot turned and caught Lanclos's eye. 'So. Let's go.'

On their way back up the drive, Jacquot paused by a stumpy vine, looked at the ground. 'Yours?' he asked Lanclos.

'Yes, Chief,' replied the sergeant, crestfallen, the bitter taste of vomit still sharp in his throat.

'And the other? Further on?'

'My corporal. Frenot.'

5

By the time Jacquot and Lanclos got back to their cars, the forensics team from Avignon had arrived in the Martner driveway and set up shop. There were seven of them, togged up in white boots and zippered Nyrex jumpsuits. Jacquot recognised most from previous jobs and nodded to the man in charge, Guy Fournier, his bald skull still brown from the previous summer, his ears reddening from the cold.

Already Fournier's team had isolated Kippi, setting up a tent-like windbreak round her sprawled body with room enough inside for them to do their work. Before they did so, their scene-of-crime photographer was shooting off a roll of film, treading lightly round the corpse, careful not to disturb anything. Even in the bright winter sunshine, Jacquot noticed, the man was using a flash. Jacquot would see the photos later that day, or the next, fanned out on his desk, then pinned up on a cork board in the incident room next to his office. All of them, all four bodies. He'd see them every day until they ceased to shock, or until the case was closed, the killer found. Big, glossy prints that missed nothing, every angle, every spray of blood, every shard of skull.

'It's messy,' said Jacquot, walking over to Fournier.

'When isn't it?' said Fournier, shaking Jacquot's hand. Like his colleagues, Fournier was wearing latex gloves. His hand felt smooth, dry and powdery. And oddly warm in the chill morning air.

27

'Three more in the house,' said Jacquot. 'Shoe in the drive. Shell casings all over.'

'I'll get you an initial report as soon as I can,' said Fournier. 'Tomorrow some time. Details later, I'm afraid.'

Jacquot nodded and left them to it. From here on in, he knew, it was nothing but grind – straightforward forensic procedure. Hours bent over the bodies, hours searching the surrounding land, hours dusting down interiors, lifting prints, making lists, inventories, taking more photographs. But with Fournier in charge, Jacquot knew it would be a thorough job. The man would miss nothing, and he'd have that report on Jacquot's desk when he said he would. While the trail was still warm. Later would come the pathologist's findings – by the weekend if he was lucky. With four bodies to examine, Jacquot knew it would take some time.

But for now he had seen all he needed to see. There was nothing more for him here. Brunet had sent a couple of men to secure the house front and back, two of the forensics team were already lugging their silver cases down the Martners' driveway to begin work on the other bodies and interiors, and on either side of the drive Jacquot could see a straggling line of gendarmes working their way between the vines.

Wherever the gun was, they wouldn't find it there, thought Jacquot, as he tossed Brunet his car keys and got into the passenger seat.

But they'd find it somewhere, some time.

And then the game would really begin.

6

A single killer, Jacquot decided.

Not two, not three. Just the one. Despite the body count, despite the scatter of shells, this was someone working alone. Of that, for no reason beyond a familiar twist in his gut, Chief Inspector Jacquot was certain. And soon enough Guy Fournier would confirm it.

A lone killer with a pocketful of cartridges and a single, heavy-calibre shotgun.

On the journey back to Cavaillon, Jacquot sat in the passenger seat as Brunet drove. As usual, after visiting a scene-of-crime, the two men stayed silent. Brunet had worked with Jacquot long enough to know that his boss liked to review the evidence, fix the progression of the crime in his mind as soon as possible, preferably on the way back to the office, and did not take kindly to interruptions. Brunet would speak when he was spoken to and not before.

And that was exactly what Jacquot was doing, sorting his initial observations into some kind of order, a sequence. Even if, in the absence of qualified reports, it was still all speculation. Guesswork.

First of all – a single killer. And then, man or woman?

At this early stage Jacquot favoured a man. In his experience it seemed unlikely that a woman could have sustained the necessary strength and pitch of ferocity to fire off what looked like close to twenty rounds, as well as chase two of the victims before gunning them down.

Also, had the killer been a woman, Jacquot believed, the daughter or granddaughter, one or the other, might reasonably have attempted to confront her, to reason or struggle with her, rather than flee. Which was why they'd both been shot in the back.

So, let's say a man, thought Jacquot, just for argument's sake; let's start from there, he decided, as they swung over the St Bédard bridge and turned out on to the Brieuc road.

A tall man, no question, taller at any rate than most women. On the steep, curving staircase leading to the Martners' bedroom, Jacquot had observed small amounts of dirt from the driveway on every second step. The murderer had climbed those stairs two at a time – not the way a woman would have done it, or the way that short-ass Sergeant Lanclos had done it during the re-enactment.

And judging by the position of the dirt on the stairs, once Jacquot had established which part of the staircase Lanclos had used, it was also clear that the intruder had stayed close to the wall, the better to mask the creak of old wood, maybe. And in so doing, his shoulder had brushed against two of the ascending line of small floral prints that decorated it, pushing them slightly out of alignment, at a height equal to Jacquot's own shoulder. And Jacquot, in his old moroccans, was a shade over six feet tall.

Also, Jacquot was in no doubt, the Martner bedroom was where the killer had been headed – the grandparents were the first to die. Because if he'd gone up there last, the Martners would have been woken by the sound of gunshots below, would have been up and struggling into their dressing-gowns, maybe already phoning the police. Also, any dirt that the killer had brought in on his shoes would have been dispersed around the ground floor, as it had been by Lanclos.

Which explained the granddaughter's body in the drive. Because she had been the last to die.

Jacquot shook his head as though to clear his thoughts, which were beginning to pile in on one another from all directions. He was getting ahead of himself. A step at a time, he said to himself, a step at a time. From the beginning.

From somewhere in the early hours, he decided.

For the murders had taken place in the dark, just before dawn, when Ilse, the Martners' daughter, awake early, had gone to the kitchen, switched on the light and started to prepare breakfast; for herself, just the two eggs. Jacquot was certain it must have been Ilse in the kitchen. Which was how she'd ended up sprawled face down in the hot-house. Younger women like Kippi, like Claudine's daughter Midou, all tousled hair and sleep-swollen faces, were rarely seen before breakfast was on the table.

And when Ilse came from the guest wing to prepare that breakfast, Jacquot was certain the killer had already entered the premises, through the Martners' front door. And that by the time Ilse switched on the kitchen lights, the killer had already reached the landing, was creeping along it towards the Martners' bedroom. Had Ilse come down any earlier, the killer would surely have dealt with her first, quietly, with a kitchen knife, say, or a blow to the back of the head, alerted by the spill of light at the end of the hallway and the sounds of breakfast being prepared.

But he hadn't. He'd gone straight upstairs, nothing to divert or distract him. Given the distance from bedroom to kitchen – the curve of the stairs, the long hallway, the darkened study, salon and dining room – it seemed unlikely that the intruder had known anyone else was up.

If, indeed, he had known anyone else was in the house. There was, after all, just the one car in the driveway. The Martners' BMW.

Which would be worth bearing in mind, Jacquot told himself.

Along with the fact that it looked likely to Jacquot that the killer knew where he was going, knew the lay-out of the house. On entering he'd gone immediately to the Martners' bedroom, even knew which of the three doors to open on the landing.

Jumping ahead again, jumping ahead. Slow down, thought Jacquot. Stand back, take a breath. Let's establish the sequence of events before anything else.

A sequence of events, so far as Jacquot could tell, that had started in the Martners' bedroom and moved to Ilse, in the kitchen preparing breakfast. Hearing shots, she'd come running down the hall just as the killer stepped out of her parents' bedroom, breaking the gun to eject the spent cartridges.

To reload? Had he known the job wasn't finished?

Whatever, the killer sees the daughter below, snaps the gun closed, raises it to fire but hits the barrel on the underside of the banister, hard enough to leave an angled dent on an otherwise smooth surface (a semi-automatic single-barrel shotgun or an over-and-under configuration?). By the time he'd wrestled the gun clear of the rails, he had had time only for a wild, instinctive shot that went wide and high, cratering the plaster way above head height.

Had it not been for that banister, Ilse would never have reached the kitchen, let alone the hot-house.

As for the crumpled rug at the bottom of the stairs, Jacquot speculated, either Ilse had slipped on it as she spun round and fled, or the killer had skidded on it as he reached the hallway and gave chase.

Although he wasn't a parent, Jacquot was certain that Ilse's first thoughts would have been for her daughter, most likely still in her bedroom in the guest wing. Her first, overwhelming instinct, Jacquot was sure, would have been to protect Kippi, to warn her. This was why Ilse had turned back into the house and not out through the open front door in an effort to escape, to raise the alarm.

So, down the hallway, through the kitchen she had raced, with the killer in hot pursuit, which was when maybe she realised she'd made a mistake, that she should have gone the other way, through the front door to scream for help, to lead the killer away from her daughter. But by now it was too late. She was trapped. All possible exits, save the front door, locked and bolted. And no keys to be found. Or the time to find them.

It was in these short, frantic moments that the killer had caught up with Ilse, maybe trying to hide herself in the hot-house, and had had his second chance at a shot, Ilse's white nightdress a bold, unmissable target in that shadowy green gloom.

And this time he had found his target.

So far as Jacquot had been able to determine, the first shot had been fired from a distance, had hit the woman's shoulder or side and sent her sprawling into the bed of flowers. The second, third and fourth, each a killing shot, had been delivered at close range, the spill of spent cartridge cases on the gravelled path witness to a bold, obsessive execution.

Hatred? Or panic? One merciless shot after another. When the first would probably have done the job.

And then what? Had the killer heard something? The sound of running feet?

Or maybe Ilse had called out her daughter's name, trying to warn her, telling her to flee. That would have been her second mistake. Alerting the killer. Unless he already knew there was someone else in the house. A fourth family member. Had he come to kill them all?

By this time, of course, Kippi would have been wide awake, roused by the sound of gunshots from the other side of the house, from her grandparents' room. She'd have flung on the dressing-gown they'd found her in, grabbed her espadrilles, then dashed downstairs to see what was going on, only to hear, let's say, her mother's screams and shouts to run, to hide, and then the second volley of gunshots from the hot-house.

And silence.

It was in that echoing silence, Jacquot decided, that three options would have presented themselves to the girl: go and see what was happening; find herself a good hiding-place; or get the hell out of there. She'd gone for the third option, dashing through the sun-lounge, the utility room and into the kitchen – Jacquot could almost see her hopping to pull on and tie her espadrilles – away from the hot-house where she'd heard the shots, heading for the hallway and the front door.

Only the killer, doubling back through the hot-house to get away himself or to cut her off, had rushed into the kitchen at exactly the same moment as Kippi.

The smear of olive oil on the floor and the upturned chair, the way the ceiling plaster, lath, onion skins and herbs covered only one section of the kitchen floor and table, furthest away from the hot-house doors, told the story here.

As Jacquot read it, the killer had slipped on the oil, crashed into the chair and, falling backwards, pulled the trigger, loosing off another wild shot that shredded the onions and garlic hanging from a beam. Giving Kippi just enough time to hightail it out of the kitchen, down the hallway and out of the house.

Which was where, like her mother, she, too, had made a fatal error. Instead of going for the cover of the vines, skimpy as it was, or making for the line of trees at the back of the house, she'd kept to the driveway, out in the open, heading for the road.

It was here, crucially, that she lost her espadrille, the ties unravelling, the rope-soled shoe wrenched away from her foot on the stony drive.

It was all the killer needed. Maybe stunned from his fall in the kitchen, her slower speed gave him sufficient opportunity to catch her up.

Like the girl's mother, another easy target.

When he judged himself close enough, the killer had stopped, taken aim and fired, pitching the girl forward. Then walked up to the body to finish her off with another wholly unnecessary volley of shots, just as he'd done with the others.

The senior Martners first, in their bedroom; then the daughter, Ilse, in the hot-house; and finally Kippi, the youngest of the family, the one with the most warning, outside the house, running for her life.

That, in Jacquot's opinion, was the way it had happened.

And at this time of year, February, who would have been surprised to hear shooting in the Brieuc valley? Hardly a daybreak went by hereabouts without hunters out on the prowl, shooting for the pot.

But it was not the whole story. Not by a long way. Jacquot may have established the how. What he needed was the why. And then, hopefully, he'd maybe find out who.

There was, however, one thing he was absolutely certain about. This had been a premeditated act. No other way to read it. Nothing random here. No chance encounter. No burglary gone wrong. Someone had come to the Martner house with the express intention to kill. With a target in mind. The whole thing smacked of something personal, something that bound the killer and his victims. There was anger and hate in the commission of this crime. An almost palpable sense of revenge. A settling of accounts. Whatever they might find out about the Martners, Jacquot was convinced that the killer had known his victims and that they had known him.

But was it just the elder Martners he was after? Or the whole family?

The killer might have come with enough ammunition to do the job a few times over, but had he reckoned on the daughter and granddaughter being in the house as well? When he came out of the Martners' bedroom did he think the job was finished?

If he did, the moment he saw Ilse at the bottom of the stairs he'd have known he had no choice but to follow and kill her. She'd seen his face, maybe recognised him, would certainly have been able to give the police a description, or tell them who the killer was.

It was the same with the granddaughter, Kippi. She'd probably seen his face too. In the kitchen. She would have had to die as well. As simple as that.

There was something else, too, that struck Jacquot about the murders. A feeling he couldn't quite shift. That the killer didn't seem particularly comfortable with a gun. Certainly it had done the job, but there was something clumsy in the way he'd used it – banging the barrel against the banister in his haste to loose off a shot from the landing; losing his balance in the kitchen and blasting off at the ceiling; and using so many shells when half the number would have done.

A killer not altogether familiar with his weapon of choice.

Or *her* weapon of choice.

Maybe, against all his instincts, the Martners' killer had been a woman. And although Jacquot was fairly confident the odds were against it, he couldn't entirely rule out the possibility. Not until he had more facts at his disposal.

A bouncing jolt shook Jacquot out of his theorising as Brunet drove over the ramp and up through the gates into Police Headquarters. He'd hardly noticed anything on their way back to Cavaillon, staring ahead through the windscreen with a quiet intensity.

Walking across the car park to the main entrance, Jacquot told Brunet what he wanted. Everything there was to know about the Martners. Back before they had come to France. The whole story.

And bank accounts – *cherchez l'argent*. Money was always a good place to start when you were looking for a motive, and might well provide a lead.

And statements from anyone who knew them, he continued; they must have had a lawyer, probably here in Cavaillon, a doctor, friends, acquaintances.

And send some of the boys up to St Bédard. Liaise with Lanclos. House to house. The usual thing.

As they took the lift to the fourth floor, Brunet nodded but took no notes. Police procedure, pure and simple. He knew the drill.

Back in his office, Jacquot shrugged off his coat, slid into the chair behind his desk and went through his messages. There was one from Claudine: if he could join them for lunch, fine; if not, well, they understood.

Jacquot glanced at his watch. A little after one p.m. There was everything to do, and nothing to do. He looked through his window at the blue sky and witch-hat belfry of Église St-Jean. Midou was leaving that afternoon for Paris and her flight home to Guadeloupe. It might be months before they saw her again. He made up his mind.

Brunet was on the phone in the outer office when Jacquot strode past, pulling his overcoat back on and winding the scarf round his neck. He put his hand over the mouthpiece. 'Chief?'

'I'll be back by three. If something urgent comes up, you can find me at Gaillard's.'

7

While Jacquot, Claudine and Midou enjoyed their farewell lunch at Brasserie Chez Gaillard, St Bédard-le-Chapitre buzzed with news of the murders.

It began, of course, with Madame Ramier.

After making her statement at the *gendarmerie*, Odile Ramier had gone straight home, startling Adéline with her unexpected return.

No, she explained to her sister, as she wheeled her Solex down the hallway, she hadn't been sacked by the Martners. And no, she assured her sister as she closed the stair-cupboard door, she was not feeling ill. Although, come to think of it, steadying herself on the back of a kitchen chair, a glass of Cognac might just help to settle her nerves. At which point, Adéline hurried off to fetch the bottle from the salon, certain now that something dreadful had happened to her sister.

And so, the two of them seated at the kitchen table, a fresh log hissing in the hearth and a busy, billowing column of smoke swirling up into the chimney, Odile told her story for the second time that morning, describing in detail her grisly discovery.

Further, larger measures of Cognac were poured as a shocked Adéline followed up her sister's account with much the same questions that Lanclos had asked.

Was she certain the granddaughter was dead?

Had she gone inside the house?

Had she seen Madame Martner? Monsieur Martner?

And what about their daughter – what was her name again? Ilse?

To which Odile replied, just as she had at the *gendarmerie*, that there was absolutely no doubt the teenager was dead, that she had seen no one else, and that she had thought it prudent to return immediately to St Bédard and inform Sergeant Lanclos rather than venture down to the house on her own.

But of course, agreed Adéline, that had been the only sensible thing to do. And thank the Lord for it. Go on to the house, indeed! Whatever was she thinking?

Which reminded her, Adéline said to her sister, someone should put a call through to Curé Foulard, advise him that his services would be required at the Martner house and that he should go there with the blessed sacrament without delay. Indeed, she would take it upon herself to do just that and, telling Odile she should go upstairs and rest for half an hour, Adéline went to the salon, closed the door and sat herself down beside the telephone.

Naturally she did not leave it at the *curé*. Shock at her sister's disclosure had quickly been superseded by a gossip's hunger to be first with the news. With her head spinning, as much from her sister's terrible news as the Cognac they had drunk, she misdialled the second number and was surprised to find herself connected to the manager of a car showroom in Carpentras. After a flurried apology, and with pounding heart, she tried again.

This next attempt was more successful, as were all the calls that followed, and for the next forty minutes Adéline Séguin passed on to her wide circle of friends and acquaintances the story of her sister's shocking discovery at the Martner house.

The success of her news service was brought home to Adéline later that morning when, calling at the *pharmacie* to pick up her prescription, she was buttonholed by Madame Héliard and informed of the discovery before she had time to tell the story herself.

In Madame Héliard's version of events, it was old Dumé's son, Patric, who'd discovered the bodies. In the Martner vineyard. According to the pharmacist, her hands dug deep into the pockets of her black cardigan, they'd been bound, gagged and terribly muti-lated.

Much disgusted with the inaccuracies of Madame Héliard's account but in no mood to correct her, Adéline had taken her prescription and wished her an abrupt good-day, realising as she stepped out on to Place Vausigne in the centre of St Bédard that the moment of her triumph was now sadly past. If Madame Héliard knew about the murders – however ill-informed of the facts she might be – then undoubtedly the whole town would know about it too.

And by Wednesday lunchtime that was certainly the case – whichever version of events the townspeople chose to believe. In St Bédard that day, their information was as reliable as their sources and the premises they frequented.

At the Chaberts' flower shop, the Fontaine des Fleurs, the Widow Blanc whispered the facts to Denise Chabert much as she had heard them over the phone from Adéline Séguin with only a few embellishments. At Tabac Fontaine, further down the road, Marc Tesserat reported to his wife Christine that six body-bags had been delivered to the Martner house. And at the grocery, Clotilde Lepantre, in apron and slacks, standing on the pavement among baskets of kale and collared sacks of potatoes, repeated Madame Héliard's account to each of her customers, with the added detail that the police had started digging for more bodies.

Across the *place*, in the steamy interior of the Mazzelli family's Bar de la Fontaine, the pool and soccer tables were deserted as Clotilde's husband, Claude, pushing up the chevroned sleeves of his purple shell-suit and bellying up to the bar with his various cronies, repeated almost word for word the version he'd heard from his wife. In Claude's possession, however, the story included not only the information about the police digging for more bodies but, significantly, the fact that the two younger women had been found naked.

It wasn't until Corporal Frenot returned to St Bédard and went to Mazzelli's bar to muster volunteers for a wider sweep of the Martner property planned for that afternoon, that the true facts of the case were finally established.

Four bodies.

All shot.

No gun.

No apparent motive.

No suspect.

In the face of this official testimony, the more lurid accounts of the murder were put aside in favour of equally fevered speculation. For everyone in St Bédard, it was no longer a question of what and how, but who and why.

Shortly after lunch, the local press arrived on the scene. In a battered Audi, Roland Lucas, from the Cavaillon evening paper, and his photographer sidekick Bernard-André Marchal pulled up at the Martner property but got no further than the taped driveway entrance. All Lucas knew was that the paper's news editor had received an anonymous phone call, an old woman by the sound of her voice, saying something about a mass murder at the Martner house on the road between Chant-le-Neuf and St Bédard, and that he and Marchal had been sent to check it out.

If it had sounded like a wasted journey in Cavaillon, the presence of the police confirmed that something was up and that the tip-off looked to be genuine. While Lucas tried to prise some information out of the two gendarmes who stood resolutely in their path, Marchal discreetly changed lenses and took a couple of snaps over the sloping vineyard towards the cluster of cars beyond the curve in the drive, with the pantiled roof of the Martner house in the background. When they saw what he was doing, the gendarmes moved the pair smartly on.

Undeterred, Lucas and Marchal headed back to St Bédard and parked outside Mazzelli's bar in the *place*. They couldn't have chosen anywhere better to continue their enquiries.

Lepantre was still pontificating at the old zinc, and the town's grocer warmed to Lucas's offer of a large brandy and the company of a man who actually wanted to write down what he had to say about the murders. When Lucas asked for his name, however, Lepantre wasn't so sure it had been such a good idea, but a second brandy put him at ease.

While Marchal took a picture of Lepantre, the top of his shell-suit pulled judiciously over his stomach to meet the band of his trousers, Lucas, excited at the prospect of such an unexpected high-profile story, moved on to Aldo Mazzelli, the bar's owner. A larger man than Lepantre, if that was possible, with a fine head of curly black hair, thick black brows and a nose the size and shape of a ripening aubergine, Mazzelli needed little prompting.

Lucas was scribbling away into his spiral-bound notebook, recording Mazzelli's recollections of the Martners – 'quiet peoples, kept themself to themself, you know' – when Mazzelli's son, Tomas, shouted from the doorway, 'TV's here,' and everyone's attention was promptly directed at the *place*. A large white van bearing the Channel 7 logo was pulling up beside the *boules* pitch.

No one in St Bédard had seen a television outside-broadcast operation before, and by the time the cameraman had shouldered his videocam outside the *gendarmerie*, a small crowd had gathered. When the videocam light came on, Tomas Mazzelli and his friend Eric Chabert, standing at the front of the crowd, were both reminded of the night lights at Cavaillon stadium when the A team played.

Sergeant Lanclos, who had left the scene-of-crime to Fournier and his team and returned to St Bédard soon after Jacquot's departure, had agreed to be interviewed and he stood on the *gendarmerie* steps, nervously straightening his jacket and tugging at his sergeant's stripes, which, years before, his wife had stitched on a little off-centre and never got round to changing.

The interviewer, a tall brunette in a belted camel overcoat and leather boots, whom everyone recognised from the local evening news, spoke a few words to him, nodded to camera and then began her introduction.

'There is a sense of shock and stunned disbelief here in the picturesque old town of St Bédard today, following the discovery early this morning of four bodies in a farmhouse only a few kilometres from where I'm standing. The victims, three generations of the same family, have been provisionally identified as Dr Josef Martner, his wife Jutta, their daughter and granddaughter. German residents who have lived here for a number of years, the Martners . . .'

Patrolling the edge of the crowd, one of St Bédard's older

residents, Simon Dumé, rolled a plump oyster of phlegm over his tongue and spat it into the gutter. '*Alors*, all this fuss for a bunch of Krauts,' he said, to no one in particular. 'You asks me, someone's done us all a big favour.'

8

Jean Brunet had been hard at work. By the time Jacquot returned from his lunch at Chez Gaillard, three green incident folders sat in the centre of his desk, a blade of thin winter sunlight slanting across the topmost cover.

The first folder contained a single flimsy sheet, the initial crime-report statement from Madame Odile Ramier who had discovered the first body, faxed through from the *gendarmerie* in St Bédard.

The statement had been handwritten, copied down in a wavering line of unsteady capitals as the cleaning lady told her story. Jacquot glanced through it as he shrugged off his coat and settled in his chair. It was simple and precise: arrival at the property, discovery of the body, her return to St Bédard and subsequent appearance at the *gendarmerie*, the four paragraphs sprinkled with spelling errors, the statement timed and dated, and the witness's signature and police counter-signature scrawled at the bottom of the page. Nothing that Jacquot didn't know already.

The second folder was a little thicker and contained photocopies of the Martners' bank accounts for the last six months, faxed through from Crédit Agricole in Cavaillon by the manager, a Monsieur Sarranne, copies of credit-card statements, phone records for the last quarter and a typewritten list of names, addresses and tele-phone numbers: the Martners' lawyer, their doctor – coincidentally Claudine's doctor – the manager of the BMW showroom in Aix

43

where the Martners had bought their car, even the name of the estate agency that had sold the Martners the Taillard property nine years earlier. Brunet had been busy.

The third folder was the thickest of all. Jacquot sat back and flipped it open. Inside were a dozen or more sheets of paper, the first of which bore the letterhead of the Cavaillon Regional Crime Squad: Brunet's faxed request to the German authorities for information concerning four deceased German nationals named Josef and Jutta Martner, and Ilse and Kippi Brauer.

Beneath this covering note were pages of photocopied official documents from Munich's Criminal Investigation Headquarters, from the Deutsche Bundesrepublik Sicherheitsdienst in Bonn and the Public Records Bureau in Zürich, Switzerland.

As he sat back in his chair, studying the file, three things surprised Jacquot: how Brunet had found out the daughter's married name so quickly; why the German and, he noted, Swiss authorities had come back so promptly; and what a doctor living in retirement in St Bédard could have done to merit so much information from such unlikely quarters.

The first question was easily answered. Leaning forward, Jacquot buzzed through to the outer office. A moment later Brunet knocked and entered.

'Brauer? How . . . ?' asked Jacquot, holding up the file as Brunet pulled out a chair, swung it between his legs and sat down, arms across its back.

'Driver's licence, passport, even a letter,' replied Brunet. 'All in the daughter's handbag, boss. I thought about it after you left for lunch. Called Fournier at the house and had him check it out. He found it in the guest wing. Ilse Brauer. Husband's name Gunther. Swiss national. Kippi is their only child.'

'And do you happen to know where Herr Gunther Brauer is right now?' asked Jacquot, feeling a prickle of excitement that the case was already moving forward, picking up momentum. An absent husband was as good a place to start a murder investigation as a bank statement.

'The letter came from New York. He's been there a month. A Treasury Bond analyst for the Swiss government seconded to CreditSuisse. I'm afraid we can count him out.'

Jacquot sighed. The first dead end. He hoped there wouldn't be too many more. 'When's he due back?'

'Our Swiss colleagues are liaising with the bank. Someone will break the news to him when he gets in to work this morning, New York time. Maybe they've already done it. Whatever, he should be on a plane out of there by late tonight. Tomorrow maybe.'

'Good work, Jean. I should go to lunch more often.'

'I just wish it was all so straightforward,' replied Brunet.

Jacquot looked at his colleague. 'I don't follow.'

'Have you read the report yet?'

'Not yet. Just your enquiry fax. Flicked through the rest.'

'When you have, you'll see what I mean.' Brunet got to his feet and headed for the door. 'My bet is high-ranking visitors any day now.' With a nod and a grin, he was gone.

Jacquot, suddenly intrigued, turned his attention back to the file. Sitting forward in his chair, he began to read.

The first few pages contained smudged copies of birth and marriage certificates.

Josef Otto Rupperich Martner, born Hamburg, August 1920.

Jutta von Diepenbroek, born Munich, February 1926.

Martner and von Diepenbroek, married Munich, September 1949.

Ilse Martner, born Munich, April 1951.

Gunther Brauer, born Zürich, July 1949.

Martner and Brauer, married Zürich, October 1976.

Kirsten Jutta Brauer, born Zürich, October 1980.

So far, so ordinary, thought Jacquot, flipping back the pages, starting from the first sheet, riffling through them again.

Except, except, except . . .

Something familiar. Something he was missing.

And then, like a light switched on in a darkened room: the names. Big names.

Von Diepenbroek! Jutta Martner's father. Ilse Brauer's grandfather. Kippi's great-grandfather.

And Brauer! Ilse's husband; Kippi's father.

Jacquot sat up sharply and turned to the following pages. Security clearances, personal resumés, a selection of blurred press cuttings.

Martin O'Brien

And anxious requests from the Swiss and German authorities for further information. Soonest.

Oh, *merde*, thought Jacquot.

Brunet was right.

Big guns, for sure.

And turning in their direction.

46

9

In St Bédard it didn't take long for the initial mood of excitement at the macabre events to turn sour and sombre. Murders. Blood. And a killer on the loose. In St Bédard of all places.

Marc Tesserat at the *tabac*, setting out his postcard racks the morning after Odile Ramier's discovery, was probably the first to notice it. Tightening the scarf round his neck, he sucked a *pastille de menthe* and looked up through the trees that shaded Place Vausigne. The previous day's high blue sky had gone and another plug of cloud had wedged itself in overnight, bringing with it a bleak, blighted sense of winter. The *place*, it seemed to Tesserat, was quieter, more forlorn, than usual, the pavements emptier than they had been twenty-four hours earlier, the normal early-morning bustle reduced to occasional figures flitting between the trees, hunched and hurrying, as if they didn't want to be seen. It was the kind of morning when, if you were able to, you sat on at the kitchen table, tarried over your coffee and delayed the start of the day.

Tesserat looked up and down the pavement. An hour later than usual, the blinds were still down on Lepantre's grocery store and the Bulots' *charcuterie*, the Chaberts had still to set out their flower racks, and not a single table had been moved out on to Mazzelli's terrace. Only the smell of baking bread from Doriane's ovens in the street behind the *place* suggested that someone other than himself was at work.

Yet somehow the aroma had less warmth than usual, less temptation, and as he remarked on it, Tesserat felt an unaccountable sadness settle on him. He and his wife had lived in St Bédard a good few years now, but in all that time he couldn't recall a more miserable morning than this one.

Back in the shop he pulled up his stool and sat behind the counter, leafing through the newspaper report that the journalist Lucas had filed, only managing a brief chuckle at the picture of Lepantre on the second page, tugging at his trousers with one hand, glass of Cognac held high in the other. Tesserat refolded the paper and pushed it aside, glancing through his shop window when he heard the grating roll up on the Fontaine des Fleurs. Between the trees he saw Eric, the Chaberts' son, step out on to the pavement, look up and down the *place* just as he had done, then disappear back inside to sort out the displays.

For the first time in years Tesserat found himself fancying a smoke. The feel of that dry paper tube between his fingers, the soft give of the filter on his lips, the first loosening of the tight tobacco as the flame caught hold and then, aaaaah, that first mouthful of smoke, a tug in the throat and the glorious filling of the lungs. If his wife, Christine, hadn't come down at that very moment from their apartment above the shop, swishing through the bead curtain at the bottom of the stairs, her shivering Pomeranian Sutti cradled in one arm, Marc Tesserat was pretty sure he'd have helped himself to a pack from the shelves behind him – and the devil take it.

Bustling round the shop, straightening the pegs of lottery tickets, tidying the pen displays and kicking the doormat into place with the toe of a zip-up bootee, Christine noticed her husband's mood immediately, recognised the look, though she failed to identify its source. The hang-dog expression, the hunched shoulders, the grey bristles on his chin and the tip of his shirt collar caught in a twist of his scarf. It was like the time he'd given up smoking, she thought: nothing could stir him, nothing could reach him.

'Go on up to Mazzelli's,' she chided, squaring off a display of chewing-gum on the counter and resetting a trembling Sutti in the crook of her elbow. 'A drink with the boys will do you good,' she said. 'Go on now, off with you. I can look after things here.' And she turned him out from behind the counter, tidying his shirt collar as he passed and reaching up to press her lips to his stubbled cheek. Squeezed between them, Sutti growled dangerously.

But as she watched him slip out of the door, giving an extra turn to his scarf and digging his hands into his pockets, Christine, too, began to sense how everything seemed to have changed overnight. Something in the air. Something strange and unsettling. Even Sutti seemed to notice it, a tiny frown puckering his brow, as she bent down and placed him gently in his basket by the radiator. Straightening up, she shuddered, pulled her fleece round her and took up the paper that her husband had put aside. Shaking it out and settling down to read the news, it didn't take her long to realise what that something in the air was.

Up at Mazzelli's, Tesserat found the mood no lighter. Aldo was behind the bar, shaking his head as he scanned the newspaper, Lepantre was perched on a stool complaining about bloody journalists and how they'd misquoted him, while Tomas seemed in no particular hurry to set out tables on the terrace. Tesserat took his usual stool, nodded greetings to those already there and ordered a *café-calva*, keeping his eyes off the cigarette that Aldo had left smoking in an ashtray while he busied himself with the Gaggia. By the time his coffee arrived, Tesserat's glass of Calvados was long gone and he ordered another.

Aldo reached for the bottle, refilled Tesserat's glass and set another two on the bar. He poured healthy measures into each, slid one across to Lepantre and kept the other for himself, swirling the liquor and staring into its caramel depths. Together, the three men lifted their drinks but made no toast.

If Doriane, Tesserat, Lepantre and the Mazzellis had been the first to start the day, then Caroline Parmentier at the Auberge de la Fontaine Dorée was not far behind, thanks to the telephone in Reception. Since a little after eight, it had been ringing off the hook. Bookings for lunch, bookings for dinner. In February, it was never this busy midweek and Caroline couldn't for the life of her understand why it should suddenly be so hectic. Normally there was time enough to get Yvette sorted out, pour herself some coffee and butter the crust of a Doriane baguette before settling at Reception with the newspaper. Just as she'd done for the last twenty years, since she'd first arrived in St Bédard, a summer job as a waitress, and the inn-keeper's son had fallen in love with her.

But not this morning. The phone hadn't stopped. It was only when she started telling callers that there were no more tables for lunch or dinner that she suddenly understood. Even if she couldn't quite believe it.

The Martners.

People had seen the TV news the night before, read their morning papers, and were keen to come and soak up the atmosphere. When she told Michel of her suspicions, he shrugged and suggested they get some more tables up from the basement, squeeze in a few more customers, maybe even open up the terrace. They had enough *magret*, he said, there was a slab of *foie gras* that needed eating and the *îles flottantes* from the night before could do with finishing up. Caroline Parmentier was lost for words. She gave her husband an icy look, turned on her heel, left him at his range and marched out into the dining room. Straightening covers as she passed between the tables, she made her way to the terrace windows and busily twitched the window drapes into order, dusting a cobweb from a fold with a tut and a shake of her head.

Across the *place*, between the trees, the Dumés' front door opened and Caroline watched as Mathilde, old Dumé's daughter-in-law, stepped out on to the pavement, shooing her three children ahead of her. Late as usual, thought Caroline. And then, as she watched, she noticed Mathilde pause as she belted up her raincoat, as though she, too, had sensed something out of kilter. Peering around the square and then up at the low, leaden sky, she seemed to shudder, pulled her coat closer, then reached out to grab her youngest as he stepped off the pavement without looking. A market van on its way to Bulot's *charcuterie* swayed out to miss him and the little fellow collected a sharp smack on the back of his bare legs to wake him up. Then, making sure the door had closed behind her, Mathilde herded her brood into shape and started them off down the slope, satchels over their shoulders, shoes scuffing the pavement. Setting a healthy pace, they looked to Caroline, the four of them, as though they were fleeing a disaster, anxious to be clear of the *place* rather than make it to school before the gates closed.

By lunchtime not even the Chaberts' racks of flowers or the happy chatter of the fountain could lighten the mood that gripped the centre of St Bédard. The *boules* pitch was empty when normally a game would be in progress, the sparrows were still and silent, and a cold, unfriendly breeze riffled its way through the trees. On the steps of the *pharmacie*, Madame Héliard and the Widow Blanc conferred, while further down Adéline Séguin and Clotilde Lepantre did the same. When a pair of police vans pulled up outside the *gendarmerie* at the bottom of the square, all four stopped their whispering and turned in that direction as a dozen gendarmes clambered out to continue their house-to-house enquiries.

Only old Dumé seemed unmoved. Standing outside the Fontaine des Fleurs, he watched the gendarmes divide into two groups and cross the Brieuc road, heading towards them. He turned to Eric and said: 'Wasn't so long ago, my son, and they'd have given the killer a medal.'

'Before my time,' replied Eric, with a mournful look as sad and lost as any, save old Dumé's, in St Bédard the morning after the murders.

10

The big guns that Jacquot and Brunet had been expecting made their appearance three days after the discovery of the bodies, shortly before lunch on Saturday.

Jacquot was at home when the call came through from headquarters, in the bath, suds to his chin and Cesaria Evora on the headphones. Claudine knew he'd never hear the low buzz of his mobile phone so she reached across the bed, where she'd been reading, snug and content after his caressing Saturday-morning wake-up call, picked up the mobile and switched it on. She recognised Brunet's voice immediately. 'He's in the bath, Jean. Hold on a moment, I'll get him for you.'

Reluctantly she slid from the warmth of the bed, pulled on a dressing-gown and padded across their bedroom to the adjoining bathroom.

The room was hot and steamy, the mirrors and marble tiles streaked and dulled with condensation. In the centre of the room, in a scroll-top tub they had bought in an antiques warehouse in L'Isle-sur-la-Sorgue the summer before, Jacquot lay stretched out, elbows over the edge of the bath and head resting on a folded hand-towel. His eyes were closed and his lips pum-pum-pummed to the tinny beat of a Cesaria Evora track. Claudine knelt beside him and tugged the hanging ponytail. He sat up abruptly, taken by surprise, and she gasped as a wave of soapy water surged over the edge of the bath. Reaching for the towel he'd been using as a pillow, she held out the mobile to him: 'It's Jean.'

Jacquot gave her a look of mock menace, as though to say, 'I'll deal with you in a moment', slipped off his headphones and took the phone. 'Yes, Jean?'

As Jacquot listened to his colleague, he watched Claudine take the towel, unfold it, drop it on to the floor and move it round with her foot, mopping up the overflow and tut-tutting as she did so, revealing her long brown legs with each sweep, the tie of her dressing-gown dancing across the taut skin of her thighs.

'Thought you should know, boss,' Brunet was saying. 'A Chief Inspector Gastal is on his way down from Lyon with two gentlemen from the German authorities. Hans Dietering from Sicherheitsdienst head office in Bonn and Frank Warendorf from BfV Munich, the federal boys.'

Jacquot sat up straighter at that. The BfV, the Bundesamt für Verfassungsshutz? And Sicherheitsdienst? Heavyweights. The real thing. And bigger guns than they'd expected.

And then that other name. Gastal? Surely it couldn't be. Not Alain Gastal. From Marseilles and Toulon. But it had to be. That was where they'd posted him. To Lyon. Gastal. Of all people. *Merde*.

'This Gastal phoned Mougeon,' continued Brunet. 'Told him to organise things. Said he wanted you and Rochet and everything we have so far.'

Mougeon was one of the desk sergeants at Cavaillon and Georges Rochet was the station head, Jacquot's immediate boss. Jacquot could imagine Rochet's annoyance at being called in on a Saturday. Not that he was too happy about it himself. There was a match that afternoon and he'd been looking forward to it – lunch with Claudine, a tumbler of Armagnac, a fat cigar and his feet up in front of the TV. Wales versus France.

And why all the rush anyway? thought Jacquot. Surely this could wait for Monday. They still hadn't received the full forensic report from Fournier's office, or the post-mortem findings from Pathology. All they had were the bare details: a statement of discovery from the house-cleaner, an initial scene-of-crime report and a plastic wallet filled with a stack of vibrant, glossy photos.

And still no sign of a weapon.

'Where are you now?' asked Jacquot.

'I got in a few minutes ago. Thought I'd get everything organised.' Brunet lived in town, in a flat near Headquarters.

'Good. When are they expected?'

It was a two-hour drive from Lyon, so maybe there was still time for a late breakfast with Claudine before he had to leave. She had finished wiping the floor and had come to sit on the edge of the bath, the satin of her wrap, he noticed, seductively tight and shiny where she'd gathered it against her legs. He watched her pick up the half-smoked joint from the stool beside the bath, reach for the matches and relight it. She pointed at the soap-dish he'd been using as an ashtray and shook her finger at him, backwards and forwards, naughty boy, smiling, then took a deep pull until the home-grown grass popped and crackled. She tipped back her head and blew the smoke at the beams in the ceiling. The front of her dressing-gown had loosened and the skin between her breasts shone, beaded with moisture from the heat and exertion, the hard brown buttons of her nipples pressing against the satin.

Maybe breakfast in bed, thought Jacquot.

'The storm's a beauty,' replied Brunet, clearly holding back bad news. 'It's sure to slow them down.'

Jacquot's heart fell.

'When are they expected?' he asked again, now certain there'd be no time for breakfast. Or anything else.

'Half an hour, at the outside.'

'*Merde*,' said Jacquot, and broke the connection. He handed Claudine the mobile, reclaimed the joint and took a puff.

'At fifty years of age, if that's how old you really are, and a police officer to boot, you should know better,' said Claudine, with a stern look.

'And so should you,' smiled Jacquot, standing up from the bath-water and sending another, smaller wave over her freshly dried floor. 'Whatever age you are.'

'Young,' replied Claudine, taking the joint back. 'Far too young to hang around with an old *blagueur* like you. All my girlfriends tell me that.'

'They don't know any better.'

'They'd better not,' she said, watching him step from the bath, reach for the towel he'd laid over the radiator and start to dry himself.

He might be fifty, thought Claudine, moving her legs to make room for him, but he still had a good body. Firm round the tummy, those hard little buttocks, the wide shoulders and trim waist, the well-muscled arms and legs strong enough, as she well knew, to sweep her off her feet and carry her upstairs. She smiled, watching him dry himself. Her own little bit of rough. Her very own *vrai dur*. But always a gentle man, an easy man to love. She remembered the first time they'd met, in that gallery in Marseilles, the off-duty *flic* buying one of her paintings, not knowing that she was the artist. And then the second time their paths crossed, a year later, here in Cavaillon, when he had raised her hand to his lips and she had felt his breath on her fingers. He had been irresistible then – even before she properly knew him – and was irresistible still.

Claudine leaned forward and ran the backs of her fingers across Jacquot's wet backside. 'It's cassoulet for dinner. And then me. So don't be late home, you hear?'

'I could make it back for lunch, if I'm lucky.' He knew there was little chance of that.

So did she. She gave him a look to confirm it.

'Dinner will do fine. Anyway, I like you when you're hungry. Maybe me first and then the cassoulet. Work up an appetite.'

'Why is it . . . ?' Jacquot began, glancing up at her. 'Why is it you never remind me of other . . . ?'

Claudine smiled in that way she had, the way he loved.

'Don't swear,' she replied, mashing out the joint in the soap-dish. 'You know how I hate bad language.'

11

Peeling potatoes at the kitchen table, Florence Picard looked up with a start as the first pellets of rain smacked against the kitchen windows of the Château de Vausigne. She'd been expecting the rain since before breakfast, but it still took her by surprise. There was a storm brewing, for sure, and not too far off by the sound of it, a low grumble of thunder following the rain and making that loose pane of glass in the kitchen door tremble.

Maybe, she thought, leaning down to her basket to pick out another potato, a good blow would help clear the air. It certainly needed clearing. Overcast one day, sun the next, then clouds back again the day after. Of course, it was the time of year . . . always changeable, you couldn't rely on it. But still . . . All this chopping and changing. It was enough to set your teeth on edge.

Except Florence knew that it wasn't just the weather that was bothering her. The last few days had been . . . She tried to settle on the right word as a length of potato peel curled on to the newspaper in her lap, tried to summon up a suitable phrase to best describe her state of mind. Uncomfortable. Everything out of sorts. That was it, that was how she felt. Out of sorts.

For the life of her, Florence hadn't known what to make of it all. When Monique, the girl from the village who came in to help three days a week, had clattered down the kitchen steps on Wednesday afternoon and told her the news, the de Vausignes' housekeeper had had to sit herself down and have the girl fetch her a small glass of *pineau*, no ice.

Murder? In St Bédard? No, it wasn't possible, surely.

But of course it was. There it was on the radio, in the paper, on TV. And while Monique's account – which she'd got from her mother, who'd got it from Clotilde Lepantre – might only have flirted with the truth, the fact remained that a dreadful, dreadful thing had happened. And on their own doorstep. Four deaths – murders – not half a dozen kilometres from the gates of the château. Just along the road. The nearest house. Why you could even see a corner of the Martners' vines from the top landing window. Close as pips.

That Wednesday, when she'd finished the *pineau* and Monique had finally started on her chores, Florence went straight to the apartment above the kitchen and changed into black. It was the least she could do, she'd decided, a mark of respect. Not that she'd known the Martners, you understand. Recognised the wife when she saw her – shopping in St Bédard, browsing through the stalls at the Friday market, driving around in that car of theirs – but they'd never spoken. A tall, distinguished-looking lady she was, straight grey hair to her shoulders; always in slacks and a man's shirt, sneakers too of all things, yet still managed to look elegant. Elegant, but also a little . . . Florence searched for the word . . . A little *masculin*.

Now, three days later, sitting at the kitchen table, the black shoes that Florence wore for funerals (which no amount of olive oil would soften around the ankles) were beginning to pinch something dreadful. Toe to heel, she eased off the tightest of the pair and sighed with relief. Working her toes and rolling her ankle, she wondered how many others would be wearing black. The Widow Blanc, but she'd been dressed in black as long as Florence could remember; Adéline and Odile, *c'était certain*; that sniffy *anglaise* at the *auberge*, of course; Denise at the flower shop; Christine at the *tabac*, Delphine at the *charcuterie*. As for Madame Héliard at the *pharmacie* (sending her husband off to some home like that, when the poor man's memory started going, and taking over the business the way she had), if she decided on the full black strip she'd look more of an old crow than she normally did.

And armbands for the men? Florence wondered. There'd certainly be some discussion about that at Mazzelli's bar. Tesserat probably would; Doriane, the baker, would; Denise's husband Fernand, no question; Clotilde's husband, Claude; the butcher Bulot. But not Michel at the *auberge*. Not after what the Boches did to his grandfather in the war. And certainly not Simon Dumé, thought Florence. No chance of that.

She seemed to remember it had been old Dumé, next door to the Fontaine des Fleurs, who'd pointed her out – Madame Martner, that is – not long after they'd first arrived, coming out of Ribaud's antiques shop on Place Vausigne.

Bought the old Taillard place, Dumé had told her, doing it up. Spending a fortune they are. Money no object. Kraut, he'd added, with a disapproving clearing of the throat.

But still, thought Florence. German or not . . .

Reaching for the last potato, breaking off a scab of mud with her thumb, Florence heard footsteps cross the hallway above – Madame la Comtesse – the front door open and close and, out in the drive, her husband, Picard, start up the Citroën. He'd been sitting out there thirty minutes now, from when Madame called down to have him bring round the car. No consideration. Off to Cavaillon for lunch, and that was all there was to it. And if Picard had to wait a half-hour while Madame got herself ready, then wait he would.

And going off to lunch anyway, at a time like this. With murders down the road. It didn't seem right, was how Florence saw it. Even if it didn't surprise her.

There'd be no black upstairs, she'd put money on it. Indeed, it was almost as if the news of the Martners' deaths hadn't filtered through to the Comte and Comtesse – even with everything in the papers and on TV. But, then, that was how it had always been. The Martners might have been neighbours but that was as far as it had ever gone. Geography, that was all it was. Not once, in the ten years they'd lived there, had the doctor and his wife ever set foot in the château. Not drinks, not dinner – nothing. Of course, being German didn't help. But Florence knew it wasn't just a question of nationality. It was class, too. A retired dentist? *Mais non.*

The news of the Martners' deaths had, of course, filtered through. Serving coffee in the library, Florence's husband had seen the Comte lay down his newspaper after reading the story and shake his head in disbelief. And Madame la Comtesse was no different. On Thursday night Florence had overheard her on the phone, telling her son Antoine about the murders.

'You think Paris is dangerous, my darling – you should live down here. Everyone's mortified. Imagine! And the killer still on the loose . . .'

God save us from that Antoine, thought Florence, wrapping up the peelings in the newspaper, straightening her stocking and pushing her shoe back on. He'd probably bring some film crew down here and do one of those dreadful films he made – straight-to-video stuff, Monique had told her. Whatever that was. Four terrible murders nothing more than a chance for the son and heir to make some money. A proper hard day's work wouldn't do him any harm, and that was certain.

Florence got painfully to her feet, hobbled over to the bin and dropped the peelings into it. These shoes would be the death of her, she thought, and as she bent down to ease a finger between ankle and leather she wondered how much longer she should wear them. A day? Two days? Maybe after church on Sunday. After all, she didn't really know the Martners. And they weren't from round here . . .

Outside, a clap of thunder ricocheted off the kitchen window and Florence started at the closeness of it.

12

Brunet had been right about the storm. It was indeed a beauty. Jacquot had seen it first from the bathroom window as he waited for the bath to fill, storm clouds looming in from Montmirail, crackling with distant thunder and threaded with silent streaks of lightning. As he wiped away the condensation on the window pane, the first scurry of rain rattled an advance warning against the glass, surprising him with its strength and suddenness, smearing his view of the valley and distant hills.

And when, twenty minutes after Brunet's call, Jacquot stepped from the house in that brief lull following the first squall, he felt a sharp, electric tension pluck at the hairs on the back of his neck, and reached his car only moments before the first real raindrops fell. As he made himself comfortable behind the wheel he listened to them tapping on the Peugeot's roof, then started the engine, reached for the wiper switch and backed down the drive. By the time he was on the road, the wind was gusting through the treetops and the tapping on the car roof had become a drumbeat.

That Saturday morning, heading for town, Jacquot drove faster than normal. Not just for the sake of his visitors from Lyon, Munich and Bonn, but for himself too. Sometimes Jacquot just felt like it. A little solo speed. A little adrenaline to start the day. Nothing more. He liked the way the old Peugeot held to the curving lane that led down from the house, his foot pressed hard on the pedal, rows of bare vines flashing past, almost unseen, to either side of him. It always gave him a little kick of pleasure, this run down the hill, and the rain hammering on his windscreen this Saturday morning added an extra little rush. Abominable conditions.

Not that driving fast along the lane that led to Claudine's house was that risky a proposition. A few hundred metres beyond the house, an old olive mill that Claudine had been gradually and carefully renovating since her mother died, the lane petered out into a grassy track leading up into the hills behind the house. And where it joined the Rocsabin to Barjas road a couple of kilometres down the slope, the *sans-issue* sign she'd persuaded the local council to put up ensured a certain privacy.

Also, there was a point a few metres from the gate where it was possible to see the entire length of the lane spooling down into the valley. Since there were no turn-offs and no other houses, Jacquot knew he could always push the old Peugeot rather harder than he ought. It was a kind of private speedway, and in the two years he'd been there he had known that, if he wanted to, he could get to the bottom of the lane before any car turning into it might pose a problem.

Jacquot kept up his speed all the way to Cavaillon, slowing only briefly when he reached the slipway on to the main road, and only using the brake again when the first of the town's traffic-lights brought him to a halt. Earlier he'd pulled past a convoy of five lorries packed tightly together in the same lane, their huge wheels sending up an almost solid wall of spray that his wipers did little to clear. He had flashed his lights and beeped his horn as he passed, hoping none of their drivers would take it into his head to pull out and overtake. Now, at the first set of Cavaillon's traffic-lights, two of the lorries drew up beside and behind him, air brakes hissing, a chrome radiator grille filling his rear-view mirror, and a pair of massive, dripping wheel arches inches from his door.

He knew what the drivers were up to, pulling in so close, releasing and applying their air brakes, revving their engines until his door panels trembled. Lorry drivers didn't take kindly to flashed lights and beeping horns if they suspected it might be personal, and they usually took great pleasure in catching up a few kilometres further on and applying a little mechanical muscle.

For a moment Jacquot wondered if he should give them a little surprise by stretching his arm out of the window, clamping the blue police light on the Peugeot's roof and sounding the siren. But he decided against it, lulled by the steady rhythm of the wipers and the rush of warm air from the heating. It was only when the lorry behind him let out a deafening blast from its klaxon that he noticed the lights had changed.

Smoking in the morning, he thought, with a wry grin. He'd been miles away.

When Jacquot reached Headquarters in Cavaillon he pulled into the courtyard and parked beside a large black Mercedes. He knew at once, with a sinking heart, that Brunet's big guns had beaten him to it.

Gastal would love that.

Pulling up his collar, Jacquot hefted himself from the car, ran through the pelting rain and up the steps into the main hall of the *gendarmerie*. Brunet was waiting for him with Mougeon at the duty sergeant's desk.

'They arrived five minutes ago,' said Brunet. 'Went straight up to Rochet's office.'

The two men headed for the lift, Jacquot tugging off his raincoat, using his scarf to wipe the rain from his hair and face. The lift bell pinged and the doors slid open. The two men got in and Brunet pressed the button for the fourth floor.

'Rochet asked me to have you join them the moment you arrived.'

'The files?'

'I took everything through to him when he got in. Give him time to catch up.'

The lift doors opened at the fourth floor and the two men stepped out.

'What are they like, the Germans?' asked Jacquot, turning left and heading for Rochet's office. There was no need to ask about Gastal. He knew all there was to know.

'Very pleasant,' said Brunet lightly. 'I think you'll like them.'

Walking a step ahead, Jacquot missed his assistant's grim little smile but the moment they entered Rochet's office Jacquot knew that Brunet had been having him on. He didn't like the look of the visitors one little bit.

The three men, sitting comfortably at Rochet's desk, looked crisply business-like and, for a Saturday, faultlessly turned out. Creases were sharp, shoe-caps buffed to a military shine, and tie knots set just so in stiff white collars. All three wore suits, the toad Gastal's ridiculously double-breasted, the ribbon of the Légion tucked neatly and unmistakably into his buttonhole.

'Ah, Daniel, so sorry to drag you in on a Saturday, but we need to brief our friends here,' said Rochet, a tall, gentle man for whom Jacquot had a large regard, a widower who loved the opera and timed his annual leave for the bird migration at Falsterbö in Sweden. 'I believe you already know Chief Inspector Gastal?'

Gastal. Alain Gastal. Of course Jacquot knew him. His old partner. As slippery as a skinned grape, a gun-slinger street cop with dubious friends turned rising star at the Lyon offices of the Direction Générale de la Sécurité Extérieure. The man Jacquot had worked with in Marseilles for just two short weeks, long enough to know there would never be anything close to friendship, just a barely civilised brew made up of Jacquot's usually quiet restraint and Gastal's dangerous self-interest.

In Marseilles, three years earlier, that fragile brew had finally boiled over and Jacquot's composure had cracked. A drugs bust had gone wrong, two hundred kilos of cocaine went missing, and Gastal had put Jacquot in the frame. When he realised what Gastal was up to, Jacquot had taken a swing in the commissioner's office and broken his partner's nose. They hadn't seen each other since.

But somewhere along the line, it was clear that the puffer-fish Gastal had picked up some clout, some *piston*. Three weeks after their spat, Jacquot the nose-breaker had been reassigned to Cavaillon to work out his pension, a long way from any fast track, while Gastal found himself transferred to the DGSE in Lyon. Although they shared the same rank, Gastal's posting at Lyon gave him a nominal superiority, which Jacquot had no doubt his old partner would use to the full.

A few years younger, Jacquot had told Claudine that morning, as he pulled on his scarf and overcoat at the front door. And ten times snottier. A hundred times snottier. Dangerous, too.

Claudine, still in her robe, had leaned up to kiss him goodbye and, with their lips still touching, had said that Gastal, whoever he was, couldn't possibly know a woman who would do what she planned doing to Jacquot when he got home that evening.

Looking at Gastal now, for the first time in three years, Jacquot reckoned Claudine was right. Or if Gastal ever did have a woman do what Claudine was planning, then he'd probably have to pay through the nose for it. His broken nose. Which made Jacquot feel, he had to admit, just that little bit better.

Jacquot was also glad he'd gone no further than jeans and polo-neck for the meeting, unconcerned by Gastal's disapproving once-over. And pleased, too, that he'd kept his weight. At forty-six, Gastal may have been a sharp operator in Toulon and Marseilles, but the good life in Lyon – all those departmental lunches at La Tour Rose, Léon and Bocuse – had fattened him up, an accomplishment only narrowly camouflaged by the shiny double-breasted suit. And fat policemen in smart new suits had always worried Jacquot, as did Gastal's thinner crop of black hair, now combed forward to a point. It gave him a wily, untrustworthy air. The Marseilles tan was gone too and his skin had the sallow bloom of a *boudin* fresh from the steamer. Jacquot wondered if he still sucked snails from their shells, as he had in Marseilles. His party trick.

The two men shook hands, Gastal with the oily smile of previous acquaintance, Jacquot with a brief nod. Gastal made a point of staying seated.

'Danny. Always a pleasure.'

'Alain.' Jacquot smiled amiably, then turned to his companions.

Unlike Gastal, the two Germans had risen to their feet. The first, introduced with a wave of the hand by Gastal as Frank Warendorf, chief inspector from Munich Criminal Investigations (Jacquot duly noted the easy familiarity Gastal had meant him to catch), was a tall, heavy-set man with wavy, mouse-coloured hair, the thickest eyebrows and blackest eyes that Jacquot had ever seen, and a sharp little smile that cut creases into his cheeks. He also wore glasses, the frames so delicate that Jacquot only noticed them when the light from Rochet's desk-lamp flashed across the lenses.

His colleague, Hans Dietering, was as tall as Warendorf but slimmer, with a gym-trained frame that showed in his shoulders and in his narrow waist. His rust-coloured hair was as sparse as Gastal's, but to compensate he'd cultivated a thin, clipped moustache, a strip

of red sandpaper that rode above freckled marmalade lips, slightly
gapped front teeth and a deeply cleft chin. Both men, Jacquot
decided, looked exactly how ambitious senior policemen should
look, both tightly Teutonic, corporate, disciplined and, he guessed,
ruthlessly efficient and just as unimaginative. And for all their
comradely politeness, their slim smiles and standing to shake his
hand (Dietering accompanying the act with the faintest click of
heels and a stiff bow), Jacquot had no doubt whatsoever that it
wouldn't take them long to get as far up his nose as Gastal had.

'Messieurs, welcome to Cavaillon,' nodded Jacquot, indicating
that there was no need for them to stand and that they should both
take their seats. Pulling up a chair, he caught Brunet's eye. His assistant looked away studiously.

When everyone was comfortable, Gastal beat Rochet to it and,
with only the slightest tip of the head in the chief's direction, got
the ball rolling. Dietering and Warendorf, he explained, had flown
down from Bonn and Munich the night before. Frank would be
returning to Munich from Lyon's Satolas airport that evening but
Dietering would be staying on as an observer.

'Observer?' asked Jacquot lightly.

'I'm booked in at the Novotel,' said Dietering, stepping in before
Gastal could reply. 'I'm here to help in whatever way I can. For as
long as it takes.'

And report back to Gastal and Warendorf every move I make,
thought Jacquot grimly, but noted that the man's voice was warmer
than he'd expected, and his tone surprisingly deferential.

'Of course,' continued Warendorf, taking over from the younger
man, maybe sensing Jacquot's unease, 'it goes without saying that
the jurisdiction and direction of the case remain yours, but Hans
here will be on hand whenever you need him. There are,' he added,
glancing at Gastal, 'certain security implications, I'm sure you'll
appreciate.'

'This is not political,' said Jacquot, before Gastal could get a word
in, looking to Rochet for support.

The older man shrugged noncommittally and laced his fingers.

Jacquot turned back to Warendorf. 'This is not an assassination,
you know. It's a domestic, pure and simple. Someone just—'

'Nevertheless,' interrupted Warendorf, 'the Bureau would like to be involved, at every level, whatever the nature of the . . . ah, assault turns out to be. Frau Martner was, as I'm sure you'll appreciate, very well connected, politically, through her father. As is her daughter's husband, Herr Brauer. So, why don't we see what you've got so far?'

And with that, effectively dismissing Jacquot's opinion, they set to work, listening intently as Jacquot ran them through progress so far, detailing his findings at the site, the lack of a clear motive, suspects, weapon, with a résumé of Fournier's initial report.

And all the way through the briefing, Jacquot wished he'd kept the joint for later.

It was past two o'clock when Rochet suggested, during a break in the conversation, some lunch.

For the first time since he'd set eyes on Gastal, Jacquot's spirits lifted. He was starving: all this talk had given him an appetite. He was about to get to his feet – maybe a late table at Chez Gaillard? Or perhaps La Dame, with a nice chilled bottle of red Sancerre? – when Warendorf suggested they send out for sandwiches. There was much to be done after all.

Warendorf looked across at Gastal, who nodded agreement.

'Good idea, just the thing,' said Gastal, though Jacquot suspected he didn't mean a word of it. Gastal loved his food.

Jacquot tried to catch Rochet's eye, but the older man avoided the look.

'Of course. Sandwiches,' said Rochet. 'Brunet, could you call Mougeon and have him rustle up something from the canteen?'

Jacquot clenched his teeth. No lunch. No rugby. No wonder he didn't like Germans.

It was getting dark by the time the meeting finally broke up. And still pelting with rain – glittering, silvery strands smacking down on to the cars in the car park. Sheltering at the top of the steps, the six men pulled up their collars and shook hands. Gastal and Warendorf were driving back to Lyon, Dietering was booked in at the Novotel and Rochet had to hurry if he was going to make the first act of *Der Rosenkavalier* at Orange. As for Brunet, he'd pulled a cape over his head, slipped on his cycle clips and was snapping down the catches on his helmet.

The Novotel, thought Jacquot. A Saturday night. A stranger in town. He looked at the overnight case at Dietering's feet and knew there was nothing else he could do.

His teeth were clenched tighter than a vice, but he managed to speak through them all the same: 'Ever tried cassoulet, Hans?'

13

Old Dumé sat at a table by the door of Mazzelli's, watched the rain slant through the streetlights in the *place* and listened to the chat across the room. They were all there, hunched round the bar: Lepantre, in a gaudy shell-suit that seemed to whistle with every movement; Bulot, twisting his butcher's whiskers; Mazzelli, perched on his favourite corner stool, a cigarette clamped between pudgy fingers; Tesserat, tapping his tin of pastilles on the zinc bar; and Fernand Chabert, on a rare visit, stirring the ice in his pastis with a long silver spoon. Behind the bar, Tomas leaned back against the Gaggia and thumbed his way through a GameBoy, glancing up every now and then to see if any glasses needed topping up.

Sergeant Lanclos, in civvies, had left the bar a few minutes earlier after fielding their questions as to progress in the Martner investigation. Now, in full possession of the latest facts, the five of them debated the single question that had perplexed everyone in St Bédard since news of the murders had broken.

Who could have done such a thing?

'It's not no one from round 'ere, that's for a certainty,' was Mazzelli's opinion, delivered in his signature mix 'n' match French and Italian. He had lived in St Bédard as long as any of them, but Mazzelli had never lost his fruity Italian accent. 'They not 'ave too many friends, I grant you, but I don't think of any enemies either.'

'I'll tell you one thing,' said Lepantre, rolling his neck out of his zippered collar. 'Whoever did it, they'll never find him. No way those cops from Cavaillon are going to crack this one. Load of schoolboys coming round asking their damn-fool questions.'

His voice took on a squeaky pitch to mimic them: '"Did you know the Martners? Did you see or hear anything unusual in the days leading up to the murders? Where were you between five and seven on Wednesday morning?"

'On the shitter is where,' said Lepantre, with a grin.

Then, in the squeaky voice again: '"And is there someone who can account for your whereabouts on the morning in question?"

'Not likely, there isn't.'

'"Well, thank you very much, Monsieur. If there's anything you remember . . ."'

Lepantre grunted, cleared his throat. 'No, no, no,' he continued. 'They're free and clear, whoever did it, and that's the truth. Long gone by now. Long gone.'

'So you don't reckon it's someone local, then?' asked Bulot, fat pink fingers working at a pimple on his chin.

'Do you?' Lepantre shook his head. 'You ask me, it's professional. Gotta be. A hit. Mafia, maybe. Or one of those German outfits – Baader-something. The Red Brigade. That lot.'

'Brigate Rosse, Claudio,' said Mazzelli. 'They're Italian, not German.'

'Whatever, whatever,' continued Lepantre. 'But I'll tell you this – I'll tell you this. There's money at the root of it. You'll see.'

'But you heard the sergeant,' said Bulot. 'There's nothing missing, nothing stolen. And all that money in the kitchen drawer. Right there. Thousands, that's what he said. Thousands.'

'What I mean is,' said Lepantre slowly, as though explaining something to a child, 'there's money maybe owed and not repaid. A debt not honoured. That sort of thing. Look at what they spent on Taillard's place, doing it up. And the holidays. All over the place they were. And he's a dentist? What dentist earns that kind of money, eh? Tell me that. They borrowed too much, somewhere shady, and couldn't pay it back.'

'Stocks and shares, that's what it is,' said Tesserat, finishing off his *Calva* and tapping the empty glass on the bar to attract Tomas's attention. 'That's where their money comes from. You should see the papers and magazines the doctor had on order. All the flower stuff, scientific and the like, that's to be expected, but there's the financials too. Lots of 'em.'

'Then they've swindled someone,' said Lepantre, lazy brown eyes flicking from one face to another, looking for agreement. 'Fraud. Some poor sod's taken a fall 'cause of something Martner's done and he's come down here looking to get his money's worth.'

'But why the child?' asked Chabert quietly, tapping his spoon against the glass before laying it on the bar. 'Why kill the child?'

Tesserat nodded his head. 'Fernand's right,' he said. 'Why kill the girl?'

'To make a point,' said Lepantre, just a little too quickly, brought up short by this new consideration. 'That's why I said Mafia in the first place. Setting an example, they were. Just to show what happens . . .'

Turning the tin of pastilles between his fingers, Tesserat continued, as though Lepantre hadn't spoken: 'I'll tell you why. Because the girl knew the killer. She recognised him. He had to kill her. Simple as that.'

Reaching for an ashtray and stubbing out his cigarette, Mazzelli looked doubtful. 'So what you're sayin', you think the killer come from round here? Or not? Someone local? Someone in St Bédard . . . ?'

'Not necessarily,' replied Tesserat. 'Maybe it's someone from where they lived before. Before the Martners came here. Maybe you're right,' he continued, nodding at Lepantre. 'Maybe it is some kind of fraud. Or something like it. Someone catching up with them, tracking them down. Maybe that's why they moved here in the first place. To get away. Keep a low profile.'

There was silence while this new possibility was pondered. But it didn't last long.

'You're all of you wrong, is my opinion.'

It was Dumé by the window, digging out the bowl of his pipe with a matchstick.

The men at the bar turned in his direction.

'So,' called out Lepantre, 'what's your best shot, then?'

'They was Krauts,' replied Dumé quietly, tapping his pipe in the

ashtray. 'I know it. You all know it. There's people still remember
. . . Simple as that.'

Another silence settled round the bar as they took this in, just
the snick of snooker balls from the table in the back room.

'So why wait ten years?' asked Bulot at last, shaking his head.
'All this time they've been here? No, no, it doesn't make sense. No
sense at all.'

'And it's not like they're the only Germans in these parts,' added
Lepantre. 'So why the Martners, eh? No, no, *mon vieux*, it's more
than that, you'll see.'

'Suit yourselves,' said Dumé, getting to his feet and reaching into
his pocket for money. 'But you asks me, it's a settling of accounts,
that's what it is. Not fraud. Nothing like that. It's for what they gone
and did back then. And Martner? Why not? He's one of them. And
old enough. You mark my words, there's something he probably
done come home to roost. And good riddance,' added Dumé,
picking up his stick from the back of his chair and making for the
door. 'Good riddance to the lot of them, is what I say.' And pulling
open the door he stepped out into the hammering rain.

14

There had always been the slim possibility that Hans Dietering would decline Jacquot's invitation to share Claudine's cassoulet.

It was the weekend after all, a Saturday night, and it wouldn't have taken the greatest skills of deduction on Dietering's part for him to realise that Jacquot was simply being polite.

But rather than decline and ask instead for a lift to his hotel, the man had said yes, he would be delighted, how kind. And please, he said, as they hurried through the rain to Jacquot's car, now that they'd be working together, to call him Hans.

'Daniel,' said Jacquot. 'Or Dan. Whichever you wish.'

'Daniel for now,' replied Hans, snapping on his seat-belt and loosening his tie with a 'do-you-mind?'.

To which Jacquot responded, pulling out of the *gendarmerie*, that no, of course he had no objection, trying as he did so to work out which of them held the higher rank. Not that Hans appeared to care that much.

Five minutes later, approaching a garage on the outskirts of town, at the junction where Jacquot had been corralled by the two shuddering lorries earlier that day, Dietering asked him to pull in, jumped from the car and returned from the garage shop a few minutes later with a paper cone of flowers, a small box of sugared almonds and a bagged bottle.

'For your wife,' Dietering explained, turning to drop the gifts on the back seat. 'And for us, too,' he added, opening the bag to reveal a bottle of what Jacquot knew was the most expensive Bas Armagnac on the shelves.

'That's very kind of you,' said Jacquot, not bothering to correct Dietering about Claudine being his wife, and as he swung back out into the rain, accelerating to fill a gap in the line of traffic headed out of town, he found himself quietly intrigued. The Christian names. The loosened tie. The thoughtful, unexpected gifts. And Armagnac too. Maybe he'd been unfair, leaping to groundless conclusions. Just because the man was German . . . Just because he looked like he ate his granary toast with low-fat margarine and drank his decaf coffee without cream or sugar didn't mean the worst. As Jacquot slowed for the turning to his house, headlights sweeping past the *sans-issue* sign, he decided to withhold judgement until he had a few more facts at his disposal.

The facts didn't take long coming.

Later, Jacquot reckoned Claudine must have seen the pair of them getting out of the car for when she opened the front door, stepping aside as they hurried in from the rain, she showed not the least surprise or irritation that he had company. And taking in his apologetic there-was-nothing-I-could-do grimace behind Dietering's back, she'd made more of their unexpected guest than she might otherwise have done, to cover Jacquot's gentle annoyance and, more important, to let him know she didn't mind the intrusion. That it was okay, she understood.

And of course the flowers and almond *calissons* helped.

As did the Armagnac.

That evening, despite Jacquot's initial irritation and contrary to expectation, Hans Dietering proved a most attentive and entertaining guest. Apologising to Claudine for his intrusion at a weekend, even though it was Jacquot who'd extended the invitation, Dietering wasted no time in making himself thoroughly agreeable.

It began almost immediately.

When Claudine led them through into the salon, the first thing she did was switch on the lights as she entered so that the candles she'd placed all round the room wouldn't appear too conspicuous. After pausing a moment in the doorway, Dietering had looked at her and, with a gentle 'May I?', reached past her and switched the lights back off.

'Candles are so romantic, don't you think? And such a perfect light,' he'd added, then stepped down into the old mill room to admire the massive wooden grinding wheels that loomed behind the sofas, the collection of Balinese masks that leered down from above the hearth and a double line of watercolour landscapes – studies of the Montmirail hills, fields of lavender, a church spire rising above pantiled roofs – that Claudine had painted for her forthcoming summer exhibition in Aix.

While Jacquot watched his colleague's performance, he tried to decide whether Dietering's behaviour was sincere natural enthusiasm or just practised charm. Despite himself, he had to admit it seemed very like the former. The man looked genuinely impressed with the way Claudine had done the place up and interested in its contents, and at no time did Jacquot get the sense that he was thinking, Some coop for a cop. Which, as Jacquot well knew, was what most people in their line of work, and out of it come to that, would have thought.

Three years earlier, after the Gastal business in Marseilles, Jacquot had arrived in Cavaillon without a friend in the world and a blot on his copybook as big and as black as a Périgord truffle. Most of his colleagues down south had reckoned on his resigning rather than take up a third-league transfer to Cavaillon. The Chicago of Provence, they called it, with a roll of the eyes and a tongue in the cheek. A dead-end posting after Jacquot's time in Marseilles.

But Jacquot had surprised them all. As far as he was concerned resignation had never been an option. He liked his job, liked the challenge, and Marseilles or Cavaillon made little difference. With a philosophical shrug and only six years to run to a full pension, Jacquot had packed a bag and headed north.

And met Claudine. For the second time. The sales assistant in that gallery in Marseilles, the one he'd missed, the one he'd wondered about. The one who'd painted that lemon on a plate he kept in his study down the hall. As far as he was concerned, leaving Marseilles for Cavaillon had turned out to be about the best thing he'd ever done. Karma.

While Claudine made things ready in the kitchen – a *salade tiède* of chicken livers to precede the cassoulet – Jacquot pulled the cork from a bottle of Chablis she'd left on ice by one of the sofas. When he had poured the wine and passed a glass to Dietering, he was about to say how work was never discussed at home, a house rule, when Dietering started asking about the house's history, as though he had not the slightest intention of mentioning the case that had brought them together.

Standing there by the fire, a chilled glass of wine in his hand, Jacquot found himself warming to the German. Somewhere between Police Headquarters and home the man had lost the polished stiffness of Rochet's office, his voice less pitched and curt, while the thin red moustache, Jacquot now decided, rather suited him. Without his tie and jacket, slipped off with his raincoat, Dietering fitted into their home as comfortably as an old friend. He could tell a good wine when he tasted one and he'd nodded appreciatively when Jacquot selected some Stan Getz as a background soundtrack.

'Corcovado,' he said, as the Brazilian sax player tooted out the first few notes. 'Do you have him playing with Astrud Gilberto? What a combination. I saw them once, you know, in Bahia.'

By the time Claudine called them through to the kitchen, Jacquot decided he rather liked the man, and was pleased he'd issued the invitation to join them for supper.

At the kitchen table, on which Jacquot had earlier planned taking Claudine before dinner, Dietering also performed admirably. He made no fuss at the livers bleeding gently on to the *mâche* leaves, and when Claudine passed him a steaming bowl of cassoulet, he'd immediately broken off telling them about the arrival three months earlier of his first child in a Bonn hospital to concentrate his attention on the food.

Which, Jacquot knew, was the kind of behaviour Claudine appreciated. A man who stopped talking about something as important as family to taste something, savour it. Which he did, shaking his head in disbelief at the first mouthful, as though he'd never had better. Dietering couldn't have known it, but it was one of the things Claudine loved about Jacquot, the way he put his hands palm down on the table, his nose over a plate and drew it all in. A man who loved his food.

As if that was not enough, Dietering then went on to remark on a sculpture he'd seen in their hallway. It was a flight of tiny silvered owls taking off from a bronze branch that Claudine had recently finished, an ascending line of birds, wingtips delicately joined. When she failed to say that she had done the work herself, along with the watercolours in the salon, Jacquot offered the information and Dietering responded with enthusiasm – how fine they were, what skill – making Claudine blush with pleasure and Jacquot smile with pride.

And then, their dinner not quite over, Dietering further excelled himself by paying not the least attention when Claudine prepared a joint. He accepted it graciously when she offered it, took a few puffs, then passed it to Jacquot as though it was the most natural thing in the world, not worth remarking upon.

It was way past midnight when Dietering finally got up to leave, the taxi he'd insisted on ordering haloed with silvery rain in the driveway. And there, standing on the front steps, that final gallantry.

Dietering had taken Claudine's hand and raised it to his lips, tipping his head but keeping his eyes on hers, Jacquot noticed, accompanying the display with the lightest of heel clicks.

'It's been a long time since you kissed my hand,' said Claudine later, as she and Jacquot folded themselves into their bed, snuggling into each other.

'I've moved on,' he whispered, burrowing down beneath the covers. 'Found more interesting places,' and she felt his hand on her hip, pulling her round to him, his mouth seeking her out.

15

March

Despite his initial misgivings in Rochet's office, Jacquot quickly discovered that Hans Dietering was as agreeable at work as he had been as a guest in their home, far more useful than a mere observer, and far less the nuisance and hindrance he had feared.

With Brunet out of the office much of the time, co-ordinating a wider sweep for the murder weapon in the Martner grounds and taking statements in and around St Bédard, Dietering was quick to fill his place, happy to take on even the most menial jobs – a hands-on, let's-not-bother-with-office-protocols approach that Jacquot thoroughly approved of.

Without being asked, Dietering called the pathologist to find out when they could expect his report, had photos of the murder scene and victims copied and distributed among the investigating team and, once he'd discovered the way Jacquot liked his coffee in the morning, he always arrived at the office with two polystyrene cups from the café on the corner. Like Brunet, Dietering had it done before Jacquot thought of asking for it. He even wrote briefing statements for the press, always seeking Jacquot's approval before sending them out.

Most important, however, was that at no time in the three weeks they ended up working together did Dietering ever once question his handling of the case, or his sense of direction.

It began with the doctor's orchids.

Jacquot had started thinking about Martner's orchids that Saturday night after Dietering left for the Novotel. As the rain rattled in gusty squalls against their bedroom windows, and Claudine's breathing descended into a soft, contented murmur, Jacquot found himself making his way through the empty, silent Martner house – down the hall, through the dining room and into the kitchen, stepping round the upturned chair and the smear of oil. And from there, to the right, into the hot-house, following the gravel path into its green, shadowy heart.

It was as good as counting sheep . . .

Which was maybe why he'd woken the following morning with an image of the hot-house in his head, the sound of clapping hands, and a million tiny petals turning to wings to flutter away like butter-flies before settling somewhere else.

'The German's Jungle', that *flic* Lanclos had called it. School parties visited. And it was, as Jacquot now knew, a remarkable place, just a fantastic set-up. He'd seen nothing like it, save at zoos and botanical gardens. Why, the heating alone must cost a fortune.

It was that thought, as he buttered a croissant at the kitchen table on Sunday morning, which brought him up short.

For Jacquot suddenly realised there was nothing he could remember seeing in the Martners' financial records to account for the expense of maintaining the doctor's hot-house. No evidence whatsoever of the kind of income or withdrawals needed to run a place like the hot-house.

And what about the travelling? Four trips in the last couple of years, according to Brunet, who'd gone through the Martners' pass-ports. To the Philippines. Borneo. Papua New Guinea. Malaysia. All expensive outings. More than a month away each time. Presumably in search of orchids.

And not a single one of those trips, Jacquot was certain, had shown up as a debit in either their bank-account or credit-card records.

The rest of the day – chopping wood in the last drizzly remnants of the storm, lying in bed beside a sleeping Claudine after their post-lunch anatomy class, and spread out on the sofa watching TV that evening – Jacquot's mind kept going back to the money. Just as he'd said, right at the start, to Brunet. *Cherchez l'argent.* Look for the money. And now he'd found it. Or, rather, the lack of it.

By the time Jacquot got into the office on Monday morning, he knew that the first thing he wanted to do was go back to the Martner place and take a closer look at that hot-house. He had a feeling there was more to it than met the eye. He didn't know what, just something . . . a shadow, a play of light and dark shifting in and out of focus at the edge of his vision.

In the normal course of events, he'd have gone there by himself, dropping in at Headquarters only to pick up the key from the property office. But Jacquot knew he'd have to play it by the book this time. From now on, as Gastal had made clear in Rochet's office the previous Saturday, Dietering was to be involved at every level of the investigation – every level.

But Dietering hadn't got in yet. Jacquot looked at his watch. Hardly surprising, he supposed. It wasn't even eight. For a moment he wondered if he should just go anyway, say nothing about it, but he dismissed the idea. Instead he picked up the phone and put a call through to the Novotel.

Ten minutes later he was pulling out of the hotel car park with Dietering snapping on his seat-belt.

'I thought you ought to have a look at the Martner place,' explained Jacquot, as they eased up into the hills above Cavaillon. 'No point working on the case if you're not familiar with the scene-of-crime. I'll give you the quick tour, then you can root about by yourself.'

'Good idea. I should have suggested it myself,' said Dietering.

Which gave Jacquot pause for thought. Admitting frailties? Very unGerman, he decided. And very encouraging. It would have been so easy for the man to say he'd been going to mention it. But he hadn't.

At the entrance to the Martner driveway, on the road between St Bédard and Chant-le-Neuf, Dietering leaped from the car to lift the police tape then rejoined Jacquot. A minute or two later Jacquot stopped the car half-way down the Martner drive and the two men got out.

Jacquot had been expecting the ring of Kippi's blood to be still visible but he'd forgotten the weekend rain. Any trace had long since been washed away. For a moment or two he wasn't even sure if they were in the right place, but then he noticed the tell-tale depression in the surface of the drive as though someone had played a high-pressure hose on to the spot. Not even the rain had softened the imprint of those savage, close-range shotgun blasts.

'The first body was found here,' said Jacquot. 'The granddaughter, Kippi Brauer. You've seen the pictures and read the initial scene-of-crime report so you won't need me to tell you there wasn't much left above the shoulders.'

Leaving the car where they'd parked it, the two men made their way to the house, pulling up their collars, their breath milky in the early-morning chill, their long shadows slicing through the bare vines. Down in the valley, a thin ribbon of mist marked out the river and on the crests of the distant hills a white capping of snow showed against a blue horizon.

'Typical Provençal house,' explained Jacquot, as the Martner place came into view over the straggle of vines – breadcrust-coloured walls, blue shuttered windows and, just visible above the sloping tiled roof, the painted glass canopy of the hot-house. 'Hundreds like them in these parts. Used to be a farm,' continued Jacquot, as they walked across the forecourt, feet scrunching over the brittle, frosty gravel.

'Were the cars out here when the bodies were found?' asked Dietering, nodding at the BMW and Volkswagen parked outside the house.

'Just the Martners' estate,' replied Jacquot. 'The Golf was in the garage,' he added, pointing to the barn doors at the end of the house.

'Did Kippi drive?'

Jacquot knew at once what Dietering was thinking. Could the granddaughter have snatched up the car keys and driven from the house?

'She might have done,' he replied. 'We don't know. But the BMW was locked when we got here, and the keys were in a drawer in the doctor's study. If she thought about it at all, I'd guess she probably figured it was better to run.'

Dietering nodded, then looked around appreciatively. At the house. The view. The tidily planted forecourt with its olive jars and stone mill wheels. 'Nice place,' he said. 'Must have cost something.'

'Three million francs. A little over half a million Deutschmarks. Small change nowadays,' said Jacquot. 'According to the construction firm the Martners brought in, they spent another million doing it up. Total, about the same amount they got for their house in Paris.'

'Did they live here while the work was being done?' asked Dietering.

'The Loge d'Épines,' replied Jacquot. 'Three months.'

'The Loge d'Épines? On the road to Barjas? We passed a sign?'

Jacquot nodded. Dietering certainly kept his eyes open. The sign was the size of a dinner plate, set in an old stone kilometre-post at the entrance to a narrow, anonymous driveway. Jacquot wondered if he'd spotted it on their way out to the Martners' or had hired himself a car and spent Sunday driving around, getting to know the area. It was the kind of thing he'd have done in Dietering's place.

'That's the one. About four kilometres outside Brieuc. You can't see the place, but it's the works. Relais et Châteaux – gold *fleur-de-lis*, spa, you name it.'

'So, no Novotel then,' said Dietering.

'No Novotel.'

Smiling to himself, Jacquot pulled the front-door keys from his pocket. 'The door was open when we got here. But no keys in the lock. And no sign of forced entry either.'

'Is there an alarm system?' asked Dietering, looking around.

'Oh yes,' said Jacquot. 'But according to the cleaner who found the bodies, the Martners didn't bother much with security. She said they only ever used it when they closed up the house and went off on one of their trips. And sometimes during the summer months when this part of the world is crawling with tourists. Otherwise . . . this time of year . . .' Jacquot shrugged '. . . it seems they just didn't bother.'

'Are all the keys accounted for?' asked Dietering.

'Every set, according to the cleaner. Not one missing.'

'So either the door was unlocked and the killer just walked in, or he . . .'

'Who said it's a he?' asked Jacquot, fitting the key into the lock, turning it and pushing the door open.

'It just feels like a he,' replied Dietering. 'Wouldn't you say?'

Jacquot shrugged and stepped aside, letting his companion go first, following after him, closing the door behind them.

Even before the door clicked shut, Jacquot sensed that the house had changed. Not that it surprised him. Once the bodies had been taken away, murder scenes like this one suddenly seemed dull, empty places. Like a bomb that had been defused. Five days earlier a family had lived here. Now they were refrigerated corpses in the Cavaillon morgue.

In any other house, Jacquot and Dietering might have been an estate agent and a prospective buyer viewing the property. What made the Martners' house different were the signs of violence that still remained. The bodies might have been moved, the plaster on the hall floor swept away, the rug straightened and the kitchen tidied up, but the hallway wall and kitchen ceiling were still cratered by shotgun blasts; light switches, door frames and handles were all smudged with the grey print powder left by Fournier's boys, and the floors taped with tiny white squares where shell casings had been retrieved.

Just as Lanclos had done, Jacquot led Dietering down the hall, through the kitchen and into the hot-house, where Dietering gave an awed whistle. Then on through the doctor's laboratory, the guest wing, sun-lounge and back through the utility room, kitchen and down the hall to the main staircase, which they climbed, step by step, side by side.

In the Martners' bedroom, the shutters were closed and the room was chilly and dark. While Dietering fiddled with the latches, Jacquot noted that the mattress, bedclothes and dog basket had all been removed; only the base of the bed, Madame Martner's dressing-table and a low armchair remained. When Dietering finally got the shutters open and early-morning light spilled into the room, Jacquot noted something else – the smeared passage of a cloth on the wall above the bed where someone had worked to wipe away the blood.

Leaving Dietering to snoop around by himself, Jacquot went back downstairs and made his way to the hot-house. As he closed the two doors behind him, grateful for a moment alone, he was surprised by the flush of unease he felt at such a small deception. If, indeed, it was a deception. After all, he wasn't looking for anything in particular. All he wanted was a few minutes alone, in the hot-house, to . . . Well, he couldn't really say.

Pulling off his coat and draping it over his shoulder, Jacquot wandered along the gravel path, breathing in the warm, loamy smell of hot soil, treading between the woodchip beds and bending beneath low, overhanging branches, just as he'd done when he'd settled into sleep two nights earlier, before dreams took the place of memory. And, he had to admit, this place did have a certain dream-like quality. More than anything it was the silence that made it so – no sound of insect or bird, no rustling of animals, no breeze stirring through the branches in this man-made jungle. Apart from the trees, the blooms, there was nothing . . . nothing natural here in 'the German's Jungle'. Not even the heat was real.

At the far end of the hot-house, Jacquot pushed through the double doors leading to Martner's lab and felt the temperature drop by about twenty degrees. He shivered and looked around, paying more attention than he had on his first visit – the notebooks lying on the worktable, the reference books and ledgers on the shelves, monthly schedule charts, a surgeon's spread of tweezers, scalpels, forceps and tongs set out on a stainless-steel tray, Petri dishes labelled and dated in black marker pen and corked flasks with thin twisting tubers held behind glass beaded with condensation.

And the equipment: Dolenz electronic weighing scales, a powerful-looking Apple Mac computer, a Zeiss microscope. Everything top-of-the-range, Jacquot noted, and pretty much brand new. And pricey, too. Say five, ten thousand francs for the scales? Maybe thirty thousand for the computer, and a bit more for the microscope. He'd have to check, but he reckoned there wouldn't be too much change from a hundred thousand francs. As hobbies go, a pretty expensive one. Equipment, heating, travel. It all added up, thought Jacquot, curling his fingers through his ponytail.

But where had the money come from? The money to pay for it all. That's what Jacquot wanted to know.

After a couple more minutes, checking through a line of drawers – office supplies, boxes of slides, computer disks – Jacquot left the lab and re-entered the hot-house, feeling the heat slide through his shirt. He shivered again, then suddenly stopped in his tracks.

A hissing sound that hadn't been there earlier. And a gentle, irregular tap-tapping.

'Hans,' he called out in the gloom.

But there was no answer.

So far as he could tell he was alone. He turned his head this way and that, trying to get a bearing on the sound, still there, light but insistent.

It sounded like gas escaping, and Jacquot tensed.

And then his head snapped up. Whatever it was, the sound was coming from above. And, as his eyes searched the canopy of branches above him, he saw and then felt the fine mist descending from the sprinklers and settling on his face.

Jesus!

Five minutes later Jacquot found Dietering in the doctor's study. It was a small, cosy room that Jacquot guessed the Martners had added on when the hot-house went up. Its stonework was newer than that of the rest of the house, there was parquet flooring rather than oak boards or worn stone tiles, and the ceiling here wasn't beamed.

Dietering was standing by the doctor's desk, flipping through a magazine taken from a shelf of similar magazines. '*Herr Doktor* took his flowers very seriously,' he said. 'Every book you see – orchids, orchids, orchids. Every magazine . . .' He gestured with the one he held. 'An expensive pastime, I believe.'

'Funny you should say that,' replied Jacquot.

16

After their visit to the Martner house, Jacquot rather surprised himself by telling Dietering what was on his mind.

The hot-house. The money. Things not squaring.

What bothered him, Jacquot explained, as he turned out of the Martners' driveway, was how the doctor afforded his hobby. Where had the money come from to subsidise his interest? Admittedly construction and installation costs would have been covered by the sale of their house in Paris, but according to the doctor's bank statements, which Jacquot had rechecked before he picked up Dietering, there appeared to be no record of any further or, at any rate, significant expenditure for the purchase of plants, materials, laboratory equipment, or the travelling.

While Jacquot was fairly certain, he said, that the orchids were not, in themselves, a motive for the murders – professional jealousy, a deranged fellow collector – and although he could see no tangible link between the doctor's hobby and the deaths, he couldn't quite shift the idea that, in some as yet undiscovered way, the hot-house and the orchids had had some small part to play.

Maybe it was something, maybe it wasn't, he said to Dietering, as they turned on to the Brieuc road. But in the absence so far of any other lead, it seemed an avenue worth exploring. 'It could be just . . . you know, a red herring,' continued Jacquot, trying to make light of his suspicions.

'Sometimes it is the red herring that leads to the fat cod,' replied Dietering, with an encouraging smile.

It wasn't quite what Jacquot had expected to hear, but he appreciated the sentiment. At least, for now, Dietering seemed to be on his side.

Which was just as well, because orchids came to occupy a large amount of their time.

For the next three days – after establishing from SudElec that the Martners' quarterly heating bills were close to four times the domestic average during the winter months and always settled in cash over the counter at SudElec's office in Aix; that the cost of the doctor's scales, computer and microscope considerably exceeded Jacquot's estimate; and that the Martners' foreign trips were paid for, as Jacquot had guessed, in cash, through a travel agent in Avignon – he and Dietering followed the orchid trail, visiting the suppliers and nurseries whose names they sourced from the doctor's laboratory Rolodex.

Names in a Rolodex, rather than company letterheads or invoices, Jacquot was intrigued to note. So far as he could see there were no records anywhere that related to hot-house expenses. Not a single folder in the doctor's laboratory or study marked 'Accounts', nor in any of the household files they looked through. Nor, so far as they could determine, was there any evidence of other bank accounts held outside France through which the doctor could have funded his hobby.

'Cash,' said a Monsieur Thibault, who ran a nursery-supply outlet in Salon and looked sad when he learned that this particular customer would not be returning. 'Always cash. Sometimes he came himself, sometimes he phoned in his orders, sending his gardener for the heavier loads.'

'Heavier loads?' asked Dietering.

'Soil, compost, gravel. Things he couldn't manage on his own.'

Another specialist supplier outside Orange, Pierre Salvaudon, told the same story. 'He just came in, bought what he wanted and left,' he said, returning the photo of Dr Martner that Dietering had handed him. 'I never knew his name, let alone where he lived.'

'Always cash?' asked Jacquot.

Salvaudon thought for a moment, then nodded. 'Cash.'

When Dietering asked how much the doctor had spent with him each year, Salvaudon looked a little nervous. As had his colleague in Salon, Monsieur Thibault.

Jacquot wasn't surprised by their discomfort. In every business he'd ever heard of, cash had a way of disappearing from balance sheets. So the two policemen agreed that double the amount Thibault and Salvaudon had suggested would probably be closer to the mark, a more realistic evaluation. And a very substantial sum it was too.

Yet there was still no sign of where the money had come from.

'Maybe,' suggested Dietering, on their way back from Salvaudon's place, 'maybe Martner was selling his orchids to other collectors for cash and not declaring the income, using it to subsidise his hobby.'

Which was how they came to visit the half-dozen collectors in the region whose names Dietering gleaned from a collectors' website. All of them had heard of Martner and two had met him.

'I visited him once,' said Paul Marquand, a retired banker whose home in the hills outside Aix had been extended, like the Martners' place, to provide space for his collection. It was, Jacquot noted, a smaller version of Martner's hot-house. And while the blooms Marquand proudly pointed out looked suitably extravagant they were not a patch, even to Jacquot's untutored eye, on those that had belonged to the doctor.

'He invited you?' asked Dietering.

Marquand shook his head, blue eyes popping behind his spectacles. 'No, no, no. Just dropped by. We'd never met but we'd heard of each other, you know how it is.'

'And he let you in? Showed you round?' continued Dietering.

'It was his wife answered the door. A charming woman. Took me to the doctor's study and said she would find out if her husband was at home. Five minutes later he was there. Five minutes after that he invited me into his hot-house, to show me what he had.' Marquand paused, as though summoning up what had clearly been a vision.

'And?' prompted Jacquot.

'And it was . . . astonishing. I couldn't believe what I saw there.

The most fabulous colours, shapes, textures. Quite remarkable. He had a magnificent set of *sanderens* that I'd never seen so heavily ladened. Like a waterfall. A cascade. And the fragrance!'

'How much would flowers like that be worth, Monsieur?' asked Dietering.

Marquand pursed his lips as though he were considering a loan request from a customer, tipped his jaw and scratched his chin. 'I would have paid him ten thousand francs without a thought. Just for one. There and then.'

'You offered?' asked Jacquot.

Marquand nodded. 'Of course. Who wouldn't? And there was enough there to spare, I can tell you.'

'But he wouldn't sell to you?'

'He just laughed, shook his head – "Nooooo, noooo, noooo, M'sieur." Something like that. Like I was surely teasing him.'

'Did you ever hear of him selling to other collectors?' asked Dietering.

'Never. Not Martner,' replied Marquand, emphatically. 'What was his was his. Just ask Balou. He would've loved to get his hands on them.'

The next morning, at the Jardins Balou a few miles outside Lucat, one of the largest nurseries in the region, the owner, Gaston Balou, told them all he could about orchids and the Martner collection. A small, chubby man in his fifties, Balou had been working with orchids for twenty years, he said, selling them in his nursery to cover his own collecting costs.

'It was quite remarkable, really,' Balou told them in his office, its bookshelves sagging, its walls crowded with antique flower prints, its windowsills, the tops of filing cabinets and his desk covered with pots of thickly leafed tubers and delicate, flowering stems. 'I couldn't believe it when I first saw what Dr Martner was doing. He'd started hybridising terrestrials and epiphytes with fantastic results. No one I know has managed to do anything like it, certainly not as spec-tacularly as Martner. Some of his specimens were, well . . . really quite something. He could have made a lot of money. But he never sold a single plant. I know collectors all over who read about his work, contacted him, asked if he would be willing to sell. Me too. But he never did. Didn't need to, I suppose,' said Balou, regretfully.

'So, what kind of money are we talking about, Monsieur?' asked Dietering. 'What are these plants worth?'

'Hard to say exactly, but blooms like his can make up to three, four thousand dollars a single stem. Often much more. Especially the ones he had. Some I'd never seen before. You might not know this, Messieurs, but the orchid business worldwide generates ooh ... billions of dollars. And illicit trade could account for half as much again.'

Balou leaned back in his chair, squeezed a thumb and forefinger into the corners of his eyes and shook his head, as though it didn't bear thinking about, then looked up at his two visitors. 'But it's a tricky business, orchids. The more you sell, the more you have on the market, the easier it is for other collectors to breed from them, to reproduce them, and then ... why, then,' he said sadly, 'the price begins to drop. Very quickly. If you want to succeed commercially, you have to keep up production – and as often as possible intro- duce new specimens, new characters. Colour, shape, hardiness, fragrance, bloom time. So many different things to consider. But he never sold a single stem. Take my word for it. I'd have known about it if he had.'

'And what kind of costs would be involved in creating these new strains, and in keeping them – heating, sprinkler systems, that whole hot-house environment?' asked Jacquot.

Balou looked out of his window, at the arched roofs of his poly- tunnels. 'A lot, Inspector. Believe me.'

'Ballpark figure?'

Balou blew out his cheeks like a submarine preparing to dive. *'Pfeu!* I only saw his place the one time, you understand, but it was the business, I can tell you.' Balou shook his head. 'Say two, maybe three hundred thousand a year? It could have been more. Could have been less. Hard to say for certain.'

Back at Headquarters, Jacquot asked Dietering to call the number Balou had given them – a Dr Heinrich Clemens of the Palmgarten Institute in Hamburg. According to Balou, Clemens was about as high up the orchid tree as it was possible to get: visiting professor of botany at Frankfurt University, director of the Palmgarten Institute and author of a dozen books on the taxonomy, reproduc- tion and hybridising of orchidacea.

Martin O'Brien

Fifteen minutes later, Dietering set the phone in its cradle. 'As Monsieur Balou told us, Martner's is a most important collection,' he began. 'According to Clemens, his research notes alone would be worth their weight in gold. As for the flowers, Clemens said it would be difficult to put a value on them. Also, as you suspected, he says it is essential they are cared for until a new home can be found, and an appropriate ownership established.'

It was at that very moment, a full week after the discovery of the bodies, that Herr Brauer – husband, father and son-in-law of the deceased – appeared in Jacquot's office.

17

They'd been expecting a visit from Herr Brauer at some time or other but no one knew for certain when he'd arrive. According to the Swiss authorities, he'd returned from the States to the family home in Zürich on the Friday following the murders.

Normally, a surviving family member would have been brought in for questioning and to provide formal identification of the bodies at the earliest opportunity. But since, in the matter of identification, there were no features left to recognise on any of the four victims, it was agreed that photos would be taken of a tattoo on Kippi's ankle, a star-shaped constellation of moles on Ilse Brauer's thigh, Madame Martner's left index finger, so swollen it had been impossible to remove her rings, and a watch that the doctor had been wearing, the photos faxed through to Zürich for Herr Brauer to identify.

As for a statement from Herr Brauer, this accompanied his formal confirmation of identity faxed back three hours later, a brief note taken by the Swiss authorities giving his whereabouts at the time of the murders – New York – along with his sworn testimony that he could think of no reason for such a brutal act, no enemies, no one with a grudge against the family.

Police authorities in Zürich also confirmed that Herr Brauer had had no idea that his daughter was pregnant, adding that they had started interviewing Kippi's schoolfriends in an attempt to trace the father of her unborn child.

But at no time had there been any indication when, or even if, Herr Brauer intended visiting. Now he was here, ushered into Jacquot's office by Sergeant Mougeon.

Tall, thin brown hair neatly parted and trimmed, casually dressed in polo-neck, grey flannels and tasselled loafers, and wrapped in a green loden coat that seemed a size too large for him, Brauer looked utterly diminished by his loss. His eyes were reddened behind oval, wire-framed spectacles, and his shoulders were stooped as though some great weight pressed down on him. He was accompanied by a lawyer who introduced himself as Pierre Boudit, of Boudit Frères in Zürich, smaller by six inches than any of them, and rounder too, by a considerable margin.

After introductions had been dealt with, and coffee declined by both Brauer and Boudit, there was a moment's pause while Dietering darted through into the squad room adjoining Jacquot's office to bring in more chairs, at the same time thoughtfully covering the glossy black-and-whites of the murder scene and victims pinned to the incident board. Indicating that Herr Brauer and his lawyer should make themselves comfortable, Dietering then began, in a gentle and most deferential manner, to express their condolences, speaking in German and glancing at Jacquot to make sure he was not out of order in doing so.

When Dietering finished Jacquot took over, bringing their visitors up to date on the progress of the investigation – no witnesses, no murder weapon, no real leads as yet. But he managed to make it sound better than it was.

When he had finished, Brauer nodded but made no comment.

'Tell me,' continued Jacquot, his tone soft, almost uninterested, 'you were in New York at the time of the . . . incident?'

'That is correct.' Brauer's reply was clipped, precise.

'And you had been there, what? A month?'

'That is also correct. A little over three weeks.'

'I believe you work in the, ah . . . financial sector?'

'That, too, is correct. I work for a branch of the Swiss Treasury, advising various clients . . .' Brauer spread his hands as though the exact details or nature of his work would be of no interest, were not germane to the inquiry, or were simply too complex, too tiresome to explain.

'Of course, of course,' replied Jacquot, indicating he quite understood and, in the brief silence that followed this opening exchange, it struck him that this was the first time he had inter-viewed anyone so closely connected with the victims. It was a prospect he warmed to, police work at its most basic. Questions and answers. The gathering of information. Not that he consid-ered Brauer a suspect. Not for a moment. After all, the man had been in another country when the murders took place, and the clumsy, amateur nature of the slaughter seemed to rule out a hit-man. However, a line of gentle questioning like this was a useful exercise, and at the very least an opportunity to tie up loose ends. 'So tell me,' continued Jacquot, 'did you know that your wife was visiting her parents? With Kippi?'

'She had said that they would be coming, yes.'

'This was before you left Zürich?'

Brauer shook his head. 'On the phone. While I was in New York.'

'You stayed in touch? Your wife and you? You spoke regularly?'

'Two or three times a week. It depended. Work. The time differ-ence. You know how it is.'

'And your wife, did she visit her parents often?'

'Maybe once or twice a year,' replied Brauer, removing his spec-tacles, taking a handkerchief from the pocket of his loden coat and carefully polishing the lenses. 'Christmas, birthdays, that sort of thing. It's not a long or difficult drive from where we live.'

'And your wife's parents . . . Did they ever come to Zürich?'

'Once or twice, I believe.'

'You were there? When they visited?'

Brauer shook his head.

'Your job?'

'Precisely. My work takes me away from home on a very regular basis.'

'And whenever your wife came here, to Provence, to visit her parents, your daughter came too?'

'Of course. As I said, I am away a lot . . . And Kippi is . . . was . . .' Brauer took a breath, steadied himself. 'Kippi was too young to be left on her own. And, anyway, Josef and Jutta loved their granddaughter. And she them.'

Brauer pushed the handkerchief back into his pocket and

replaced his glasses, shifting them on the bridge of his nose, blinking to refocus.

Short-sighted, thought Jacquot. And judging by the thickness of the lenses, quite badly so. Had the killer been short-sighted? he wondered. Was that why the shot had missed, the shot in the Martner house that had cratered the wall beside the front door? Did the killer have to get up close to be sure of a killing shot?

'And you, Herr Brauer, did you ever visit? Here in Provence?'

Across Jacquot's desk, Brauer shook his head. 'No. Never.' There was something in his tone, something final, something . . . disapproving.

'So when did you last see your parents-in-law, Dr Martner and his wife?'

Brauer gave it thought. 'Some time ago now.'

Jacquot spread his hands. 'A year? More? Less?'

'At least five years.'

Jacquot paused, took this in, then began again: 'That seems a long time, living so close as you said. Tell me,' he continued. 'Did you get on with your wife's parents?'

Brauer took a breath, sighed. 'No, I did not.'

'Might I ask why?'

Brauer glanced at Boudit. The lawyer shrugged, nodded.

'Soon after they moved here . . . from Paris . . . I discovered they had borrowed money from us. From my wife.'

'A lot of money?'

'Enough.'

'And?'

'I told my wife it must stop. I was not prepared to . . . subsidise their extravagances.'

'And she did as you asked?'

Brauer shrugged, as though there could be no doubt that his wife would not do as she was told. 'Of course.'

'You said "extravagances".'

'Their lifestyle, if you like. The holidays . . . They were always going off somewhere. And living here, in Provence. It was all . . . well, unnecessary.'

Jacquot nodded, as though in agreement. 'Have you any idea how much money your wife gave them?'

'At least a hundred thousand francs,' replied Brauer, crossing his legs and pulling at the crease in his trousers, arranging the folds of his coat. The subject of money seemed to animate him. 'It was too much. And they had their own investments. If the returns were not enough to keep them, then they should have . . .' Brauer cast round for the right word. 'They should have . . . economised.'

Jacquot nodded once more, leaned back in his chair. 'And was this money, this loan . . . repaid?'

'Not that I am aware of.'

'You asked your wife?'

'No, I did not. It was enough for me that my wife gave her word that no further payments would be made. Whether the money was repaid was her concern. For her to deal with. I did not want to be involved. I made that clear.'

'And your wife understood?'

'Completely.'

For a moment, Jacquot wondered what kind of marriage they had had. Clean. Lean. Cold? Not the kind of relationship Jacquot would have wanted, that was for certain. He decided to change tack.

'Tell me, Herr Brauer, did your daughter drive?'

'She has no licence. But, yes, she knows how.' Brauer lifted a hand to his mouth, coughed, replaced the hand in his lap. 'Knew how.'

'And you had no idea that your daughter was pregnant?'

'No idea at all. It was a shock.'

'Did your wife know?'

Brauer sighed. 'Apparently.'

'But she didn't tell you?'

'No. She did not.'

'So how did you find out that your daughter was pregnant, and that your wife knew about it?'

'There was a letter . . . when I got home. It was addressed to my wife. In the circumstances . . .'

'And . . . ?' Jacquot pushed.

'It was from a clinic. The Brücke. It is well known.'

'So, your wife had made arrangements for the pregnancy to be terminated?'

'It appears that that would be the case. Yes.'

'And did your daughter have a boyfriend? A particular friend? In Zürich?'

Brauer shook his head. 'Not that I am aware of. Although . . .'

'Although . . . ?'

'Kippi was at a difficult age, you know. Just seventeen. And, like most girls her age, she was starting to live her own life and did not particularly . . . communicate with us. Or appreciate any interference. It's not unusual, I think . . .'

Jacquot nodded again, watched Brauer slide a finger beneath his glasses, lifting them slightly, wiping at something in the corner of his eye.

'Well, thank you for your co-operation, Herr Brauer. I know how difficult all this must be. All these questions. You have been most helpful.'

There was silence in the room, a creak of chairs, a phone ringing in the squad room. Someone picked it up, a mutter of voices. For a moment no one moved, no one spoke.

And then the lawyer, Boudit, leaning across and placing a hand on his client's shoulder, piped up: 'I wonder, Chief Inspector, whether it would be possible for my client to visit the Martner property?'

18

An hour later Monsieur Boudit, Dietering and Jacquot made themselves comfortable in the Martners' salon while Brauer prowled
the house. They could hear floorboards creak, cupboard doors opening
and closing, drawers sliding. And once, from the kitchen, a painful,
pitiful sobbing. Jacquot and Dietering looked at each other, wondering
whether one of them should go to comfort the man, but Boudit saw
the look, shook his head and they remained where they were.

When Brauer finally joined them, he took a seat beside his lawyer,
thanked them for their patience and then, turning to Boudit, rattled
off a volley of rapid-fire Schweizerdeutsch. It was the first time he
had spoken anything but French.

Jacquot looked at Dietering who shrugged, meaning either he
didn't understand what was being said or, as Jacquot sensed, that
it was of no great significance.

When Brauer had finished, the round, squat Boudit turned to
the two detectives and began speaking in a high-pitched wheeze:
'My client, Herr Brauer, wishes to make arrangements for his wife's
and daughter's personal belongings to be sent to the family home
in Zürich. If that is acceptable to you, Monsieur?'

Jacquot nodded. The property was no longer a secure scene-of-
crime, he told the lawyer, and, so as far as he could see, Herr
Brauer's removal of personal effects could no longer compromise
any evidence.

'And the house? The cars? Those items belonging to Herr Brauer's parents-in-law?' asked Jacquot, turning from Boudit to Brauer, already well aware from talks with the Martners' local lawyer that there were no direct beneficiaries beyond the son-in-law, via his wife and daughter, and a couple of minor institutional bequests.

Once again Monsieur Boudit leaned forward, spoke for his client. 'Herr Brauer has instructed me to ask that the property be put on the market as soon as you are satisfied you have everything you need. My office will be happy to confirm that this is in keeping with the terms and spirit of the principals' various wills. As for the contents, there are certain items belonging to his parents-in-law that my client would like to keep – albums, photos, family things. A list will be provided. As for the rest – the cars, the furnishings and so on – it can be disposed of locally. Auctions, that sort of thing. Of course, if anything still has some pertinence to the investigation . . .'

Jacquot shook his head. The house could be cleared.

There was a short pause, and then Boudit began again: 'As we have seen, there has been some damage done to the property.' He covered his mouth and coughed diplomatically. 'If you have no objections, Monsieur, we would like the house repaired and repainted prior to it being offered on the market. I am sure you will appreciate that prospective purchasers might find its, ah . . . current condition, how shall I say . . . ?'

'Off-putting?' supplied Jacquot.

'*Exactement*, Monsieur.'

'I have no objections,' replied Jacquot, nodding to Brauer. 'And the orchids? Dr Martner's collection?'

Monsieur Boudit's brow knotted. 'Orchids?'

It was clearly the first Boudit had heard about orchids. Even Brauer looked puzzled.

'Monsieur Brauer's father-in-law, Dr Martner, was an authority on orchids,' explained Jacquot. 'One of Germany's foremost taxonomists and an expert hybridiser. I am reliably informed that the collection, along with the good doctor's library, forms a most valuable legacy. Also, if the collection stays here uncared-for . . .'

Boudit conferred with his client who shrugged, as though the orchids were of no interest.

Once more Boudit put his hand on his client's arm as though to quieten any concerns he might have, then turned back to Jacquot. His tiny black eyes flickered between the two policemen as he spoke. 'We will make enquiries, of course, as to the best course of action and my office will be in touch. For the time being, I will make arrangements locally for the collection to be cared for in whatever way is considered appropriate.'

Cared for . . . and evaluated, thought Jacquot, who'd taken a mild dislike to the Swiss lawyer from the moment he'd padded self-importantly into his office.

With a sigh, Boudit put his hands on his knees and pushed himself to his feet, followed by Herr Brauer.

'So. If that is all, gentlemen?'

Five days after Brauer and Boudit's visit, Jacquot and Dietering found out what Herr Brauer had decided to do about the orchids. According to a letter from Boudit Frères, signed in Pierre Boudit's absence, the collection would remain in place until the sale of the property had been effected, at which time Martner's orchids, library and research notes would be shipped to Dr Heinrich Clemens at the Palmgarten Institute in Hamburg. It was understood by Boudit Frères that the Institute had made a significant contribution to a charity of Herr Brauer's choice in return for the collection.

In the meantime the Martner hot-house would be monitored by the Dassy Nursery in Aix.

19

For ten days following Brauer's visit, the investigation ground on with little real progress.

By then pretty well everyone within a ten-kilometre radius of the Martner property had been interviewed regarding their where-abouts at the time of the murders, and questioned about any rela-tionship they might have had with a member of the murdered family.

In St Bédard there were a number of such relationships. The Martners had held accounts at Lepantre's grocery, the Bulots' *char-cuterie* and with the baker Doriane. Each of these accounts, the suppliers were sad to note, was overdue for payment. Then there was Eric Chabert at the Fontaine des Fleurs, who'd been the Martners' gardener, working there when Denise and her husband Fernand could spare him. And the Parmentiers too. The Martners had dined at the *auberge* on a number of occasions, most recently that last weekend. Sunday lunch. A birthday celebration. The daughter and granddaughter were vegetarian but the old couple had liked their meat, Madame Parmentier had told the gendarme who questioned her, and all of them had seemed in good spirits.

It was the same story three doors down from the *auberge* at Au Broc Fontaine, the antiques dealer André Ribaud reporting that Jutta Martner was a regular visitor and that she had called by just the week before with her daughter. In a tense piece of negotiation, Ribaud had sold the daughter a fabulous thirty-piece blue Delft

dinner service he had discovered at a snip in . . . Well, he didn't like
to say. She had paid by cheque and given details for the service to
be sent to Zürich. Given the tragic turn of events – and since the
items had still to be wrapped and delivered – Ribaud would, he
assured Brunet, have his bank return Ilse Brauer's cheque.

Almost without exception, Brunet and his squad of gendarmes
had managed to establish that most people in St Bédard – save early
risers like Tomas Mazzelli, Eric Chabert and Georges Doriane –
had been in bed when the murders took place, some time between
five and seven in the morning, according to Fournier. Or in the
bath, or shaving, or getting ready for work or, in Lepantre's case,
engaged in his morning constitutional. Impossible to verify any of
them one way or the other.

As for friends, it seemed the Martners had kept to themselves.
Their address books provided no real leads and no one the police
interviewed would volunteer anything more than a passing acquaintance with the family.

Which surprised Dietering.

'Ten years here and no friends? No dinner parties? No lunches?'
he said, driving Jacquot back to Cavaillon after they had called on
the heating engineer in Avignon who'd installed the doctor's hot-
house system.

'You have to remember,' said Jacquot, carefully, 'that they weren't
from round here.'

'You mean they were German.' Dietering accompanied the
remark with a smile, red moustache twitching as he glanced across
at his passenger.

Jacquot shrugged. 'We're not known for our warm welcome,
Hans. It takes time in these parts. And ten years? A tick of the
clock, my friend.'

'It didn't take you ten years.'

'Maybe the Martners didn't have my charm,' replied Jacquot
lightly.

What he wanted to say, what he felt, he kept to himself. Memories
were long hereabouts. People hadn't forgotten. Especially the old
ones. Sometimes wars never ended.

'Could it be racial? National Front? The war?' It was as though
Dietering had read his mind.

For a minute or two Jacquot didn't reply, simply looked out at the slanting rain and the rows of bare vines flicking past.

'At the last count there were more than two hundred German families living permanently in Provence,' he began at last, 'excluding the Côte d'Azur. And there are a further fifteen hundred, Hans, who maintain properties here and in the Languedoc. They stay for a month in the summer, a week at Christmas, and rent it out the rest of the time. Usually to other Germans.'

Jacquot shifted in his seat, reaching for his cigarettes. 'Then there are the tourists,' he continued, lighting up and letting out a stream of smoke. 'Last summer – April to September – we estimate more than a quarter of a million German visitors. A month. And that's just hotel records. There may have been many thousands more putting up at *chambres d'hôtes* and the like. Or camping. Or coming here on business. In and out the same day. Border controls being what they are, it's difficult to estimate exactly.

'But what we can estimate is this. In fact, it's not "estimate", it's "know-for-certain". Because we do have figures. In the last seven years, excluding the World Cup, only seventy-three German nationals have been the victims of crime in Provence. Any crime. And only six of those were fatalities. Most of them drug-related.'

Jacquot might not have remembered the figures exactly, but the spirit of his message was the same that Brunet had given him a few days after the murders, when Jacquot had considered the race card and had Brunet check it out.

He turned in his seat and gave Dietering a grin. 'Believe me, Hans, race is not a factor here. The Martners were not killed because they were German.' It was almost exactly what Brunet had said when he handed Jacquot the figures. But the moment the words were out of Jacquot's mouth he felt a strange twist of discomfort, knowing somehow that, despite the statistics, the words didn't quite ring true. He knew all too well what people felt about the Germans, even after more than half a century. For himself, he had no feelings one way or the other. The past was the past. Learn from it, remember and move on, was the way he looked at it. Yet he was in no doubt about how some of his compatriots regarded their northern neighbours.

He wound down the window and flicked his cigarette into the rain. 'Anyway, how about dinner?' he said, keen to change the subject. 'Claudine's got a *gigot*. She said to ask you.'

'She could be offering burnt toast,' replied Hans, pulling in to Headquarters, 'and I would still find it impossible to decline. So. Yes. Thank you. That would be fine.'

Sharing their cassoulet that first night hadn't been the only time that Dietering visited the Jacquot home. As well as fitting in easily in the office, he'd become a regular and increasingly welcome guest, joining Jacquot and Claudine for supper on several occasions. If he'd stayed in town at weekends, it would probably have been more often. But with a new family back home in Bonn, Dietering had persuaded his superiors to agree to a five-day week rather than a permanent posting to Cavaillon. That meant flying out of Marseilles each Friday evening and back again on Monday morning. Which was when, Jacquot was certain, Dietering submitted his progress reports.

From the moment Dietering had joined the team, what surprised Jacquot was that there'd been no questioning of the handling of the case from Lyon or Munich. The least he'd expected, when he'd gone off on his orchid thing, was that Gastal and Warendorf would come barging in, insisting the murder was political and that chasing flower-fanciers was not the name of the game. But they hadn't. Not a word. Which could only mean that Dietering, their man on the spot, was reporting back favourably, for which Jacquot was grateful.

This had been confirmed the previous week when Jacquot and his boss, Rochet, had shared a lift together. Although Rochet probably knew as well as Jacquot that the Martner investigation was going nowhere fast, it was equally clear that he was as grateful as Jacquot that the right noises were being made by their German friend. According to Rochet, Gastal and the German authorities were well pleased with the way things were going, the leads that were being pursued – interesting angles, they'd said. But although everyone now seemed to agree that the murders looked less and less likely to have been political, Dietering remained at his post.

Très bien, said Rochet, as the lift doors opened, keep it up.

The message was clear. So long as I don't have any flak from Lyon and Munich, then neither will you, *mon ami*.

That evening, as the two detectives joined the queue of traffic out of Cavaillon, Jacquot brought up the question of reports.

At first Dietering didn't speak, as though he hadn't heard what Jacquot had said, making Jacquot worry that he might have offended the man. 'I tell them everything we do, with a personal recommendation. I may have . . . coloured our leads and our progress on the case, but I have always said the truth,' explained Dietering, punctiliously. 'As I see it.'

And then, glancing at Jacquot: 'Also, anything that keeps your esteemed colleague Herr Gastal off our backs is, like an invitation from you and Claudine to dinner, a pleasure quite impossible to resist.'

Jacquot was stunned at this disclosure. 'You don't like him, then?'

'Do you?'

'As a matter of fact . . . not one little bit. We used to work together.'

'You have my sympathy,' said Dietering. 'He is not a man I would like at my side in a difficult situation.'

'Usually he's behind your back.'

'And you know something else? There's nothing I dislike more than a fat policeman. In a smart suit.'

That evening the two men drank more Armagnac than they should have and, instead of taking a taxi back to his hotel, Dietering passed out on the sofa.

The following morning, arriving at the office an hour late, tongues dry, heads hammering, they discovered the Martner case had taken a new turn.

Orchids were forgotten.

Nearly a month after the murders, someone had found a gun.

20

When Jacquot and Dietering entered the office, both slump-shouldered and squint-eyed, Jean Brunet was standing at his desk, hand clamped over his phone. 'A man called Benedict. Says he knows you, Chief. Says he's found a gun.'

It took a moment or two for the information to sink in, skimming like a pebble over a foggy lake of Armagnac. That name. Benedict. Not Max Benedict? It couldn't be.

And a gun.

The gun. Jacquot was suddenly sure of it.

He took the phone. 'Jacquot,' he said, more briskly than he felt. 'Why, Chief Inspector. *Quel plaisir*. Such a long time.'

Three years, thought Jacquot, recognising the low, bourbony drawl, remembering the last time he'd heard it, that bar off Marseilles' Vieux Port, the day he had packed his bags and come north.

'And such a small world,' continued Benedict. 'I heard you'd been transferred but I had no idea we'd end up in the same place.'

'You live round here?'

'About four miles west of Rocsabin. A marvellous little farm I found a few years back. I've been letting it out most of the time, but I moved back in last week.'

Which explained why Jacquot had seen no statement from Max Benedict. With a house so close to St Bédard, he'd certainly have been interviewed in the days following the murders if he'd been in residence.

'My colleague tells me you've found a gun, Monsieur Benedict,' said Jacquot, steering the conversation back to business.

'I have indeed. I'm looking at it now.'

'And you are . . . ?'

'On my mobile.' ·

Jacquot sighed, smiled. 'What I mean is . . .'

'Where am I?'

'That would help.' Jacquot put up a hand to stop Dietering taking off his coat.

'A hundred metres off the Brieuc road,' continued Benedict. 'On the border, if I'm not mistaken, of the Martner property.'

Of all the people to find the murder weapon it had to be a journalist, thought Jacquot, as he and Dietering sped out of Cavaillon.

And not just any journalist.

Max Benedict. *The* Max Benedict.

A lean, rangy Texan, bald as a *boule*, suspiciously single and somewhere in his sixties, Benedict's speciality was high-society crime – scandal by any other name – and he was a master at getting his stories. And telling them. He and Jacquot had first met in Marseilles where Benedict had covered the murder of an American heiress called Susie de Cotigny, only daughter of the Wall Street Delahayes, followed by the suicide only a few hours later of her husband Hubert. For a man like Benedict, and the magazine he wrote for, the double-header was a natural.

Three years later, Benedict was back in Jacquot's life.

Benedict was sitting beneath an olive tree when Jacquot and Dietering arrived. They'd parked by the black Chevy jeep he'd told them to look out for in a lay-by off the Brieuc road and they'd followed the path he'd described, climbing up through a stony scrub of garrigue and wild olive trees, both men wishing they'd drunk a little less the night before.

'Over here,' came Benedict's voice over the barking of dogs, somewhere ahead, close enough for him to have heard their approach but still hidden among the trees.

The next minute the path opened up into a small clearing and there he was, legs stretched out in front of him, ankles crossed, back resting against the trunk of an olive tree. The bald brown head was nestled in the sheepskin collar of an expensive leather jacket, blue eyes twinkled behind his signature tortoiseshell spectacles and a pair of Weimaraners strained at their leashes towards Jacquot and Dietering.

'Mailer, Vidal. Behave yourselves. *Taisez-vous*.'

'Monsieur Benedict,' said Jacquot, wincing from the climb.

'Why how nice to meet again, Chief Inspector,' said Benedict, remaining where he was. His French was slow and precise, society French, ordered and correct, the words only gently ghosted with a Texan drawl. 'A pleasure indeed,' he continued, and then, eyes straying to Dietering, 'I don't believe we've met,' he said.

Dietering introduced himself.

'Dietering? Dietering? Germans working with the French,' said Benedict, with a wry smile, clearly knowing exactly why the Germans would be working with the French. 'My, my. What is the world coming to? Herr Dietering, a pleasure.'

Dietering, whom Jacquot had briefed on the way out, nodded a greeting but left the running to Jacquot.

'You said you'd found a gun,' said Jacquot, wishing the pain behind his eyes would ease.

'I have indeed. I was with the dogs, on my way into town, when Mailer here got caught short. I stopped the car to let him out and he just chased off. So, of course, I had to follow him – and since I could hardly leave Vidal, I brought him with me. I managed to get Mailer on the leash and I was just walking through this little glade here, back to the car, when I saw it.'

Jacquot and Dietering looked around. The ground was hard and bare, the dry spear-tip leaves on the trees rattling lightly with the breeze. A pale sun left thin trails of light between the branches.

'And it is where exactly, Monsieur?' asked Dietering.

'Why, right above my head, Herr Dietering. In the branches.'

And there it was, hanging over Benedict's head, the wooden stock caught in a fork of the tree and the barrel, supported by a branch, pointing off to the left. It looked as though it had been thrown there, hurled from a distance rather than placed deliberately. For all the world it might have been another branch in the tree.

'It's the gun that killed the Martners, isn't it, Chief Inspector?' said Benedict, as Dietering stepped forward to retrieve the weapon.

The Weimaraners bristled.

In the absence of gloves, Dietering pulled off his scarf and Jacquot watched him step round the gun and reach up for the stock. Jacquot nodded to himself – no point in pulling it out barrel first. It might still be loaded. The trigger might catch on a twig. Things like that happened when a policeman let his attention slip. There was no chance of that with Dietering.

'Oh, come on, Chief Inspector,' Benedict continued, watching Dietering's attempts to dislodge the gun but making no effort to help or get out of the way. Then he turned to Jacquot. 'You know I'll find out soon enough. Why not spare yourself all my phone calls and visits? You know what an absolute pest I can be.'

When Dietering had a secure grip on the trigger mechanism, he started to ease the gun free of the branches. When he'd pulled it clear, he snapped open the breech. Two empty shell casings flew from the twin barrels and the Weimaraners growled, then sidled forward to investigate, ears pinned back, noses sniffing. Benedict pulled them away as Dietering, using the other end of his scarf, picked up the casings. He looked at Jacquot and nodded. The same make and gauge as the others.

'Should I call Brunet?' asked Dietering, looking round the area.

Both men knew that a month's weather would have badly compromised the site, along with the herd of goats they could hear bleating somewhere above them, bells clunking dully, not to mention Benedict and the Weimaraners. But they both knew, too, that there was still a possibility that something might be found, something that might point them to the killer.

'No need for Brunet,' replied Jacquot. 'Have Mougeon send out a couple of men to search the area. Fifty metres all round. The roadside too. And tell them to look out for any tracks or paths between here and the Martner place and follow them.'

Tucking the gun under his arm and pocketing the shell casings, Dietering pulled out his mobile and tapped in the number.

'Well? What do you say?' said Benedict. He'd loosened his grip on the dogs and they were close enough to stretch out and sniff at Jacquot's boots.

Jacquot looked down at them. Benedict pulled them back.

'I say, thank you, Monsieur, for bringing this to our attention.' No matter how hard Jacquot tried to dislike Benedict there was something disarming about the man – even if he was a journalist. Despite himself Jacquot rather enjoyed their sparring. He suspected that Benedict did too.

'And?' said Benedict, scrambling to his feet, brushing off his Levi's. 'Go on, Chief Inspector. You can tell me. It *is* the Martner gun, isn't it?'

'Maybe, Monsieur. Who can say?'

Dietering pocketed his mobile. 'Mougeon's sending out a couple of men. Do we have any tape in the car to mark the tree?'

Jacquot shook his head.

'Then I'll leave my scarf,' said Dietering, passing the gun to Jacquot who cradled it under his arm.

With the scarf tied to a branch, Jacquot and Dietering started back the way they had come.

'It's a grand story, you know. Just my sort of thing,' said Benedict, following behind them, the dogs straining at their leashes, reaching for the detectives' heels. 'Well-connected German couple and their young family killed in a bloody massacre. Did you know I can see their house from mine?'

The men and the dogs broke through the last of the olive trees, scrambled down the bank and out on to the lay-by.

While Jacquot stowed the gun in the boot, Dietering hefted some stones into a pile to mark the path for Mougeon's men. He flagged them with an old carrier-bag he found in the ditch.

'Get the accreditation, Monsieur Benedict,' said Jacquot, settling himself behind the wheel, 'and, as always, I will be happy to oblige.' He snapped on his seat-belt, then started the engine. Dietering slid in beside him, brushing off his hands. 'You and all the other journalists.'

And with that Jacquot's old Peugeot lurched off, leaving Benedict looking after them, a canny smile playing across his features, his two Weimaraners sneezing in the dust.

21

It didn't take long to get the results from Ballistics.

Dietering and Jacquot had just returned from a late canteen lunch when Brunet came into the office.

'It's the gun, all right,' said Brunet, handing Jacquot the report. 'And there are prints too, badly deteriorated but maybe enough to run a match. One thumb and a partial finger. Probably a man, Fournier says.'

'And the serial number?' asked Jacquot. 'The owner of the gun?'

Twenty minutes later Jacquot and Dietering drove out of Cavaillon along the Brieuc road. At the St Bédard turning, they crossed the old stone bridge, climbed up to the hilltop settlement and squeezed through the battlemented west gate.

'Busy,' said Dietering, as they drove along the lower end of Place Vausigne, following the sign for Chant-le-Neuf. The Friday market was in full swing, the *place* filled with tented stalls set up among the trees. Even at this time of year it was crowded with shoppers.

'Come summer, you can't move here on a Friday,' said Jacquot, slowing down to let a family loaded with carrier-bags cross the road to the car park behind the *gendarmerie*. 'It's one of those places they put on all the travel posters. Gordes, Roquebrune, Bargemon, St Bédard. *Le vrai Provence.*'

'No wonder the Martners liked it here.'

A few minutes later, six kilometres on from the Martner property, they pulled off the road and drove between the set of stone pillars and wrought-iron gates that Brunet had described. After a hundred metres or so the wooded driveway swung up to the left, levelled off for a few metres then sloped down past terraces of fig and olive to the pantiled, turreted roof of the Château de Vausigne.

'They should photograph this for their posters too.' Dietering whistled. 'What a place.'

What a place indeed, thought Jacquot.

Occupying a small bowl of land a few hundred metres from the road, concealed from passing traffic by the pelt of pine, holm oak and spindly-tipped cypresses they'd just driven through, the château was an impressive sight. Built in southern style, its tiled roof lay almost flat, pegged out between four corner turrets, its windows were bracketed with blue-grey shutters and its pale limestone walls looked soft enough to spread on bread.

They'd be thick too, Jacquot knew – the house cool in summer, and even without central heating just about bearable in winter. And the colour of the stone changed with the season, the time of day, absorbing light like blotting paper. In summer, it would be a pale ochre at dawn, glaring white at midday, rose in the evening. At this time of year, the beginning of March, it was the same grey as the sky, the wisteria still to bloom from a tangle of wrist-thick branches that wove round the shutters and covered the lower half of the house. Jacquot took the car out of gear and let it coast down the slope, past alternating terraces of fig and olive, the wheel playing lightly between his hands, gravel crunching as they swung through a final border of palms and boxed orange trees into the château's sloping forecourt.

As they got out of the car, the front door opened and an elderly gentleman in a striped waistcoat appeared. A green apron was tied round his waist and his shirtsleeves were rolled up past bony elbows. He wore a pair of white cotton gloves and held a silver plate in one hand, a cloth in the other. He came down the steps to greet them, walking carefully, one step at a time.

'Inspectors Jacquot and Dietering from Cavaillon, to see the Comte de Vausigne,' said Jacquot. 'We are not expected.'

111

The old man nodded. 'Please, Messieurs, if you would follow me. I believe the Comte is at home.'

Slowly, laboriously, he climbed back up the steps, then stood aside, ushering Jacquot and Dietering into a stone-flagged ante-room large enough to accommodate a long oak table. A bowl of unseasonably scented flowers from the château's hot-house sat in its middle.

He put aside the plate and cloth, took their coats and laid them on one of a pair of high-backed tapestried chairs set at either end of the table. Then, remarking on the chill snap and mournful grey skies, he limped ahead of them down a stone-walled corridor and showed them into a library. Its walls were lined from floor to ceiling with bookshelves and its french windows, Jacquot noticed, opened on to a terrace with a distant view of the roofs of St Bédard.

'If you will wait a moment, I'll let the Comte know that you are here,' he told them, and with that he inclined his head and left the room.

While they waited Dietering strolled around, hands clasped behind his back, looking at the paintings, the furnishings, the books, then turned to Jacquot, who'd made himself comfortable in an armchair by the fire. 'You know something, Daniel, the house looks so great from outside, but inside it is, how do you say? A little—'

At which point the manservant reappeared and asked them to accompany him.

'A little what?' asked Jacquot, as they followed the old fellow down the hallway.

'A little . . . worn, tatty. *Schäbig*, we would say in German. Not cared-for.'

Before he could say any more, a door was opened and a voice like crystal, pure and brittle, rang out: 'Messieurs, good afternoon. And how can we be of assistance?'

As though posing for a portrait, Hélène de Vausigne stood behind her husband, hands resting lightly on the back of his armchair. Back straight as a peppermill, shoulders squared and turned slightly away, her head was tilted upwards as though the eyes needed the bridge of the nose to take aim.

Her husband, Gilles, legs crossed, put down the paper he was reading and smiled lazily in their direction. He looked as lean and haughty as his wife, narrow features tanned and lined, hair lustrously waved and corrugated. He was, Jacquot judged, a man who took care of his appearance and probably enjoyed the pleasure it provided.

'Monsieur, Madame,' replied Jacquot, then introduced himself and Dietering.

'Please, Messieurs, make yourselves comfortable,' said the Comtesse, waving to a matching pair of daintily upholstered chairs that looked as though they'd been set out specially for the occasion.

The two policemen sat down with frightening creaks, and tried to make themselves comfortable. It was no easy task. Jacquot decided that crossing his legs was simply not worth the risk: he'd end up on the floor in a bundle of kindling for sure. He wondered if people like the de Vausignes did such things deliberately. 'I'm in the comfy armchair, you're on the box of matches.' He guessed they probably did. He'd only been in the room a minute or two but already he'd taken against the pair of them.

For a moment he wondered which of them to address. Both were looking at him intently, as though they'd never seen his kind before and didn't know what to expect. He settled for the Comte, whose name was on the gun licence, and got down to business: 'I believe you own a Beretta shotgun, Monsieur. An over-and-under,' he began.

Which was a mistake. It was clearly Madame who did the talking in this house, regardless of whose name was on the licence.

'Four actually, a mixture – twelve, sixteen and twenty bores. Then there are the Brownings, Perazzis and Ayas,' she added, coming round to perch on the arm of her husband's chair, clasping her hands and placing them in her lap. 'Also, there's my husband's collection of muskets, most of which don't work, and our two Purdys.'

'It's the Beretta we're interested in. A twenty bore,' said Jacquot.

'You're not going to tell me you've found it,' said the Comtesse, clapping her hands. 'How marvellous.'

Jacquot was startled. 'Did you know the gun was missing, Madame?'

'Why of course,' she replied, eyes twinkling with delight. 'We reported it stolen. When was it, my dear? Back in November?'

The Comte nodded. 'November, yes. Some time around then.'

It was the first time he'd spoken, a low, silky drawl as lazy as his smile.

'There was a break-in,' continued the Comtesse, now fingering the pearls in her necklace. 'Nothing of any real value taken – my husband's wallet, which he'd left on his desk in the study, a portable TV and video from next door. A CD player. A few other trinkets. And the gun, of course. They found the keys for the cabinet in my husband's desk. Fortunately they left the Purdys. Much more valuable, of course, but they weren't to know that.'

The Comte waved across the room. 'They came in through that terrace door there. Smashed a window pane and forced the lock. Glass all over the place. We called Lanclos in St Bédard and he came out, took all the details.'

Jacquot groaned. Lanclos. Three months earlier a twenty-bore shotgun had been reported stolen and three months later the same gauge shotgun had been used in a murder. And Lanclos hadn't thought to connect the two – even as coincidence. No wonder the man had been put out to pasture in St Bédard where he couldn't do too much damage.

Jacquot heard Dietering cough and felt the slightest pressure against his sleeve as his colleague nudged him. The Comtesse was looking at him, head cocked to one side, a smile on her face. She must have asked him something.

'Madame was wondering when she could have the gun back? Now that we've found it,' prompted Dietering.

'You see, it has sentimental value,' she explained. 'I bought it for my husband on his fiftieth birthday.'

'Of course, Madame. As soon as we have finished with it,' said Jacquot.

'Finished with it?'

'The gun will be held as evidence.'

'Evidence? I'm afraid I don't follow.'

'We have reason to believe the Beretta was used in a crime, Madame. A murder,' said Dietering.

'Well, well,' said the Comte, shifting in his seat and recrossing his legs, straightening the crease in his trousers. 'What about that?'

'Not the Martners?' asked the Comtesse, making the connection. 'A month or so back?'

Dietering nodded. 'The last week of February.'

'And they used our gun?'

'I regret . . .'

'But that's dreadful,' said the Comtesse, softly. 'I'm not so sure that I want it back now. Not after . . . that.' She looked genuinely stricken at the very thought.

'Did you know the family?' asked Jacquot, catching her eye.

'The Martners? Only the name. The story was in the papers, wasn't it? And television. Of course, we never actually met. We knew they lived nearby but . . .' The Comtesse let the words hang, looking with a gently complicit smile at Jacquot. 'We told that to the police when they questioned us after the murders. I believe everyone in the neighbourhood was spoken to.'

Jacquot nodded and turned to her husband. 'Might I ask where you keep your guns, Monsieur?'

The Comte pointed to a door by the fireplace. 'Through there. In my study. I'll show you if you like.' He heaved himself out of his chair, indicating that they should follow.

With a polite nod to the Comtesse, who stayed where she was, and with much creaking from their chairs, the two detectives got to their feet and followed him into the study. It was smaller than the library and the morning room and occupied one of the château's four corner turrets. It had a snug, clubby feel, its curved stone walls decorated with the tusked heads of two boars and the horned skulls of twenty or more deer, the bone polished and varnished.

The Comte took a ring of keys from his desk drawer, unlocked a cabinet and pulled open the doors. It was lined with scarlet baize and the guns were lined up in a chained rack. The Comte selected another key from the bunch and undid the clasp, sliding the chain through the trigger guards, stepping aside for Jacquot and Dietering to examine his collection. The wood stocks glowed a deep, burred mahogany from frequent polishing and the gunmetal barrels glinted a malevolent blue-black. There were twelve spaces but only eleven guns.

'How many people know about this cabinet, that you keep guns here?' asked Jacquot.

'My wife, son, the staff,' replied the Comte, playing the clasp and security chain between his fingers, 'and any friends who come to stay and like to shoot. It's no secret that we keep guns, Chief Inspector. Around here, who doesn't?'

'And the keys? Do you always keep them in that drawer?'

'Not always. In the drawer . . . on the desk . . . It depends.'

'And on the night of the robbery?'

The Comte shrugged.

'And where did you find the keys, after you discovered the break-in?'

'Still in the padlock,' he replied, lifting the chain as though offering it for inspection. 'Just like this. Whoever broke in just dropped it on the floor, where you're standing.'

'Was it only the gun that was taken, or cartridges too?' asked Dietering.

'Oh, yes. Cartridges too. Three or four boxes, I seem to recall.'

'And where do you keep the ammunition?' continued Jacquot.

'The drawer there,' said the Comte, pointing below the rack.

Jacquot slid it open. Inside were a half-dozen boxes and a few loose cartridges – the .20s the same make and colour as the casings collected at the Martner house.

'You do a lot of shooting, Monsieur?' asked Jacquot.

'Now and again, Chief Inspector. But not as much as I used to.'

'Anyone else?'

'Eric the gardener – rabbits, crows, mostly. And then, as I said earlier, there're friends who maybe fancy a walk around the estate. Nothing formal, you understand. Not any more.'

'Your wife?'

'Used to, a fine shot as well. But not now.'

'And your son?'

'Antoine? Not so often. He lives in Paris now. But he's a good shot when the mood takes him.'

Jacquot nodded, taking it in. 'And you are the keyholder? There are no copies for the cabinet?'

'Yes, and no.'

'So when your gardener, say . . .'

'If he needs a gun, he'll ask Picard, who'll ask me.'

'You get him the gun yourself?'

'If I'm here. Otherwise I leave it to Picard.'

116

'Does he have a preference? Your gardener? Twelve bore? Twenty bore?'

The Comte shrugged. 'I honestly don't recall. Whichever comes to hand, usually.'

'And who cleans the guns, Monsieur?' asked Dietering.

'Picard.'

'And how often?'

'Whenever a gun is used. He's meticulous. Always. Without fail.'

Back in the morning room the Comte eased into his chair, as though answering so many questions had thoroughly exhausted him. Jacquot and Dietering remained standing.

'Is there anything else we can do to help, Chief Inspector?' asked the Comtesse, patting her husband's shoulder.

'As a matter of fact, there is,' replied Jacquot. 'We will need to take fingerprints.'

'Fingerprints?' She looked greatly taken aback.

'From you and your staff, Madame. An unfortunate formality, but a necessary one. Purely for the purpose of elimination. I'm sure you understand.'

'I see . . . Well, I suppose if you must, you must.'

'And your staff? Who exactly . . . ?'

'Well, there's Picard, of course,' she replied, 'and his wife, Florence, our cook and housekeeper. They have an apartment above the kitchen.'

'And how long have they worked here?'

'As long as I can remember, Chief Inspector. There have been Picards with the family for generations. As for the others, there's Monique, who comes in three times a week, and the gardener, Eric, both of them from St Bédard.'

'And how long have Monique and Eric been with you?' asked Jacquot.

'Monique came first. About five years now,' replied the Comtesse. 'Eric . . .' she looked at her husband. 'A year, maybe two. He's a little . . .' the Comtesse spread her hands '. . . a little slow, but a good worker all the same. Picard speaks highly of him, and the garden is always immaculate.'

Forty minutes later, Jacquot and Dietering pulled away from the house and followed the drive up the hillside. In Dietering's briefcase was a set of prints from the de Vausignes, Picard and his wife, and the maid Monique. As for the gardener, Eric Chabert, no one seemed to know where he was. Picard thought he was out chopping wood, Monique was certain he'd gone into Cavaillon for a new hose, and Florence simply shrugged her shoulders.

'The lad could be anywhere,' she said, wiping the ink from her fingertips. 'Who knows? But wherever he is, you can be certain he'll be putting his back into it.'

Rather than wait for his return, Jacquot decided to have Brunet call in on the gardener at his home in St Bédard.

No point leaving it to Lanclos, he thought, as they pulled out through the château gates and on to the St Bédard road. He'd probably send in his own fingerprints by mistake. Fournier had already lifted more than a dozen of the sergeant's prints from around the Martner house.

22

According to Lanclos's report, which Jacquot called up from Records after dropping Dietering at the airport for his weekend flight home, the break-in at the château was exactly how the de Vausignes had described it.

November 26. At night. Window pane smashed and lock forced. Nothing of value taken beyond a wallet containing six thousand francs, a TV, video and CD player. And the gun and cartridges. To all appearances it seemed to have been a simple but professional break-in. Whoever had done it had left no fingerprints at the scene, no footprints in the garden, and no one had heard a thing.

Jacquot tossed the report on to his desk, swung round in his chair and wondered about the six thousand francs. Somehow he doubted the de Vausignes ever carried that kind of money in cash. As Dietering had noted, the château was not in a state of repair that suggested a wad of six thousand francs left lying around.

What was the word he had used? *Schäbig*. Shabby, down-at-heel. And it was an accurate enough description. The house might look imposing from the outside, with its terraces and turrets, but its interior was . . . well, *schäbig* caught it exactly. The curtains were threadbare, the paint was flaking on the mouldings, the floorboards dulled and the carpets worn to the weave, as though the de Vausignes had other, more important, things to occupy their minds than domestic concerns. A house like that would certainly need more than a

Florence and Monique to keep it in order. And for a family that had been around for centuries, the place was hardly brimming with treasures.

Six thousand francs? No, no, no. Jacquot didn't think so. As for the TV, video and CD player, he was willing to bet his pension they'd been stacked upstairs, window-dressing contrived by the de Vausignes to increase the value of their claim. Insurance companies. Jacquot shook his head. If they used their brains they'd save themselves millions in pay-outs. No wonder everyone tried to con them. Even the de Vausignes of this world. And if the burglar was ever caught, it was just his word against theirs. A *comte* and *comtesse*? No competition.

Which meant, so far as Jacquot could see, that it was the gun the intruder had come for. Not videos, not TVs, not wallets, not cash. All he wanted was a gun. A weapon.

A murder weapon.

Which meant, more than likely, that the man who had broken into the de Vausignes' home in November was the same man who, three months later, had slaughtered the Martner family.

Whichever way he looked at it, Jacquot couldn't help but think he was right.

23

It was Dietering, at a little after eleven o'clock on Monday morning, fresh off the flight from Bonn, who took the call. 'The prints,' he said, coming through into Jacquot's office. 'We have a match.'

There was a gleam of excitement in the younger man's eyes, but it was an excitement that Jacquot found hard to share. After more than twenty years in the job he knew that a fingerprint, like a murder weapon, was only half of the story. And sometimes not as much as that. Finding one or the other might bring focus to an investigation, and finding both might provide a certain impetus. But that was all. In Jacquot's experience, the two were never more than starting points. Signposts. But signposts that any policeman worth his badge was duty-bound to follow. Even if the signpost in question pointed back to the Château de Vausignes.

If the prints on the gun had been matched to a known felon, Jacquot might have felt differently. But the prints – a partial right index finger on the trigger guard and a smudged thumb on the underside of the barrel – belonged to Eric Chabert, the de Vausignes' gardener. As far as Jacquot was concerned, it would have been astonishing if his prints had not been found – or those of Picard, or the Comte, or even the Comtesse. But a signpost was a signpost and, really for want of anything better to do, Jacquot called up all the information they could source. It didn't take long.

Name: Eric Gérard Chabert. Nineteen. Only child.

Parents: Fernand and Denise Chabert, owners of the flower shop Fontaine des Fleurs on Place Vausigne, St Bédard-le-Chapitre.

Education: École du Clos, Cavaillon. According to the school's director, Chabert had been as poor at academics as attendance. 'If I remember, not a naturally gifted student,' the man had told Brunet, with a dismissive gesture.

Employment: worked at his parents' shop, and part-time gardener at the Château de Vausigne. And at Mas Taillard – the Martners' home.

Police records were checked for previous convictions – nothing – and the gendarme who'd taken Chabert's statement the day after the murders was promptly hauled in. His name was Barlisse and he looked uncomfortable, standing there at Jacquot's desk.

'Eric Chabert. Impressions, please,' asked Jacquot.

Barlisse looked blank.

'St Bédard. The flower shop. You interviewed him,' Jacquot prompted gently.

The man thought for a moment, then nodded vigorously. 'Yes, I remember. Good-looking kid,' he replied. 'Well-built. But not the sharpest knife in the drawer, if you get my meaning. You know those village types – live at home, love their *mamans* . . .'

'Friends?'

'The Mazzelli lad across the *place*. Chabert's a bit older but they hang out. Play for the same rugby club.'

'Position?' asked Jacquot.

Barlisse looked suddenly anxious. Had he forgotten something? 'Scrum, by the look of him.'

'Girlfriends? Boyfriends?' continued Jacquot.

'Seemed straight to me, boss. Shouldn't have had too much trouble with the girls, but nothing serious I heard about. Nobody particular, so far as I know.'

'What did he think of his employers?'

The gendarme seemed lost now.

Jacquot sighed. 'The Martners.'

'The Martners. That's right. No complaints, so far as I recall. He said they left him pretty much to his own devices. The doctor wasn't bothered with the garden, only the hot-house. Sometimes Chabert picked up supplies for the old man, but usually it was Madame Martner dealt with him when something needed doing or fetching.'

'And where did he say he was at the time of the murders?'

'Having breakfast. Getting the shop ready.' There was a note of uncertainty in the gendarme's voice, the information delivered almost as questions. He dug in his pockets and pulled out his note-book, scrabbled through the pages.

Jacquot waited a moment before he continued. 'And what time did he get up that morning?

Barlisse ran a finger down a page in his notebook. 'Between five and six. As usual.'

'Anyone vouch for his whereabouts?'

'He shared a cigarette with Tomas Mazzelli,' replied Barlisse, glancing at his notes. 'Around seven, Mazzelli said. Then he went back to the shop, helped bring in the flowers from the outhouses and set up the racks. Just like normal, according to Mazzelli.'

'But until then, the smoke with Mazzelli, Chabert was on his own?'

Barlisse thought for a moment, then nodded. 'That's all we got, boss.'

And that was it. Everything to go on – and nothing.

Two days after confirming the print, Jacquot gave the nod. Early evening, midweek, a good time to go calling. Chabert was having supper with his parents in the back parlour of the Fontaine des Fleurs when Brunet and three gendarmes knocked on the front door to bring him in for questioning.

It was all done very quickly. An hour after putting down his fork to answer the door, Eric Chabert was sitting in an interview room at Cavaillon Police Headquarters, his parents huddled anxiously in a waiting room behind Mougeon's front desk.

Two hours later, as Jacquot and Dietering followed Brunet down the second-floor hallway towards the interview room where Chabert was being held, Jacquot felt no real sense of expectation, no stir-ring in the gut. It was just a fingerprint, after all. And it was just a gun. And he knew that they needed a great deal more than a murder weapon and a matching fingerprint. According to Picard, the boy used the Comte's guns regularly – rabbits, crows or other vermin on the estate – a fact confirmed by Fournier who'd lifted partial

Chabert prints from three other guns in the cabinet. What they were looking for now was information, something to move the investigation along. As for a motive, a reason why Chabert might have killed these people, well, he wasn't holding his breath.

As things turned out, everything happened faster than any of them could have imagined.

24

Chabert looked up when they came in, anxious eyes darting between them, taking their measure. He had short blond hair, all awry as though he'd been running his fingers through it, a broad, honest face, bulky shoulders and large, strong hands. The hand-knitted sweater he wore was tight across the chest and the cuffs and collar of his white shirt were grubby and curled. He sat at a Formica-top table stranded in the centre of the room, and seemed confused, uncertain. Which was why they'd left him alone for the last two hours, save visits from Mougeon with coffee from the machine. There were three empty polystyrene cups on the table, standing in a mess of rings.

As planned, Brunet took a seat across from Chabert, while Dietering and Jacquot settled in two chairs set against the wall by the window. Someone had opened it for air – maybe Chabert – although a few barred centimetres was as high as it would go. The glass was frosted, but it was still possible to make out the dark smudge of the spire and belfry of Église St-Jean across the gendarmerie's car park.

Brunet made himself comfortable, shot his buttoned cuffs, shrugged his shoulders inside his sports jacket and loosened his tie. Only then did he open the file he'd brought with him, shuffling through its contents, then shuffling through them again, as though he'd lost something, left something behind. He closed the file and sighed deeply.

125

Next, Jacquot knew, he'd pull a pen from his pocket. Roll it in his fingers. Remove the cap. Then place the pen on the table, positioning it just so. It was a great act. Burglar, wife-beater, rapist or murderer, they all got the same performance. In three years, Jacquot had seen it many times.

As expected Brunet searched for his pen, found it in an inside pocket, pulled off the cap and laid it on the table, squaring it up beside the file.

Like many before him, Chabert was mesmerised.

Brunet sighed again. Then, leaning across the table, he switched on the tape, introduced himself, gave the names of the other officers present and began the questions. The same ones they'd asked on the door-to-door.

Straight into it. Just like that.

Right through the first time. Just questions. One after another. And not a word about Chabert's fingerprints on the murder weapon.

Then again. Just as fast.

Then a third time, Brunet moving about a bit, skipping the order, coming back to things, feints to left and right. 'You said earlier . . .' and 'But I thought you said . . .' and 'Now you're telling me . . .'. That sort of thing, trying to throw the boy.

Over and over.

And Brunet was a master.

But four times through and Chabert's story seemed to hold, never really faltered: where he was at the time of the murders; what he was doing; how the Martners treated him; what he thought of them; what he did for them. Not a step wrong. The doctor. His wife, Madame Martner. The daughter, Ilse Brauer.

And then Kippi.

Chabert had trouble with the name. A catch in the voice, a clearing of the throat, a swift cuff across the eyes.

Jacquot and Dietering sensed something.

So did Brunet. 'Tell me about Kippi,' he probed. 'Pretty girl, wasn't she? Really pretty.' Brunet looked to the ceiling, shaking his head. 'I tell you, I seen the photos. Beautiful.'

Then he turned back to Chabert, leaned forward. 'How often did she visit? You see much of her? You ever go out with her? Take her into town?' He moved his elbows forward, dropped his voice.

'You and Kippi have something going on together, Eric? Yeah? You did?'

Brunet sat back and slapped the table, which made Chabert and Dietering jump. Not Jacquot: he'd known it was coming.

'Not bad,' said Brunet, chuckling darkly. 'Not bad at all.' He nodded, as though considering the prospect of making love to a girl like Kippi. Idly, he reached into an inside pocket, pulled out a tiny silver tube, unscrewed the lid and shook out a toothpick. When the silver tube was back in his pocket, he set to work. On his teeth. And Chabert.

'And then what? Don't tell me. She goes and gives you the boot. Over. *Fini*. Just when things are getting good. Is that how it was? Is that how it happened?'

Which was when Chabert put his elbows on the table, hands to his face, and began to weep. 'I didn't know she was pregnant. I didn't know. I swear it.'

Jacquot had heard that voice many times. He caught Dietering's eye. So had the German.

Brunet too. He waited a beat, working on a tooth in the back of his mouth, then removed the toothpick and bore on. 'Why should you? Why should you know she was pregnant?'

'I didn't.'

'I mean, why would she tell you? Come on, Eric. She might have been banging you, but you are just the gardener, right?' Leaning back in his seat, Brunet started working the dampened toothpick at his cuticles. Another beat, and then: 'I mean, hey, it wasn't going anywhere, was it? Surely you knew that?'

And then the silence.

Brunet rode with it.

Chabert shook his head but his hands stayed where they were. Big and pink with knuckly fingers and dirt-rimmed nails. A bunch of hair stood up at his fingertips.

Jacquot and Dietering didn't move.

Brunet gave it a few more moments.

Jacquot knew what he was going to say before he said it.

'You loved her, didn't you?'

No reply. Head in hands.

'You loved her like you never loved anyone in your life, right? You didn't want to lose her, did you?'

Silence.

'Did you?'

The head shook. A mournful, muffled, 'No,' rose from behind the hands.

'And it's driving you crazy. I mean, you haven't seen her since, what? New Year? The last time she's down here, right? And now, all of a sudden, here she is giving you the cold shoulder. The heave-ho. Party's over, *liebchen*. Let's call it a day. Thanks for the memory.'

'If I had known . . . If only I had known . . .' he whimpered.

25

May

It was old Dumé who saw her first. On his afternoon walk. The last Sunday in May.

Closing the front door behind him, pushing it with his stick to make sure the latch had caught, Dumé glanced round the empty *place*. All his. Just a few late lunchers on the Parmentiers' terrace across the way, the splashing of the fountain in front of the church and the chatter of sparrows in the plane trees that shaded the square.

After a moment's pause, taking all this in with a beat or two of satisfaction, the world to himself at last, Dumé stepped away from his house and, leaning on his stick, set off for the Brieuc road.

Winter or summer Dumé wore what he always wore – a pair of baggy *bleus* cinched by a brown leather belt, a waistcoat polished to a shine with old stains and a pinstripe jacket that hung from his shoulders like the night cover on a birdcage. In the opening of a collarless flannel combination that reached to his ankles, a red bandanna was knotted with a flourish and on his head he wore the beret his wife had bought him in the market at Arles the summer before she died. In his jacket pockets, which bulged even when they were empty, were his pipe, a box of matches and a leather pouch. An easy stroll and a quiet smoke, that was what old Dumé was after.

Martin O'Brien

The Brieuc road was his favourite walk. It began at the lower end of the *place*, to the right, in the shade of what remained of St Bédard's medieval fortifications, along a single pavement that led to the town's west gate, an arch of honeyed stone rising above the road like a giant keyhole. Beyond this gate, its sides scored by the brush of passing traffic, the countryside began: hillsides ribbed with vines, fields rustling with early maize and down in the valley the black ribbon of road that led from the heights of Rocsabin to Brieuc and Cavaillon.

In the cool shadow of the arch Dumé waited, listening for the sound of a car or the low-gear groan of a lorry labouring up the hill. From where he stood it was maybe ten metres to the first of the plane trees that lined the valley side of the road. He'd be out in the sun for those ten metres and Dumé knew it would be hot. So far as he could recall, today was the first white sky of the year, any blue long since bleached away. If there was a cloud up there you'd never see it now.

As he'd expected the sun clamped down the moment he stepped from the arch. Gripping his stick he made for the nearest tree as fast as his old canvas boots would carry him. As he reached its skirt of shade, he felt a cold dampness in his armpits and a broad ache in his chest. Tomorrow, he decided, catching his breath, he'd leave his walk for later in the day.

From tree to tree, from one puddle of shade to the next, Dumé made his way along the road, surrounded by the busy ticking of insects and the scent of hot dust and wild fennel. Behind him the stone arch and crumbling walls of St Bédard were soon hidden by the trees, and ahead he could see now where the road began its first gentle descent. Here the walking became easier and after a few more steps the valley opened up before him, its distant heights scabbed with limestone bluffs, slopes freckled with olive trees and the course of its river piped with poplar and linden.

It was here that Dumé did what he always did. Turning his back to the road, he hooked his stick over his arm and, tottering slightly, fumbled at his trouser front. Satisfactorily unbuttoned, he pointed himself to the valley, to the folding slopes of the Luberon, and waited.

And waited.

130

Despite a tickling promise – nothing. After a few muttered moments, tightening and loosening old muscles to persuade a trickle that wouldn't come, he tugged himself back into shape and walked on, head shaking at the cussedness of it all.

Old age, he thought. Who'd want it?

A few years back, he'd been able to take a pee when he wanted and make it all the way down to the bridge to smoke his pipe. But now the journey was too steep – both ways – too long and, even this early in the year, already too hot for him. Now it was enough to walk to the first bend and turn off, as he did now, along a stone-studded path between the vines. About twenty metres along this path, where the land began to rise again, stood a copse of twisted olives where Dumé liked to sit, on the low stone wall that terraced them into the hillside, with nothing but the sky and the land, the hum of crickets and the occasional flutter of a bird in the branches to keep him company.

Wedging a bony arse between the stones, Dumé propped his stick against the wall and felt in his pockets for his pipe and pouch. Carefully, he pulled out a wad of black tobacco, loaded it into the bowl and tamped it down with a finger. Too tightly packed and it was the devil to draw, too loose and the smoke made him cough and catch his breath. With his second match, the tobacco caught and, lips pop-pop-popping on the stem of the pipe, Dumé pocketed the matches and pouch and looked back towards the road.

It was then, through a curl of blue tobacco smoke, that something caught his eye, something down in the valley, somewhere beyond the trees that marked the course of the river, a flash of sun on metal or glass. He waited for it to show itself again, and when it failed to do so he knew it wasn't a car, or it would have passed the St Bédard turn by now. Whatever it was, it was still in the trees.

And then, moments later, he caught another movement, closer than he'd expected, something streaking towards the St Bédard bridge, pulling out to negotiate the turning off the Brieuc road, disappearing into the slope of the land at his feet.

A bicycle. He was certain. Had to be.

Dumé waited in the shade beneath the olives, smoking his pipe, occasionally tamping down the tobacco with his thumb, the bowl warm in his palm. From somewhere behind him came a tap-tap-tapping sound, but he didn't bother to turn. He knew what it was. A blue jay with a snail, smacking the shell against a stone to loosen the treasure inside. A good French bird, he thought with a chuckle, fishing for his matches to relight his pipe. But as the flame licked down, he tasted the end of his smoke and heard the pipe-stem start to bubble. Tossing away the spent match, he drew the pipe from his mouth, tapped it against the stone wall and stamped on the smoking black dottle of tobacco that dropped beside his boot. And all the while he kept his eyes on the slope of the road.

Not that a bicycle would make it this far in such a short space of time. Whoever was riding it would be forced out of the saddle after the first hundred metres and then, as Dumé knew well, it was uphill all the way. A long, hard push.

Slipping his pipe into a pocket, he followed the route in his mind's eye: past the memorial – 'Tué par les Allemands, Juin 8, 1944' – through a tunnel of chestnuts to the ruins of the old mill, round the first long turn to the left and then a steep climb, with the valley dropping away to one side.

Maybe he dozed in the warm, chirruping afternoon shade. Dumé couldn't decide. But the next thing he knew the bike was there, the rider leaning into the slope, pushing up towards St Bédard, the circular passage of the spokes speeding and slowing, speeding and slowing with every tired step. For a moment Dumé fancied he could hear the rhythmic ticking of the back wheel against the disengaged gear, but the distance was too great for that. It was just the song of the crickets that made him think it.

Not moving in the shadow of the olives, Dumé peered between the vines and watched the bike's approach. There were panniers at either side of the back wheel, a saddlebag above the rear mudguard and a large wicker basket on the handlebars, the weight of the load tipping the bike towards the rider.

Was it a boy or a girl? Dumé wondered. A man or a woman? All he could make out was a bob of black hair, a short-sleeved brown shirt, creased shorts that came to the knee, bare legs and socks tucked round boots.

It was a boy, Dumé decided. And then he revised that opinion, for the legs were too narrow and smooth, the arms too long and thin, and the line and curve of the body altogether softer. It was a woman. A girl.

And then, right there, at the very end of the path, no more than twenty metres distant, where the road began to level, she stopped pushing and looked ahead, gauging what was left of the gradient. Dumé nodded. She could start riding now, for sure, even with the weight she was carrying. And that was what she did, stepping across the bike – it was a woman's model, he could see now – lifting a foot to a pedal and taking a long, deep breath as though mustering herself for the effort.

And in that pause, she turned in his direction, caught his eye – as if she'd seen him from the moment she'd rounded the bend, as though the cover of the olives concealed nothing from her – and waved to him, arm high in the air, hand fluid at the wrist. A big, strong wave, a wave made for long distances, an extravagant, happy gesture, which shook down through her body.

And shook through his too.

Then she was off, standing on the pedals, weaving forward, front wheel twisting left and right until it steadied with the power from her legs. A moment later she had passed from sight and he was alone again.

Dumé breathed out, as though he'd been holding his breath all that time, and gulped in the warm, still air. He hadn't moved an inch, but his heart was beating fast. His beret felt suddenly tight and he pulled it from his head. Across his scalp he felt the heat of the sun and the cool of the shade in a single instant and he shivered.

'*Dieu*,' he said, to the tangle of spear-tip leaves above his head, followed by the conviction: 'Here's something.'

And, without knowing precisely why, he started after her, out of the shade of the olives, between the vines and back the way he had come.

26

Odile Ramier had no good reason to go into the salon. She'd thought she had, but now that she was there she couldn't for the life of her remember what she was supposed to be doing. Or what it was she had wanted. And as she stood there, the tips of her fingers playing across the soft scarlet velour of her late mother's *chaise-longue*, she thought, with a jolt: You're getting old, Odile. You're getting just like your sister.

That Sunday there'd been three of them for lunch at their home on Place Vausigne. Just as there always were on the last Sunday of the month when Odile Ramier and Adéline Séguin entertained the Curé Foulard. Two hours earlier he'd been ushered into the salon where Odile now stood, had accepted a small aperitif, then followed them through the kitchen to the tiny walled garden where the sisters had set out a table in the shade of a plum tree.

Their lunch – a cool *pistou* soup, a crisply turned *roti de porc*, a salad, some cheese and a little wine – had been much praised by the *curé*, and both sisters had been greatly relieved. The last time he had visited, the cream, lemon and tarragon sauce they'd prepared for the chicken breasts had cruelly separated in the heat of the kitchen and they'd had to make do with a thin, watery *jus*.

As for their conversation over lunch, it had probably taken much the same direction as every other conversation in St Bédard that day.

'What an anxious time for Denise,' said Adéline, dabbing her napkin at the corners of her mouth.

'And poor Fernand,' added Odile, shaking her head at the thought of it. 'However will they get through it?'

'It won't be long now,' continued Adéline, 'one way or the other. Do you suppose they'll stay here in St Bédard – if the worst comes to the worst?'

'Let us pray that it doesn't,' replied Curé Foulard, gently. 'But . . . if it is God's will . . .'

'And Eric, of all people,' said Adéline. 'Do you know I still can't believe it. Such a quiet, good boy. So considerate, so . . .'

It was exactly then that Odile had pushed back her chair, got to her feet and gathered the plates, saying she would make them all some coffee.

And that was what she'd started to do – listening to Adéline's chatter through the kitchen window as she spooned coffee into the percolator and put a flame to the gas. But then, for some reason she couldn't now fathom, she'd left the kitchen, walked up the hallway and come into the salon.

But what on earth for? she thought, tut-tutting at her memory and allowing herself a chuckle of irritation. Then, behind the net curtains that concealed their salon from the *place*, Odile heard a fly tapping against the window. She wondered if she should let it out, but decided to leave it. So much easier to dust away the brittle black husk of a body later.

Out in the kitchen, the percolator started to bubble and spit on the range.

'Odie? Odie? Do you need any help?' Adéline called, from the garden.

'No, no. I'm fine,' she called back. 'I'll be there in just a moment.'

But still Odile stood where she was, trying to remember, trying to think why she should have come to this room. And then she noticed that the fly had stopped buzzing and beating against the glass. She walked to the window, parted the curtain and inspected the window ledge. Not a sign of the creature anywhere. Maybe it had sensed a draught through the open door and escaped without her seeing it.

But flies were never like that, she thought. They beat against a window until they could beat no more – even if there was a door open and another way out. That was the obstinate nature of flies. Intrigued, Odile stooped down to inspect the floor, looking for the stiffened black body.

Which was when a movement caught her eye, through the window, out across the square.

Had Odile been standing, as she had been a moment earlier, the lowest branches of the plane trees would have obscured her view of someone leaning a bicycle against a lamp-post on the other side of Place Vausigne. But from this angle, looking through the window at sill level, she was able to make out a pair of brown legs, sturdy boots and creased khaki shorts. She could also see there were bags on the bike's back wheel and a basket on its handlebars. And no crossbar. It was a woman's bike.

Not that Odile needed any telling that the rider was a woman. You could see it from the shape of the legs, the way she walked away from the bike until the peeling trunks of the plane trees and the square's incline conspired to block her view.

All she could say, as she poured coffee for the *curé* and her sister, was that the Chaberts had a visitor.

27

'I really think I should stay,' said Denise Chabert, unpinning her hat, lifting it off and placing it on the parlour table.

Fernand Chabert, putting away the last of the lunch plates, turned to his wife and managed a smile. The poor woman looked worn-out, he thought, at the end of her tether.

But worn-out or not, he knew his wife didn't mean what she said about staying in St Bédard, knew there was only one place Denise Chabert wanted to be right now. And that was in Lyon. With Eric. To be at his side, or as close as she could manage, for every one of the days or weeks – however long it took – that lay ahead. She was fretting, that was all. Anxious about the shop, the business. But, most of all, about Eric. And the trial.

'It won't be much longer, *chérie*. You shouldn't worry so.'

'I know, I know,' she replied, in a tight, strained little voice. 'It's just the time. They said midday. And midday's midday. Even on a Sunday. He should be here by now, that's all . . .'

For want of something better to do, she sat down at the parlour table, pushing aside her hat and the pearl-topped pin that had held it in place. She was fifty-two, a little stout now in the shoulders and hips, fuller in the face perhaps, but with the same small strong hands and long fingers that, Fernand knew, could grasp the stems of twenty tulips tightly enough to cut away the ends with a single, straight slice. Along the edges of those same fingers, which she now clasped and unclasped, was a cross-hatching of tiny black lines, the nicks and cuts she had collected not from the blade of her knife but from the sharp edges of the paper they used to wrap the flowers.

'It's just . . . it's just so vexing,' she said, with an anguished sigh.

Coming through from the kitchen, he pulled out a chair, reached over the table and touched her fingers.

She looked at him for a few moments, his touch making her mouth bunch and her eyes brim with tears. She couldn't bear this. Couldn't bear it.

'I just want it all to be over,' she whispered, holding back the tears. 'I want him home again. I want it . . . like it was.'

'It will be, I promise. You'll see,' replied Fernand, with a strength and a certainty that he didn't altogether feel.

She nodded, and sniffed, then cleared her throat, gave him a tearful smile, and turned once more to the clock on the parlour wall as though constant referral to the time would somehow hasten the arrival they were waiting for.

That Sunday, Fernand and Denise had missed Sunday mass. Shortly after ten o'clock, when the bells from the church fell silent, Denise had crossed herself and left it at that. Fernand didn't press the matter. Later she said to him: 'I couldn't face them, you understand. Not today.'

And he'd nodded: yes, of course he understood.

Not that the Chaberts had anything to fear from the congregation of St Bédard. In those dreadful days after the police had come for Eric, their black Peugeot parked across the pavement in front of Fontaine des Fleurs as though to block any chance of escape – as if there'd been some possibility their son might try to make a run for it – everyone had rallied round. Curé Foulard had been first to call by, with gentle words, the evening they returned from Cavaillon after being told that their son would not be coming home with them.

And it hadn't stopped with the *curé*.

As news spread about Eric being held for the Martner murders, friends and neighbours all made a point of visiting the shop. So many signs of concern, offers of support: Aldo and Tira at the Bar de la Fontaine across the *place* volunteering their son Tomas, who'd be happy, they said, to help out at the shop or make any market trips they wanted; the Parmentiers, Caroline and Michel, shooing away a journalist from one of their tables when he tried to wheedle information out of them; Delphine Bulot from the *charcuterie* passing by at the end of the day with odds and ends from her shelves; and dear old Adéline Séguin coming across every Thursday with one of her sister's terrines prettily wrapped in a damp gingham cloth

A mistake, they all said. Ridiculous! Eric, a killer? Whatever next? It'll soon be sorted out, you'll see. It was as though their son had been taken to hospital, not prison.

If they'd given it any thought the Chaberts might have anticipated these small kindnesses from their neighbours. But there was no way they could have been prepared for the letter from Gilles de Vausigne, which arrived two days after formal charges were made against Eric. The Comte had written to inform them that a distinguished cousin, Maître Messain of Lyon, would be contacting them shortly regarding Eric's defence and that he and the Comtesse had taken it upon themselves to settle in advance the fees for this action.

Such an unexpected profession of faith in their son's innocence had stunned the Chaberts. Why, the boy was only their gardener, a four-afternoons-a-week handyman, who'd been with them just a couple of years. Such a generous offer seemed inconceivable. But when Fernand, against Denise's wishes, phoned the Comte and Comtesse to decline their kind offer with his most grateful thanks he was cut off mid-sentence by the Comte's growling voice, which Denise, standing beside her husband, could clearly hear.

Dear Monsieur Chabert, the old man had drawled, there was to be absolutely no argument. He and his wife were in complete agreement. A mistake had been made. Of course Eric was innocent. As for the good *maître*'s fees, *alors*, such a small thing, the matter was settled and there, dear fellow, was an end to it. The sooner they got their gardener back, the better for all of them. When Fernand put down the phone, there was a tightness in his throat that made speaking difficult.

That Sunday morning Denise had prepared only a light lunch, which they had eaten in silence at the old oak table, the two of them expecting at any moment the doorbell to ring, the man from the agency to arrive.

Midday, Sunday, they'd said.

Fernand, of course, supposed the word 'midday' allowed some leeway, particularly at a weekend. Their train for Avignon and Lyon didn't leave until after five, so there'd be plenty of time to do what needed to be done. Show him the cold store, the hot-house; run him through the suppliers, the orders and account books. Explain the locks, the old Citroën van, the house. It wouldn't take long. A methodical man, Fernand had written it all down anyway, like a hotel directory.

But Denise would not settle. Midday was midday in her book – twelve o'clock sharp – and after their lunch she'd taken to going through to the shop to peer through the slats in the metal grating that was rolled down over the window. On the last of these checks, as he rinsed their lunch plates, Fernand heard her unlock the front door to look out, heard the fountain splashing in the *place*.

'Old Dumé out for his stroll,' he heard her say. And then, as she came back to the parlour: 'It's too hot. He should wait for evening.'

He likes it, Fernand tried to explain, turning from the kitchen sink and watching her pace the parlour. He has the world to himself, he said. His son, Patric, his daughter-in-law, Mathilde, the children – the house was too busy and loud for the old man. He deserved his moment of peace.

Denise looked unconvinced, disapproving. For the hundredth time that day she glanced at the clock and pursed her lips.

'Why don't we have some coffee?' suggested Fernand, getting up from the table. Truth be told, he was as troubled and anxious as his wife, desperate now to fill the time.

Denise made a *moue*. 'If you want . . .'

Out in the kitchen he poured two cups from the pot brewing on the stove and brought them through to the table. By the time he returned with the cream and sugar, his wife had taken up her hat and was pinning it back into place.

Which was when the stranger arrived.

The girl.

Afterwards, in the taxi to Cavaillon, they talked about her.

Denise began it: 'I thought they said a man,' she said. 'What did she say her name was? I've forgotten already.'

'Buhl,' replied her husband. 'Marie-Ange Buhl. A stand-in. The man they were going to send was ill. We were lucky they found someone.'

They watched the countryside flashing past, then the first few houses, and the empty Sunday streets of Cavaillon.

'Do you think she'll manage,' asked Denise, 'all on her own? She looked so . . .'

'Of course she will. Don't fret, my darling. Everything will be fine, you'll see.'

'She was beautiful, wasn't she?' said Denise, as the taxi rocked over the railway line and she spotted the station ahead. 'What I wouldn't give to see their faces tomorrow.'

Fernand turned to his wife. 'Maybe I should stay, help her out,' he said, smiling at her.

She looked at him, uncertain again. Then saw his smile and smiled too, her first real smile for many days. She slipped her arm through his, leaning against his narrow frame in the bouncing rear seat of the taxi. 'Don't even think about it, Monsieur Chabert. Don't you even think about it.'

28

June

That first Monday in June, Marie-Ange Buhl awoke in a stranger's bed. Eric Chabert's bed. Without moving she felt him there. All the warm hollows and soft depressions, the unfamiliar angles and unlikely curves. Over the years, he'd given this bed his form, moulded its surface, a set of unfamiliar contours, which Marie-Ange had burrowed into the night before, and fitted to the shape of her own body. Just as she'd known she would. Now, rubbing the sleep from her eyes, she stretched slowly, limbs unfolding under the crumpled sheet, all tousled black hair and sleepy face.

Here, at the front of the house, above the topmost branches of the trees in the *place*, with only thin cotton curtains to cover the window, the room grew light early. Marie-Ange liked that. And the sounds she'd woken to she liked as well: the brooding of doves and the chalky scratch of their claws on the roof tiles, the first chirruping of sparrows in the branches below her window, a clattering of footsteps across the cobbles in the *place* and the distant splash of the fountain.

Shifting up in his bed, resting on her elbows, Marie-Ange looked around, taking it all in. A boy's room still, she decided, not yet quite a man's room. Sparsely furnished, as she'd expected, but still cosy in a low-ceilinged, under-the-eaves way. And oddly out of kilter, she noted, closing one eye and taking a bead on the room: the uneven walls, the casement window crookedly recessed in the slope of the roof, the bare boards tipping the opposite way to the window. There was something precarious about it all, she decided, like being in a nest at the top of a tall tree.

And everything in its place: a teetering wardrobe with a mirror-panelled door against one wall and, facing it, a bulky chest of drawers with white china knobs and a highly polished walnut veneer. On top of the chest stood a radio-cassette player, a neatly stacked selection of tapes and a row of paperbacks, curled and fattened from reading, held in place by carpentry-class bookends of darkly stained wood. A varnished black stone had been set in the angle of each bookend to provide the necessary weight and a crocheted cloth had been laid beneath to save the veneer from scratches. A matching crocheted cloth had also been placed under the flexi-lamp and digital clock on her bedside table. It was the way Denise Chabert probably liked the room to look, neat and ordered, with nothing save the hollows of the mattress to bear the true imprint of the room's owner.

Of course, she'd been shown to the spare room the previous afternoon, at the back of the house, smaller than the one she now occupied. It overlooked the glass roof of the hot-house, the metalled cold store, and a shadowy garden set with rows of salad leaves and a tented frame of beans, bordered by a section of crumbling battlement that blocked a proper view of the valley. She'd professed herself delighted with it, of course: such a perfect little room, she'd said, turning to Madame Chabert who stood in the doorway, hands clasped in front of her.

'We hope you'll be comfortable,' Eric's mother had replied, with a curt little nod.

But when the Chaberts left and Marie-Ange was alone, she hadn't hesitated. She'd moved her things one floor up, into this room, Eric's room, stripped off her clothes and run herself a bath in the bathroom across the landing. After the long ride in, she'd been looking forward to a good hot soak.

While the bathwater cooled, Marie-Ange had explored her new home, from Eric's bedroom at the top of the house to the kitchen and parlour behind the shop, feeling the old place surrender its secrets one by one as she padded round in his dressing-gown, feet bare, fingers trailing.

Although the house was warm that late Sunday afternoon, there were certain places – on the top landing outside Eric's room, in the room she'd chosen not to sleep in, and between the parlour and kitchen – where the skin puckered on her shoulders, arms and belly. It was a familiar sensation and Marie-Ange was not unduly perturbed.

Here in the parlour a rising battery of words – not the Chaberts' voices – and the sharp sound of a slap still echoing between dresser and table; the distant whisper of a scream in the hallway; a cool, regretful note of departure in the spare room; and, on the top landing outside Eric's bedroom, a terrible, haunting melancholy. Not that any of this surprised Marie-Ange: the house was old – two hundred, maybe three hundred years of domestic history. She'd have been amazed if it had been any different.

Back in the bathroom, feeling the first gentle crampings she'd been expecting all day, Marie-Ange spent an hour in the hot soapy water. Head resting where his head had rested, she'd listened through the open door to the Sunday-evening sounds of St Bédard that he would have heard: the tap of *boules*, the metal scrape of a chair at the bar across the *place*, the church bell tolling for Benediction, a motorbike accelerating away, braking at the bottom of the square, then accelerating off again along the road to Brieuc. And in the twilight silences between, always there, the splashing of the fountain.

After her bath Marie-Ange decided to go for a walk, to explore this hilltop town that she'd come to, but by the time she'd unpacked her bags, she'd thought better of it. Instead, naked, she'd lain down on Eric's bed and watched the window darken. It was the last thing she remembered.

Now, shoulders aching, Marie-Ange pushed herself up and with a sigh, as though sorry to leave it, she slid from his bed, feeling the boards give as she walked to the window. Drawing apart the curtains, she looked out across the rooftops of St Bédard, the sky a pale lilac shot with shifting bars of rose and lavender, a dawn breeze from the open casement chasing across her breasts.

It was all just as she'd imagined it.

29

Whatever the time of year, St Bédard woke early.

The baker Georges Doriane, driving in from Chant-le-Neuf, was always the first to appear. Parking his car behind the *gendarmerie* on that first Monday in June, he crossed the Brieuc road without checking for traffic and hurried across Place Vausigne, hands dug deep in the pockets of a flapping overcoat, hair a nimbus of grey like a dandelion gone to seed.

Early morning was Doriane's favourite time of day – a useful preference for a baker – regardless of the season. He loved those bitter winter mornings when the rain spattered in gusts across the *place* and those long summer dawns when the sky cracked open like a lifted lid. He loved the early-morning stillness of a small country town at an hour when no one stirred, loved the sound of water tumbling from the fountain, the way his sabots rang out over the cobblestones and those welcoming scents of charred beech, hot brick and warm dough when he unlocked the bakery door and pushed it open, pinging the bell on the spring that his grandfather had put up.

Doriane's was an old St Bédard name, a fourth-generation baker whose grandfather's father had secured premises a block back from the *place* behind what was now Mazzelli's bar. The side-street property had a suitable basement for brick ovens, a small space on the ground floor for a counter, bread baskets and papered shelves, with three floors above, including a loft, to house his family. In short order Great-grandfather Doriane had moved in and rapidly established a reputation that none of his successors had in any way diminished – the Doriane *fougasses* and *ficelles*, their *couronnes* and *campagnes*, their *brioches*, *croissants*, *baguettes* and extravagant *pâtisseries* still celebrated throughout the region and still baked in the same ovens.

Georges Doriane had worked these ovens six days a week for twenty years. And every year – every month it sometimes seemed – some salesman would call by in the hope of selling him the latest gas or electric installation. But Doriane had never given in. Dressed in singlet and baggy whites, his face, shoulders and arms ghosted with flour and rivered with sweat, he'd tell them wearily that if the old wood-burning ovens had been good enough for his father, for his father's father and for a generation before that, then they were good enough for him. And with that he'd clap them on the back, bid them *adieu* and leave them, though they only realised it later, with his white handprint on the shoulder of their suits – the Doriane signature.

But if some things didn't change, others did – like moving away from St Bédard. Since Great-grandfather Doriane's day, the family had always lived above the bakery, but with two children and a third on the way, Georges and his wife Brigitte had decided to sell the three floors above the bakery and move into a new villa off the Chant-le-Neuf road. They'd been there now for three years, and apart from a dispute with a neighbour over fencing and boundaries – something that had never happened when they'd lived above the shop – Doriane and his wife both agreed that the move had been worth it. The new house was bigger, the views were better and the kids had a garden to play in.

And as of the mail that morning – the news telephoned in by Brigitte as Georges finished scooping out the last batch of *croissants* from the ovens – it looked like everything was about to get even better. Three months after the deaths of the Martners, Georges's bid for a half-hectare of the doctor's land had finally been accepted. Brigitte was beside herself. The swimming-pool she'd been planning for the last three years was as good as built.

And what about a pool-house? she'd asked excitedly. She'd seen the perfect one in a magazine. Like a log cabin. And what about a hot tub? The kids would love it. Just imagine.

30

Woken by Doriane's sabots clattering along the cobbles outside his bedroom window, Tomas Mazzelli swung out of bed, pulled on jeans and a T-shirt and padded down the back stairs in bare feet so as not to disturb his parents. He carried a trainer in each hand, and left them off until he pushed through the bead curtain that separated the bar from the Mazzellis' private quarters. Leaning against the old zinc counter, which his grandfather had plastered with mortar and painted black when the Boches had come looking for spare metal, he pulled them on, bent to tie them, then stepped up on to the duckboard pallet behind the bar and switched on the Gaggia.

As the metal flanks of the coffee machine began to tick with heat, Tomas set about his morning chores. First he unbolted the terrace doors, folding them back into their pillared recesses and then, the *place* still chill, deeply shadowed but filled with the first scents of fresh-baked bread from Doriane's, he hosed off the terrace, chasing away the cigarette ends and scouring through the spilt-drink stains from the night before. Next he set out tables and chairs from where he'd stacked them inside the night before and then, when the red light was glowing and the water in the Gaggia was scalding, returned to the bar to make himself a cup of strong black coffee.

He gave himself the usual double measure, then took the cup, helped himself to a cigarette from the packet his father always left by the till and sat himself down at one of the inside tables close to the terrace. It was his moment, his time away from the watchful eye of his father. He stretched out his legs, crossed his ankles and lit the cigarette.

Tomas was nineteen, beefily well-built like his father, with broad enough shoulders, he hoped, to see him promoted to the Cavaillon A team in the coming season. Like his team-mate Eric Chabert, he'd done two substitutions for the senior team the previous year. He might have spent no more than a dozen minutes on the pitch but everyone in St Bédard agreed that he'd acquitted himself well.

And that was all Tomas wanted right now, a place in the Cavaillon senior scrum, a hand up Yvette's skirt as often as she'd let him and enough money to keep up payments on the Suzuki trail bike he kept in the backyard. And with Eric Chabert otherwise engaged, possibly for some time to come, it looked like he was set to get all three.

Tomas was stubbing out his cigarette, wondering if he dare take another, when he glanced up and saw her. Just a glimpse, just the briefest moment. A movement at the window, at the top of the house across the *place*. A shape, lit by a streak of sun. He tipped forward for a better view, squinting between the trees, but the moment was gone. Just the open window and a stirring of curtains in the breeze.

Tomas got up from his seat, went behind the bar and helped himself to a second cigarette. Back at the table he lit it, finished the last of his coffee and tried to convince himself he hadn't just seen a naked girl at his friend's bedroom window.

31

Sitting at the table in the Chaberts' parlour, Marie-Ange read through the instructions that Monsieur Chabert had left with her the previous day and sipped at her coffee.

Printed neatly on three sheets of paper, the first page contained information on opening and closing times, the various suppliers and their usual delivery times, and a list of useful telephone numbers: Denise Chabert's sister in Lyon where they would be staying for the duration of the trial; Sergeant Lanclos at the *gendarmerie* (Marie-Ange remembered the name from the first press cuttings she'd collected); the local plumber, electrician and garage mechanic; the refrigeration people in Cavaillon in case something went wrong with the cold store; and the security firm in Brieuc if the alarm played up.

The second page listed the Chaberts' regular clients, their orders and delivery details. There were only three standing accounts she would need to deal with. On Tuesday, Thursday and Saturday mornings she must prepare and deliver the table and room decorations for the Fontaine Dorée across the *place*; on Wednesday afternoons (half-day closing) deliver four boxes of Canna lilies to the funeral parlour in Brieuc; and on Saturday afternoons put together those blooms that wouldn't last the following week for the *curé*.

Telephone orders were normally delivered between twelve-thirty and two o'clock when the shop closed for lunch. Takings were to be kept in the safe in the parlour and deposited weekly, preferably Wednesday afternoons, at Crédit Agricole in Cavaillon.

On the third sheet Monsieur Chabert had drawn a map of the ground floor with circled numbers that corresponded with the ring of number-tagged keys lying on the table beside her. There were five keys in all: for the front door to the house, the padlock for the metal grating that rolled down over the shop window, the back door that opened on to the garden, the cold store and the hot-house. There were also two cars – a second-hand Renault and a dusty old Deux Chevaux van kept in the car park behind the *mairie* – either of which, he had told her, she could use whenever she pleased. The keys for both vehicles were kept on a hook by the back door.

It was all quite straightforward, Marie-Ange decided, though Monsieur Chabert had made it seem far more complicated the afternoon before. She supposed, correctly, that it had been his nerves.

Madame Chabert had been on edge too, bothered about the time, telling her from the moment she arrived that they'd expected her earlier. She'd apologised, of course, explained that the agency had told her she should get there in the early afternoon, and left it at that. Monsieur Chabert had nodded and smiled politely as though he quite understood, but his wife had frowned and muttered on.

It had been strange meeting the Chaberts. After all this time Marie-Ange had felt she knew them. When Monsieur Chabert answered the door – a tall, angular man with sharp blue eyes, dark, tilting eyebrows and a round brown mole the size of a centime peeping over his collar – Marie-Ange recognised him immediately from the television and newspaper photographs. His wife was equally familiar, though shorter, heavier than she'd expected. As she followed them round the house – one after the other, first with Monsieur Chabert in the shop, the cold store and hot-house, and then upstairs with Madame showing her to a bedroom, the bathroom, the airing cupboard – she'd wanted to put them at their ease, explain that she could find her way round, that there was no need for their anxiety. But she'd said nothing, let them walk and talk her through it, which, she knew, was what they wanted.

Afterwards, in those final moments before their departure, standing on the pavement outside the shop, while the cabbie packed away their cases in the boot, they shook hands and Marie-Ange wished them well.

Madame Chabert thanked her, summoned a smile from some-where and, with much tugging of coat hems, got herself into the back of the cab. But Monsieur Chabert seemed to want to say some-thing, held her eyes for a beat too long, as though he suspected something, as though he sensed something, before he let go of her hand and joined his wife in the back seat. Which was when he had remembered the keys and the instructions in his pocket, winding down the window to pass them to her.

Finishing her coffee, Marie-Ange folded Monsieur Chabert's instructions and tucked them away in a drawer of the dresser. Then, hefting the keys, she went through to the stores at the back of the house.

There were things to do.

It was time to prepare the Fontaine des Fleurs.

32

If Tomas Mazzelli was the first to see Marie-Ange, it was Adéline Séguin, with one of her sister's terrines, who was the first to speak to her, relaying the conversation almost word for word to Odile the moment she returned home.

Planning to steal a march on her sister, whose discovery of the Martner bodies four months before still rankled, Adéline had left the house a little before eight, bound for Doriane's. But instead of using the back gate at the bottom of their garden and taking the short-cut, she'd deliberately opted for the *place*, a steeper, longer route altogether. She bade good-day to her neighbour Marc Tesserat as he set up his postcard racks outside the *tabac*, nodded a greeting to Delphine Bulot laying out her *pâtés*, *salades* and *saucissons* in the Charcuterie Bulot's window, passed the still-closed *pharmacie* and at Ribaud's antiques shop paused, pretending to look at something on display but actually inspecting the reflection in his darkened window of the Fontaine des Fleurs through the trees.

Half an hour earlier than usual, the Chaberts' shop was open. Its metal grille was rolled up, its windows panels folded back in their slots, and beneath the shop's striped awning its display shelves were laden with blooms, step upon step of flowers, more than Adéline had ever seen, arranged in tiered ranks larger, grander and more extravagant than anything Denise Chabert had ever achieved.

Having taken the short-cut home from Doriane's and told her

sister about Fontaine des Fleurs being open early and how it looked, Adéline now stood on the pavement in front of the Chaberts' shop, holding a china dish covered with a damp cloth. She carried it in both hands, like the *curé* with the sacrament.

'Hello, dear. Is Madame Chabert at home?'

The girl was standing with her back to Adéline, among the blooms in the middle of the central display rack, a hose in her hand, directing the finest spray the gun attachment would deliver over the flowers she'd set out that morning.

When she turned and smiled, Adéline's heart seemed to miss a beat.

It was a marvellous effect, simply took my breath away, Adéline told her sister when she got back home, this young woman set against the flowers like that, lost to her shoulders in the blooms, surrounded by rainbow clouds of colour from the sun catching the spray.

But what did she look like? her sister Odile prodded, already certain that this was the person whose bare brown legs she'd seen through the parlour window the previous afternoon.

Oh, such a beauty, replied Adéline, such a beauty. Like a painting. You wouldn't believe your eyes. And the older sister started counting off on her fingers what she could remember of the newcomer.

Let me see, she began . . . Her hair is cut short, and very dark, almost black, like a shiny cap. High, strong cheekbones, like Maman's in the album, you know? And deep black eyes. Or maybe brown. So dark you can't really tell. And then, with a chuckle: The men will make fools of themselves, that's for certain.

And? And? Odile wanted more, standing at the kitchen sink with her plastic gloves held just so, dripping on to the breakfast things she'd been washing up when Adéline returned.

Elegant, you know, continued Adéline. And tall. She holds herself so well, like they did in the old days. Like a lady. A proper lady. Quite unlike other girls her age. Somehow very grown-up. She looks . . . Adéline searched for the right word . . . she looks wise. Wise for her years.

And how old is she, do you suppose? asked Odile.

Which flummoxed Adéline. She tried to set the girl in her mind's eye and make a guess, but the familiar process of calculation seemed suddenly to elude her.

Young, certainly, she replied. In her twenties, I'd say. And then, suddenly not so certain: No, no, older than that. Oh, goodness, said Adéline, beginning to laugh at herself. Do you know? I couldn't really say for sure. One minute she looks so young, the next she seems . . .

And what did she say? continued Odile, determined to winkle every last possible detail from her sister, not a little indignant that it was Adéline in possession of the facts and not her.

"'I'm so sorry, Madame. The Chaberts have gone away. To Lyon. They left together yesterday evening. I'm looking after the shop in their absence. Maybe I can be of help?'"

'Oh, how silly of me,' Adéline had replied. 'Of course they have. How forgetful I'm becoming. You see, well, usually on a Monday morning, I bring over . . .' She lifted the china dish. 'Just a small terrine my sister, Odile, makes. It's a favourite of Denise's. On a Monday, you see, and it being . . .'

And then, suddenly, Adéline had felt oddly flustered. She knew she was not being altogether accurate – she'd known very well that the Chaberts had left the previous day, just as she'd known that her sister's terrine was usually delivered on a Thursday – but, she told Odile, she'd never anticipated such a small distortion of the truth causing her so much . . . well, discomfort.

And all the time there was this beautiful girl, giving her the most charming smile, trying to be of help. Those dark eyes looking right through her, their owner somehow seeming to know she'd been telling a fib.

'Perhaps . . . since you've just moved in,' she stammered, offering the dish, 'you might like to . . .'

'How kind,' said the girl, squeezing between the blooms and stepping out on to the pavement. She put down the hose, wiped her hands on the blue apron she was wearing and took the dish. Clasping it to her, she lifted a corner of the cloth. 'Goodness, it looks delicious. Such a pretty pattern.'

The lemon crescents, Adéline explained to her sister.

And then she held out her hand, long and straight, fingers together. 'I'm Marie-Ange. Marie-Ange Buhl.'

Is that all? asked Odile. Did you say anything else? Did she?

I told her my name, replied Adéline.

'Adéline Séguin. I live with my sister, Odile. Across the square. Over there.'

And then, she told Odile – just the kindest thing. This Marie-Ange reached into the display of flowers and picked out the most glorious blossom, just snipped the stem with her scissors, then and there, from the middle of the display, and gave it to me. Here, look. It's perfect.

And as her sister turned it admiringly in her gloved fingers, Adéline found a small vase, filled it with water, placed the flower in it and set it on the kitchen table.

Just perfect.

33

Not long after a flushed Adéline Séguin retreated across the square with her flower, Sergeant Lanclos left Frenot in charge of the *gendarmerie*, crossed the Brieuc road and headed up to the Fontaine des Fleurs. As he climbed the slope, he tugged at his cuffs, rolled his shoulders and eased his chin over his collar. He was going to introduce himself to the new arrival, just as he'd promised Fernand he would. Take a look at the fellow, get his measure.

A few steps further on Lanclos came to a halt where Adéline had stood and peered into the shop's shadowy interior. At first he could see no one and then a shape rose from behind the counter and came towards him. She'd removed the blue apron, and the flowery print dress she was wearing seemed to cling and whisper round her as though it were a part of her.

'*Bonjour*, Monsieur.'

Like Adéline before him, Lanclos took a moment to collect his thoughts. This was not what he'd expected. A girl? A young woman?

'Mademoiselle,' replied Lanclos, touching his fingers to the peak of his kepi, not quite certain how to continue. And then: 'Mademoiselle . . . ?'

'Buhl. Marie-Ange Buhl.' She held out her hand as she had with Adéline, and Sergeant Lanclos took it. It made his own seem large and rough and ham-like.

157

'Lanclos, from the *gendarmerie.*'

'Ah, Sergeant Lanclos. Of course. I have you on my list.'

Lanclos looked uncertain. 'List?'

'Monsieur Chabert. He gave me a list of all the important people I'd need to get to know.'

Lanclos let the word 'important' settle warmly on his chest; he liked the sound of it. 'Of course, of course. I was just . . . you know . . . passing, as it happens, thought I'd call by, see how everything was going. Settling in and all. Anything you needed, you know. That sort of thing.'

'How kind, Monsieur.'

And Marie-Ange smiled the smile she had given Adéline and, like Adéline before him, Lanclos felt a curious coil of discomfort as though he'd been caught out somehow, seen through. It was the same kind of feeling he'd sometimes experienced in the witness box, that same sense of being second-guessed, when some smart-arse city advocate turned everything upside down, confused him, got the better of him.

He also found himself wishing he was thirty years younger. And it was a very long time since he'd experienced that particular pang.

'I have some coffee in the back,' Marie-Ange continued. 'Will you join me, Sergeant?'

And though he'd already drunk enough coffee that morning to float a battleship, Lanclos saw no reason not to take another, particularly in such company as this, and pulling off his kepi he shouldered his way through the flowers and into the shop.

Across the square, leaning against the terrace shutters, Tomas Mazzelli watched Sergeant Lanclos talking to the new girl at the Fontaine des Fleurs. He licked his lips and longed for a cigarette.

By now, of course, his father was up and about, fitting a new roll of paper into the till.

'What's wrong with you this morning? Looks to me like you see a ghost,' Mazzelli *père* called out, closing the front of the till and ringing up a sale to see if the roll was operating correctly.

'There's a new girl at the Fontaine des Fleurs,' replied Tomas. 'Talking to Lanclos.'

'So it's not a ghost, it's a vision.'

'You should see her.'

Satisfied that everything was in order, Aldo came round from behind the bar to join his son. But by the time he'd pushed his way through the tables to the terrace, Lanclos and Marie-Ange had disappeared into the shop.

'So? Where I see this vision then?'

'Well, she's just gone inside, with Sergeant Lanclos.'

Aldo peered through the trees, established that there really wasn't anything to see, then turned back to Tomas. 'So? You going to hang around out here till she make another appearance or what? When the barrels at the back need bringing in? And the fridges are near empty? And the dishwasher to stack? Eh? Eh? Time enough for visions when the work's done and dusted, *mon brave.*'

Back at the Fontaine des Fleurs, it was the sudden ringing of the telephone that brought Lanclos to his senses.

He'd sat at the counter for what seemed like a few minutes, sipping his coffee while Marie-Ange snipped away at the stems of flowers, the trimmings caught in a black plastic bucket she'd pulled between her ankles. Yet when he glanced at his watch, Lanclos was astonished to see that he'd been there closer to forty minutes, breathing in a heady mix of scents he'd never noticed when the Chaberts ran the shop. It was as if he'd nodded off in front of the television.

Pulling himself together, he dragged his eyes from the soft valley of the girl's dress draped between her open thighs, and from the tight rise and swell of her breasts as she cradled the phone to her shoulder – Madame Parmentier by the sound of it. He waited until the call was over before he got to his feet. 'Well, Mam'selle, I'd best be going . . .' he managed.

'Then I'll join you,' she replied brightly, taking up a pen and notebook from the counter. 'I'm on my way to Madame Parmentier's. It's across the *place*, isn't it?'

'That's right,' said Lanclos, leading the way out of the shop. 'Next to the *pharmacie.*' Then he stopped on the pavement and turned to her. 'But you're not leaving the shop unattended?'

'Oh, it'll be fine, Sergeant. Don't you worry,' she said.

And although Lanclos was pretty sure he should worry – some of these tourists – somehow he felt he needn't, not this morning, not in this company, and together they crossed the *place* to the Auberge de la Fontaine Dorée.

34

Caroline Parmentier was sitting at a table in the dining room, twisting her wedding ring, checking through Doriane's monthly bill for the hundredth time, when she'd looked up and spotted Sergeant Lanclos lumbering across the terrace. And there beside him, ushered gallantly along, the girl she'd been speaking to on the phone, the one looking after the Chaberts' shop. She was certain of it. And as Sergeant Lanclos confirmed the fact with introductions, Caroline felt a great weight lift from her shoulders. A dozen reservations for lunch already and a party of forty-two – the annual dinner of the Confrérie des Amis du Vin – booked for that evening. And not a flower in the place.

Caroline Parmentier had been dreading the first Monday in June ever since the secretary of the Confrérie had called three weeks earlier to make the booking. Usually, he explained, the society met in an upstairs room at the Brasserie Chez Gaillard in Cavaillon, or at the Loge d'Épines outside Barjas, but they'd heard such good reports . . .

Of course, Caroline had been thrilled to think the Fontaine Dorée would be hosting this year's Confrérie dinner, but the moment she'd put down the phone she'd begun to fret. She might have lived in the country for twenty-five years, but she'd never quite managed to shake off that peculiarly English sense of impending doom. Refugee mentality, her mother had called it. What happened when you stopped running. You might be safe, but you were always looking over your shoulder, waiting for the knock on the door, the sound of boots in a stairwell. And her mother knew all about that. She and Caroline's father had left their respective families in Cracow, and for two years had made their way across Europe, always managing to stay one step ahead of the Nazis. It was what had killed her father in the end, her mother always said, never shaking off that fear.

If only she'd inherited more of their grit, Caroline thought, or had some of her own husband's shoulder-shrugging insouciance. Stretched back in the bath that morning, cupping his balls fondly, he'd tried to put her mind at rest. Everything would work out, he'd told her airily, everything would go splendidly, nothing-to-get-worked-up-about, his usual just-you-wait-and-see sort of thing.

But Caroline was having none of it. Indeed, her husband's easy-going attitude simply exasperated her. He didn't understand – men never did: it wasn't just Michel's cooking that made their name, it was the way the place looked – the drapes, the napery, the *toilettes*. There were twenty-one members in the Confrérie and every one of them would bring a wife or a girlfriend. And if the men didn't pay too much heed to their surroundings, then certainly the women would. In the last three weeks, Caroline had had the swagged curtains in the dining room dry-cleaned, two new rugs positioned just so in the entrance hall, and had ordered a range of prettily wrapped designer soaps for the ladies' powder room.

But on the morning of the dinner there was not a single flower in the place, those from the weekend well past their prime despite Denise Chabert's assurances the previous week that they would last. After she had tried to revive them with a little trimming and some fresh water, Caroline had given up hope and had the maid, Yvette, collect them up and take them to the bins. Which was when she'd called the Fontaine des Fleurs.

Of course, she had no good reason to suppose that Denise's replacement – a man, she'd thought – would prove any more accommodating. Yet now, less than an hour later, here was this delightful girl, full of energy and enthusiasm, with half the job done already.

'It sounds an awful lot,' said Caroline Parmentier, as Marie-Ange jotted notes in her book. They were sitting in the dining room while

Dumé's son, Patric, worked on the air-conditioning units at the other side of the room. From behind the kitchen door came a muted rattle of pans, a radio playing, someone whistling. 'Are you quite sure you can manage it all?'

Marie-Ange looked up from her notebook. 'Not a problem, Madame. I have some irises just about to bloom that will look great in Reception, some garrigue gorse and cornflowers for the bar, and those yellow petit-points with the black eyes for the bedside tables. Also, there's a dozen or so small bouquets I've nearly finished preparing – daisies, jonquils and pettyfar. Add a tiny spray of gypso-phylla and honesty and they'll look just glorious in here. And not too big. They'll take up very little room.' Marie-Ange closed her notebook and got to her feet. 'I could bring some over before lunch, if you like, and the rest this evening?'

And that was that.

Thank you, God. Oh, thank you, God, thought Madame Parmentier, as she watched Marie-Ange make her way across the *place* to the Fontaine des Fleurs.

35

André Ribaud arrived late at Au Broc Fontaine. And still a little shaken from the night before. For the second time in a week, his companion Didier Houssaye had come home late – and clearly the worse for wear. The stale smell of straw on his clothes, whisky and cigars on his breath. The way he swaggered into their apartment, threw himself on to the sofa without bothering to remove his riding boots, saying how he'd been held up at Rocsabin, at the stables, and how the traffic into Cavaillon had been *affreuse*.

Excuses, excuses, excuses. André had heard it all before. Hadn't he driven back from Barjas himself that very evening? And had the traffic delayed him? Really. But for the second time that week he had let it pass, refusing to be drawn by his lover. So much easier than confrontation, he'd decided, placing the *daubière* back in the oven to reheat, so much safer. And Didier could be so wounding. The things he said. The temper on him.

Pushing open the door of Au Broc Fontaine, André picked up the mail and made his way to the back of the shop. Shuffling through the letters and circulars at his desk, his mind kept going back to the night before. Didier's appalling behaviour. Coarse. Inconsiderate. Deliberate. Daring him to say something, contradict him. Just waiting for an excuse to have a row. And then, when supper was ready, playing with the food on his plate, his favourite *daube*, pushing the meat around with his fork, reaching for the wine bottle and accidentally – or not – tipping his glass on to their best linen tablecloth.

But still he'd said nothing, chattering on about the faience bowls he'd picked up for a song at the Sunday market in Barjas, just the tiniest chip on one, a dab with the paintbrush and you'd never see it, until Didier pushed back from the table with a healthy belch and stumbled into the salon to sprawl in front of the television. And never a word of thanks.

By the time he came through from the kitchen, nerves jangling like the cymbals on a tambourine, Didier was snoring loudly. So André had left him there, hadn't even bothered to take off his boots. And that's where Didier had slept, fully dressed, on the sofa, creeping out early before André was up.

Of course André knew what it was all about. Some new stable-lad out at the stud making Didier feel his age. Close on sixty and he still thought he could pull the young ones. And when he couldn't, he didn't like it, took it out on André. It wasn't the first time it had happened and it wouldn't be the last.

But that didn't make it any easier. André could just about cope with the black moods and bad temper when things weren't going Didier's way. What was not so easy to bear was the prospect that one of these days Didier might just strike it lucky. And be gone. Out of his life. After ten years together.

With the last of the letters, André started to fan himself, opening his shirt a little to feel the draught on his chest. He'd started perspiring, and he hated that. The stress of it all. The tension. He shouldn't have driven so fast; he shouldn't have been in such a hurry to open the shop on time.

André left the desk, still fanning himself, and moved among the display tables: the snuff boxes and pomanders, the netsuke and chinoiserie, the Paul Duboy busts and *blanc de Chine* cherubs, and there, on the Louis Philippe buffet table, the blue Delft dinner service he'd almost sold to Ilse Brauer but hadn't been able to shift since.

And then he stopped, looked round the dark, tapestry-walled interior and shook his head. Something was missing. Something he'd forgotten. And then he had it. Flowers. Monday morning. Some flowers to brighten up the shop. And brighten him up too.

But what to have? Something small, he decided. Something white . . . No, creamy white – to set against the Flemish tapestries and hanging Bijar rugs and lacquer screens.

And something for lunch, he thought, stepping from the shop a few minutes later and locking the door. Something from Doriane's. Something sweet. Maybe a couple of his *crème abricots* if they hadn't already gone.

36

Sitting in the small parlour, old Dumé heard the front door open, the wiping of boots on the mat and Patric's heavy tread come down the hallway. Whenever his son had a job in Chant-le-Neuf or Barjas or Rocsabin, the boy took sandwiches for his lunch. When he had a job in St Bédard, like this morning, he usually came home.

Normally, father and son would share a wedge of Doriane's *couronne* at the kitchen table, smear it with *pâté* or *rillettes* or whatever Mathilde had left in the fridge, and wash it down with a glass or two of *rouge*. But Mondays were different. Even if he was working away from St Bédard, you could bet your last *sou* that Patric would find some excuse to make it back home for lunch.

Because Monday was Mathilde's day off.

For most of the morning, Dumé had sat in his chair by the parlour hearth, reading his paper while his daughter-in-law worked her way through the house – the whine of the vacuum-cleaner on the floors above, the whirring and spinning of the washing-machine and dryer, and a thwack-thwack-thwacking of rugs being beaten on the clothes-line out back. She was a good girl, no doubt about it. A bit boyish in the looks and figure department, which had surprised old Dumé the first time Patric brought her home – not the boy's usual style – but a good worker all the same, a good mother to the children. And not a bad cook either, the tumult of her Monday spring-cleaning replaced an hour before Patric's return by the sound of the radio in the kitchen and the smell of lunch being prepared. For the last hour, Dumé's mouth had been watering. A soup to be sure – Dumé's favourite: some left-over ham bones and chunks of smoked sausage from Delphine Bulot put to boil, a whole head of garlic and vegetables from Clotilde, with a cupful of Puy lentils to thicken the broth.

But, good as it always was, Dumé knew that it wasn't just the prospect of Mathilde's cooking that brought Patric home on Mondays. With the children at school and, more often than not, old Dumé snoozing in his chair for an hour after lunch, there were other things on Patric's mind these Monday lunchtimes. Namely Mathilde. The lad's enthusiasm astonished old Dumé – eight years' married and his son still had an itch in his pants. Astonishment, but also a certain pride, Dumé was pleased to concede. A chip off the old block, that was a certainty. Even if, one of these days, the lad was sure to come a cropper. Because if Mathilde wasn't in the mood, Patric was not the kind of man to hold himself back. More than one job, Dumé suspected, had been lost when Patric took it into his head to play away from home – cosying up to a client when hubby was off at work – and in Dumé's opinion it could only be a matter of time before Mathilde got to hear about it.

That Monday, seated around the parlour table, tucking into their broth, Dumé's ears pricked up when Patric happened to mention how he'd met the new girl, the one looking after the Chaberts' place, over at the Parmentiers'. Like everyone else in St Bédard, Dumé had been told by the Chaberts that a man would be looking after the shop in their absence, but when he'd spotted that bike against the lamp-post outside the Fontaine des Fleurs the previous afternoon Dumé had been in no doubt that it was the girl he'd seen on the Brieuc hill who'd come to do the job. Dipping a crust of bread into his soup, Dumé listened intently as his son described the encounter.

Patric had been at work on the air-conditioning system, he told them, when Madame Parmentier and the new girl had come in, discussing flower arrangements for the tables and terrace. Patric went on to explain how he'd been lying on his back under one of the tables with his arm wedged behind one of the units and how, at first, they hadn't noticed him. All he could see were their legs through the tables, moving across the room – Madame Parmentier's thickly ankled and precariously heeled, the newcomer's slim and brown with feet comfortably shod in espadrilles. Which was when the Parmentier woman had spotted his toolbag, realised who was lying there and seen fit to make the introductions, the new girl and him, the two of them being neighbours and all.

As he emptied the last of his wine into the remains of his soup and mopped it up with a wad of bread, Dumé decided it was the details that finally set the cat among the pigeons. The espadrilles, the brown legs, the thin cotton dress, the cap of black hair, her eyes, her voice – Patric's close attention to detail was all it took to set Dumé on the alert, that and the tightening of his daughter-in-law's lips.

Didn't his idiot son realise he was digging a hole for himself with all his admiring comments? Didn't the man have eyes in his head? Couldn't he see how Mathilde was responding?

And then, during a pause in Patric's dreamy recollections, Mathilde waded in, just as Dumé had known she would. Not about the girl, you understand, but about some bill that needed paying, some job that needed doing, their eldest needing new shoes, anything that gave her the chance to dig in the blade and twist it.

Dumé pushed back from the table as Mathilde got into her stride, retrieved his newspaper from the chair and made himself comfortable. He pretended to read, but he listened to every word. It was better than TV.

And if Patric, for one instant, believed that he and Mathilde might go upstairs after lunch for a brief nap, as they usually did, Dumé had little doubt his son was in for a big disappointment.

37

It was a little after seven in the evening, at the end of her first day, when Marie-Ange rolled down the metal grille on the Fontaine des Fleurs and snapped the padlock into place. In the shop's shuttered gloom, the air heavy with the scent of flowers, she pulled out the chair from behind the counter and put up her feet on an upturned bucket.

It felt like the first moment she'd had to herself all day, which, despite her fatigue, was the way Marie-Ange liked it. Busy, busy, busy: setting out the displays (wondering how the Chaberts had managed with so little shelving), sorting through the stock, ordering a few new things, putting together the table decorations for Madame Parmentier, then finding that thin bale sacking in the cold store and cutting it up for pot-pourri bags. No time to think beyond the flowers, the customers and her new neighbours on the *place*, all of whom had found some pretext to introduce themselves, take a look at the newcomer. Just as she'd known they would.

First, the old lady from across the *place*, Adéline Séguin, with her sister's terrine; then the policeman Lanclos with his skew-whiff sergeant's stripes; Madame Parmentier at the Fontaine Dorée fretting about her flowers; Delphine Bulot from the *charcuterie* with a little sliced sausage and a *crottin* at lunch; and the grocer's wife, Clotilde Lepantre, dropping by to ask if she had any ten-franc pieces for change when she could more easily have called at the *tabac*.

And after lunch that sweet little man with the white shoes, the pink cords, and the stripy shirt – André Ribaud, from the antiques shop across the *place*, looking for some flowers for his window display. She'd recommended some billias, creamy white, that she'd found that morning at the back of the cold house, and he'd been delighted. Just what he'd been looking for, he told her, and offered one of his *abricots* as a thank-you. From Doriane's, he'd told her. In the street behind Mazzelli's. A billion calories, but who cared?

The strangest of her visitors, however, came later in the day. The lady from the *pharmacie*, Madame Héliard. Unforgettable. Tall and hunched, with a widow's peak and beetling brows, she looked like a crow just settled on a branch. Marie-Ange had been ringing up a sale when she made her appearance, black cardigan over white dispenser's uniform, the white plimsolls, Marie-Ange could clearly see, pinching her corns.

'Broken aspirins,' the pharmacist began, when Marie-Ange's customers were safely out of earshot, holding out a paper bag across the counter. 'Not for you, of course. For the flowers. Denise swore by them.' And then, with a curt little nod, shifting her weight from one foot to the other: 'I'm Madame Héliard. From the *pharmacie*. Just across the *place*.'

Of all her visitors that day, Madame Héliard was the only one who brought up the real reason why Marie-Ange was looking after the shop in the Chaberts' absence.

'Poor dears. Simply dreadful,' she said, burrowing her hands into her cardigan pockets and giving a little shudder.

'You mean the murders? Their son, Eric?'

Madame Héliard tipped her head, narrowed her eyes. 'You know about . . . all that?'

'The agency told me. I suppose they had to.'

'Yes,' sighed Madame Héliard. 'I suppose they did.' She sounded disappointed, as though someone had stolen her thunder.

'So terrible for the Chaberts,' continued Marie-Ange, squaring up the wedge of wrapping paper on the counter between them. 'They must be so worried.'

Madame Héliard nodded. 'It was a shock, that's for sure. No one could credit it. Eric of all people. Such a good, quiet boy . . .'

Marie-Ange nodded, waited.

'Of course,' continued Madame Héliard, 'it's always the quiet ones, isn't that what they say?'

'So you think Eric's the one. The killer?'

Madame Héliard's sharp little eyes latched on to Marie-Ange. 'Stands to reason, I'm afraid. The girl being . . . you know. And the Martners finding out. Poor boy must have gone and lost his head. Mind you . . .' Madame Héliard paused, glanced around to see that they couldn't be overheard. Another couple had come into the shop and were working their way along the shelves of flowers towards the counter. 'Mind you, Eric wasn't the only one had cause to . . . I mean, if it hadn't been Eric, there's plenty of others round here had as good a reason to see those Martners . . .' She took a breath, sank her chin to her chest. 'Well, there's some might have you believe there's more to it, that's all I'm saying . . .'

She cut herself short as the couple approached the counter. 'But I mustn't be holding you up,' she'd said regretfully, shifting her bony shoulders as though to signify there was more to the Chabert story than Marie-Ange might imagine, facts to which only she, Madame Héliard, was privy. 'I ought to be getting back.'

Putting down the bag of broken aspirins, Marie-Ange reached for one of her pot-pourri *sacs*, leaned across the counter and pressed it into Madame Héliard's hands. 'In return for the aspirins,' she said.

For a beat, Madame Héliard looked quite taken aback, but then her surprise softened into a smile.

'Why, how kind,' she said, 'and so pretty,' sniffing at the tiny purse of petals, leaves, bark and seeds. 'And such a glorious scent.'

Madame Héliard wasn't the only one who thought so. By the end of her first day, Marie-Ange had sold a half-dozen, and by the time she had brought in the pavement displays, closed the window screens and finished off the Parmentier order – the posies for bedside tables, and some ribboned sprigs of lavender for the *toilettes* – she was down to her last three.

Loading the Parmentiers' order on to a trolley, she'd trundled it across to the Fontaine Dorée and helped Yvette set them out, supervised by a beaming Madame Parmentier.

'Have you eaten?' Caroline asked and, without waiting for an answer, had Yvette show Marie-Ange through to the kitchen. 'We overdid it on the *poulet* and *rognons* for the Confrérie, so there's no shortage. Please. I insist.'

Which was what Marie-Ange had done, suddenly famished, nothing to eat since breakfast save André Ribaud's *abricot*. As she sat on a stool in the *auberge* kitchen, an attentive Michel had cut her a slice of truffled *foie gras* while Jean-Claude spilled some Cognac into a pan of tumbling *rognons*, set them aflame with a whoosh and a billow, then gave them a final shuffle.

And now, an hour or so later, here she was, back at the shop with her feet up on a bucket and her stomach groaning, as much from the *foie gras* and *rognons* as the niggling twists and cramps that had been playing with her innards all day. She looked at the laden flower trolleys waiting to be wheeled out to the store-rooms but decided they could wait. She pushed herself out of her seat, went upstairs and ran a bath.

It was after ten when the cramps began to ease. The bath had helped but it had taken some of Madame Héliard's broken aspirins and a foetal curl under the bedclothes to get the better of them.

Out of sorts, tired but not tired, trying not to hear the sounds all around her, Marie-Ange got out of bed, pulled on a pair of jeans, a T-shirt and trainers and went downstairs.

A little night air might do the trick, she decided.

That and a hot *chocolat*, if they had it, at the bar across the *place*.

38

Marie-Ange was Mazzelli's last customer.

He'd seen off Lepantre, Bulot and Tesserat, watched the first of the Confrérie des Amis du Vin stagger from the Fontaine Dorée in search of their cars and been about to call in Tomas from the back yard to shut up shop when he saw her coming across the *place*.

In his direction.

Mazzelli needed only one look to know who she was. The Chaberts' replacement. And coming in for a nightcap by the look of it. So he made himself busy behind the bar, pretending not to see her until she'd pulled out a stool, the one he liked to sit on, and climbed up on to it. When he turned, hands on the counter to take her order, he felt as if the breath had been snatched from his lungs.

Tomas had been right, and so was every man who'd expressed an opinion that day in his bar.

A vision. Radiance. The good almighty Gods, he thought. They hadn't got the half of her. And without being able to do anything about it, Aldo felt his head start nodding, as though the bearing in his neck had finally worn away and the whole apparatus was about to topple from his shoulders, his eyes widening, as though he'd dug up a chest of gold and couldn't believe his good fortune when he prised open the lid.

'Signorina,' he managed, with what little breath he had left, and a smile that let her know he knew who she was. 'Aldo Mazzelli,' he continued, attempting composure, extending a pudgy hand.

'Marie-Ange,' she replied, taking his hand and shaking it.

'Marie-Ange. Marie-Ange,' he repeated, looking to the ceiling as though the sound of the name would bring forth angels. 'A beautiful name, you don't mind my saying. Welcome to St Bédard, Marie-Ange. And Bar de la Fontaine, of course. And what can I get for you this evening, *per favore*?'

'A *chocolat*? You do them?'

'Only the best in the whole of the south,' Aldo replied, turning back to the Gaggia, selecting the superior cacao and adding an extra spoonful to the mixing tumbler. 'I'm not mistaken,' he said over his shoulder, pouring in the full-cream milk and whooshing it up under the steamer, 'you lookin' after the Chabert place? Am I right or am I right?'

Marie-Ange nodded.

'Nasty business,' Mazzelli intoned, shaking his head. 'Nasty business. And couldn't have happened to nicer people.' He reached for a mug, poured the *chocolat* and turned back to the bar. 'There. The house speciality, young lady. You taste it one time, you never forget.'

Marie-Ange took a sip. 'Delicious.'

'So, anyway. What you think of our little community, eh? Very pleasant. Very pleasant, no?'

'It's just how I imagined it,' Marie-Ange replied. 'Only nicer.'

'Of course. Nowhere like it.' Mazzelli beamed, then turned to the shelves behind him, selected a bottle and whisked two glasses between them. The bottle was uncorked and the liquor poured before his visitor had a chance to say anything.

'So, there you go,' he said, pushing a glass towards her, filling his own. 'A little something to keep the *chocolat* company,' he added, tipping his glass for a toast. Their glasses chinked. 'So, here's to the Fontaine des Fleurs. And new friends.'

'New friends,' replied Marie-Ange, closing her eyes as the grappa scalded its way down her throat.

Across the bar, Aldo watched. Not a cough, not a splutter. Just the closed eyes. Not bad, he thought, and smiled wickedly to himself. Tomas would have a stroke when he came in from mending his bike

175

out back and saw the two of them at the bar chatting away. As for the wife, Tira, she'd gone up to bed an hour ago, blessed be the mothers of all the saints, and would be fast asleep by now. No chance of her coming down and looking all cat's-arse about it. For now he was on his own.

'So? Busy day?' he asked, loosening his watch-strap, his collar, pushing back his hair.

'You could say,' said Marie-Ange, putting down her glass and picking up the *chocolat*, cupping the mug in her hands and licking at the froth with the tip of her tongue.

A shiver passed through Mazzelli's limbs. Taking up the bottle for a second shot, he pulled the cork with a squeaky plop.

'No, no, please,' she protested, covering her glass with her hand. 'I couldn't. There's so much to do at the shop. Flowers to put in the stores, floors to be swept . . .'

Which was the moment that Tomas, coming in from the back-yard and hearing voices, trotted down the hallway and into the bar. He rocked to a halt when he saw who his father was talking to.

Aldo slid him a purring look, then turned back to Marie-Ange.

'Oh, you not to worry about that, Marie-Ange,' said Mazzelli, saying her name with a comfortable intimacy that he knew would stun the boy. 'Tomas here will lend you a hand, won't you, Tomas? Tomas,' he continued, noting with pleasure his son's open mouth, 'meet Marie-Ange, from the flower shop.'

Five minutes later, having held up his hand when Marie-Ange made to pay for the *chocolat*, Aldo Mazzelli watched the two of them cross the *place*.

Nice girl, he thought. A real cracker.

Then he chuckled to himself. Wait till Tomas got back and took a look at that face of his, a fingered smear of grease from the Suzuki slanting across his cheek from nose to ear like a scar of sooty snot. The chuckle subsided into a wheezing laugh. That'll teach him, thought Aldo. Way out of his league anyhow.

39

Denise Chabert had been right about Marie-Ange Buhl. Within a month of her arrival, everyone who lived and worked on the Place Vausigne in the centre of St Bédard had something to say about her.

Among the men there was only the one opinion shared, greedily, like a glass of beer in the middle of a desert. An angel, a stunner, a gem; what I wouldn't give . . . if I were twenty years younger; a roll of the eyes from Bulot, a wink from Mazzelli, a low whistle from Tesserat, a nudge from Lepantre to accompany these judgements. And when those who still did so made love to their wives, it was with Marie-Ange's face on the pillow and her slim, willowy body beneath them.

Though his interests lay elsewhere, even André Ribaud had to admit the girl was a beauty, and such a winning smile, while Georges Doriane, no man more contentedly wed, just sighed when he saw her across the counter, sliding a warm *baguette* under her arm, the clasping between arm and body gently swelling a breast, throwing shadow and edge to the smooth valley between them. Not even the Curé Foulard was beyond her charms, always making sure he was on hand when she made her weekly delivery, sometimes even seeing her face when he prayed before the Virgin and feeling a tight coursing flush when he found his attention wandering. And though they knew it was wrong, there wasn't a man among them who didn't hope that up there in Lyon the Chabert trial would last a good long time.

As for the women of St Bédard, they were split. While the sisters Adéline and Odile, the Widow Blanc and Madame Héliard had only good words to say for her, the rest were not so certain.

Caroline Parmentier might have loved her flower arrangements and the pretty little posies Marie-Ange brought over for her guests' bedside tables, but she also knew what her husband was like.

The same held true of Delphine Bulot. She might have persuaded her husband to decorate the marbled, meaty slabs of their display window with the knotted wreaths of tarragon and myrtle that Marie-Ange had made for her, but she didn't miss the look in her husband's eye when the newcomer called by a few days later with some pretty twists of vine for the shelf edgings.

The same went for Clotilde Lepantre and Tira Mazzelli, though both acknowledged with a grim chuckle that neither of their husbands would prove too much temptation for Marie-Ange. Which happy thought made both women feel somehow sad and dissatisfied in a way they couldn't quite pinpoint.

As for the shop, of course, the Fontaine des Fleurs, there was more general agreement. Talk to anyone in the *place* and they were all agreed that the Chaberts' place had never looked prettier. New varieties, new arrangements and each morning a fresh display – cacti and flowering succulents one day, everything red the next. Or blue, or purple, or pink. And the racks and shelves in front of the shop reconstructed, repositioned, realigned daily to show the blooms to best effect as islands, pyramids, towers and magic bowers. And always a basket of those delightful little sachets of dried herbs and flowers and fruits she put together when the shop was empty – which wasn't often. Within a fortnight the place had been transformed.

Even a blind man, the Widow Blanc commented to Odile and Adéline, would have come up short when he got within fifty metres of the shop front. He might not see anything, she said, but the fragrance . . . those jonquils, paper-whites, stocks and jasmine. They'd never known anything like it.

By the end of the month, almost every house on the *place* and a few further down the slope had one of Marie-Ange's sachets in a bedroom, salon or parlour. And no one needed any telling that the *curé's* new altar decorations were Marie-Ange's handiwork. Not the usual tired arrangements that Denise Chabert spruced up for Sunday service from what was left in the shop the afternoon before, but great sheafs of canna lilies and irises stepped around the altar, ropes of blood-red roses tumbling from the cross, banks of nasturtium woven into the Communion rail and fist-sized knots of wild lavender and rosemary at the end of every pew, blooms that easily lasted through to Wednesday evening's Benediction.

Little wonder, then, that everyone in St Bédard was talking about the new girl at the Fontaine des Fleurs.

Which was how Hélène de Vausigne came to hear of her.

40

It was Picard, early one Wednesday morning, who delivered the summons. Letting the de Vausignes' Citroën Légère idle at the pavement outside the Fontaine des Fleurs, he made his way to the Chaberts' door, pulled the note from an inside pocket and pushed it through the letterbox, letting the flap slide gently over his gloved fingers as he withdrew his hand. No need to let it snap back at this hour of the morning and wake everyone.

As he came back round the bonnet of the Citroën, pausing to flick a bug from one of the headlamps, Picard glimpsed a figure darting between the plane trees, tall and skinny, skirting the *boules* pitch. It was Doriane making his way across the *place*.

Picard's cheeks puckered. A Doriane *gâteau*. It was a long time since he'd had one of those. Now, there would be a treat for the wife. He patted his pockets. No heavy lump. No happy jingle of change. Not a *sou*. Another time, he thought, as he sank back into the driver's seat.

By the time Marie-Ange came down for breakfast, Picard and the Citroën were long gone, only the envelope on the hallway mat to tell of their passing. She picked it up, read her name and slipped it into her apron pocket. Only later, when the shop was open, the awning down, the flowers set out to her satisfaction, leaves and blooms winking with droplets of spray, did she retrieve the envelope, slit it open with her scissors and pull the letter free:

an invitation to visit the Château de Vausigne at five o'clock that afternoon. Just that. No need to reply. Signed simply 'Hélène de Vausigne'.

Since her arrival in St Bédard Marie-Ange had heard all about Hélène de Vausigne. From all the usual sources. Madame Héliard, of course, the Widow Blanc, Adéline Séguin, they'd all had something to say.

'Marvellous woman,' Adéline told her over a glass of *pineau* one Sunday morning in the Séguin salon. 'The energy. The drive. The woman's unstoppable.'

Madame Héliard, typically, wasn't so certain. 'She can be sharp, that's for sure. Likes her own way, too, if she can get it. And she usually does,' she'd added, with a roll of her shoulders.

'Tight as a screw-top jar,' the Widow Blanc told her, 'but there's nothing wrong with that, *chérie*. Not these days. Prices what they are. You keep a leash on things or you're lost, *n'est-ce pas?*'

Marie-Ange had seen the family too, at church every Sunday. The Comtesse, thin as a rose stem and, according to Madame Héliard, just as thorny; her husband sprawled in the family pew, making only the merest motion when the time came to kneel. And, a few Sundays back, their son Antoine, somewhere in his thirties, taking a nip from a silver hip-flask when the congregation went up for Communion, lighting a cigarette the moment he was out of the church.

'Lives in Paris,' Clotilde Lepantre had told her. 'And just as well too. Got to watch yourself with that one. Trousers on a rip-cord and hands like an octopus. Just like his father, you ask me.'

And, of course, Marie-Ange had read about the family.

Their shotgun.

Their gardener.

Their neighbours.

Le Figaro had done a big spread the week Marie-Ange arrived in St Bédard, the story written by an American journalist called Benedict, who'd actually found the murder weapon and lived nearby. The feature had taken up four pages, with photos of the Martners and their house, the Brauer family and a blurred team photo of the Cavaillon B squad with the head and shoulders of Eric Chabert circled in the back row. There'd even been a picture of the Comtesse, looking sad yet resigned on the steps of the château.

All in all, Marie-Ange decided, driving back to St Bédard after delivering the canna lilies in Brieuc and dropping in with the week's takings at Crédit Agricole in Cavaillon, she was rather looking forward to the encounter.

Back at the shop, she busied herself behind the rolled-down grating, shafts of light slanting through its grillework. After she had packed away the flowers in the store-rooms, she swept the floor of cuttings and then, when she was satisfied, went upstairs and ran a bath. While it filled, she went to her room, swung open Eric's wardrobe and fingered her way through half a dozen summer frocks, settling finally on a floral-sprigged outfit with high neck, tight bodice and elbow-length sleeves. She stripped off her work clothes, went to the bathroom and, as she slid down into the soapy water, she wondered whether to drive to the château or take her bike. She decided on the bike.

An hour later, tucking the folds of her skirt into the saddle, she pushed away from the pavement outside the Fontaine des Fleurs and free-wheeled across the square, between the plane trees, waving to Adéline and the Widow Blanc chatting at Adéline's door before she swung left at the bottom of the *place* and headed for Chant-le-Neuf.

The first couple of kilometres out of St Bédard sloped gently towards the valley and the bike quickly picked up speed, the breeze whipping her hair and making her sing out as the bike hurtled along. But soon enough the road levelled, then rose for a few kilometres. By then, however, Marie-Ange had built up enough speed to save herself too much legwork and when she pulled in through the open gates of the château she was neither too hot nor too tired, though she felt an unexpected shiver course through her as she swooped down the drive and the first of the château's four corner turrets showed through the trees.

At precisely four fifty-nine she pulled the bell-chain.

'Marie-Ange Buhl,' she said, when Picard opened the door.

The old man's eyes settled on hers, narrowed. 'You are expected, Mam'selle.'

41

Gilles de Vausigne had spent the day at leisure. As he spent almost every one of his days. He liked it that way. It suited him. He was seventy-one after all, old enough to qualify.

That morning, as usual, he'd risen late, had Picard lay out cream linen trousers and a blue cotton shirt, and soaked in his bath the full half-hour, pleasurably contemplating his forthcoming visit to Aix. Afterwards, dressed in a silk gown and velvet slippers, he'd shaved, patted his cheeks with a palmful of Givenchy's Monsieur and taken clippers and dye brush to his thickening eyebrows. Colouring and containing the thatch. Just so.

Now, what to wear with the blue shirt? he wondered. A cravat should do nicely. But which one? He slid open a drawer and riffled through his collection for a suitable match. Yellow, perhaps. Or gold? Paisley, plain or stripe? The yellow, he decided, sliding it from the drawer. The silk St Laurent with the tiny red dots. He lifted his chin, slid the cravat round his neck, tied it and tucked it into his shirt, puffing it up between the collar points. *Ça va . . . bien.*

On his way downstairs Gilles knocked at his wife's door and softly called her name. No answer. He pushed open the door and looked in. As expected. Long gone. Just that dreadful cloying scent of hers still heavy in the air despite the open windows. He wondered how long she'd been up. Since they slept in separate rooms now, it was difficult to know for sure. Certainly well before him. But that, he supposed, as he settled down to his breakfast, wasn't so difficult a feat to achieve.

The morning had flown by. Breakfast done, he'd strolled the terrace, smoked one of the cigars he'd picked up in Aix on his last little outing, and looked out over the land that spread down to the valley and across to the distant blue slopes of the Luberon. A fine view, he conceded, no doubt about it. A generous holding to be sure. But there was always one thing missing. The sea.

As plain Gilles Sallère, distantly related on his father's side to the Haut-Sallères of Poitou, the Comte had spent his childhood roaming Brittany's rocky headlands and beaches. He remembered it as a dozen dreamy seaside years, which ended abruptly when his father drowned in a sailing accident and the creditors came calling. Dispossessed of their small *manoir*, his mother, Béatrice, had taken an off-season lease on a small set of rooms in Deauville where, stalking its gaming tables, she'd chanced upon the recently widowed Edouard de Vausigne, softly seduced him and promptly accepted his invitation to move south.

Here to St Bédard. The Château de Vausigne. A pleasant enough life, to be sure. But no sea in sight. Even now, sixty years on, Gilles missed it. Its swell and movement, its changeable moods, the briny green scent of it. Fresh, invigorating. Nothing like it.

At a little after midday, the Comte took lunch in the small dining room. Of all the rooms in the château, this was his wife's favourite, the room where his step-father's great-grandfather had entertained Napoleon on his way to Elba, at the same round rosewood table where he now sat, and where, according to family lore, a soon-to-be-exiled emperor had complimented his host on the sweetness of the family figs. It was probably one of Hélène's greatest regrets that that long-ago lunch had not been dinner, and the emperor an overnight guest. Monique, with her vacuum-cleaner, cloths and polishes, was never allowed anywhere near the room, and whenever he chose to take his lunch there, Gilles could be assured of his wife's lemon-lipped irritation if she found out, as though the room was some museum piece and Hélène its disapproving curator. Typical, of course.

The trouble was, he thought, as Florence ladled out a bowl of consommé, the old girl just took it all too seriously. The having.

The history. Obligations and duty. It really was all rather boring, the way she went on about it. The title he'd given her might not have been a blood title, but it was a title all the same. And for Hélène de Vausigne that was all that mattered. She lived and breathed it.

Mopping away a spill of consommé, Gilles rang the bell at his side. A moment later, Florence reappeared with a plate of trimmed cutlets, swapped them for the empty soup bowl, and retreated to the kitchen.

Just like her husband Picard, thought Gilles. Never a word unless you spoke directly to her and then the same sideways shift of the eyes as though looking at him might pain her in some way. Ridiculous. Should have got shot of the pair of them when he had the chance, when his mother died. But Hélène wouldn't hear of it.

'Picards have been with the family for generations,' she'd said. 'You can't possibly.'

So of course he'd given in, and now had to suffer for his generous heart.

Cutting out one of the *noisettes* and popping it into his mouth, Gilles wondered at his wife. Extraordinary woman, he mused. Such energy. Such enthusiasm. Bold and decisive. But cold as a winter snap. He tried to remember the last time he'd gone to her room and not been sent packing. Impossible to say exactly. Antoine was what? Thirty-six? Thirty-seven? Gilles chuckled to himself. Some time soon after that, he reckoned. Astonishing she'd ever got pregnant in the first place. He should have known when they went on their honeymoon, back to Brittany, staying at all the best addresses. Once, if he remembered correctly. Once in ten days. Some southerner, he thought, compared with the others who'd come his way since.

Gilles sometimes wondered if Hélène knew of his straying – an idle speculation – but he guessed not. Never a word, never a look to hint that she was on to him. And he was always discreet, of course.

He pushed away the remains of his lunch and finished his wine. Coffee in the library, he decided, and maybe a small brandy. Hélène wouldn't be back before five, so there was time enough. Apparently the new girl, the one looking after the Chaberts' place, was coming to discuss flowers for the party. He'd suggested Lasouhaitte in Paris but Hélène had told him quite firmly that the Chaberts should get the business. And it would save them a fortune, she'd told him. So much more sensible.

Settling himself in the library, he hoped Hélène didn't start getting bothersome about money in front of the girl. Young women, he well knew, liked nothing more than an older man who knew how to spend money – as though it was of no concern. Which was what he liked to do. As often as he could get away with it. He might not have looked at the books for a while but he knew that the vines were always full, the trees on the terraces loaded with those famous family figs and Hélène's business at Rocsabin, from what he heard, performing tolerably well. Which was all he needed to know. Good harvests, a full pot and a hard-working wife to keep everything ship-shape. It was why he'd married her in the first place. Someone to do the dirty work.

Gilles was dozing in his chair when Picard knocked on the library door, entered and announced that a Marie-Ange Buhl was in the morning room.

He started up and looked at his watch. Five o'clock. How time flew.

'Is my wife back?' he asked, heaving himself from his chair and straightening his cravat in the mirror above the fireplace.

'Not as yet, sir.'

'Better bring her in here then,' he said gruffly, pushing back a wisp of hair that the wing of the armchair had set out of place.

Picard nodded and withdrew.

42

For some unaccountable reason, waiting in the morning room, Marie-Ange felt a great ache of lassitude sweep over her and the muscles between her shoulder-blades tighten. She should have driven, she thought. The bath. All that cycling . . . She'd gone and caught a chill. She wiped away a thin film of sweat from her brow and was beginning to wonder how on earth she'd make it back to St Bédard when Picard reappeared and indicated that she should follow him. A moment later she was shown through into the library. She could see a pair of crossed legs and a newspaper, which, with a cough from Picard, lowered with a rustle.

'Mademoiselle Buhl,' said Picard. 'From the village, sir.'

As Picard retreated, Marie-Ange watched the Comte put aside the paper, haul himself from his armchair and come across the room to shake her hand. And as his hand touched hers it was as if a spill of cold water had trickled down her spine. For a moment she thought she would faint, but then recovered.

'Mademoiselle, a pleasure,' he said, eyes raking over her, noting with satisfaction the effect he had on her, his hand keeping hers to draw her into the room. 'What a delight. So good of you to come so far.' He gestured to the sofa. 'Please, do take a seat,' he said. 'I'm afraid Hélène . . .'

And then, preparing to sit beside her, his eyes registered a slow sadness as the library door swung open. His wife had returned.

Marie-Ange turned as the Comtesse pushed the door closed behind her and tumbled an armful of ledgers and an attaché case on to a chair.

'Ah, Hélène. You're here at last. My dear, this is . . .' Gilles turned back to Marie-Ange, questioningly, although she knew he remembered the name well enough.

'Buhl, Madame,' she said, getting to her feet, pulling the thin material of her dress away from her aching body, holding out her hand. 'Marie-Ange Buhl, from the Fontaine des Fleurs. You sent a note.'

'Of course, of course, so good of you to come.' Hélène de Vausigne shook her hand, then went to her husband and kissed his cheek. 'So sorry I'm late, darling. Have you been looking after Mademoiselle Buhl? I do hope so.' And then, turning back to Marie-Ange, clasping her hands: 'Gilles said we should go to Paris, organise things from there, but I told him no. The Chaberts should have the business. Especially given their current concerns. So. There we are. The anniversary.'

'Anniversary?'

'Fifty years together. A half-century, doesn't that sound terrible? The first weekend in August. It's to be quite big,' said Hélène, almost regretfully. 'And more people than we anticipated. So we've decided on the ballroom and the terrace, with a small marquee on the back lawn. And a dozen house-guests as well. Rather a lot to get done, I'm afraid. And not much time. I was rather hoping you could help?'

'I should be delighted,' replied Marie-Ange.

'*Très bien, très bien*. Shall I show you round? No time like the present.'

'Of course,' said Marie-Ange, gathering herself, turning to the Comte and holding out her hand.

'Mademoiselle,' he said. 'It's been a pleasure. I look forward to hearing your suggestions.' He was tempted to raise her hand to his lips but he made do with a tight, pressing little handshake. Such a remarkable young woman, he thought to himself. Such a perfect, perfect little body.

'If you'd care to follow me,' said the Comtesse.

Part Two

Abbaye de Laune, Salon, Provence: July

'*Crack! Crack-crack! Crack-crack, crack!*
That was what it sounded like, you know. Sharp, like stones hit together, like a branch breaking, slowly snapping. But louder than you might expect, Sister. Maybe a dozen shots, single and overlapping . . . So quick. So fast. Over. Like that . . .'

The old lady sat in her chair by the window. She paused, nodded, fingers gripping the blanket they had tucked round her legs, and wondered again if anyone heard what she had to say, whether anyone heard the words she heard.

'*But the echo, alors, that was the worst, you know. That's what I really remember. That terrible, terrible echo. Not just a dozen shots, Sister, but a hundred, a thousand, hurrying away into the sky. Fading, till there was nothing left but silence.*'

If she could have cried, she would have. But all the tears were gone, years ago, her eyes dry and dim now. '*That's . . . that's when I knew he was gone.*'

Her mouth trembled a moment, then pursed as though to smother the memory, bleached eyes searching the space around her, brows clouding.

'*They shot him, you know. Rat-a-tat-a-tat. Just like that. I watched it all. I saw. And I will never forget.*'

191

The old woman's head nodded. Her eyes closed.

Later – ten minutes, an hour, another day, she couldn't tell – she opened her eyes, lifted her head from a pillow, then let it sink back. What was the use? She was in her room, that was all she knew. She could smell the jasmine curling round her window, hear a bee or wasp buzzing somewhere close, feel the warmth of the sun across her bed.

'We were betrayed,' she said, for she sensed that somebody was there, sitting beside the bed. 'Someone . . . talked. The Boches. They knew. They were waiting for us.

"'Hande hoche!" they said. "Hande hoche!"'

She could feel the rough words rattle in her chest, heard them fill her head. They made her reach for breath, and then cough.

'And there they were,' she continued, eyes widening, staring back into the past. 'There they were, rising out of the mist like strange green ghosts. A clatter of boots. Running. Shouts. Firing. There was nothing we could do, you see. The game was up. Fini.'

She felt a hand take hers, stroke her crooked knuckles. She'd been right, there was someone beside the bed.

'We called him . . . Stephane. Stephane,' she repeated gently, as though just the sound of the name was enough to bring her peace. 'But all of us knew that wasn't his real name. It was the way we worked, you see. The way we worked then. Only our given name. It was safer that way. Me? My name was . . . I forget now . . . A flower? Rose? Something. Not Sandrine. Never Sandrine. Only Stephane knew my real name. And I his.'

Somewhere she could hear a bell, a distant murmur of voices. Her brow creased as though she was trying to catch hold of something, something she knew. But the harder she tried to grasp it, the faster it slipped away.

'Someone talked, you see. And that was that. All over,' she sighed, 'all over . . .'

And as the words left her she wondered again whether anyone had heard her, whether anyone was listening. Whether she should try to take another breath, whether she was able to take another breath. Say the name again. It didn't seem to matter any more. So long ago. All so long ago.

But she said it anyway, a whisper, just as she'd said it a thousand times.

192

And then she felt a sleeve brush against her cheek, felt a finger touch her forehead, this way, that way, leaving something there. Something cool, slick. And a single voice, soft, lilting, sad, caring. Familiar words. Words she understood, words she remembered. Church words.

'All over . . .' she whispered. 'There, you see? All over . . .'

43

Jacquot sat in cloudless midsummer sunshine. It was late morning, and Place Vausigne was bustling with life. Women with shopping bags, children swinging from their grip; shopkeepers in their doorways warming to the prospect of custom; a couple of old-timers watching a game of *boules*; and a party of rickety American tourists mopping their brows after the climb from the coach-park on the lower levels, looking around as they came out into the *place* and realising it had been worth the effort after all. The crescent of teetering townhouses set at either side of the church, the pastel-wash façades, wrought-iron balconies and sun-pinked Provençal roofs following in stepped lines the slope of the hill on which St Bédard stood. It was just as the guidebooks had said.

Jacquot watched them make for the *tabac* and gather round the postcard racks. There was an urgency about them – so little time, so much to do and see before their coach moved on. And in another hour, Jacquot knew, it would all close down. The shops. Everything. Just the sparrows swooping through the trees and the clatter of lunchtime plates from the shade of the *auberge* parasols.

Across the road St Bédard's fountain splashed like a baby in the bath – an extraordinary sound, thought Jacquot – the lapping water caught in its mossy edges flashing and winking in sunlight that was hard as diamonds in the open, dappled and shifting in the leafy shade where Jacquot sat. Now and again a car negotiated the sloping one-way route round the square, curtains shifted in open windows, billowed, caught on wrought-iron railings. There was the warm, floury smell of bread from a bakery somewhere close by and behind him, inside the Bar de la Fontaine, the muted sound of a jukebox.

Jacquot sipped his beer, wiped away the froth with the back of his hand. Good beer. *Pression.* Drawn from the barrel. The colour of old Sauternes. Sweetly metallic. Icy. He put down the glass, lit a cigarette, the second since he'd arrived in St Bédard, and took it all in, just as he'd done the last time he'd sat there, putting names to faces. Not the visitors, but the people who lived and worked in St Bédard.

They were easy to spot, thought Jacquot. They belonged. They had that air about them, a certain purpose. They didn't look up at the church, or point out the ornate balcony railings, or take pictures, or buy postcards. They were the ones whom Jacquot looked out for.

Of course it wasn't easy. That man in the shell-suit, stepping into the bar, who was he? Or the tall, gangly fellow crossing the *place* with that plumber's bag slung over his shoulder. Or the lady in a straw hat and housecoat carrying something under a cloth, in her sixties, maybe, but still a striking woman. But not so striking that Jacquot could remember her name. Or any of the other names. Brunet and his boys had taken the statements, done the house-to-house during those chill-whipped days following the murders. They'd probably remember who was whom. Jacquot, he'd just read through their flimsy report sheets.

Time and again. Over and over.

Name, age, address, occupation.

'Did you know . . . ?' and 'Where were you . . . ?' The litany of investigation. Yet three weeks into Eric Chabert's trial, Jacquot knew that something was missing. Something not ringing quite true.

Through the trees a flash of black caught his eye and he turned to see the *curé* dart across the *place*, side stepping the corner of the *boules* pitch, soutane snapping at his ankles, head forward, reaching into his sleeve for something. And there, beyond the priest, on the far side of the *place*, through the trees, stood the Fontaine des Fleurs. In the shade beneath its awning, a customer was pointing out blooms in the display and a girl was reaching for them, collecting the stems in a bouquet. The last time he'd been in St Bédard, Jacquot had asked about her. Came from an agency, he was told, looking after the Chaberts' shop while Monsieur and Madame were away in Lyon.

She'd be there a while, thought Jacquot. A month at least, possibly more. The first week of the trial, it had looked like the charges might be reduced to manslaughter, with the defence counsel Maître Messain arguing for a discontinuation – the boy's mental state and all. But by the start of the second week his pleas had been rejected and the murder charge stood. Four counts.

There was no doubt in Jacquot's mind that the shake of the head had come from Lyon. From the prosecutor's office. Aided and abetted by the Direction Générale de la Sécurité Extérieure. Gastal. That man wanted a trial, no matter what, and Jacquot knew that no mitigating plea for diminished responsibility was going to keep him off the front page. Something big. Above the fold. That was what Gastal was after. Something to show his superiors that this was the way it was done when Chief Inspector Alain Gastal was in charge. Make his name lodge somewhere useful. Reputation. Jacquot grunted. But that was the kind of man Gastal was. He should have learned by now. What was it Gastal used to say? Back in Marseilles. Bad-a-boum. That was it. Point his fingers like a gun and go, 'Bad-a-boum.'

As he sat there in the sunshine, Jacquot remembered his own day in court, at the end of the second week. The waiting on a hard bench in a marbled hallway, the windowless, panelled courtroom, the black swirl of the lawyers' gowns, the amplified voices and the snicker-ticker of the stenographer's machine. His moment in the witness box. His recital of the known facts.

Hunched over folded arms beside his bloated counsel, Maître Messain, Eric Chabert had never once looked up as Jacquot testified.

Afterwards, on the steps of Lyon's Palais de Justice, Gastal had caught Jacquot's arm. Maybe next time, Gastal had said, he could try to be a little more convincing.

Jacquot had pulled his arm free, given Gastal a look and found himself a table in a *bouchon* beneath the hill of St Croix. He'd been a little drunk when he caught the train south.

''Scusez-moi, M'sieur . . .'

Jacquot looked up. It was the owner of the bar. Mazzelli. Aldo Mazzelli. So, he'd managed to rouse himself from his stool, thought Jacquot.

There was a frosted glass of beer in one hand – rivered with drips, a spill of the white head covering his fingers – and a saucer of Lucques olives in the other. He set both down in front of Jacquot with a gruff '*Eh, voilà*', slicing the air with the hand that had held the saucer, palm down, as though to deflect any argument, before Jacquot could reach for his pocket.

Jacquot knew at once what it was all about.

'M'sieur, a pleasure. And an honour. It really is you.' Mazzelli wiped the beer from his fingers, reached for Jacquot's hand and shook it. And then, as they always did, he looked away, summoning up the moment. 'Twick-en-ham. Those English thugs against *la France*. Injury time. I never forget it. Inside,' he said, thumbing back to the murky interior of the bar. 'Inside there. All of us around the TV. No one speaks. No one breathes. And then – *oouff* – from nowhere . . . *Formidable. Assolutamente formidabile.*'

Jacquot nodded. Thanked him for the beer and olives. It was very kind. He shouldn't have. The usual things.

Sometimes it happened like that. Sometimes, still, he was recognised. All these years later. A drink. An autograph. Despite himself, he'd grown used to it. Sometimes he liked it too.

And all for sixteen seconds' work.

As he picked up an olive and popped it into his mouth, Jacquot was back there in an instant. Time concertinaed.

A low, steely sky, sheets of freezing rain pelting down through the floodlights, the English pitch a thick churn of mud, hardly a blade of grass left standing. And Jacquot, substitute flanker, sitting it out on the benches, groaning with every English try, flooding with hope when his team-mates fought back to bring the game level. And then, with only minutes to go, England two points up, the coach tapped his shoulder, told him to warm up. He was going on. He couldn't believe it – playing for France. The moment he'd been waiting for. A minute later his stomach rolled, his heart vaulted and the crowd roared him on to the pitch. They roared again two minutes later when, springing away from an English scrum-down on the French five-metre line, Jacquot suddenly found the ball cradled in his arms and the field ahead of him clear. Just the English posts beckoning down the length of the pitch. All Jacquot had to do was run, as fast as he could, and hang on to that ball.

But Jacquot wasn't alone. The English winger might have been wrong-footed as Jacquot burst through their line with the ball settling into his chest, but it didn't take an instant for the fellow to turn and give chase.

For sixteen seconds Jacquot galloped down that pitch – an Englishman hot on his heels, his boots sinking and sucking at the mud – waiting for the tackle that he knew had to come. Which it did, as he closed on the English posts, a final, fatal tap on the heel of his right boot followed by a giddy, desperate lunge that sent him sliding across the English line.

'You'll never buy another drink, my friend,' his team-mate, Touche, had told him, as they hauled him out of the mud and hugged him.

And Touche was right. All these years and people still remembered that winning try, in injury time, against the English, at Twickenham. And sometimes, too – just like Touche said they would – they even bought him a drink.

'My son plays,' Mazzelli was saying. 'Cavaillon A's next season. So he tells me. Who knows?'

'A good team. We never liked Cavaillon when I played with Béziers,' replied Jacquot, spitting an olive pit into cupped fingers.

'*Oouff*. Those Béziers boys. You had to be tough, *hein*?' Mazzelli spread his arms as though to say, 'Of course you had to be', enjoying his moment in the sunshine, the camaraderie, the shared knowledge, the closeness.

Jacquot nodded. You had to be tough, all right. Only he hadn't been quite tough enough. Maybe that was what Mazzelli meant.

That last game against Toulouse for the Regionals. He'd already been selected for a second outing in his country's colours – against Wales – and was playing this local match cautiously. Until the second half when he got caught in a running ruck, which sank to the ground and the second row forward from Béziers, his own side, stamped down on his heel and snapped his Achilles tendon.

Jacquot's career on the rugby field was over. Thirty years old. One cap. Sixteen seconds of glory.

'Well, as I was saying, an honour and a privilege,' concluded Mazzelli, reaching down to shake Jacquot's hand one more time, then stepping back, arms spread again. 'Please, enjoy your beer, enjoy the sunshine.'

And he was gone, weaving his way self-importantly between the terrace tables to report the conversation to his pals, to confirm once and for all that, *oui, certainement*, it was indeed Jacquot. Daniel Jacquot. Number Six. Flanker. Twickenham. The try. The man. Right there at the Bar de la Fontaine. Yes, indeed.

Jacquot sighed, and shook his head. Sixteen seconds. That was all it had been. And people like Mazzelli still remembered. Not the stretcher off the field, for ever, ten days later. Just that glory dash across the Twickenham turf to score against the English.

But what good had it done him, Jacquot thought, apart from the free beer? All these years later here he was, after everything in Marseilles, marooned in a back-end posting in the Vaucluse. Another six years to a full pension and nothing more challenging than a furniture-warehouse fire to investigate.

But it wasn't all downside, Jacquot decided, reaching for Mazzelli's beer. There was always Claudine. The glorious, captivating, wonderful Claudine. The gallery assistant in Marseilles and her gentle deception; the painter and sculptor here in Cavaillon. And the home they now shared. If he hadn't met up with her again after that first time in Marseilles, he really would have gone crazy. But some things were meant to be. Like Gastal, the business in Marseilles and then ending up here. The very place she lived. Fate. And thank God for it.

But still Jacquot made no move to go, even though he knew he didn't have time to sit around in the sunshine, accepting free drinks from *le patron*. He had a job to do, like everyone else. He should be in Rocsabin, sifting his way through the charred remains of a burned-out warehouse, talking with the fire officer, going through the drill with Brunet. Yet here he was, sitting on the terrace of the Bar de la Fontaine in St Bédard-le-Chapitre. The third time in as many weeks. Feeling oddly distracted. But knowing, somehow, that he was in the right place. Doing the right thing.

For a moment more Jacquot sat absorbed in his thoughts until the sound of a metal grating being hauled down brought him spinning back to the present. He searched out the sound and saw a flash of ankles as the metal screen rolled down the final few feet on the front of the Fontaine des Fleurs. The shop was closing. And others too. The shades lowered on the *charcuterie*, the postcard racks rolled back into the *tabac* and the blinds snapped shut at the *pharmacie*.

Jacquot finished his beer, stood and squared his shoulders. Time for Rocsabin and that warehouse fire, he told himself, whether he liked it or not.

44

They'd all seen it, the glow in the night sky across the valley, heard the wail of sirens, but it was Tira Mazzelli, whose friend Madame Deslandes lived in Rocsabin, who'd been first with the news that Wednesday morning. The warehouse outside town. Burned to the ground, it was. Not a stick of furniture left. Tremendous heat. Scorched the leaves off the trees, Tira reported, with all the authority of someone who'd actually seen it herself. And the smell! All that plastic, the foam, the rubber. By midday in St Bédard the details had been debated a hundred times over, and the various consequences considered.

They were all there at Lepantre's grocery store, gathered round the counter, when Marie-Ange called by on her way to the car park. The Widow Blanc, of course, absently stroking the bristles on her chin; Clotilde, whittling her way through a sack of cauliflowers behind the counter; and Madame Héliard, hands dug deep and disapprovingly into the pockets of her dispenser's uniform. On the outer edges stood Christine Tesserat, cradling a wide-eyed Sutti, while Odile Ramier nodded along to the chat, wishing she had something to contribute. It was Tira Mazzelli, however, perched on a sack of *flageolets* in the centre of the group, tugging at the creases in her slacks, who held the floor.

'The smoke. You wouldn't believe it,' she said, the slacks too tight and her cardigan too short to conceal the balloon of fat below her waistband. 'And old Monsieur Deslandes just finished painting his window frames, would you believe? Black specks all over them. Poor man. Of course, he'll have to do everything again.'

'She's lucky she's got someone to do it at all,' said Clotilde, sweeping the cauliflower cuttings off the counter and on to the wooden floor where she tidied them into a pile with her foot. 'The nearest my Claude gets to a tin of paint is when he passes the *quincaillerie* in Cavaillon. Usually on the other side of the road.'

It was as it always was in St Bédard, thought Marie-Ange, pulling a brown-paper bag from a butcher's hook and sorting through a box of apples. Something happens and the men head for Mazzelli's (she'd seen them all morning sloping in for a drink and a chat) while the women huddle around Clotilde's grocery counter. Or at Christine Tesserat's *tabac*, or outside the *pharmacie*, or at the Widow Blanc's front door.

It was like some strange physical phenomenon, she decided, slipping an apple from its tissue wrapping and taking a bite. Two people, stopping for a chat, suddenly become three, and four, and five – and so on until the mass, the energy of communication, becomes so great and so unwieldy that it simply disperses.

Only the week before, these women had assembled outside the Fontaine des Fleurs to discuss the latest news from the courthouse in Lyon. One minute there was just Madame Héliard stopping by with her broken aspirins and asking if Marie-Ange had seen the latest report in the newspaper (Hélène de Vausigne testifying at Eric's trial and running rings round the prosecuting *advocat*), and then there was Clotilde (in the time it took her to cross the *place*) and, before you knew it, Christine and Sutti (on a lead this time), Adéline Séguin (the two sisters never seemed to appear together), Delphine from the *charcuterie*, the Widow Blanc and, lastly, Caroline Parmentier (come by to pick up one of Marie-Ange's arrangements for the Fontaine Dorée's reception desk), pausing to add her observations to the brew.

And then, in an instant, they were gone, like shrapnel from an exploding bomb. Just Marie-Ange standing there, spray hose in hand, flowers dripping. It struck her then that this had been the first time they'd gathered outside her shop, the Fontaine des Fleurs, and she'd felt a real warmth rise up in her. She was twenty years younger than any of them, but they'd accepted her. She was one of the gang. One of the girls.

Lifting a tangle of plump, purple cherries and dropping them into a bag, Marie-Ange turned and was making her way to the counter when Delphine came bustling down the aisle, brushing past the collared sacks of vegetables, red-faced and breathing heavily. The assembled company stopped talking and turned in her direction.

'Out at Rocsabin,' she began. 'You'll never guess . . .'

45

Driving to Rocsabin, playing the wheel between his fingers, Jacquot acknowledged that, like his other visits to St Bédard, this latest outing had failed to comfort him.

There was no getting away from it, he thought, pulling down the visor as he took the first bends up to Rocsabin and the sun flashed across his windscreen.

The Chabert case.

Try as he might, he just couldn't shake it.

Which had as much to do with his own worming intuition as the letter in his pocket.

And the others in his desk drawer.

The first had arrived a week after Eric Chabert's arrest and three days after Dietering had returned to Bonn. The envelope bore an Alsace frank and was addressed 'L'Inspecteur "Martner"'. After Jacquot's name had appeared in the papers in connection with the case, the letters that followed had all been correctly addressed. Letters from Alsace, Île-de-France, Brittany, Poitou-Charentes. All in the same hand, a girlish slant, the 'Private and Confidential' heavily underlined.

The letters were brief. The message clear.

You have the wrong man.

As though someone was trying to chivvy the police into looking at the case again.

It was a message that coincided exactly with Jacquot's feeling about Chabert. They had the wrong man. Eric Chabert was not – could not be – the Martners' and Brauers' killer.

It was at the end of that first session with Brunet, after they'd found out about Eric and Kippi, that Jacquot realised they'd got it wrong. Right at the very end of the session, when Brunet switched off the tape and Mougeon came in to take the boy down to the cells.

When Mougeon reached for his arm and Chabert got to his feet. That was when Jacquot knew they had the wrong man.

The moment Eric Chabert stood up.

Sure he had access to the Comte's guns, sure he might shoot rabbits, crows, be used to blood, skinning for the pot. And he certainly had the strength, and motive, to kill four people, blasting away their heads with up to four shots apiece, when the first would have done the job.

It was just that . . . Eric Chabert wasn't tall enough.

Simple as that.

No way, as he climbed the Martner staircase, could Chabert have knocked those floral prints out of line. No way, Jacquot was certain, unless the boy had done it with his head, and even then he'd have had to reach a bit.

And neither, more significantly, was Eric Chabert clairvoyant. Which he must have been if he'd thought to steal the murder weapon in November. Kippi was certainly pregnant then, but she hadn't given him the push – hadn't provided him with a motive – until she and her mother had visited that last time for Jutta Martner's birthday.

Like the orchids. Like the money. It just didn't add up.

But everyone else went for it. They had their man.

Rochet, Gastal, Warendorf, Brunet. No doubt in their minds. Confession or no confession, they had what they needed: access to the murder weapon; access to the same make of ammunition used; his prints on the murder weapon; and, later, a DNA test confirming the boy's paternity.

And motive, of course.

The two letters.

When they found the letters, Jacquot knew it was all over. The note from Jutta Martner, discovered in a pocket in Chabert's overalls, terminating his employment, presumably after Ilse Brauer had told her mother the boy had made Kippi pregnant. There was also the note from Kippi herself, dated four days before the killings, scrunched up, lodged half-way down behind the chest of drawers in Eric Chabert's bedroom, telling him to stop pestering her, she didn't want to see him any more. It was over.

Enough. They had enough. To arrest. To secure a conviction. Nothing political. Nothing to worry about.

Even Dietering, he recalled, had seemed happy with the outcome. But, then, he had a wife and a three-month-old baby to get home to. 'It adds up, Dan. He's the one,' said Dietering, as Jacquot drove him to the airport for the last time.

Jacquot wondered when Dietering had started calling him Dan. He couldn't remember. 'He's not tall enough, Hans. I told you.'

Dietering shook his head. 'You mean the pictures on the stairs? He could have done it with the gun, running downstairs after the daughter.'

'And the shells?'

Dietering knew what Jacquot was getting at. Prints on the gun, but not on the shell casings?

'And the break-in. November?' continued Jacquot.

'He had to cover his tracks. Put some distance between him and the murder weapon.'

'But in November, Hans, there were no tracks he needed to cover. He didn't know back then the girl was pregnant, didn't know she was going to dump him, did he? The kid was in love, for God's sake.'

When they pulled up outside the departures hall, Dietering looked at him hard. 'You really don't believe it was this Chabert boy, do you?'

'No, Hans, I don't. Not Chabert. It just doesn't work for me.'

'But the evidence is compelling, don't you think? And the motive? Opportunity?'

'Oh, sure, compelling – but real? No,' said Jacquot. 'Not real.'

The two men got out of the car, the engine still running.

'Leave it,' said Dietering, as he pulled his bag from the back seat and closed the door. 'Things like this have a way of sorting themselves out.'

'I'm surprised to hear you say that, Hans.'

'In the end, Dan, there is always the truth,' he said, and reached out to shake Jacquot's hand.

'"In the end" can be a very long time,' replied Jacquot, taking his friend's hand, not to shake it but to draw the man towards him.

A hug. They'd parted on a hug. Which was good.

Leaning back in his seat, Jacquot felt the latest letter crumple in his pocket. No different from all the others he had received following Chabert's arrest. The same message: 'You have made a mistake. Eric Chabert is innocent'. Each letter signed: 'A Friend'.

No different in any respect. Except this last letter bore a Brieuc postmark. Someone was telling him something, and this time it wasn't just that Chabert was innocent.

Find me. I'm here. We need to talk.

That was what someone was telling him. Jacquot was sure of it.

46

Canna lilies delivered to the funeral parlour in Brieuc, the week's takings deposited at Crédit Agricole, Marie-Ange Buhl crossed the cobbled yard at the Rocsabin stud and breathed in the scent of cut straw damped with urine. Warm, pungent. Exciting. She was still some distance from the stall but she could hear Pierrot stamping and snorting. He knew she was there.

Twenty minutes later, down the lane from the stud and through the gate that opened on to the slopes of the valley, Marie-Ange leaned forward, whispered, 'Allez-y,' into Pierrot's flickering ears and touched her heels to his flanks. It was enough. They were off. In seconds the wind was batting through her hair, his mane whipping against her cheek and his hoofbeats thudding up inside her. She took a breath and whooped with delight.

For the last three Wednesdays, Marie-Ange had come to Rocsabin and ridden Pierrot. She'd known about the stud from her delivery rounds, but it was André Ribaud who'd set it all up, as a thank-you for the window displays Marie-Ange had helped him put together for Au Broc Fontaine. When she happened to mention how she loved riding, he'd taken her straight out to Rocsabin and introduced her to Didier Houssaye. And it was Houssaye who had introduced her to Pierrot.

According to Ribaud's lover, none of the regulars would touch the old grey and the stud wouldn't dare let him out with a tourist.

Spirited, mean-tempered when he wanted to be, Pierrot was just about the best ride at the stables, he told her. If you were up to it, he'd added, with a hard, wicked look. It was that challenging look from Houssaye that had done it.

Between her legs Marie-Ange felt the grey change pace, the reins pull in her hands. As usual Pierrot had ridden fast for the first few minutes, galloping across the side of the valley, then settled back into a gentle canter beside a field of shuffling sunflowers. Once past them, he'd put on speed again but was now pulling up, snorting and stamping as the land levelled.

Marie-Ange stood in the stirrups. Up ahead she could see the river winking through the linden trees and poplars that marked its course. Border Sweets, that was what Pierrot was after, the lush green shoots that lined the riverbanks. Try to keep him away from them, Marie-Ange had discovered, and you'd regret it. Give him his head, let him graze, and he'd pay you back in spades.

She nudged him forward and they followed the river until Pierrot found what he was looking for – a gentle, muddy slope between the trees. Forelegs stiffened to keep himself steady, hindquarters lowered, he slithered down the bank and into the water. Stepping delicately among the pebbles, he headed downstream. Ten metres on, Marie-Ange loosened the reins and his neck swooped down to a bright girdle of shoots and buds.

These flowers, Marie-Ange knew, made the sweetest *tisane*. She should pick some while she was there, she decided, and make something up for Agnès Héliard, to ease her bones and help her sleep at night. Gripping the pommel, she leaned down from the saddle and pulled up a handful, two, three, before Pierrot angled his hindquarters out into the stream, putting distance between Marie-Ange, the bank and the flowers he considered his own. She could have spurred him back, or waited until he moved on to a fresh bed, but she didn't. She had enough. She wadded the pickings into a ball, stood in the stirrups and pushed them down into her pocket.

The first time Marie-Ange had given Madame Héliard the *tisane*, the pharmacist had peered into the bag, eyebrows beetling down over her nose as though they, too, wanted to see what was in it. When she realised what the bag contained, those same brows shot up in astonishment, almost bracketing her widow's peak.

'I didn't know these grew here any more,' she'd said, a surprised smile breaking across her face.

'Along the riverbank,' replied Marie-Ange. 'Try it with a teaspoon of pastis at bedtime.'

'I prefer Cognac,' said Madame Héliard, tucking the bag into a cardigan pocket, and with a wink she was gone.

With a satisfied snort Pierrot lifted his head from the Border Sweets and swung back out into the stream, stooping once for a quick gulp of water, then making for the far bank, springing up between the trees and cantering into the open pasture beyond. For a moment he paused, shaking his head, snatching at the reins, waiting for Marie-Ange to let him know where she wanted to go.

Marie-Ange smiled to herself. Payback time.

With a flick of the reins and a squeeze from her heels she swung Pierrot to the right, opting for a gentle walk along the riverbank, letting him find his own path, away from Rocsabin to the other side of the valley. At a little after four, the sun was still strong enough to burn and the trees on this side of the river promised at least some protection. Beside them the water chattered along – faster over the shallows, slower across the pools – unseen crickets hummed and cackled in the grass and the sun sparkled through the branches like a spill of fractured diamonds. They'd go as far as the large oak, she decided, where the river turned towards Cavaillon and the first three arches of St Bédard's bridge came into view. That was where she'd pull up Pierrot and turn him back for Rocsabin. She knew if she went any further, drew any closer to the bridge, the skin on her arms would pucker into shivery life and she'd get that dry, dusty taste in her mouth. And Pierrot wouldn't like it either. He'd stamp and snort and skitter and pull at his bit. The one time they'd got too close, he'd almost unsaddled her.

Not a nice place, the bridge that led to St Bédard. She'd glimpsed its coppery memorial from her bike the day she arrived, and she passed it every time she drove to and from Brieuc. But she'd never stopped to read the inscription.

She didn't need to.

What she heard there told her all she needed to know.

The stuttering of guns, the shouting, the revving of engines and the clatter of boots.

Panic, desperation and fear.

That familiar shivering chill.

Like the marshalling yards at Metz.

47

'There's a body,' said Brunet, when Jacquot arrived at the smoking remains of the HacheGee furniture warehouse. Behind him, the building's corrugated, red plastic roof sagged down from the brick retaining walls, the A-frame beams that had once held it in place crumpled and blistered from the heat. Through the rising coils of smoke a blue sky smiled on cheerfully as though unaware of the blackened scab beneath it.

A body? Jacquot frowned. This was not what he'd expected. Another insurance job, he'd decided on his way out to Rocsabin, the owners looking to make something from a business that was not performing. Jacquot had been to the warehouse when he first arrived in Cavaillon, bought a desk and a bookshelf for his cramped apartment because someone had told him there was always a sale on, bargains to be had, items marked down, every day a sale day. Arson almost certainly, he'd decided. But he hadn't figured on a body. Suicide? Murder? Or maybe it had been an accident, an insurance scam gone wrong. Leaping to conclusions again. Jacquot reined himself in.

'Name?'

Brunet shook his head. 'Fournier's there now. In the office at the back. What's left of it.'

Brunet led Jacquot between the fire engines assembled in the front car park, stepping over the canvas snakes of empty, flattened hose, shards of window glass blown out by the inferno crunching underfoot. Firefighters sat on their footplates, taking a rest, chatting, smoking cigarettes. They looked done in, shoulders hunched, faces oddly clean where oxygen masks had protected them from the soot and smoke.

According to Brunet, the fire had been called in at twelve twenty-seven a.m. and had taken most of the night to subdue, fed by the melting plastic roof, the plastic display units, sofa and cushion fillings, rolls of rubber-backed carpet, lino tiles and plastic packaging.

Poisonous fumes, thought Jacquot, the acrid scent of burnt timber laced with a cool, chemical note. It had been a blaze all right. He'd seen the glow from his bedroom window. Even against the night sky you could see the roiling black clouds blotting out the stars. It was astonishing they'd even found a body.

Jacquot and Brunet skirted the edge of the smouldering ruin and turned into the back yard. A delivery van stood a few steps from what had once been the back wall. The side panels facing the fire were scorched and peeled, bumpers at front and rear grotesquely warped, and the van's nearside tyres had burst, making the vehicle tilt drunkenly to one side. The white lines marking out the bay where it stood were blackened and bubbled, and the ground was gritty and wet underfoot. Everything was running with water, or steaming gently. They must have poured millions of litres on to the place.

'Through here, boss,' said Brunet, passing an intact section of brick wall no more than shoulder high and stepping through what remained of a doorway.

Fournier was down on his knees sifting through a mound of ash, the sleeves and legs of his white Nyrex suit smeared with black. He looked round when Jacquot came in and got to his feet.

'Don't ask,' he said, peeling off his gloves. 'Impossible to tell anything right now. If we hadn't spotted the wristwatch,' he continued, 'she'd have been cleaned out of here with the rest of this mess.' He gestured to the ruined heart of the warehouse behind him.

'She?'

'Seems likely. It's a woman's watch. Rolex. Still working, would you believe? Maybe the ads are right.'

Jacquot looked at the cindery mound where Fournier had been working. At first he could see nothing but a coal-black square, but as his eyes adjusted he was able to make out a kind of pattern to the chaos: the twisted metal legs of a desk, its wooden surface reduced to a warped, wrinkled sheet of carbon; a tumble of metal filing cabinets toppled forward like blistered black pillars; the puddling melt of a computer monitor – screen long gone, innards burst and scorched; and there, between desk and cabinets, what looked like a chair, tipped over, its charred metal frame outlining a familiar form. The two objects, it seemed to Jacquot, appeared attached, spoonlike in their closeness: the bunched curve of a body, the crook of an elbow, a glimmer of metal, rounded and calcified like the bodies they had found at Pompeii, baked to a crisp.

Odd, thought Jacquot, sitting at your desk in the middle of the night. With the building burning down around you. Heart-attack? Suicide? Something else?

'Who runs the place?'

'Guy called Joel Filbert,' replied Brunet.

'What's his story?'

'Holiday. Corsica. Been away a week.'

'He the owner?'

Brunet shook his head. 'A Madame Grace Bartolomé. Lives out at Lucat the other side of Rocsabin.'

'She around?'

'According to one of the staff, she's away on a buying trip. Back later today. Tomorrow.'

Or maybe lying there at his feet, thought Jacquot grimly. 'Tell me about the fire,' he said, turning to Fournier.

'Deliberate, no question,' said the forensics man. 'Petrol all over. Starting here . . .'

Before he could say any more a fireman stepped up behind them, yellow helmet in hand, short hair standing up in sweaty spikes, face smeared with soot. The three men turned to him.

'*Un autre,*' he said, pointing the helmet across the blackened, smoking interior.

Jacquot and Brunet exchanged glances.

Another body.

Fournier bent down for his bag and they followed the fireman, picking their way through a landscape of tangled metalwork, breeze-shifting ash and flame-quilted timbers to the front of the ware-house, Fournier's Nyrex suit swishing with every step.

Crossing the roofless warehouse, Jacquot looked around him, trying to recall the layout – the sections for beds and mattresses, bedside units and dressing-tables, the kitchen sets, office supplies – matching them to the charred, shapeless islands that remained. When they reached the fireman's colleagues grouped around one of these mounds, Jacquot remembered that a large cash desk had stood here – a bank of tills – where customers like him had paid their money or signed the credit forms. Buy now, pay later. One of Fournier's team was there already, shooting off a roll of film, the flash attachment weak in the sunlight but still catching the drifts of blue smoke. Beside him, a member of the fire-investigation crew was doing the same with a videocam.

Jacquot looked where everyone else was looking, where the cameras were pointed. This time he had no trouble identifying the shape. The fire here had not burned so greedily. The clothes might be scorched to the body, the features blackened beyond recogni-tion, but the shoes were unmistakable: a man's, one foot crossed over the heel of the other as though the victim had tripped and fallen. Jacquot knew the feeling.

Fournier got down on his knees and opened his case. 'It's going to take a while,' he said, to Jacquot. 'I'll be able to give you more when we get them out of here. Tomorrow some time,' he said. 'You're lucky. It's been a quiet week.'

Out in the car park, Jacquot paused in the sunshine. 'So, how do you see it?' he asked Brunet, nodding back at the warehouse.

'Right now we're missing a third party, boss. That's to say, there's someone else involved. Has to be. Does the deed – a bullet, a blow to the back of the head – then starts the fire to cover his trail. Prints, fibres, blood . . . whatever. Can't see it any other way.'

'Security cameras?'

'We checked but the fire got to the film before we did.'

'Sprinklers?'

'Fire boys said they were active. But not enough to do the job. The blaze was way too strong.'

'Alarms?'

'Not in the office. Only tripped when the fire reached the main hall.'

They watched Fournier walk to his car and open the boot. In the smouldering remains of the warehouse, two of his white-suited colleagues were laying out blue plastic body-bags.

'I've asked the local boys to handle Rocsabin,' continued Brunet. 'Door to door. And staff too.'

Jacquot pulled his ponytail through his fingers, then looked at the half-dozen cars parked in the bays.

Brunet knew what he was thinking. 'Four accounted for, boss. Mougeon's checking the other two.'

Jacquot glanced at his watch. A little after four. 'Seems about all we can do right now.'

Brunet nodded, straightened his tie.

A new one by the look of it, thought Jacquot. 'Why don't we call it a day?' he said. 'Sleep on it.'

Brunet brightened. With the discovery of the bodies he hadn't expected to get away so early.

Jacquot gave him a look and Brunet's lips flickered close to a smile. Clearly his assistant had something else on his mind. Jacquot should have known: the haircut, the new jeans that morning in the office. And now the tie? But he said nothing.

'See you tomorrow, then,' said Brunet, eager to be gone before something else cropped up that might detain them.

'À demain, oui,' replied Jacquot, with a smile, getting into his car and starting up the engine.

A few hundred metres from the warehouse car park, he pulled over for Brunet to pass.

As he came up alongside, Brunet slowed and looked at him anxiously, but Jacquot waved him on. It's okay . . . nothing . . . just looking for something, he motioned, leaning over to the glove compartment.

But it was all show. With Brunet ahead of him, there'd be no

216

problem making the detour he'd planned. Right now the last thing Jacquot wanted was Brunet knowing what he was up to, where he was headed.

48

Sounds and voices. That was what Marie-Ange heard. Like some far-off signal picked up on a radio, something from the furthest reaches of the dial, beyond the usual frequencies. And always accompanied by an icy dance of shivery skin, like Pierrot's flanks when a horsefly settled, and that dry, dusty taste on her tongue.

And it always happened in the same way, in a deepening silence that seemed to isolate her, as though she'd put her fingers into her ears. Distant sounds and voices floating in that only she could hear. Like the whispering in the Chaberts' home, the sobbing on the top floor of the Fontaine Dorée – and like that evening in the *place*, sitting out on Mazzelli's terrace, when everything around her had grown quiet – no jukebox, no snap of snooker balls, no clatter of dishes from the Parmentiers' kitchen. And in that silence a sudden, heavy brush of leaves in the tree closest to her, the creaking of a branch and the tightening squeak of a rope as though some hefty weight was suspended from it.

Then, of course, there was the Martner place. The reason she'd come south. Where it had all happened.

Marie-Ange had gone there the first time with the representative from Agence Florale in Aix, an older lady who shouldn't have worn jeans or so much make-up, a bleached-blonde, leathery-faced woman with pale lipstick whose voice . . . whose voice had just dropped away into an indistinct whisper the moment the front door

218

closed behind them, at the very edge of a silence that had wrapped round Marie-Ange like a smothering blanket, muffling the woman's words as though she were listening to them from somewhere deep under water.

There, on her left, were the stairs, her eyes drawn to the last of the three doors on the landing above; ahead, the long hallway where she felt an urgent desire to run, to push past her companion as though her life depended on it; then the kitchen, filled with a desperate panic; and finally the hot-house, dense and stifling with memories. And out of the silence, at a bend in the gravel path, the terrible blasts of a shotgun, battering her ears with a percussive force that made her want to duck down. Right there, among the rich, dripping green foliage.

'Are you all right, dear?' the woman had asked, and the silence was gone.

'Fine,' Marie-Ange had managed to reply, the dryness in her mouth giving her words an awkward thickness. 'Fine, just fine. Fancy shivering in such heat.'

And the two of them had walked on.

They were neither pleasant nor unpleasant, these 'moments', but over the years Marie-Ange had grown used to them, learned to accommodate them.

She had been eleven when they had begun, in the house in Metz where the Buhl family moved in the winter of 1983. Her father, an administrator for French Railways, had been transferred from Colmar, and the house the family moved into overlooked the Metz marshalling yards, a vast, flat landscape of sheds, sidings and fenced turnplates cross-hatched with steel rails and overhead electric cables.

Her first night in her new room she fell asleep quickly, lulled by the sounds beyond her window – the distant rattle of coupling chains, the sliding clang of doors and buffers, the whistling of released steam – too exhausted by the excitement of moving to a new house and getting to choose her own bedroom to be surprised that there should be so much activity at night or by the sound of a steam whistle when the yards were electrified. It was Metz after all, not Colmar, on the main line between Paris and Strasbourg. That's what her father had told her, adding that his new posting meant a ski holiday, come winter, hoping to make up for her leaving all her friends and having to make new ones.

On her second night, however, no matter how hard she tried, Marie-Ange simply couldn't get to sleep. She tossed and turned until the bedclothes were twisted round her like a shroud, listening to the sounds from the railyard beyond – an endless shunting to and fro, a rattle of box-car doors being pulled opened and slammed shut, the bark of dogs and distant voices.

At last she gave up on sleep, unwound herself from her bedclothes and went to the window to see what was going on so late at night. The moment she parted the curtains, her skin crawled with shivers and her mouth turned as dry and dusty as the thin carpet beneath her feet.

For there was nothing there. Nothing to see but the moon glinting off the rails and the distant lights of the main station. No movement. No activity. Nothing below her in the yards. Yet still the sounds continued, receding gently until all she was left with was an icy puckering of skin that raced up her neck and over the top of her head, prickling and tightening at her hairline.

If she'd been confused when she was eleven, she knew what was going on by the time she was fourteen. She'd read the books, seen the films, and knew now that she was different. If not exactly psychic she was, she realised, a great deal more sensitive to her surroundings than anyone else she knew, particularly in the last days of her cycle, with an increasing awareness that was as sure an indication as any twisting cramp or spotting.

Most often this 'awareness' presented as nothing more than a kind of intuition, about people, places – a certainty that someone was not telling the truth, or that something had happened at a particular place. A moment of clarity. But sometimes, as with the marshalling yards of Metz, her 'awareness' manifested itself a great deal more dramatically. And it didn't matter where she was or what she was doing: that isolating silence was her only warning.

But it was only ever sounds and voices.

She never saw anything. Or anyone.

Until Kippi.

It was March, cold and wet outside, a bitter wind from the Vosges mountains sweeping a sleety rain along the streets of Metz, tugging at umbrellas, snapping coat hems and stooping those brave enough to venture out. But in the polythene-lined tunnels of the Jardins Gilbert where Marie-Ange worked, it was close and humid, the air thick and moist.

It was shortly after nine in the morning, potting a tray of seedlings, when she became aware of someone at her side, talking to her. At first she thought it was Pascale, off for a cigarette and wanting some company.

So she shook her head, no, then realised it wasn't Pascale, couldn't be Pascale, because Pascale had left for a nursery in St Maxime the week before.

Then Marie-Ange noticed how quiet everything was – no radio from along the bench, no sound from the wind and rain blustering against the sides of the poly-tunnel, no scuffing of gloves on plastic pots. But she didn't stop work, just glanced round.

A young girl, a teenager, blonde, pulling at a strand of hair, licking its end. And talking to her, telling her something. In German. Over and over again. The same words. Something about a young man.

'*Ein junge. Ein junge ich liebe. Er ist Französisch.*'

And then a word she did recognise: '*Er ist ein gärtner.*'

A gardener.

Something about a young man who was a gardener.

And then, in French, so softly Marie-Ange had to strain to hear: '*Pas lui. Pas lui.*'

And then the girl seemed to drift behind her.

And not be there any more.

That was when Marie-Ange did stop working, fingers icy cold in her rubber gloves, expecting to be frightened but relieved to find she wasn't. Rather, she felt an odd elation. It was just like the voices, only much, much more real. More . . . exhilarating.

It was another week before she put it all together, reading a newspaper story about a killing in Provence, the arrest of a suspect. The moment she saw the picture that accompanied the report she knew immediately that the man in the photograph was not the murderer. She couldn't explain how she knew this, or why she should think it, until she reached the final paragraph where she read what the suspect did for a living.

A gardener.

And that was when Marie-Ange made the connection with the girl in the poly-tunnel, knew instantly what her 'visitor' had been telling her.

The young man, the gardener, he is not the killer.

That evening she started writing her letters.

It wasn't the first time that Marie-Ange had 'worked' with the police. A year earlier, a month after she had graduated, she'd heard about a local woman who'd jumped to her death from a fourth-floor window. She couldn't say what made her go to the street where the woman lived, but when she got there she knew immediately that the woman hadn't jumped. Or fallen.

She'd been pushed.

There was no appearance, of course – no Kippi. But the silence was as deep as it ever was and the iciness that gripped her as she walked up and down the street as sharp and piercing as anything she'd ever felt.

That night she'd gone home and written a letter to the policeman heading the investigation.

'It's not a suicide, it's not an accident,' she wrote. 'It's murder.'

And then, from somewhere she couldn't identify, the words just came to her. Details. Shadowy, sketchy, but unmistakable.

There is a man, she wrote. Tall, fifties. With a beard. He bore a grudge. He wanted revenge. But it didn't turn out the way he wanted. Things got out of hand. He didn't mean to kill, just to frighten.

And then: 'He's a teacher', she added, at the end of the letter, almost as an afterthought, looking at the word, admiring its shape, form and meaning, knowing she was right.

And that was exactly what he turned out to be. A week later, a fifty-six-year-old man was arrested for the woman's murder and the newspapers gave his profession as teacher.

Of course, no mention of her letter was made in the press coverage that followed, so Marie-Ange couldn't say for sure whether her involvement – her letter – or straightforward detective work had led to the man's arrest. All she knew for certain was that they had the right man. And when, a few days later, she returned to the street where the woman died, the chill had gone. Just as the sounds from the Metz marshalling yards had stopped when she learned what had happened a half-century earlier, down there among the sidings and the turntables, in the lines of steaming, wailing box-cars and rattling cattle wagons headed east for Germany, Poland and the camps.

And now she was doing it again – sending letters to say what she felt, what she knew. From Île-de-France, from Brittany, from Poitou-Charentes, from the various garden centres and nurseries she was sent to by Agence Florale, the outfit Pascale had told her about, working two weeks here, a week there, a month somewhere else, filling holiday shoes mostly.

'*Cher* Monsieur Jacquot,' her letters began. 'You may remember . . .'

And although she had nothing more to add, no details like the Metz case, no teacher she could identify, she continued to send the letters. Like a reminder. Simply stating that the gardener Chabert was innocent. They had the wrong man. They should look again. Nothing more.

In time, of course, the Chabert story was lost as other news took its place, but Marie-Ange kept writing. And then, at the beginning of May, working at a nursery in Angoulême, she had read in the newspapers that a trial was imminent, and known in an instant that letters weren't enough.

That same day she'd called Agence Florale and requested a transfer as soon as the permanent worker she was covering for returned from her holidays. A transfer from Angoulême to the Fontaine des Fleurs, she told them, in St Bédard.

Yes, the agency said, they were aware of that posting but they'd already put a man in place. So sorry. But for some reason, when she put down the phone, Marie-Ange felt no sense of loss. Things, she was certain, would work out.

And, of course, they had. In the last week of May, the agency had called her back. Their original placement, the man, was unable to make it, they told her. Something had cropped up and he'd had to back down at the last minute. If she was still interested . . .

Three days later Marie-Ange was pushing her bike up the hill to St Bédard, the place where Eric Chabert lived.

Into his home. Into his bed.

49

Twenty minutes after leaving Rocsabin, with the sun settling over the distant Alpilles, Jacquot turned into the Martner property, coasted down the drive and pulled up in the gravelled forecourt.

And there was the horse. A grey. Tethered in the shade, a hind leg raised, hoof dangling indolently.

Jacquot climbed from the car and looked around.

Someone passing by? he wondered. Someone working the vines? He gazed across the slope of the hill but could see no one. He turned back to the house. The studded front door was closed and the windows shuttered. Apart from the buzz of insects, the crunch of gravel underfoot and the old grey's occasional nickering there was nothing to be heard.

At least it wasn't a burglary in progress, Jacquot decided. Who ever heard of a house-breaker making their getaway on horseback? Or breaking into an empty house, come to that. Apart from the hot-house collection, all the Martners' belongings had either been put into storage outside Cavaillon, placed with an auction house in Avignon or moved back to Zürich. The place was empty. But four months after the murders, Herr Brauer had still to achieve a sale.

As though it might supply some answers, Jacquot walked over to the horse.

He approached carefully. Jacquot didn't like horses. Too big. Too heavy. Too stubborn. How could anyone claim to control such a beast? If a horse wanted to do something, there wasn't a whip, a spur or a bit that would stop it. And anyone who said different, thought Jacquot, was as stupid as their horse.

From a safe few feet away Jacquot inspected the beast: an English saddle polished to a smooth, mahogany shine, reins looped through an olive branch, its salt-and-pepper tail twitching away the flies and a large brown eye rolling back to give Jacquot the once-over. Like most people who don't much care for horses, Jacquot stretched out a hand and ran it along the old grey's flank, patting the animal in a familiar, confident manner as though he wasn't that worried. But when Pierrot jittered and snorted at his touch, he promptly snatched away his hand.

Leaving the horse, putting some distance between himself and its back legs, Jacquot walked to the Martners' front door feeling in his pocket for the keys – a shiny brass Métalux and a key that must have been cast a century earlier, long and heavy with a ring at the top you could squeeze four fingers into. He selected the Métalux, slipped it into the lock and immediately felt resistance. Already unlocked. Without bothering to try the second key he pressed down the old latch and the door swung open.

Whoever owned the horse, he decided, was probably in the house.

In the old days, in Marseilles, Jacquot would have kept his hand near his gun, every sense keening. Now he just stepped inside the house, wiped his boots on the mat and shouted, '*Allo*', like a friend of the family, just calling by. That was the way it was in the Vaucluse. After three years, he'd grown used to it. As for his gun, it was back at Headquarters, in the drawer with the letters.

Jacquot closed the door behind him and stood in the shadows at the bottom of the stairs, listening, for a moment, waiting for a reply, for someone to make an appearance. But no one did. There was not a sound, just the creak of cool floorboards between sun-heated walls and the resinous scent of fresh paint and plaster, the wall by the front door once cratered by a shotgun blast now replastered, the whole house redecorated.

Stepping away from the door Jacquot made his way down the hall, peering into a shuttered, shadowy salon, dining room and study, expecting at any moment to turn a corner and come face to face with, well, presumably the owner of the horse.

Jacquot called again, but still no answer. In the kitchen, he noticed the courtyard shutters were open and tried to recall if they'd been that way the last time he'd visited. Since Eric Chabert's arrest he'd been to the house a couple of times, both occasions on his own, walking through these rooms, searching for something he couldn't quite put his finger on.

From the kitchen Jacquot knew he could go two ways: left, to sun-lounge and guest wing; or right, to the hot-house. As he'd done with Lanclos that first visit, with Dietering, and on the last couple of times he'd visited, he turned right and opened the first of the double doors leading to the hot-house. As he closed it behind him, breathing in the musty, stale scent of an enclosed, airless space, he reached forward, opened the second door and stepped into the hot-house gloom.

The heat was stifling, just as he'd been expecting, a warm, wet blanket that crept under his collar, seeped into his shirt and made his linen trousers cling to his thighs. The next instant he felt a bead of sweat trickle into the small of his back. He peeled off his jacket and swung it over his shoulder, but seconds later the shirt beneath the jacket was sticking to his skin. Instead, as he followed the gravel path snaking between the trees and banks of foliage, he held the jacket in his hand, let it hang by his leg.

Jesus, he thought, it was hot.

And suddenly he came to a halt.

Something was different. Very different.

He looked around. For a moment he couldn't grasp what it was, what had brought him up short. And then he had it. The last time he'd been there, a few weeks before, the hot-house had seemed drab, February's radiant blooms reduced to a steaming, vegetative green. Now, suddenly, there was colour again – pinks and reds, blues and greens, the softest creams and purples, the petals of a thousand blooms speckled and freckled, spotted and striped, reaching upwards from the beds at his feet and draping down from the branches above him.

Maybe it was the season for orchid blooms, he thought, for it was more glorious here than he could ever remember, more colourful and lush and luxuriant than any of the garden centres, nurseries and private collections that he and Dietering had visited on their orchid trail. Somehow even more spectacular than it had been the first time Jacquot had visited, on the morning of the murders. The place felt alive with growth, felt alive with . . . with . . . Jacquot tried to think what it was.

Sex. That was what it was. Hot, luscious sex. The flowers looked, well . . . sexy – gloriously, gaudily sexy. And weaving through the dripping, drenching air was their fragrance – soft and subtle one moment, hot and spicy the next, like the sinuous, slinking scents of a Marseilles' whorehouse.

Jacquot looked about in amazement, and for the first time he began to understand the fascination – the obsession – that must have gripped the good doctor, and every orchid-fancier he and Dietering had spoken to. No wonder Martner had been loath to sell anything. He wished Claudine was there to see it with him – the shapes, the colours, the textures . . . She'd have had her brushes out in a moment, a canvas on an easel, palette prepared . . . just as Jutta Martner had done.

Jacquot moved on, heading in the direction of the doctor's lab, stunned by the massed cluster of blooms that crowded round him – bursting up through the soil, clinging to the branches of the trees and plunging down in delicate curtains of colour. He was about to push his way through one of these curtains when he remembered what Lanclos had told him, about the pollen. The devil to get out. Instead he stooped beneath the lowest blooms, and strolled on.

About half-way through the hot-house, beyond the stream fed by the overflow from the fountain in the courtyard, Jacquot rounded a bend and stopped in his tracks. A pace or two ahead, at the side of the path, a step-ladder had been set up, a box of tools and a trug loaded with browned, twisted clippings on the ground beside it. Whoever had been working there had placed the ladder beside a cascade of orchids, a three-metre shawl of pink and white slipper-like blooms reaching up to a distant, lichened branch. They were the most magnificent flowers Jacquot had ever seen and he was tempted to reach up a hand to touch them, just to see if they were real.

Martin O'Brien

'*Vanda curvifolium cristata*. Very striking, don't you think?'
The voice came from behind him.
He'd heard nothing. Sensed nothing. He spun round.

50

She was wearing jodhpurs, black riding-boots and a man's white cotton shirt, which billowed round her waist. Her hair was tucked behind her ears and her cheeks had a rosy, healthy glow. She seemed not the least surprised to find him there.

'They come from southern India,' she continued, 'but the poor things have no scent. So strange, for such a beautiful bloom.'

'Jesus, you scared me,' said Jacquot, without thinking. Just blurted it out, as though the words would somehow help his heart return to normal. And then: 'Who are you? What are you doing here?' although he knew the answers already. It was the girl from St Bédard, the girl running the Chaberts' shop. He'd only ever caught a glimpse of her, but Jacquot was certain of it.

'Buhl,' said the girl. 'Marie-Ange Buhl. I'm looking after the Fontaine des Fleurs in St Bédard. My agency asked me to take on this extra job, looking after the hot-house.' She paused, looked around her. 'It's beautiful, don't you think?'

Reaching past him, she swept away a tangle of cobwebs from the branch of an overhanging fern. As she did so, Jacquot smelt the farmyard on her – horse, hay, cooled sweat. She turned back to him, working the filaments of the web between her fingers, rolling it into a tiny black ball, letting it drop to the ground, holding his eye the whole time. 'And you are?' she asked.

'Daniel Jacquot. Chief Inspector Jacquot. Cavaillon Regional Crime Squad.'

She gave him a closer look, a grin hovering on her lips. 'Haven't I seen you before somewhere? Up in St Bédard? Didn't I see you there this morning? With Aldo, at Mazzelli's?'

Jacquot nodded. 'I go there sometimes. It's a good place to . . . sit in the sun, have a beer.'

Another dark, appraising glance. 'So, what brings you here, Chief Inspector?' she said.

'Scene of crime,' Jacquot replied. 'A few months back. Sometimes I call by.'

'The Martner family.'

'You know about it?'

'Of course I know about it, Chief Inspector. I'm filling in for the Chaberts while they're away. Living in their house. Not to mention looking after the doctor's collection. I'd have to be pretty dim not to know about it, don't you think? Added to which, it's all anyone ever talks about.' Then she frowned, tipped her head to one side. 'But surely it's all over and done with? The investigation, I mean.'

Jacquot shrugged, left it at that.

The frown eased, disappeared. She looked around her 'Tell me, Chief Inspector, do you know anything about orchids?'

'I know they're expensive.'

She laughed, and Jacquot felt every nerve-ending sing. It was the most beautiful laugh he'd ever heard. Briefly he felt childishly pleased that it was something he had said that had made it happen.

'Oh, they're much more than that,' replied Marie-Ange, looping a fall of hair behind her ear. 'Would you like the tour?'

'My mother always said an education was a fine and noble thing,' replied Jacquot, trying to regain some sense of composure.

'Your mother was a wise woman,' said Marie-Ange, stepping past him, her arm brushing his. 'Come with me, I'll show you,' she continued, and led the way deeper into the hot-house, pausing every now and again to point out the blooms – gaudy sprays of *christiearas, ascocendas, coeruleas, tessellatas, sanderianas* – the names tripping off her tongue with easy familiarity. Since the path was too narrow for them to walk side by side, Jacquot kept a pace or two behind her, close enough to hear what she said, and close enough to smell

the soap beneath the horse, close enough to reach out a hand and
. . . touch her.

'The word "orchid" comes from the Greek,' she was telling him.
'Did you know that? *Orkhis*. It means . . . testicle. Not the flower
you understand, but the tuber. Look, here,' she said, pointing to
some browning, oval balls peeping through the soil, each one tipped
with a tiny green spear.

Jacquot nodded, not sure how to respond.

'Orchids are also one of the largest flowering-plant families on
earth,' she continued, walking on, 'found on every continent except
Antarctica. So far, more than thirty thousand species have been
identified, but there may be many thousands more still to discover.
It is that possibility,' she said, glancing over her shoulder, 'the possibility of discovery, that drives the orchid-collector. The chance to
find a flower never seen before, never catalogued.

'Tell me,' she asked, pushing aside a curling spike of blossom,
holding it for him to take and step past, 'do you have a garden of
your own?'

'You could say. Enough to grow this and that,' he replied, thinking
of his own small patch in Claudine's garden where she'd let him
grow his favourite plant, the heads already swollen, strongly scented
and sticky to the touch.

'What about something like this?' she said, coming to a stop a
few steps further on, pointing to a cluster of delicate green buds,
forty or more, the size of fat, juicy grapes, clinging to a single stem
above their heads. Some of the buds had already burst their skins
and their spiky petals twisted and beckoned like a witch's fingers.

Jacquot looked up and shook his head. 'A little beyond my capa-
bilities, I'm afraid.'

It was then, without warning, that he felt the strangest sensation,
a kind of shiver dancing over his forearms. He looked around, trying
to get his bearings. And then it struck him. In February a body had
lain here. Right here. At this exact spot – not two steps from where
he now stood. He was certain of it.

Beside him, Marie-Ange seemed not to notice his sudden lack
of attention. '*Phalaenopsis deliria*,' she continued, reaching up her
fingers to touch the petals closest to her. 'One of my favourites.
First hybridised in the nineteenth century by an English grower

called John Dominy, using *Phalaenopsis delanatii* and *casteria*. Look here, you see? From the *delanatii*, he's captured the frilled edge of the petals, and from the *casteria* that peachy colouring at the tips. Which is what hybridising is all about – years of trial and error to produce a flower like this.'

'You seem to know a great deal about it,' Jacquot said.

'I studied plant hybridisation at college,' she replied, turning her back on him and walking ahead.

Jacquot stayed where he was, watching her.

'Orchids were my speciality. It wasn't much, but I always thought it was enough. Until I came here.' She stopped, as though sensing he hadn't moved, looked back over her shoulder, turned towards him. 'These . . .' she gestured to the plants around them '. . . well, these are different.'

Although she gave no sign of it, Jacquot suspected that she knew he'd been looking at her figure, the way she moved. He felt oddly flustered that she might have caught him out.

'Exquisite,' she said. 'Don't you think?'

Another unnerving look. Jacquot managed a nod.

'I'm not an expert,' she continued, 'but Dr Martner could have taught Dominy a thing or two and that's for sure. He's done some incredible work here.'

'Hybridising epiphytes and terrestrials,' said Jacquot, recalling what the nurseryman Balou had said about Martner's work.

'So you *do* know about orchids?'

Jacquot smiled. 'Not really. Just something I picked up during the investigation. Are all Martner's orchids hybrids?'

'Quite a few,' she replied. 'It was his speciality after all. But not all of them. He must have travelled, brought back specimens to experiment with. Just look,' she said, lifting a single stem looping down to her right, letting the flowers rest in the palm of her hand, droop against her wrist. '*Zygopetalum aspasia violacea*. It flowers only twice a year – July and late December, never more than ten days each time. You could set your watch by it. A real collector's orchid, and a perfect specimen for hybridising. The colour of that tongue, the throat, there, you see it?' She pointed a long finger into the heart of one of the flowers. 'That's what he'd have been after. That red is just so . . . incredible. I can't think of another orchid that has such an intensity, such a . . . depth of colour. Like the skin of a dark cherry where it touches the flesh beneath.' She took her eyes off the orchid and looked straight at Jacquot. 'Have you ever seen a colour like that? Such a shape?'

Again Jacquot spoke without thinking, but managed to catch himself in time. 'It looks a little . . .'

'A little . . . ?' She tipped her head. 'A little rude?' she prompted.

'Well, I suppose . . .' Again Jacquot felt flustered, this young woman rendering him as soft and stupid as a starstruck teenager.

'Which is what it is, Chief Inspector. Rude. And flagrant. A come-on. Seduction. That's what it's all about, you see. Where this plant is found, in the rainforests of Brazil, there are many like it fighting for attention, for some insect to come and . . . well, pollinate them. And it is up to each flower to create its own, unique . . . enticement, to provide whatever it is their particular seed-carrier needs or desires. And this one . . . this one plays the game like no other. She is, if you like, the greatest seductress of them all. Here, come closer,' she said, holding up the fall of flowers to him. 'Just look. This single petal, the pink one, like a tiny open hand, so delicately veined . . . this is where the insect lands, attracted by the colours, the patterns, the apparent ease of access, all deliberate, external devices – like expertly applied make-up – to draw him on. And here, at the top . . .' pointing with her fingertip '. . . where the pink lip darkens to scarlet, at the entrance to the flower's interior, here is the promise of nectar. A sweet, succulent scent to lure him forward, deeper into the bloom. Which is when, sensing the entry of this intruder, the flower shudders and pulses, showering the insect with a spray of pollen. Job done.'

She paused for a moment, then let the stem of blooms slide from her hand. 'I think it is the sexiest flower I know. You should only give it to someone you love. Or someone you want.'

'Maybe you could write the name down for me,' said Jacquot, reaching into his jacket pocket for a pen and paper, passing them to her.

She grinned. 'Of course.' And then, after a beat: 'Had you anyone in mind?'

'Oh, yes. Yes, I have someone in mind.'

She cocked her head as though wanting to know more.

'A friend,' replied Jacquot. 'It's her birthday in a few weeks.'

'But the blossom will be gone by then,' said Marie-Ange. 'It will be too late.'

'Christmas, then,' he said, nodding for her to write the name anyway.

She smiled, then started writing. When she had finished, she folded the paper and handed it back with the pen.

'Well, Chief Inspector, I must get on. Still a lot to do.' She held out her hand and he took it. 'It was good to meet you.'

'*Et vous aussi*, Mademoiselle. And thank you for the tour.'

'I enjoyed it as much as you,' replied Marie-Ange, eyes twinkling.

Ten minutes later, sitting in his car, Jacquot pulled the paper from his pocket and unfolded it.

And gave a grunt of laughter.

She'd written the orchid's name in capitals.

51

After leaving the Martner house Jacquot skirted Cavaillon and drove straight home. On the way, he called the office and left a message for Brunet. 'Any information you can get on a woman. A girl. Marie-Ange Buhl. Start with that lawyer fellow of Brauer's. Boudit. Which agency he used for the Martner hot-house job. Anything you can get. See you in the morning.'

By the time Jacquot arrived home, the breeze through the open driver's window had dried the hot-house sweat on him. His shirt was stiff and creased and he knew he needed a bath. That was what he was thinking – a bath and a joint – when he opened his front door and heard muffled sobbing coming from the kitchen. He knew immediately it was Claudine. His first thought was Midou, Claudine's daughter. Something had happened to Midou. His heart vaulted into his throat. He hurried down the hallway and pushed through the door into the kitchen.

Claudine was sitting at the table, head in hands, shoulders shaking, a tangle of auburn hair hanging round her wrists. At the end of the table the portable TV combo they kept in the kitchen was playing a video, a silent black-and-white film transferred from Super Eight of a young girl doing cartwheels in a garden. Jacquot had seen it before. It was an old family film of Claudine, aged ten or eleven, performing for her aunt, a frail figure sitting in a garden chair and clapping silent hands. Beside the television was a long tin box, its glossy black paint chipped and scratched. It looked like an old deed-box, the letters 'J.E.' painted on the lid in a yellowed, curling copperplate.

Jacquot pulled out a chair and sat beside Claudine, reaching for her hand, which she gave him gratefully, looking up with a sad, tearful smile that told him that whatever was wrong, it was suddenly bearable with him there, that all she wanted was sympathy, love, a hug. He breathed a sigh of relief. Not Midou, then. If it had been Midou . . . Jacquot didn't dare try to imagine.

Perching on the edge of his chair he took Claudine in his arms and felt a hot wet cheek press against his neck and the heave of her body as a fresh spring of sobs arrived. 'There, there,' he said, brushing the hair from her face where the tears had plastered it to her skin. 'Now tell me, tell me. What's wrong, my darling? What's wrong?'

Claudine took a deep breath, held back the hiccuping for long enough to say: 'It's Tatine . . .'

Jacquot took it in, relieved but saddened too.

Tatine. The old lady in the video. The last of Claudine's family. Sandrine Eddé. Seventy-nine, eighty. Somewhere around there. For the last four years she'd been cared for by the Sisters of Laune, in a seventeenth-century abbey run as a private hospice in the hills above Salon.

'She died this morning,' sniffed Claudine, pulling a tissue from the box by her elbow and blowing her nose. 'They called at lunchtime. I went over straight away. Saw her. She looked . . . she looked . . . at peace, at last.'

'I guess we knew it was coming,' said Jacquot, gently. 'And maybe better this way.'

Jacquot remembered the last time he'd seen the old lady, March, April, not long after Dietering had left. She was sitting in the conservatory, head nodding, eyes shifting from their faces to the garden and back again, or towards the hall when something caught her attention. At no time during their visit did she speak, just the mouth moving, as though the words were sticking to the back of her tongue, like hairballs she couldn't quite get a purchase on. Often, in the silences, when her eyes wandered and Claudine just stroked her hand, Jacquot wondered whether she even knew they were there, let alone recognised them.

Four years earlier, while Jacquot was still in Marseilles, Tatine had lived with Claudine and Midou in a self-contained ground-floor apartment off the kitchen, which Claudine now used as a studio. It was there, one morning, that Claudine had found her aunt, stretched out on the floor of her bathroom. She was breathing but unconscious. Claudine had called an ambulance and the old lady had been rushed to Avignon's general hospital. For three days she was on a monitor, the inside of her oxygen mask dusted with shallow, inaudible breaths. On the fourth day a priest was called and the last rites administered.

But slowly Sandrine rallied, enough for the oxygen, glucose drip and monitor to be disconnected, enough to be propped up in bed, then to be dressed and sat in an armchair, in a day room where she gazed at the world passing by with a blank stare and shaking hands as though trying to applaud everything she saw around her.

It was a stroke, the doctors told Claudine, a multiple *infarc dementia* they called it, a terrible bleed, from which it was unlikely her aunt would ever fully recover.

But Claudine would have none of it. Not a stroke, she'd insisted. Not a bleed. Not a multiple . . . whatever. It was a *tristesse de coeur*, a sadness of the heart, a sadness that had finally got the better of the old lady.

For as long as Claudine could remember, Tatine had suffered from it. The war, she'd told Jacquot the first time she took him to Laune to meet her aunt. Something had happened then. Something that had emptied her heart. Afterwards Tatine never spoke, only smiled. Maybe a '*chérie*' now and then, a nod, a shake of the head, the quietest '*je t'en prie*' you can imagine. And now that hollow place in her heart had caught up with her. Engulfed her.

Sitting there at the kitchen table, holding Claudine's hands, Jacquot remembered that first visit to Laune – the abbey's silent cloisters, its trickling fountain, walled gardens and tree-shaded walks, the cracked bell that rang out the Angelus twice a day with a single, discordant note. And the old lady. Tatine. Agitated, anxious, her shoulders slumped to one side but still tall in her armchair, beady-eyed and frowning as though for the life of her she couldn't work out what she was doing there, or who all these people were.

He remembered standing in the doorway of her room while

Claudine sat beside her aunt, reached for her crumpled, gossamer hand and made the introductions. Back then, there still seemed to be some thin tatters of understanding and Jacquot recalled the way the old lady looked at him, in astonishment – the ponytail, the cowboy boots, the jeans – as though she was wondering despairingly where on earth her niece could have found such a specimen.

Claudine pulled another tissue from the box and blew her nose.

'I asked that she be buried at Laune. The *abbesse* said there would be no problem. The service has been set for Monday. Is that all right?'

'Of course,' said Jacquot. 'If you want me to be there.'

'I think Tatine would. That's the important thing.'

'Then I will be there, of course,' replied Jacquot.

Claudine squeezed his hand and tried a smile.

On the TV, the video had ended and a blaze of shifting static filled the screen. Jacquot leaned over and switched it off, then reached across to the metal deed-box, turning it to read the writing on the lid.

'Tatine's,' said Claudine. 'When I left this afternoon they gave it to me. All her private things – just one box. She kept it under the bed. Here and at the *abbaye*. She never liked to be far from it, but I never saw it open.' Claudine sniffed, wiped her nose. 'I'd completely forgotten about it.'

Jacquot pulled it towards him, tried the lid.

'It's locked,' she said. 'One of the nuns was certain she'd seen a key for it somewhere and they said they'd look. They promised to give me a call when they found it. Maybe Monday . . . It seems a pity to force it.'

Jacquot lifted it and shook it gingerly. There was something heavy and loose inside. When he tipped the box, he could feel it slide with the tilt.

He put it down and squinted at the tiny opening for a key, then ran his fingers over the copperplate script. 'J.E. Any ideas?'

Claudine nodded. 'Jacqueline Eddé, Tatine's mother. My grandmother.'

'Well, I'm sure they'll find the key,' said Jacquot, getting to his feet and moving the deed-box to the sideboard. 'I'll put it here, out of the way, until they do.'

And then, looking around, a little uncertain: 'I don't suppose . . . I don't suppose you're really very hungry?'

Claudine smiled bravely. 'No, but I'm sure you are.' And then, wrinkling her nose: 'You smell smoky. And sweaty. Have a shower and I'll get something organised.'

52

Later, after a put-together supper of sausage, bread, cheese and wine, they went to bed, Claudine wriggling herself into the contours of Jacquot's body, pulling his arm round her waist and holding it tight, as though to stop it straying. He understood she just wanted to feel him there, nothing more.

'I love you, Monsieur Jacquot,' he heard her whisper, in a soft, sleepy voice.

'And I love you too, Mademoiselle Eddé.'

For half an hour or more, he listened to her small, sad sighs and felt her gentle sobbing and held her close. But when, finally, she fell asleep, Jacquot slipped silently from their bed, pulled on his night-shirt and, in darkness, tiptoed downstairs.

He knew what he wanted to do, couldn't help himself. And Claudine need never know.

He closed the kitchen door behind him and switched on the light, then made straight for the sideboard where he'd left the deed-box. He carried it to the table and sat in front of it, peering down to examine the lock. Whatever key opened it must have been as small as a paperclip. Which was what he pulled open the table drawer to look for, sorting through household odds and ends – screwdrivers, a ball of string, pliers, tape, various round tins filled with screws and nails – clearing a way down to the bottom of the drawer until he found one.

He prised the clip apart and began to shape it as he'd learned to do so long ago, not with the police but in his wild, ruffian days with the Chats de Nuit gang in Marseilles – breaking into cars, apartments, anything with a lock that needed attention.

Some things you never forget, thought Jacquot, as he poured a drop of olive oil on to the wooden table and dipped the end of the paperclip into it. Tilting the box, he inserted it into the lock and played for a connection. Twice he caught it and twice he missed, the olive oil that lubricated the tip making his fingers slip on the metal. The third time he was successful. He felt the obstruction he was looking for, gently applied pressure and the mechanism clicked into place. He put down the paperclip, wiped his hands on his night-shirt and, with a dry, metallic creak, lifted the lid.

Opening the deed-box was like stepping into a room that had been sealed for a century, a dry, tomb-like staleness rising from its interior like a dying gasp. A final, dusty exhalation. Age and decay. As he pushed back the lid Jacquot wondered when the box had last been opened. Years ago, judging by the smell that seeped from the canvas envelope carefully wrapped round the box's contents.

Folding back the canvas and draping it over the sides of the deed-box, the first thing Jacquot saw was a cloth wrap, a dirty piece of oiled chamois, which he knew contained a gun, the loose weight he'd felt sliding around in the box. That was what had brought him down to the kitchen: the gun, and the frustrating prospect of having to wait until Monday to know for sure.

He lifted the bundle from the box. Its weight and shape confirmed his suspicions even before he unwrapped it. It was a service revolver, an old Smith & Wesson, six chambers, its hand-grip and body blackened. Given the few chips along its bevelled barrel it looked as though someone had painted it. So the barrel wouldn't glint in the sunshine? In moonlight? Jacquot broke the weapon. The chambers were empty. He sniffed at its innards. Nothing through there in years.

But what on earth was Tatine doing with a gun? And where had it come from? She'd seemed so frail, the Tatine he knew; it was hard to imagine her having the strength to lift such a weapon, let alone fire it. And then he recalled Claudine telling him about Tatine's work in the war. With the Maquis, the resistance, she'd said.

Something clandestine. Which also seemed unlikely, the old woman he knew.

But she'd been young once. Pictures of her from those distant days hung in the salon – a rather fine chalk and pencil sketch on faded rose paper, a more formal portrait in a cardigan, with folded hands and pearls – and there were all the photos in the family albums: in a black swimming cap at Antibes, leaning over ski poles with a line of snowy mountains behind her, and arm in arm with her brother and sister, both of whom she'd survived. A self-possessed, beautiful young woman, who had held the camera's eye firmly, unflinching, challenging, even when she was laughing. Just as, presumably, she'd have held that Smith & Wesson: single-handed, as sure and steady as her gaze. Tatine, Jacquot suspected, would not have been a woman to underestimate. Even if, since those far-off days, she had settled into a muddled and confused old age, stooped and broken by Claudine's *tristesse de coeur*.

It ran in the family, thought Jacquot, hefting the gun, squinting down its barrel. Claudine was no different. Self-assured, defiant, up for anything.

Laying the gun carefully on the table, Jacquot turned back to the deed-box, and removed a thin top-sheet of canvas stiffened with age, to reveal the rest of its contents.

First out was a man's wristwatch with a strap of military webbing, a cracked glass and fat luminescent numerals. Jacquot cupped his hand over the face – the numbers still shone bright and green. Not surprisingly the watch had stopped. Five-forty. Evening or morning, who could say? He tried the winder but it refused to budge. Rusted? Wound too tight? Impossible to determine. He turned it over. Engraved on the backplate, still clearly incised in the metal, were the letters 'à SE de AV'. To Sandrine Eddé, it had to be. From 'AV', whoever that might have been.

Jacquot placed the watch beside the gun, then lifted out a neatly folded cotton handkerchief embroidered in one corner with the same 'AV' initials and a small cigar box secured with a rubber band. Jacquot eased off the band and opened the lid. Inside was a blackened twig of what might once have been a sprig of rosemary, its scent long gone, stem withered and bare, the splintery foliage littering the lustreless silver-foil lining.

He put aside the handkerchief and the cigar box, then brought out another layer of canvas, revealing beneath it a tightly squared fold of paper, which crinkled stiffly when he opened it, creases brown with time and split at the corners with overuse.

It was an old survey map, one centimetre to one kilometre scale, reaching from . . . he turned it in the light . . . from the northern bank of the Durance river across the Luberon hills to the Vaucluse plateau. And from Cavaillon in the west to Manosque in the east. There were no relief marks to indicate elevations and no colour to indicate forests or flats, just a cobwebbing of routes and various place names printed in either small or large capitals according to size of population.

Beside a number of them, scratched in thin pencil marks, were what could only be times and dates – 'Pertuis: 3am – 6/iv/43; Céreste: midnight – 16/v/43; Roussillon: 5am – 14/iii/43; Apt: 4am – 23/ii/44; Barjas: 3am – 28/iv/44.'

Jacquot refolded the map and laid it on the table. The blackened gun, the map, the pencilled codes – Jacquot didn't need to be told what he was looking at. It was just as Claudine had said. The war. *Résistants*. The Maquis. *Action directe*. Dating, so far as he could tell, from Manosque in February 1943 to St Bédard in June 1944. Fourteen notations, fourteen separate strikes. In only sixteen months.

The next documents confirmed it, a wad held together with twine. Jacquot slipped the knots and spread out the papers on the table.

First an identity card, *'carte d'identité de citoyen français'*, the picture of Sandrine in the top left-hand corner clearly recognisable. It was a head-and-shoulders shot, Sandrine looking directly at the camera, no smile, hair drawn back, her left shoulder indented with part of the official seal, validated with the regulation thirteen-franc stamp.

What drew Jacquot's attention, however, were the personal details, written in what he could only assume was Tatine's hand. So far as he could tell, both date and place of birth looked okay, but the name was different. Rose Valence.

There was a second *carte d'identité* as well, this time for a man named Stephane Beaumont, the details written in another hand. The photo showed a youngish man in an open-necked shirt. He wore spectacles with one lens clear and the other blackened. '*Demi-aveugle*', Jacquot saw in the space for 'Distinguishing Features'. Blind in one eye.

False papers. They could be nothing else.

Jacquot put them to one side, picked up the last documents and unfolded them one by one. What he saw brought a whistle to his lips. Stiff vellum pages with crested letterheads and extravagant seals. Awards for gallantry to Sandrine Eddé: Médaille de la Résistance, 5 October 1945; Croix de la Libération and L'Ordre de la Libération, 14 February 1946; Chevalier de la Légion d'Honneur, 17 April 1946.

And here, one after another, the justificatory reports:

'. . . planned and carried out several dangerous and vital missions with total disregard to her own safety . . . '
     Colonel Hugo Rascousse (Renard)
     Head of Network F2

And another:

'. . . provided information of the greatest importance at great risk to herself . . .'
     Lieutenant Colonel Jacques Mazin
     Head of the Fighting France Service

Jacquot laid down the documents, turned back to the box and lifted out a small velvet bag. It was weighty. He could hear the chink of coins. He untied the knot that secured it and shook the contents into the palm of his hand.

Not coins but medals, four of them, the gold and silver catching the kitchen light, the milled edges still sharp, the colours of the silk ribbons to which they were attached only slightly faded.

So Claudine had not been exaggerating. Tatine had had a colourful – and dangerous – past. For a moment Jacquot wished he'd known about this while the old girl was alive. But then, in the next instant, he was glad he hadn't. It would have been that much harder to see her so reduced.

Jacquot tipped the medals back into the bag and retied the knot.

By now he judged he was about half-way through the deed-box. He was about to lift out a pack of letters tied with string when a hand reached down and picked up the gun.

53

It was Claudine. He hadn't heard a thing, hadn't heard the stairs creak or the kitchen door open. Caught fair and square. Too long away from Marseilles, he thought.

Gathering her robe round her, Claudine sat down beside him, hefting the Smith & Wesson.

'Well, well, Tatine,' she said, in a who-would-have-thought-it tone. And then, looking at Jacquot, an eyebrow arching: 'So you found yourself a key?'

Jacquot picked up the paperclip. 'You could say.'

Claudine gave him an admonishing smile, like a parent catching out a child.

Jacquot felt a lift of relief. She wasn't angry.

'And?' she asked.

'You can see. Looks like mementoes from the war.'

Claudine put down the gun and reached for the handkerchief, ran her thumb across the embroidered initials, picked up the watch and turned it over. 'The same initials.'

'Do they mean anything to you?'

'Perhaps.'

Jacquot gave her a look.

She picked up the identity cards. Sandrine's first. Then Beaumont's. She studied the picture.

'It was always said there had been a man in her life,' Claudine began. 'In the war, you know? I remember Maman telling me. How much in love they were. He sounded like a fairy-tale prince. And that was what I thought he was. A fairy-tale prince. But then, when I was older, I learned he was real. A resistance fighter. That he was captured and shot by the Germans. In Cavaillon. Actually, in what is now your car park. At police headquarters.'

'Police headquarters? He was shot there? Where I work?'

Claudine nodded. 'From November 1942, when the Germans occupied the Southern Zone, they used your building as their *Kommandantur*, their regional headquarters. Gestapo too. You didn't know?'

Jacquot shook his head. 'I've only been here three years, remember?'

'Some policeman,' said Claudine.

Jacquot ignored the jibe. 'And what about the name? AV?'

'That I do not know. Tatine never spoke of him. And my mother was so much younger, you see. Ten years, I think. They were never . . . confidantes. And later, after the war, well . . .'

Claudine reached into the box for the pack of letters that Jacquot had been about to pick up, undid the string bow and let them spill out on to the table. Some were still in envelopes, others simply folded. Only a few bore stamps. Jacquot and Claudine took one each from the pile.

'Love letters,' said Jacquot, after he had read a single page. '"*Ma chère Dédé*". Eddé? Sandrine?' He turned the letter over. 'No signature.'

Beside him Claudine's lips flickered with the words. 'It's so beautiful. And so sad.' Her voice caught. 'Listen,' she said, and began to read: '"My darling Dédé. It is only two days since we met at Bonaire's yet it seems like a year. Two years. A lifetime. You looked so calm, so strong, so beautiful . . ."' Claudine's voice quivered again and she took a deep breath. '"In all my life I have never known anyone like you, never been so proud of someone, never been so happy, so complete. My heart breaks with love for you. One day, all this will be over and we will be together. Always. *Je t'aime follement*. Albert."'

'Albert . . . The "A" in "AV", I assume. But Albert who?'

Claudine reached for another envelope and as she lifted it a photo slid free, its edges creased, its surface a creamy, sun-faded sepia.

Claudine picked it up, looked at the two figures and turned it over. 'Voilà,' she said. '"Albert de Vausigne. July 1943". And that's Tatine in the picture and her handwriting too.'

At first the name failed to register.

'What did you say?' asked Jacquot. 'What was the name?'

'Vausigne. Albert de Vausigne. And better with an eyepatch, if you ask me. Look.'

Jacquot reached for the picture and studied it. It was a long shot, Sandrine with her head resting against the shoulder of a tall young man, his arm clasped in hers. With his free hand he was waving to the camera and smiling widely, maybe saying something.

Stephane Beaumont. There was no doubt about it. The man in the identity card. The man with the spectacles. Jacquot turned the photo over and read the name and date scrawled on the back. Only here he was Albert de Vausigne, forsaking the spectacles in favour of an eyepatch, which, as Claudine said, suited him better, its black strap angled rakishly across his forehead, lost among blond curls.

'Familiar?' asked Claudine, sensing his interest.

Jacquot nodded. 'You could say. The family lives near St Bédard. The Comte and Comtesse de Vausigne. On the road to Chant-le-Neuf. Maybe thirty kilometres from here.'

Jacquot turned back to the photo of Sandrine and Albert.

They looked good together, no question about it. Lovers for sure, the way they held each other, the way they touched. Behind the couple, Jacquot could make out a stone wall covered with ivy and the corner of a low doorway or window.

'They're brothers, Albert and the present Comte?' asked Claudine, taking the photo back from him.

'Step-brothers, I think,' said Jacquot, trying to remember what he knew of the family, what Brunet had told him when they found the Beretta and traced it to the de Vausignes. 'Albert was the heir, next in line. Mother died in the thirties some time, and the old Comte married again. Someone from Brittany, Normandy maybe. The second wife had a son, Gilles, by a previous marriage, younger than Albert. The old man adopted him.'

Jacquot put the photo beside the letters and tipped up the box to look inside. He reached in and pulled out a newspaper. It was dated June 1944. He opened it and scanned the front page. In the bottom corner he found a single paragraph reporting the execution of four resistance fighters in Cavaillon. No names were given, just a warning that further attempts to attack occupying forces would be met with vigorous reprisals.

But Jacquot was certain he knew one of the names. Monsieur Beaumont. Albert de Vausigne. The cause of Tatine's *tristesse de coeur*. Had to be.

A few months later, thought Jacquot, handing the newspaper to Claudine and pointing out the story, those same occupying forces were retreating up the Rhône with the Allies hot on their heels. A few months later and those four resistance fighters would have been spared a firing squad. And Albert, not Gilles, would have inherited the title when the old Comte died. And, who knows? Tatine might have been his *comtesse*.

While Claudine read the report, Jacquot looked back into the box. It was empty. He pulled out the canvas envelope to make sure, and as he did so a half-dozen silvery bullets, nestled in the folds of the canvas, dropped out and thudded on to the faded pink cover of a notebook. Jacquot picked up the shells, the same calibre as the revolver, then turned to the notebook.

It was a school exercise book. He flipped through it.

Then stopped and flicked through again. More slowly this time.

Every page was written on.

Different-coloured ink. Different pens.

But he'd been right. Only one word.

Over and over again.

Rocsabin.

54

It was widely agreed at police headquarters, among uniforms and detectives alike, that Jean Brunet was a tomcat. He even had the look of a tomcat: always a little ruffled in the mornings, a tad fatigued, and every now and again altogether far too pleased with himself.

Like this morning, Jacquot decided, the cat who'd definitely got the cream. He came into Jacquot's office carrying a file and wearing a satisfied smirk. 'Buhl. Marie-Ange,' he said, sliding the dossier across Jacquot's desk. 'As requested.'

Jacquot, as usual, was impressed. He may have come late to the office, taking most of the morning off to be at home with Claudine, but the moment he sat at his desk, Brunet was there with the information he'd requested the previous evening.

'Anything I should know?' asked Brunet, nodding at the file.

Jacquot knew what his assistant was getting at. He wondered whether he should involve Brunet in a case they'd put to bed months before. Finally he reached into his pocket, pulled out the letter and handed it over.

His assistant read it through. 'You think this could be the Buhl girl?'

Jacquot shrugged. 'Maybe. Maybe not.'

'Anything to it?'

'They never say anything new. Just that we got the wrong man.'

Brunet held up the letter. 'This isn't the first?'

Jacquot opened his desk drawer, pulled out the others he'd received.

Brunet whistled. 'All the same handwriting?'

Jacquot nodded.

'And you think it's the Buhl girl?'

'Could be. Who knows?' replied Jacquot, dropping the letters back into the drawer and sliding it shut.

'You want me to keep an eye on her?'

'You don't have enough on your plate?'

It was time to change the subject. Jacquot didn't want Brunet thinking the letters had got to him. The tactic worked.

Brunet frowned, mock-innocent, giving Jacquot a kind of I-can't-think-what-you're-getting-at look. Jacquot was used to it.

'Mademoiselle Gaillard?' prompted Jacquot. 'Suzi? At the Brasserie?'

'Aaah,' replied Brunet, as though finally making the connection, then pushing out his bottom lip as though he'd been asked to assess the chances of a trotter at Chantilly. He shrugged his shoulders. A contemplative nod, as though giving the matter due consideration, the jury still out. And then, slowly, as though recalling some pleasurable little detail, Brunet gave that smile of his, the smile that always won them over.

The smile transformed him. Even Claudine said she loved Brunet's smile. He might be a little short, she told Jacquot, when she first met his assistant, but there was something about him. The way he moved, the look of his body, the snappy way he dressed.

And, of course, that smile.

Jacquot couldn't see it, but he had no doubts about Brunet's score card. So far as Jacquot could figure it, Brunet had never failed in the three years they'd worked together.

Jacquot guessed it was the way he went about things. Like his interview technique. Just so determined once he got the scent. Single-minded. It could take a day, a week, sometimes longer, but Brunet never gave up. The widow in Roujac who found her husband drowned in the pool? Three days after the funeral Brunet was in her bed. Then there was the usherette at the Ritz in Cavaillon. And her mother, too, according to one of the boys in uniform. The insurance assessor from Aix. Some nurse at the hospital. That secretary in the *mairie* . . . Jacquot had a problem keeping track of them all. And now Suzi Gaillard at the brasserie. Only the owner's daughter, for God's sake.

In Brunet terms, he'd put in the hours with Mademoiselle Gaillard and, for a time, it had looked like he was getting nowhere fast. But last night, by the smug, rumpled look of him, Brunet had stamped her papers well and good.

Yet, somehow, Brunet still managed to be about the best assistant Jacquot had ever come across. He might stagger home at dawn, but he'd be at his desk, ready for anything, when Jacquot arrived – with whatever it was that Jacquot had asked for. In this case, information on the Buhl girl.

And a lot else besides.

Knowing he'd get nothing more on Suzi Gaillard than that lip-licking smirk, Jacquot moved on. 'Anything from Fournier on the fire at Rocsabin?' he asked.

Brunet took a chair. Down to business. 'Let's just say there have been developments.'

'I like developments. What kind?'

'Looks like the open-and-shut variety. Well, as good as.'

Jacquot gave him a startled look.

'Like I said, there's a third party. No question. Both victims shot. Fournier called it in this morning. And the first body's been identified,' continued Brunet. 'Grace Bartolomé, the warehouse owner. Early fifties. Married. No kids. A looker, they say. They're matching dental records for confirmation.'

'Identified? How?'

'The watch. One of the staff recognised it. Last night, after we left.'

'Husband? What's he got to say for himself?'

'Not a lot,' replied Brunet, stretching back, sliding his hands behind his head. 'Which is why I'm saying open and shut. On account of Monsieur Guy Bartolomé having shot himself in the head.'

Jacquot's eyes widened. 'You're kidding?'

'After they identified the watch, one of the Rocsabin boys went out to Lucat where they live. Locked tight. No one home. So this morning, first thing, they go out there again. Still no answer. But there's a dog howling in the front room, pawing the window. So they force the lock and there he is. Sat at the kitchen table, gun in his hand.'

'And the gun belongs to?'

'Registered to Madame Bartolomé. A pearl-handled twenty-two. Three bullets fired. Ballistics are working on it, but you ask me . . .'

'Any note?'

'No note. But they found an empty ten-litre petrol can in the boot of his car.'

'What do we know about him?'

'Used to be a teacher. At the Rocsabin *lycée*. Retired early. Health reasons.'

'Which were?'

'He had a breakdown. Four months in a clinic outside Grenoble. We've got reports coming down some time today.'

'So the story is this Guy Bartolomé discovers his wife's playing around . . .'

'. . . and decides to do something about it. Catches them at the warehouse. Sorts them out. Torches the place to cover any trail he may have left. But when he gets back home, he goes to pieces. Tops himself. Something like that is my guess.'

'What about the second body. Any names?'

'Nothing yet. Except the shoes.'

'Shoes?'

'Hand-made. Badly burned, of course, but Fournier found a maker's mark. Some place in Aix. I've got one of our boys down there checking it out.'

Jacquot was impressed. As Brunet had said, it all looked like a done deal.

'Course, we might not have to wait that long,' his assistant continued.

'You got something else?'

'Maybe.'

'The cars in the yard?'

'Could be,' said Brunet, stretching out his legs, just about managing to muffle a yawn.

Jacquot waited. As always Brunet's performance was impeccable. He looked like he was getting ready to lick himself all over. 'Whenever you're ready . . .' Jacquot said at last.

'We traced both cars. The Peugeot belongs to a Louis Simon,' began Brunet. 'I called him this morning. He runs a travel shop here in Cavaillon – Voyages Simon on Cours Bournissac – but lives out in Rocsabin, pretty much next door to the warehouse. According to Simon, the manager Filbert lets him leave his car overnight in the warehouse car park when he can't get into his own garage.'

Jacquot gave him a look.

'Tourists,' continued Brunet. 'They're always blocking his driveway. Apparently he likes to let down their tyres, get his own back. Especially the Mercs and the BMWs. Lost his parents in some wartime round-up in Lyon. They were coming out of the cinema and the Fritzes were waiting for them. Took every last one. The whole audience. Management too. Never saw them again. Seven when it happened and never forgotten it.'

Jacquot marvelled at the information Brunet could dredge up in the space of a single phone call.

But Louis Simon was only half the story. Brunet's smile was still there, hovering in the wings.

There was something else.

'And the other car?'

Brunet turned down his lips as though what he'd learned about the second car was of even less interest than the Simon story. 'Aaah. The Citroën. A beauty – 1952 Traction-Avant. Immaculate condition, you wouldn't believe . . .'

'And the owner?'

Brunet smiled. 'Just the Comte de Vausigne.'

55

Jacquot had Brunet drive out to the château. It was the same route he'd taken with Dietering – along the Brieuc road, over the bridge and up through St Bédard. But in July the journey took longer, Brunet beeping at a couple of slowcoaches dawdling along to better admire the slopes of thickening vines, the fields of sunflowers below and the distant, blue-shadowed heights of the Luberon.

Through the open window the wind was warm, buffeting Jacquot's hand and fingers. It smelt of dust, wild lavender and sweet melons ready for market. But neither the scent nor the view was getting through to Jacquot as he tapped his fingers against the car door and reviewed the evidence. Brunet was right. Tracing the shoe would confirm it, but Jacquot was certain they already knew the identity of the second body.

The de Vausigne Citroën at the burned-out warehouse, a man's body found among the ruins and, according to Fournier who'd phoned in just as he and Brunet were leaving the office, a set of keys in the dead man's pocket, one of which unlocked the Citroën. Fournier had checked it himself. There was even an overnight case in the boot. And a pair of shoes with the same maker's mark. It had to be the Comte.

Watching the vines flash by, Jacquot tried to get a fix on Gilles de Vausigne, recalling the first and only time they'd met, when he

255

and Dietering had gone out to the château to ask about the gun Benedict had found. Somewhere in his early seventies, Jacquot guessed, but still a good-looking man, tall, tanned and aristocratic even if he wasn't family blood. That lazy smile of his, the honeyed drawl. The kind of man who took care of his appearance – looks and clothes. The kind of man a fifty-year-old woman like Madame Bartolomé might easily take a shine to.

As Brunet passed through the château gates, Jacquot sighed. This was not going to be an easy call.

By the time they'd unbuckled their seat-belts and climbed from the car, Picard had appeared on the front steps. When they reached him, Jacquot explained that they'd made no appointment but Picard assured them that the Comtesse was around somewhere. If they would care to follow him. Turning on a *sou*, he led them into the château and showed them to the library.

'Glad to see your leg is better,' remarked Jacquot. 'The last time I was here . . .'

Picard frowned, as though trying to remember, then smiled. 'You have a good memory, Monsieur. An old war wound. The cold weather plays the very devil with it.'

Jacquot nodded, thinking about his heel, the snapped tendon all those years ago on a rugby pitch in Béziers. Cold weather, he knew, was certainly no friend to old injuries.

'Looks like they've had the decorators in,' said Brunet, as Picard closed the door behind him. 'About time, you ask me. The last time I was here the place was a right shambles.'

Jacquot looked around, as though he were seeing the room for the first time. Brunet was right. The scuffed paintwork and fading drapes that Dietering had pointed out, the threadbare upholstery and brass light switches smudged with fingermarks were no more. The room had been given a makeover. Fresh paint, new covers, even the books looked buffed to a shine.

But before Jacquot could reply the door swung open and a young man strode in, stopping dead in his tracks as though surprised to find anyone there. Somewhere in his late thirties, Jacquot judged, he wore a pair of well-pressed jeans, a blue Lacoste polo shirt and boat shoes on bare feet. He was tall, tanned and fit-looking, as though he'd just swung off a horse or stepped ashore. Jacquot recognised him immediately. His mother's manner and his father's features.

'And you are?' he demanded, looking them over.

Brunet made the introductions. The young man nodded.

'And you are?' asked Jacquot back, already knowing the answer.

·It was a while before the man replied, as though considering whether he was obliged to provide any information to a . . . to a policeman. Whether he could be bothered.

'Antoine de Vausigne,' he said, and swung the door wider, indicating that they could now leave the room – where to was no concern of his. 'If you don't mind, I have a phone call to make.'

'Just the one phone is there?' asked Jacquot, turning back to the bookshelves as though he had no intention of going anywhere.

Before the young man could reply, Picard reappeared. He gave de Vausigne a deferential nod, then informed Jacquot and Brunet that the Comtesse would see them now.

'Monsieur,' said Brunet, as he passed de Vausigne at the door.

Jacquot simply nodded on his way out.

The door closed abruptly behind them.

On their previous visit, Jacquot and Dietering had been taken to the morning room. This time Picard led them past that door to the end of the corridor where he pushed open a section of panelling and ushered them into what was clearly the Comtesse's study – low cream sofas at either side of a cream marble fireplace, louvred blinds casting zebra stripes of sunlight across the floor and furnishings, the air filled with a strong, musky scent. Sitting at a *secrétaire* just large enough to accommodate a laptop computer, a telephone and a small vase of violets, Hélène de Vausigne was tapping away at the keys when they were shown into the room. She was dressed in a tailored silk blouse and the same coloured jeans as her son's, though not so snugly fitting. She made no move to greet them, rise from the chair, shake their hands. Instead she gave them a questioning look.

'Chief Inspector Jacquot, isn't it? And . . . I'm so sorry . . . ?'

'Brunet. Inspector Jean Brunet.'

'Of course, yes.' She looked hard at Brunet. 'Aren't you the gentleman who took our statements? Back in . . . when was it? February?'

'That's correct, Madame. You have a good memory.'

'So, please, do have a seat, Messieurs,' she said, sweeping her hand towards the sofas while she repositioned herself to face them, sliding her knees to one side, crossing her ankles and laying her hands in her lap. A suitably helpful, attentive smile was switched on. 'Now, tell me, how can I be of help? Is it something to do with the trial? Our gardener, Chabert?'

Brunet shook his head. 'No, Madame. Something else entirely.'

The Comtesse looked intrigued. 'Really,' she said. 'Do tell.'

'I believe you own a 1952 Citroën Légère. Registration number—'

'That's correct. No need to quote the number, it's the only 'fifty-two Légère in the *département*.' She looked from Brunet to Jacquot, then back again. 'And?'

'And do you happen to know where that car is at the moment, Madame?' asked Jacquot, taking over from Brunet.

The Comtesse turned to him. 'Of course I do,' she replied.

'And that is?'

'Aix. The Hôtel Pigonnet. My husband is staying there for a few days. On business. He drives down every few weeks. He usually leaves it in the hotel car park and takes taxis. Traffic is so monstrous at this time of year.'

'Business?' asked Jacquot.

For a brief moment Hélène de Vausigne assumed the same expression as her son in the library, as though the Comte's business was no concern of his.

'My husband has certain . . . interests in the north,' she began. 'Brittany. A few family holdings. His lawyer is in Aix.'

'And when did your husband leave for Aix, Madame?'

'Why, Monday afternoon.'

'And have you spoken to him since then?'

'No, I haven't. There's no need. He's back tonight.'

'Not without his car, Madame,' broke in Brunet.

Jacquot let the moment hang, and Brunet knew not to add anything more.

And then, for the first time, the Comtesse looked unsure of her ground. These were policeman, after all. Had something happened?

'You're being very mysterious, Chief Inspector. Has the car been stolen? I'm sure if it had been that Gilles would have let me know. He absolutely adores it.' Then she looked alarmed as another possibility dawned on her. Icily, composing herself, she asked: 'Has there been an accident?'

'Not an accident, Madame,' said Jacquot, 'so far as we can tell. We just need to account for your husband's Citroën. What it's doing in Rocsabin when you say it's in Aix.'

'In Rocsabin? But that's ridiculous. I told you. My husband drove it to Aix. Like he always does.'

She swung round to the desk, opened a drawer and found her address book. 'Let me call the hotel, speak to Gilles. I'm sure we can sort all this out,' she said, riffling through the pages.

She found a page, a number, dialled and waited for the connection. Putting her hand over the mouthpiece she was about to say something when the hotel came on the line.

'Ah, yes. Hello. Hôtel Pigonnet? . . . I wonder if I could speak to the Comte de Vausigne . . .'

Jacquot folded his hands in his lap. He knew how this was going to end.

At her desk, the Comtesse looked suddenly puzzled, perplexed. 'Are you sure? . . . That's right, Monday evening . . . Yes, three days.' There was a short pause. The Comtesse began to twist the telephone cord. 'I see. Yes. Thank you.'

She put down the receiver, the earlier studied looseness of her limbs starting to constrict. She straightened her back and minutely turned her head away from them as though expecting a blow. 'It appears that my husband spent only the one night in Aix. According to the hotel he checked out on Tuesday evening.' She bunched a small fist to her lips, cleared her throat. 'Perhaps, Chief Inspector, you would be so kind as to tell me what all this is about.'

'You may be aware, Madame, that early on Wednesday morning, a little after midnight, a fire broke out at a furniture warehouse in Rocsabin . . .'

'Yes, yes, I saw it on the news yesterday. The HacheGee warehouse. A dreadful business. I've been calling Grace all day.'

Jacquot sat forward. 'You know Madame Bartolomé?'

'Of course I know her. For some years now. We are partners.

HacheGee – Hélène and Grace. My husband and I have a stake in the business.'

'A stake, Madame?'

'Well, a little more than a stake, to be precise. We have done since the beginning. The warehouse is built on family land, you see. In addition to rent from the holding company, we take a small percentage of profits as non-executive directors. In fact, I was going out there this afternoon to . . .'

'Might I ask when you last saw Madame Bartolomé? Or spoke to her.'

'Last week. Thursday. Friday. She was going on a buying trip. I asked her to look up some suppliers for me.' The Comtesse gave Jacquot a questioning look. 'Why? What is all this about, Chief Inspector?'

'As you already know, Madame, the warehouse was destroyed. What you will not know is that Madame Bartolomé perished in that fire.'

The Comtesse took a sudden breath, shook her head. 'You can't be serious? Surely not.'

'I'm afraid there's no doubt, Madame. I am very sorry.'

'Does Guy know? Grace's husband? I must call him. Poor, poor man. He'll be devastated . . .' The Comtesse reached for the phone.

'I'm afraid, Madame, he knows already. In fact, it would appear from our enquiries that it was Monsieur Bartolomé who started the fire, and is, as far as we can establish, responsible for his wife's death.'

Hélène de Vausigne shot Jacquot a hard, disbelieving look. 'But that's ridiculous, Chief Inspector. He couldn't possibly—'

'May I ask why you say that, Madame?'

'Because he loved her, to distraction. She was the most important thing in his life. She – she – I mean, if it hadn't been for Grace . . .'

'You're referring to Monsieur Bartolomé's illness?' asked Jacquot.

'You know about that?'

'We have his records coming through. From a hospital in Grenoble.'

'That's right. He suffered a breakdown. Two, three years ago. Such a dreadful time, they had. Grace was . . . Grace brought him through it. Cared for him. There was nothing she wouldn't do for him.'

Jacquot nodded, knowing that the worst was yet to come.

There was a short silence and then the Comtesse frowned, as though she had made some connection. 'But what has all this to do with my husband? And his car?'

Jacquot took a deep breath. The moment had come.

'As I said, your husband's Citroën has been found in Rocsabin. In the warehouse car park . . . As well as Madame Bartolomé, a second victim was found. So far we have been unable to confirm identity but . . .' Jacquot paused, spread his hands. He might not like the woman but he felt a swell of sympathy for her. '. . . given the presence of your husband's car, and a set of keys to that car found on the second body, and having failed as yet to establish your husband's whereabouts, there seems a strong likelihood . . .'

The Comtesse, he could see now, knew exactly what was coming. She swallowed hard, took a breath, and, turning to the *secrétaire* let it out in a low moan that grew by degrees into a rising wail of grief.

It was then that the study door swung open and Antoine was there. In an instant he was at his mother's side, getting down on his knees to wrap her in his arms, his eyes fixing hard on Jacquot and Brunet over her heaving shoulders.

56

The moment they arrived back at Cavaillon headquarters, Jacquot asked Brunet to put a call through to Aix to confirm the Comte's hotel reservation and departure details. He had no doubt that they would tally with what the Comtesse had told them, but there was no harm in double-checking. 'And find out whether he was on his own or accompanied,' added Jacquot, heading for his office. 'Also, whatever you can get on the de Vausignes.'

He closed the door behind him, snapped down the blinds between him and the outer office and stretched out behind his desk. Feet up, ankles crossed, Jacquot cradled his head in his hands and stared at the ceiling.

Gilles de Vausigne. Dead. Murdered. The man who owned the gun that had been used to murder the Martners. The man who employed Eric Chabert. The man who was covering the boy's legal costs. And, as Jacquot had discovered the previous evening, the man whose step-brother had fallen in love with Claudine's aunt, a man who would never have been a *comte*, never have been a de Vausigne, if not for a firing squad in the car park below Jacquot's office window.

Across the road from police headquarters, the bell of Église St-Jean sounded the third quarter. Jacquot turned his head to the window and his eyes settled on the church's square tower with its side-boxing of overlapping wood slats. So many ties, he thought, so many strange, unexpected links.

But there was work to be done and, as the last note from St-Jean's belfry faded, Jacquot put aside thoughts of what might have been, could have been, swung his legs off the desk, and started up his computer. There was something he'd been meaning to do, something he wanted to check out. He pulled the keyboard towards him, typed an e-mail and, with a click of the mouse, sent it off.

Turning away from the computer he noticed the file that Brunet had brought in earlier that morning, the one on Marie-Ange Buhl, the file he hadn't bothered to look at after Brunet dropped his bombshell about the warehouse killings and the de Vausigne Citroën.

He opened it and skimmed through the first two sheets of paper, photocopied brochure details of Agence Florale, part of the FranceFleurs organisation. The third page was a copy of a fax from Boudit Frères' offices in Zürich, dated 10 March, instructing FranceFleurs to supply care to the hot-house of Josef Martner until further notice. According to FranceFleurs' records on the following page, Agence Florale had put the Dassy Nursery in Aix in charge of the doctor's hot-house. This arrangement had lasted until June when the Dassy Nursery contacted Agence Florale to say they were no longer able to do the job: the hot-house collection needed more specialised care.

Jacquot flipped to the fifth page, a copy of Mademoiselle Buhl's personnel file held by Agence Florale.

Name: Marie-Ange Buhl.

Date of Birth: 23 November 1972.

Place of Birth: Ribeauvillé, Alsace.

Educated: Salon Schongauer and Lycée Saulcy in Metz; graduated 1992 – botany – from the Fondation des Jardins des Plantes, Paris.

A small passport photo had been attached to the personnel file but the copying process had reduced it to a black blur.

On the final page there was a record of her employment with Agence Florale, a list of gardens and nurseries in different parts of the country where the agency had placed her.

In the last six months, Jacquot noted, Marie-Ange Buhl had worked in a half-dozen different locations – Alsace, Île-de-France, Brittany, Poitou-Charentes . . .

The significance of these postings was not lost on him.

57

Two days after the fire at Rocsabin, with a molten sun beating down from a cloudless blue sky and the air as dry as onion skin, Marie-Ange turned the Chaberts' delivery van off the Chant-le-Neuf road and followed the drive through pine and holm oak to the Château de Vausigne. As she coasted down the slope past the terraces of vine and fig, she saw a blue Mercedes saloon pull out of the château's forecourt and head up the drive towards her. The car, she knew, belonged to the Comtesse's son, Antoine, but Picard was at the wheel, with the Comtesse, small and diminished, huddled in the back seat. She was wearing a black veil tucked into the collar of her suit and her eyes were hidden behind large black sunglasses.

As the two cars drew closer Marie-Ange saw the Comtesse lean forward to speak to Picard and, as they came abreast, the Mercedes slowed, the driver's window slid down and Picard said would she please wait at the house until the Comtesse returned. It wouldn't be long, he assured her. An hour at most. As the Mercedes moved on, the Comtesse gave no indication that she had seen Marie-Ange and looked resolutely ahead.

Marie-Ange had been expecting the mourning black, ever since news of the Comte's death had reached St Bédard the previous day. Crossing from the *pharmacie* where he'd heard it from the Widow Blanc and Agnès Héliard, who'd heard it from the de Vausignes' maid Monique, it was old Dumé who had filled Marie-Ange in on the details: burned in that warehouse fire in Rocsabin, the clothes on his back melted on to him, all that was left of him a single shoe, this information followed up with Dumé's usual energetic throat-clearing.

And only a week or so to go before the de Vausignes' *anniversaire*, he continued. It must surely be cancelled now. Couldn't possibly go ahead in the circumstances. As for the *fête* the town council had arranged to go in tandem with the de Vausignes' private function – dancing in the *place*, an ox roast, a band from Cavaillon – well, that would surely be cancelled too. Out of respect, *n'est-ce pas*? The council members, he told her, were meeting at the *mairie* the following day to discuss the matter. And it was serious. Apparently the band had already been paid for and the ox that had been ordered through Jacques Bulot could not be unordered. Though for himself, old Dumé assured Marie-Ange, he didn't see anything remotely disrespectful. If it had been him who had died, he said, jauntily tapping his stick against his leg, he'd have loved the idea of a party – even if he couldn't be there to enjoy it.

Parking the Chabert van at the side of the château, near the basement entrance to the kitchens, Marie-Ange skipped down the steps, tapped on the door and found Florence sitting by the range, shelling peas from a trug at her feet.

The Comtesse was devastated, reported the housekeeper, as Marie-Ange helped herself to some coffee and sat down at the kitchen table. She'd taken to her bed the moment the policemen left, Florence told her. Nothing to eat, just her pills and Antoine at her side until the call from Police Headquarters that morning. According to Picard, Madame was needed in Cavaillon to identify certain items – personal belongings, most likely – found at the fire.

'First, young Eric. And now the Comte,' she said, shaking her head. 'Whatever next?'

Like Dumé the old lady was in no doubt. The party would be cancelled for sure. And then, realising what this would mean, Florence settled a sympathetic eye on Marie-Ange: 'All that work, *ma jolie*. For nothing.'

Marie-Ange sighed. All that work, preparing the decorations for the de Vausignes' party. For nothing. Florence didn't know how right she was.

Or maybe she did.

Since her initial meeting with the Comtesse, Marie-Ange had come to the château twice a week, scaffolding the ballroom with trellis-work for the weave of jonquils and honeysuckle they'd agreed on, devising floral arrangements for the marquee on the south lawn, and advising the Comtesse on decorations for the half-dozen bedrooms upstairs that had been spring-cleaned for the arrival of friends and family from the north.

Yet not a *sou* to show for it, nothing to cover the orders she'd made or the time she'd spent at the château. And as if that wasn't enough, she'd had to endure every single one of her estimates being questioned and picked over by the Comtesse as though they were targets to be shot at rather than the best quote for the work involved. If it hadn't been for the promise of extra income in the Chaberts' bank account, Marie-Ange would have told the Comtesse to look elsewhere for the displays she wanted – she'd find no better price. But Marie-Ange had said nothing, negotiating with a gentle tolerance of the older woman's bickering parsimony until they had reached an agreement that satisfied them both – just. For the Chaberts' sake.

And it wasn't only the woman's meanness that Marie-Ange had had to contend with. Whenever the Comtesse was out of the house, her husband had always contrived to be around, with his scraggy neck and gaudy cravats, following her with his greedy little eyes and always on hand to steady her ladder as she climbed up to secure the trellis-work. She might not have minded the admiring glances of the men of St Bédard, but there had always been something . . . dangerous, something . . . unsettling about the Comte's attentions.

And now it was the son she had to deal with, Antoine, down from Paris to stay through the festivities. Just as Clotilde had described him, nothing less than a younger version of the father – the wavy hair, the shiny lower lip, those same hungry eyes licking over her like a cold, wet tongue. A film producer, apparently, though no one in St Bédard could say for certain what kind of films he produced.

Marie-Ange shivered.

'Devil over your grave, *chérie*?' asked Florence, popping a pea pod and running a thumbnail down its middle. A half-dozen peas skittered into the bowl in her lap.

'Something like that,' replied Marie-Ange and, finishing her coffee, she decided that while she was waiting for the Comtesse she might as well start dismantling the decorations in the ballroom. Florence and Dumé were surely right: there'd be no party now.

Leaving the old lady to her peas, Marie-Ange climbed the kitchen stairs and pushed through the service door that led into the main house. She was half-way across the hall, heading for the ballroom, when suddenly she stopped, as though someone had caught her sleeve and pulled her to a standstill.

Normally the château's interior was cool and comfortable whatever the heat outside, kept so by metre-thick walls and flagstoned floors. But now, it seemed to Marie-Ange, the cool had sharpened to a chill, making the skin on the back of her neck pucker, and the tiny hairs on her forearms quiver like the minutest antennae.

There was something else, too, that she noticed as she stood there – a damp, cindery smell drifting in from the terrace windows, stirring the muslin drapes. She considered the possibility of a hillside fire somewhere close by. It was the season for it after all, crackling hot outside, tinder dry, with just enough breeze to fan the smallest spark. Or maybe, she thought, it was the remnants of the blaze at Rocsabin, carried across the valley by the same breeze.

But she wasn't convinced and, compelled by some impulse she couldn't quite place, Marie-Ange turned on her heel and headed for the staircase leading to the château's upper floors. With the Comtesse and Picard at Police Headquarters in Cavaillon, Florence busy with her peas in the kitchen and Antoine, according to the old housekeeper, still in his bed in the guest cottage by the pool, she had the house to herself. Although why this should be of any significance, she couldn't really say.

Yet as she climbed the wide stone sweep of stairs, Marie-Ange felt a rising certainty that something was about to happen, and she began to prepare herself for the insulating cloak of silence that preceded one of her 'moments'.

But there was nothing. No voices. No sounds. No enveloping silence or dry, dusty taste in her mouth. Just the ropey slap of her espadrilles on the stairs and the distant smell of burning to draw her on.

At the top of the staircase, Marie-Ange paused, hand resting on the banister. Here the stone gave way to wooden floorboards, wide and polished, running left and right into distant shadows. For a moment, undecided, she stood there, contemplating the narrow strip of scarlet carpet, faded to pink and foxed with patches bared to the weave, which ran down the centre of the corridor, the length of the house. To the right, she knew from her visits with the Comtesse, were six of the château's guest bedrooms, three on either side of the corridor, and to the left a suite of rooms she had not yet visited, the private quarters of the de Vausignes.

It was to these that Marie-Ange now made her way, turning down the corridor as though led by the hand, scalp prickling, skin shivering, the smell of burning stronger with every step.

58

Scratching the triangle of hair on his chest, Antoine de Vausigne stood in his boxers and peered through the windows of the guest cottage.

Beyond the reflection of his tousled hair and puffy, sleep-creased face, he watched the swallows dive at the still surface of the swimming-pool, scooping beakfuls of water and leaving only circular ripples in their wake, as though single, unseen drops of rain were falling. He yawned, rubbed his eyes, then ran his hand under the band of his shorts, tugged at his cock, loosening a wedge of pubic hair caught in his foreskin. At least the Jews had got one thing right, he thought, with a wince and a chuckle.

It might have been close to midday but the new Comte was still sleepy enough not to be able to decide whether to shower first or to swim. Hot water or cold? Thanks to his mother vetoing his suggestion for solar panels to heat the pool, an early-morning dive could still snatch the breath from your body.

Antoine turned his back on the pool and walked over to the small kitchenette, divided from the main living room by a narrow breakfast bar. While the coffee percolated he found his wallet, pulled out a fold of white paper and tipped some of its contents on to the smooth Formica top. With the base of a coffee spoon he crushed the lumpy white powder and then, with its handle, arranged the cocaine into a careless, ragged line. He picked up the same two-hundred-franc note he'd used the night before, rolled it into a tight tube, then leaned over the line about half-way along its length. Sweeping the note left and right in one practised motion, he took it up in a single snort. He'd seen Duc do it like that and he'd adopted the style as his own. Left. Right. Tip the head. Deep exhale. Ye*sssss*.

He wetted a finger, mopped up what remained of the line, then rubbed it over his gums, working the powder round with his tongue until his mouth started to tingle and fade. Oooh. Yes.

Antoine had brought the coke from Paris. He'd got it at Duc's. Trade. Four grammes in a single fold. A week later there wasn't much left. He wasn't too concerned: he could always get more in Cavaillon. Not as good, of course, but not as pricey either.

Sniffing contentedly, squeezing his eyes shut, then opening them wide, Antoine poured himself coffee and looked around the room. Furnished simply in Provençal rental style, like dozens of other *gîtes* that dotted the Luberon for people who couldn't afford anything longer than a fortnight, it felt as homely as a hotel room. His bedroom in the main house was far more comfortable but at least here he was certain of some privacy. The last time Antoine had stayed, on his way to Cannes a couple of months earlier, the old man had walked into his bedroom without so much as a tap on the door at exactly the moment that Antoine entered the willing loins of his latest star-turn. God knows how long the old man had stood there, taking in the scenery.

Now, of course, there was no old man to bother about. Burned to a crisp. Tough break. Antoine tossed back the last of his coffee and smiled fondly. The stupid, lazy fuck. He'd had it coming, of course – him and his ladyfriend. Another few years and the pair of them would have bled the family dry. Now all Antoine had to do was cope with his mother. She'd taken the news badly, far worse than Antoine had expected. Which was a bore. Things were happening in Paris and he wanted to get moving. He'd wait another week, he decided, but then he'd have to have a serious chat with her.

Pulling down his shorts and stepping out of them, Antoine wondered idly if his mother knew what the old man had been up to. His *petites affaires*, his liaisons, particularly the latest. But he thought not. Give the old boy some credit, he'd always been discreet. Opening the french windows Antoine wandered naked to the pool, squinting into the sun, still sniffing. It was surrounded by a screen of red-barked firs, and although the house was no more than a hundred metres distant there was no sign of it except the topmost tiles of one of its four towers.

As he stood there, he heard the Mercedes start up, at the front of the house. Picard taking his mother into Cavaillon. She'd called him earlier, saying the Citroën was still not back from Rocsabin and could she have Picard drive her in the Mercedes? The police, she told him, had phoned to ask if she'd come in to town, identify the old man's personal effects.

Perfect timing, thought Antoine to himself, toes curling round the paving at the edge of the pool. Perfect timing. And, holding his nose like a little boy, he pushed up and away from the side of the pool, hugged his legs to his chest and dropped like a bomb into the cold, blue water.

Forty minutes later, hair brushed, teeth cleaned, dressed in shorts and sports-shirt that Florence had provided with knife-edge creases, Antoine helped himself to the last of the cocaine. Then, hands in pockets, kicking at the pine cones that littered the path, he strode through the trees and up to the house. He was on a mission. Things to do. And now, with Maman and Picard out of the house, and old Florence hobbling around the kitchen, he had the run of the place. No time like the present, he decided, as he crossed the terrace, stepped through the french windows and headed across the hall. He'd start with those cufflinks of his father's. And that antique Zoffany silver cigarette case with the family arms.

Whistling softly, head buzzing pleasurably from the drug, Antoine climbed the stairs, turned to the left when he reached the landing and headed for his parents' apartments. Which was when he noticed something out of place, the white mucus thickening at the back of his nostrils suddenly cut through with a sweet, sharp scent he didn't recognise. Certainly not his mother's. She wore Arpège in the evening and Dior during the day. He knew that well enough, bought her the requisite bottles every birthday and Christmas.

No, Antoine decided, this was a different scent altogether. Younger, fresher . . . some kind of flower, he thought, following it down the corridor. Monique, perhaps, on her rounds? Was this one of her days at the château? He couldn't remember. Beautiful eyes she had, and gorgeous hair. But those teeth of hers, and those tiny, itsy breasts . . .

The door to his parents' suite was open and Antoine pushed through into the small salon they shared. From here, two doors led to his parents' private quarters, their separate bedrooms and bathrooms. He was about to head for his father's door when he heard the tell-tale creak of the old *armoire* in his mother's bedroom. He stiffened, senses alert.

Easing off his shoes he stole across the salon and peered through the gap between door and frame, wide as its ancient hinges. At first he could see nothing, but as the *armoire* door continued to swing open he saw a woman bending down to sort through his mother's things.

He couldn't see the cap of black hair, but the long brown legs and the floral print dress were immediately familiar. Not Monique this, but the town florist who'd been working in the ballroom.

But what on earth was she doing up here, going through his mother's wardrobe? Looking for money? Something to steal? Who cared? She wouldn't find anything. He'd tried the same thing himself, a hundred times, feeling through his parents' pockets, but never a *sou*.

Taking care not to touch the door – as notorious a squeaker as the *armoire* – Antoine crept round it and into his mother's bedroom, expecting the girl to turn, suddenly aware there was someone in the room with her, caught in the act.

But she didn't. Instead she stood up from the drawers, still with her back to him, and slid her hand through the rail of coat-hangers, one outfit after another.

Astonished he'd got so close without being detected and enjoying the thrill of being there without her knowing it, Antoine sat quietly on the edge of his mother's bed and watched the way the girl's body moved through the thin material of her dress.

59

Marie-Ange was puzzled. The silence she'd been expecting, the distant sounds and voices, had failed to materialise. Even the puckering chill and scent of burning had faded. Yet here she was in the de Vausignes' private quarters with no real idea why she was there. Was it something to do with Eric? Something to do with the Martner murders? The death of the Comte? Or something else altogether?

For a moment she was tempted to go back the way she had come, down to the ballroom and the trellising. But something held her there, a sense that she was where she was supposed to be. It was, she realised, the same feeling she had had when she made her way to that street in Metz after reading about the woman's 'suicide'.

Standing in the salon, Marie-Ange cast about for inspiration. A chintz-covered sofa, a pair of sagging armchairs, a compact TV and video combination in the corner. A twin-bar electric fire in the grate, dwarfed by its massive marble surround. Ornaments on the mantel. A few crusty-framed prints of country views. Books on the coffee-table. But no drawers, no cupboards that she could see. Nothing closed, nothing hidden away. No clue to explain why she'd been drawn there.

Two doors led off the salon, both closed. Without thinking, Marie-Ange opened the first and stepped into a bedroom. It had clearly belonged to the Comte – the lemony scent of aftershave, a pair of pyjamas neatly folded on a single bed, a line of shoes beneath a chest of drawers, prints of sailing boats, and a gorgeous seascape in oils above the fireplace. Pulling open the drawers in the chest, Marie-Ange shifted through balled socks and cotton underwear, piles of neatly-folded shirts, cashmere sweaters, silk cravats, embroidered waistcoats, cummerbunds and ties. But whatever it was she was searching for, it eluded her. This was not the place. Instead she crossed to the Comtesse's bedroom, opening the door with a soft click and healthy squeak, letting loose a swarm of scents – lotions and potions and the warm, musty lingerings of sleep.

Like the Comte's room, the bedroom was large and brightly sunlit, occupying a corner of the château at the front of the house where one of its four turrets provided a semi-circular canopied space in which she'd set her dressing-table. The windows to either side of this turret had been thrown open, looking out over the gravelled courtyard and rising terraces.

Marie-Ange went to the dressing-table and slid out its tiny drawers, a nest of three set at either side of a shield-shaped mirror. The ones on the left were filled with hairpins and clips, corn plasters and pads, rolls of crêpe bandaging, tubes and tongs; the ones on the right with a tangle of brooches, pearls and pins – the day-to-day *batterie de la boudoir* for a woman intent on her appearance.

For an instant Marie-Ange felt guilty, uncomfortable, at this intimate intrusion. And then, the next moment, ridiculously exposed, vulnerable. What on earth was she doing, she thought, prying through the Comtesse's bedroom like a common criminal? What on earth had possessed her? If someone should catch her . . .

But if she couldn't explain it, neither could she resist it, the lure to go on, to be there, waiting for something to happen. Whatever it might be.

Comforting herself that she would hear the Mercedes returning from Cavaillon, and have easily enough time to get back downstairs before the Comtesse reached the front door, Marie-Ange moved from the dressing-table to the bed, a wide *bateau lit* covered with a quilted, pink satin counterpane. On each side stood a delicate empire chest on curled, spindly legs, each with a matching lamp and frilled shade, each with a single drawer and small cupboard.

It was easy to tell which side of the bed Madame la Comtesse slept on. The left-hand chest had a small alarm clock set for six, a pot of moisturiser, a book and a small carafe filled with water, a matching glass set over its top like a stopper. Marie-Ange picked up the book and read the words on the spine – a biography of Napoleon by Edmond Lévy. She flicked through the pages. Tiny print, endless asterisks and copious, scholarly footnotes. Judging by the position of the bookmark – only fifteen pages in – either the Comtesse had just started reading or was finding it heavy going.

Marie-Ange replaced the book exactly as she had found it, then searched through the bedside table's drawer and cupboard, both equipped with tiny keys but both unlocked. Finding nothing of interest she went round to the other side of the bed and did the same.

Or tried to. On this side, both drawer and cupboard were locked. Marie-Ange went back to the first table and pulled out the two keys. It was a long shot, she knew, but it might work. And it did: both bedside chests shared the same keys. A true pair. With a tiny click, the drawer lock gave and she slid it open.

At first it looked empty, nothing but a few hairpins and a worn emery board. Then, peering down its length, she noticed a narrow rectangle of white with some writing on it. She slid it towards her, picked it up and read the script:

'AV et PR, Rocsabin. Célébrations Noël, décembre 1937.'

Turning it over she saw it was a photo, a still-glossy black-and-white snapshot of a young man and an older man standing together by a fireplace. Behind their heads, strung across the length of a stone mantelpiece, was a wreath of Christmas pine.

The younger man looked to be in his early twenties, eyes twinkling with merriment, mouth curled into a grin, a hand pushing back a fall of wavy blond hair. He had, Marie-Ange decided, that eager, expectant expression you have when you begin to understand what the world has to offer.

Marie-Ange turned her attention to the older man. Without a doubt he was the Comtesse's father – the same thin lips, black eyes and that certain haughty set to the chin and eyebrows. With the red of his cheeks a shade of grey in the photo and a well-upholstered stomach stretching the buttons of his waistcoat, his thumbs pressed into its tiny pockets, he looked as if he might have been a jovial sort of a fellow. But in that instant of the flash he looked anything but jovial: there was something uncertain about the line of his mouth, something anxious at the back of his eyes, as though he were somehow uncomfortable with his young companion. It was as if the two men had just reached some kind of agreement and the older man wasn't certain he liked the terms.

Marie-Ange put the photo back as she had found it, slid the drawer closed and relocked it. Then, settling in front of the cupboard, she fitted the second key into the lock and turned it. As with the drawer above, the lock gave and, with a thin, resisting squeak, the door opened.

Inside was a stack of ledgers, leather-spined, cloth-covered, one atop another. But what caught Marie-Ange's attention was a brown envelope wedged between the ledgers and the side of the cupboard. The flap had not been sealed, which meant that the contents were clearly visible. And immediately recognisable. A meaty wad of emerald green and the engraved head of Marie Curie. Creased, dirty but unmistakable. Five hundred-franc notes. A thick bundle bound at either end with rubber bands. She lifted the envelope, felt the weight. Fifty thousand, she estimated. Easily. Maybe more. For someone who quibbled over a few hundred francs it was an astonishing amount of cash to stuff into an envelope and keep in a bedside cupboard.

Tight-fisted old carrion, thought Marie-Ange, resisting the temptation to slip out a few notes to cover her costs. Instead, carefully, she replaced the envelope, locked the cupboard and put the keys back where she'd found them.

Which was when a bird, perched on a windowsill overlooking the side of the house, suddenly took flight, chattering away into the trees. Marie-Ange's heart lurched and her legs turned to water. If she'd been watching a scene like this in the movies, she'd be saying, 'Get out of there! Now! While you still can!'

But she didn't. She bottled up her fear, screwed down the lid and continued her search, riffling through a chest of drawers that matched exactly the one in the Comte's bedroom. Again nothing. Which left only a tall, panelled *armoire*. With a volley of heart-rending squeaks, she eased open the door and looked inside. Above

Martin O'Brien

her, the top shelf was packed with hatboxes. Beneath this, a single rail held a selection of clothing – jackets, suits, dresses, blouses, slacks – and at knee level another shelf and a pair of deep drawers. Tipping the hatboxes to gauge their weight and quickly discounting them, she ran her eyes along the line of clothes, all sleeves and shoulders, blues, greys and browns, then bent down, pushing aside the clothes to see into the *armoire*'s depths.

It was at exactly that moment, when both her arms were deep in one of the drawers, that a pair of hands grabbed her round the waist, dragged her away from the *armoire* and heaved her backwards.

Frantically she tried to pull free, twisting and turning, reaching behind her for something to get at. But she was held too tightly, one of her assailant's hands now reaching up to cup a breast, fingers spreading around it. And, unbelievably, laughter, as though this was some kind of game.

Desperately now, unable to believe what was happening, she pulled at the hand on her breast, trying to lever it away, only to have the other hand reach down, slide between her legs, hoisting her back to where she knew the bed stood.

With a supreme effort Marie-Ange jerked her hips to one side trying to face her attacker, squirming away from the hand on her breast and the fingers between her thighs, feeling as she did so a familiar stiffness press against her hip. But it was too late. Half turned in an attempt to beat off her assailant, she lost her balance, felt her feet leave the floor and the two of them fell back on to the bed.

From beneath her the laughter was cut short by a winded '*ouuff*' and the hands released her. Taking advantage of the spring in the mattress, Marie-Ange leaped away, panting, hair swinging across her face, and spun round to confront her attacker.

'What the hell do you think you're doing?' she screamed, in a breathless whisper, her face red with fury, fists clenched.

On the bed Antoine pushed himself up on an elbow. His lips were wet, his shorts removed, his cock waving stiffly. He grabbed it in a fist and shook it at her, chuckling lightly.

She glanced down and saw she was standing on his shorts. She took a step back.

'And what the hell, *exactly*,' replied Antoine, shifting his elbows and now stroking himself with the backs of his fingers, 'do you think you're doing, Mam'selle? Sneaking around in my mother's—'

Which was the moment, somewhere beneath them, that a door, caught in a breeze, slammed shut and a voice floated up to them.

'Marie-Ange? *Où es-tu*, Marie-Ange?'

It was Florence.

'*J'ai préparé un déjeuner*. Some soup. Come quick.'

Which was just what Marie-Ange did.

60

Jacquot watched Hélène de Vausigne's blue Mercedes draw away from the steps of the Cavaillon *gendarmerie* and head for the entrance to the courtyard. A moment later it dropped down the ramp opposite Église St-Jean, turned into traffic and was gone. He loosened his tie and breathed a sigh of relief.

It had been a gruelling encounter. In a small, windowless room next to the property office, he'd watched the Comtesse identify her late husband's belongings. Hands shaking, she'd reached for the sealed plastic bags that Mougeon placed in front of her, taken one by one from a cardboard box on the table. It wasn't much. A metal comb, a strapless watch, a signet ring, a set of keys, the charred remains of a wallet.

After the first positive identification – the Comte's watch – she could have stopped, not bothered with the rest. But she didn't. She carried on, as though keen to see and hold each object, turning them in the light, feeling them through the plastic. And all the time she said nothing, just nodded to signify recognition before she reached for the next bag.

When it was over Jacquot pulled back her chair and helped her to her feet, offering his condolences. She'd thanked him, tried a brave smile, but then turned away quickly, busying herself with her sunglasses and veil. When she turned back she'd regained her composure, her mouth grim and tight. Jacquot might not like the woman but he felt for her in her loss, wondering whether she'd gone far enough through her grief to give any thought as to what her husband might have been doing in that furniture warehouse with an attractive fifty-year-old woman so late at night.

Five minutes after Picard had settled the Comtesse in the back of the Mercedes and driven off, Jacquot stepped from the lift and headed down the corridor to his office. The phone began to ring the moment he reached his desk.

'You have mail.' The clipped tones from a thousand miles north were unmistakable. Jacquot couldn't help smiling at the familiar voice. He pulled out his chair and turned to his computer screen. The envelope icon in the top right-hand corner was blinking.

'I have indeed,' he said, opening the file, scrolling through it. 'Thanks, Hans. I'm very grateful.'

'So you still haven't given it up, Dan?'

'They reckon another week or so for the trial. So, still time,' replied Jacquot, setting the file to print.

'And then?'

'If the ball comes your way, you play it,' he said.

'And has it?'

Jacquot shrugged, as though Dietering were in the room to see it. 'Not so far, it hasn't. But you never know,' he replied, watching the pages spill out of the printer. 'Anything interesting. About the Martners? Anything you found?'

Brunet came round the door, dropped a file on to his desk and returned to his office. Jacquot pulled it towards him. The name 'de Vausigne' was scrawled across its cover

'Since I'm not sure what you are looking for, it's difficult to say,' replied Dietering, 'but I did what you asked. Every obituary I could find. German and Swiss.'

A few minutes later, after they'd said their farewells and hung up, Jacquot scooped up the pages from the printer, picked up the file Brunet had brought him and went through to the outer office.

'I'll be gone for an hour or two. Back by three latest.'

Brunet glanced up and nodded. 'Anything you need?'

'Spare file for this?' Jacquot held up the sheaf of print-out.

Brunet pulled one from a drawer and handed it over. 'Anything else?'

Yes, thought Jacquot, there was something else, but in this particular instance Brunet wouldn't be able to help. What he needed was space to think, somewhere without the blare of phones, the constant interruptions. 'Nothing, thanks,' he replied and, swinging his jacket over his shoulder, he headed for the door.

There was only one place he knew.

61

Passage Cabassole was a brisk seven-minute walk from Jacquot's office, an unremarkable alley-way off Cavaillon's main square, a canyon of tall, tilting buildings rising to a band of blue sky, so close at the top that, leaning out of a window on one side, it seemed quite conceivable you could touch the fingers, even clasp the hands of someone leaning out from the other side.

Low doors furnished with brass knockers led into these narrow, teetering houses, and lace-covered windows concealed their shadowy interiors from the cobbled passageway that ran between them. Most of the houses on Cabassole were private residences. The exceptions were an antiquarian bookseller, a carpenter's work-shop that filled the passageway with the scent of freshly sawn wood and, half-way down the alley, on the left-hand side, Jacquot's favourite restaurant. A sign above the door proclaimed three simple words – Brasserie Chez Gaillard. Jacquot passed beneath it and pushed through the door.

'Monsieur Jacquot. A pleasure, *comme toujours*,' said the brasserie's owner Laurent Gaillard, darting forward from the bar when he saw who it was, busily shaking his hand, drawing him in as he did so. 'Come in. Come in. A little lunch?'

'Afternoon, Laurent. No lunch today but a small table if you have one. And a *café-calva* to clear the head.'

'Of course – please,' replied Laurent, leading Jacquot through the bar and into a restaurant humming with chat and the clink of glass, china and cutlery.

The room was low and long, closely beamed, the floor stone-flagged with a dozen tables crowded into a space not big enough for ten. In the middle of the room Laurent's daughter, Suzi, was taking an order. She gave Jacquot a swift nod and a knowing smile, a smile that told Jacquot there was no need to be concerned or embarrassed on her behalf, a smile that said, 'I can handle that tomcat of yours.' And as Jacquot nodded back, smiled, passed by, he knew she could. A tough, wiry young woman who looked like she'd have Brunet dancing to her tune whenever it pleased her. Maybe this time Brunet had met his match.

'How's the family?' asked Jacquot, as Laurent steered him to a corner table in the back. Four months earlier he, Claudine and Dietering had taken the same table on Dietering's last night in Cavaillon.

'Oh, fine, just fine,' said Laurent, glancing up at the portrait gallery of Gaillard *patrons* who'd run this brasserie before him 'Although the old man gets more curmudgeonly by the day. It takes all our wits to keep him out of the kitchen. That, and a sharp knife.' Laurent laughed and pulled out a chair for Jacquot. 'Old men, eh? Who'd want to be one? And who'd want to live with one? Please, Monsieur, make yourself at home. *Café-calva, toute suite.'*

While Laurent hurried away to prepare the coffee and Calvados, Jacquot made himself comfortable, shrugging off his jacket and re-arranging the tabletop to make room for his two files. His office outside his office, thought Jacquot contentedly. He pulled up his chair, rested his forearms on the table and opened the first file, the one from Dietering.

There were more than a dozen pages in all, a raft of obituaries for Josef Martner, Jutta Martner and their daughter Ilse, taken from both German and Swiss publications, everything from the *Frankfurter Allgemeine Zeitung* and the *Hamburger Abendblatt* to the *Neue Zurcher Zeitung* and *Die Welt*. Not surprisingly, the majority of obituaries were devoted to Dr Martner and his work with orchids, and only a few to his wife and daughter.

Obituaries, thought Jacquot, nodding his thanks as Laurent put down a double espresso and a vast *balon* of Calvados. Such a mine of information. And someone else did all the work for you, found all those interesting little snippets that, more often than not, a police inquiry failed to uncover.

There was only one problem. As he leafed through the pile, Jacquot soon discovered that every single obituary was written in German. It was only when he reached the last three pages that his spirits lifted, a typewritten report from Dietering, God bless him, and in passable French as well:

Dear Dan

As requested every obituary I could lay my hands on. Most, as you will see, are for the good doctor, but his wife and daughter also feature. Much of it will be familiar, old ground we went over in February, and in case your German isn't up to it (?!) I give you a short précis.

Martner, Josef, only child of Hilde and Gerhardt Martner. Father in the shipping business – mercantile insurance – mother did not work. Although Martner's birth certificate says Hamburg, he was actually born in the family home at Quickborn, now about twenty minutes from the city – longer then. Attended all the right schools, did passably well, and in 1939 started a medical internship at Heidelberg University. Half-way through the course his father died and Martner switched to dentistry. And got called up. Expecting to find himself on the Russian front like most of the call-ups at that time – this was 1942, remember – he was seconded to the Abwehr in your newly occupied Southern Zone, France. As a medical orderly, no less. And a long way from any action.

According to Die Welt, *he was posted first to Toulouse and then – you will like this, Dan – to Cavaillon. Small world – hah?*

Jacquot felt a sudden twist of excitement. Posted to Cavaillon. A small world indeed. Without him noticing, Laurent reappeared with fresh coffee and more *calva*.

Jacquot read on:

Martin O'Brien

It was in Cavaillon that Martner ended his war, captured by the Allies, August 1944. Imprisoned Aix-Luynes for eighteen months, released without charge and repatriated.

So much for the blameless. Now for the fortunate.

Two years after returning to Germany, Martner completed his internship, got his licence to practise dentistry and, in 1949, married the only child of widower Ludwig von Diepenbroek. As we know, Diepenbroek was a very big name. Minister for internal reconstruction after the war, rising to second secretary – a little like your deputy prime minister – during the Adenauer years. Like Adenauer, von Diepenbroek was a Christian Democrat, and like Adenauer was imprisoned in the late thirties for his opposition to Hitler's Nazis.

According to the wife's obituary in Neue Zürcher Zeitung, *this thing between her and Martner was a real love-conquers-all affair. Aristocratic Prussian family and solid, middle-class bourgeoisie. Doomed to fail. But despite the odds it worked. Seven years later, old von Diepenbroek died and Jutta inherited over two million Deutschmarks in today's currency. Less than six months later, Martner's mother died and left him the family home in Quickborn.*

Dentistry, not surprisingly, was ditched. They sold the house in Hamburg and started travelling – all tropical destinations: the Far East particularly, but also South and Central America. Anything up to six months away. Purpose of travel? Well, we know that, don't we? Botanical expeditions. A shared passion, apparently.

Before CITES and the endangered-species list made a collector's life miserable, the Martners brought back some amazing orchids and he made a name for himself contributing to some serious scholarly journals. I've listed the main ones on page nine. Quite the expert, as we already know.

By the end of the seventies, however, the Martners tired of travelling and settled full-time in Germany. Or maybe they don't tire, exactly. As we already know from their tax submissions, their original capital had decreased dramatically – inflation, one or two bad investments – and it's clear they had to rein in. But the new Germany no longer seemed to

*their liking. As we know they moved to Paris, and then, in
1987, they went south. We know the rest.*

*All this tells us is that Dr Martner came from a comfortable
family background, was well educated and enjoyed an easy
war helping you French with your dental hygiene. After the
war he married well, paid his taxes and kept himself to himself.
No criminal record, not even points on his driving licence.*

*It's much the same story with Jutta. Old family
background, average at school, marries not well as far as
her old man's concerned, but he comes round. From all
accounts she appears to have been happy, lived well, travelled.
She also did some writing – for magazines, 'Postcard from . . .'
that kind of format. And all good publications, though not in
the same league as her husband.*

*As for their daughter, Ilse . . . likewise, clean as a whistle.
Well educated, boarding-schools in Switzerland while the
parents travelled. Worked for Bertelsmann, the German
publisher, after graduation and was highly regarded. Met
Gunther Brauer, son of Helmut Brauer, the Swiss finance
minister, on a skiing holiday in Zermatt. They married in
Zurich. Lakeside. Big ceremony. Very powerful names. Old
and new. Diepenbroeks, Brauers. Ludwig would have
approved.*

*As for Kippi, not surprisingly there are only small
mentions, nothing beyond being related to the Martners, the
granddaughter of von Diepenbroek and Brauer. Suspecting
you might want more than that, I contacted a colleague in
Zürich and he made some enquiries. From what he tells me,
she was clearly a handful. Expelled from two schools for
disruptive behaviour. A caution from Zürich Police, drunk
and disorderly. Six months later, arrested for possession.
Marijuana. Held overnight, remanded into care of mother
the following day, case dismissed. And she's only sixteen.*

*So, that's it. I'm sorry if there's too much repetition – what
we already know. But maybe these few extra details will help.*

If you need anything else, call.

TschüB,

Hans

62

Jacquot finished the last of his coffee and took a gulp of the *calva*, flicking back through the file, looking for anything that might catch his eye, quietly giving thanks for Dietering. Without his colleague's covering report, he'd have been wading through this for days.

Jacquot was also grateful for the way Dietering saw it. Now that *was* interesting. 'Blameless'. 'Fortunate'.

After he had read through the report, those were the two words that stayed in Jacquot's head. The second was certainly true – a safe and spoiled middle-class upbringing, a secure war and an advantageous marriage. But Jacquot wasn't so sure about the first. Blameless. Blameless. Blameless. No, it couldn't be. Couldn't be. There was something there, something in his past – maybe in Toulouse, or here in Cavaillon – that they didn't know about, a connection they hadn't found, Jacquot was sure of it.

'Another *café*, Monsieur?' Laurent was at his side. 'Another *calva*?'

Jacquot gazed at him, as though he were trying to place him. And then: 'How many of these have you given me, Laurent?'

'It will be the third, Monsieur.' And then, with a smile: 'But only the first was given, on the house.'

Jacquot glanced at his watch. 'No *café*. Maybe later,' he said. 'Is it too late for a little lunch?'

'First you say no, and now you say yes?'

'Can't a customer change his mind?' countered Jacquot, with a grin.

'*Jarré?*'

'If you have it.'

Laurent sniffed, gave him a we'll-hunt-around-see-if-we-can't-find-you-something look, and was gone. Jacquot knew better than to ask about wine: seconds later Laurent was back with a *pichet* of his favourite Côte d'Or, tipping it into a glass.

As Jacquot pushed aside his files, reset the table and tasted the wine, he looked around him, nothing obtrusive, just the way you do when you eat alone, taking it all in: local businesspeople who knew the Gaillards kept a good table, housewives leaning close over their coffee and petits-fours to exchange gossip, and a sprinkling of tourists, camera bags at their feet and guidebooks by their elbows, a chatter of German, Dutch and English, a sense of delight at having found such a marvellous little place.

'Ah, Monsieur Jacquot,' said Marthe Gaillard, Laurent's wife and Suzi's mother, a large tureen clasped to her bosom, bending her knees to plant a kiss on his cheek. 'And how are you?' she asked, ladling the soup into his plate. 'And Claudine?'

Jacquot made all the right noises as Madame Gaillard filled his bowl and set the tureen on the table: '*Et voilà.* You help yourself, yes? *Et bon appetit.*' And she was gone.

Bread roll broken, glass refilled, spoon in hand, the meal began.

If you'd asked Jacquot after lunch what he'd eaten, he'd have probably remembered. Because you didn't easily forget a Gaillard meal. But as he ate it – the *soupe au potiron*, the *jarré*, a *salade frisée*, some cheese, a slice of pear, more coffee, another Calvados, older this time – he tasted nothing.

All he could think of was Martner, tracing in his mind the man's life, from a cradle in Hamburg to a deathbed in St Bédard. He followed the path, so far as he was able, recalling the photographs from the Martner house that they'd copied for their files – the grainy picture of a lanky child on a chill, hair-whipping beach with his mother; a studio portrait of an earnest teenage student; a beaming twenty-nine-year-old with his bride; a proud father with his daughter; a fifty-year-old academic at his desk, glasses in hand, weightier now in the face; and, most recently, the gentle, doting grandfather.

He'd have made a good dentist, thought Jacquot. He looked kind, caring, considerate. Sleepy blue eyes, few wrinkles, thinning white hair at the end. And good teeth, of course. An easy smile.

And, save just the one detail, absolutely no pattern to the man's life that Jacquot could detect beyond the normal formalities of growing older – childhood, schooling, marriage, fatherhood, retirement, grandfatherhood.

Save that one small detail, that single repetition – the only thing out of place.

In 1943, after a brief stay in Toulouse, Josef Martner finds himself stationed in Cavaillon.

And nearly fifty years later Josef Martner comes back.

A childhood home Jacquot could understand, a pleasant place to play out one's final years. But choosing somewhere you've spent two years of your life as part of an occupying army? Even if it was in Provence.

That was what surprised Jacquot.

Oh, it was done, of course. There were enough Germans of a certain age living in these hills to prove it. Big-bellied, brash. Even in Marseilles Jacquot had marvelled at their insensitivity, their boldness: the way they strutted into restaurants, the way they counted their change, squared their shoulders and lifted their chins as though somehow superior to those around them.

And there were still so many *vieux français* left who remembered. Maybe, thought Jacquot idly, enough still around for someone to take their revenge, to settle accounts.

Then, of course, there was the money. Always the money. By 1987, the year they had come south, it was clear there were problems in the Martner household. As Dietering had said, interest on their capital had dwindled to maybe three hundred thousand francs a year, after tax. Hardly the kind of money to subsidise the extravagant lifestyle they were used to but, with the land and property in Provence covered by the sale of their home in Paris and enough left over to fix the place up, there remained just about enough to live carefully.

Yet from the moment Martner arrived in Provence, his fortunes had turned. There might not have been much in the bank but he and his wife had lived well, even if they didn't have to worry about their daughter. She'd married one of the richest families on the Zürichsee, so no problems there.

But how, thought Jacquot, had they done it? How had the good doctor been able to underwrite his abiding passion – his orchids and his hot-house? And the travel? During their last four years in Hamburg and three years in Paris they hadn't taken a single trip. Yet two years after arriving in Provence, they'd started again – Belize, Honduras and Guatemala, all in the space of eighteen months. So where had the money come from? For the hot-house, for the supplies, for the travelling? Even the Martners' BMW. It might have been second-hand but it was still worth a substantial amount. And nowhere any record of withdrawals to account for it. Everything paid for in cash.

Cash. Cash. Cash. And over the years a lot of it.

Which was why, Jacquot was now certain, someone had decided to kill them. Not this unrequited-love twaddle they'd used to put the kid Chabert in the dock. No, no, no. This was much more than that. This was all about money. A lot of money. Cold, hard cash. You could twist Jacquot's arm till it came off at the shoulder, but he wouldn't change his mind on that score.

But where was the link? thought Jacquot, knotting his brow. What was the story? Where had the money come from?

The war?

Martner's time in Toulouse? In Cavaillon?

Something he'd done? People he knew? People he'd met back then?

Or could it have been something to do with the wife? Jutta. Maybe it was her, not her husband. Maybe they'd been looking in the wrong place.

Jacquot groaned.

And then: 'A grand family once,' came a voice beside him, all gravel in mucus. 'A sham now.'

Jacquot looked up. It was old man Gaillard, Laurent's father, a halo of white hair, purple nose and ponderous jowls, as solemn and disapproving as his portrait on the wall. His pouchy, red-rimmed eyes were fixed on the table, on the second of Jacquot's two files.

'The de Vausignes,' he continued, gesturing at the name with the handle of his stick. 'I knew the old Comte, Edouard. Came here, you know. Oh, yes.' Grandpère Gaillard nodded. 'Fine man, *le tout gratin*, you could say. Real upper class – *ancien*. Noble. And his son, Albert. I knew him too. One of the first to fight back, you understand my meaning? *Un homme de la première heure.*'

'I didn't know that, M'sieur,' Jacquot lied smoothly, sitting back to show he was ready for a chat, happy to hear anything the old man had to say, but knowing there was little point in inviting him to sit. Jacquot knew he wouldn't. He'd offered a chair just the one time, when he was roundly informed why such a thing could not be. Jacquot was a guest, the Gaillards his hosts. It would never do to mix the two.

'*Beh oui*,' continued old Gaillard. 'No one like him. Some of the things it turned out he did! And we never knew,' he said. 'Like a shadow he was. You'd never have guessed. Until they caught him. Three weeks with *la Gestapo*.' Gaillard shook his head and turned down his lip. 'You could always tell them by their green fedoras,' the old fellow mused. '*La Gestapo*, that is. Did you know that?'

Jacquot shook his head.

'Always very fond of green fedoras they were. Never liked them myself. Fedoras. Head's too big.' He chuckled.

'So what happened? To Albert? The Gestapo?' asked Jacquot, knowing the answer but bringing the old man back on track.

'*La Gestapo?* Shot him, of course. That was when we found out. Heard the stories. Set up, he was. So they say. Some action out on the Brieuc road. A few months later and the Americans were here. *Fini*. All over.'

'Set up?'

'There were rumours. Only rumours. It was a time for that then. But no one knew for sure.'

'What about you? What do you think?'

The old man shook his head. 'You're too young to remember, Monsieur. Back then, towards the end of the war, things happened it's best to forget. Even though, sometimes, it is hard to do,' he added, casting a disapproving glance in the direction of the German table.

'Albert was married, wasn't he?' lied Jacquot again, knowing full well that he hadn't been.

'Albert de Vausigne? *Non, non*, M'sieur! You are mistaken. *Absolument pas!*' The old man shook his head vehemently, but then a twinkle lit his eye as though some memory had come fleeting back from nowhere, unbidden, unexpected. But pleasurable all the same.

Jacquot saw it and waited.

'There was one, though. One woman. Blonde. Oh, a beauty, you wouldn't believe.'

Claudine's aunt, Jacquot wanted to say. But he kept silent.

'They were always together, came here a few times. I think her name was . . .'

Sandrine, thought Jacquot. Sandrine Eddé. Or maybe Rose. Rose Valence.

The old man looked at the floor, brows furrowed, wrestling with the handle of his stick. 'No, it's gone. Like so much else, M'sieur, eh?' And he chuckled again.

Jacquot nodded and smiled.

'Anyway,' Gaillard continued, 'they were tight. You could see it. Which didn't please everyone, I can tell you.' He nodded at the file again, as though the answer lay between its buff covers.

Jacquot was caught on the hop. 'Albert's father? He didn't approve?'

'*Non, non, non*, M'sieur. The Comtesse. The one now. Set her sights on Albert the day they met, so they say. Never anyone else but him. Thought she had a chance. *Bouff*, some chance! But it's only when that blonde turns up, she sees her goose is cooked. The writing on the wall, *hein*? And then, what do you know? Albert's dead and she's married the step-brother, half-brother . . . whatever . . .'

'Gilles de Vausigne?'

'That's him. That's the one.' Gaillard sniffed. 'Got what she wanted in the end.'

'Got what she wanted?'

The old man looked at Jacquot as though the answer was plain to see. 'Why, the title, of course. What else? At Rocsabin they had the land, at St Bédard they had the title. She might not have got the man she wanted, but at least she got the title.'

Old Gaillard paused, scratched at a dribble of white spittle that had dried at the corner of his mouth. 'Course they've frittered it away – sold off the land, here, there – until there's pretty much nothing left. A few hectares, maybe. And the son? *Bouff*. Low class. With pretensions. Not the true *gratin*, not by a very long chalk.'

The old man gave Jacquot another look as if to say, 'I know you know what I'm saying here.'

But Jacquot wasn't listening any more. He was leafing through the file that Brunet had given him. Somehow he sensed he'd stumbled on something, a piece in the jigsaw puzzle there wasn't even space for.

The name, the name, the name.

And there it was. The second page.

Rocsabin.

Hélène de Vausigne, née Rocsabin.

63

Marie-Ange lay still in Eric's bath, the twin islands of her knees all that showed above a blanket of *bain moussant*. But Marie-Ange knew what lay beneath, out of sight. The scarlet, pinching tracks of that pig Antoine's fingers on her breast, her hip and between her thighs, and the dull red rash at the side of her neck where his bristly mouth had rubbed against her skin. She'd run the water as hot as she could bear, misting the panes of the window beside the bath and the mirror above the wash-basin. But still she shivered.

She'd known there'd be marks on her body, felt them beneath her dress as she'd sat at the kitchen table with Florence, breathless from her rush down the stairs, hand trembling as she lifted the soup spoon to her mouth, voice unsteady when she tried to speak, as though his fingers were still there, hot and coarse, reaching for her.

But it was only later, in Eric's bedroom, standing naked in front of his mirror, that she'd seen them, examined the damage. She was startled by how bright and livid they still were, like red worms branded on her tenderest places, and she shuddered as she traced with her fingertips the paths they'd left across her skin.

Loathsome, loathsome, loathsome, she thought.

Even if he had caught her snooping.

Even if she had had no good reason to be in the Comtesse's bedroom.

So what?

He had no right, no right whatsoever . . . How dare he? How *dare* he?

Lying back, the sweat standing out on her brow, her limbs humming with the heat, what concerned her now was not that Antoine would tell his mother what he had found her doing, but that he would use it against her, threaten her with exposure to have what he so clearly wanted. That was the kind of man he was – that was what he was probably planning, she decided. She would have to watch her step when she visited the château, stay out of his way if she wanted to avoid a repeat performance. Lying there, she wished now that she hadn't run, that she'd gone for him, hit him, punched him, torn him limb from limb, ripped his wrinkled little *couilles* from his sad, winded little body . . . done him some horrible, horrible kind of damage. Bastard, bastard, *bastard*. If she'd had a knife, a gun . . . well, he'd have been dead meat. *Dead* meat.

How she'd got through the afternoon, she couldn't imagine. How she finished her soup and bread, how she managed the chit-chat with Florence, she'd never know.

And then, just when she'd decided to make a run for it, get out of the house and back to St Bédard, they'd heard the Mercedes pull into the courtyard, the sound of Picard's boots on the steps down to the kitchen and the information that the Comtesse was waiting for her in the ballroom.

Which was where, creeping across the hallway, on the look-out for Antoine, Marie-Ange had found her.

'I regret, Mademoiselle Buhl, that we must forgo our planned festivities,' the Comtesse had told her, looking at the trellised walls of the ballroom, confirming Dumé's earlier speculation. And then, with steel in her voice: 'It's the Comte's funeral we have to arrange now,' she continued, unbuttoning her coat and passing it to Marie-Ange. 'And as usual there's a great deal to do and very little time. I'll help, if you don't mind. Best to stay busy. It'll keep my mind off things.'

For the rest of that afternoon, the two of them had dismantled the flower frames that Marie-Ange had erected, so much quicker to take down than they had been to put up. And, but for a few directions, the whole job was done in silence.

And not once had Antoine made an appearance.

Light-headed from the heat of the water, Marie-Ange heaved herself from the bath, wrapped herself in a towel and went to her room to dress, a pair of jeans and a rollneck sweater high enough in the collar to cover the red rash on her neck. Afterwards she went to the kitchen, thinking to eat, but decided she wasn't hungry. Instead she curled herself up in Monsieur Chabert's chair in the parlour and watched TV.

Remote in hand she flicked through the options – news, a chat show, a game show, a football match – settling for the last half of the film *Léon*. She'd seen it before, knew the end. But it didn't seem to matter. It would take her mind off her horrible day, and that horrible, horrible man.

The next thing she knew the film was over. Another football match. She'd dozed off, and it took her a few moments to remember where she was and what she'd gone to sleep thinking about.

She frowned.

Marie-Ange's eyes strayed to the screen. The referee in his black strip. Whistle in hand. Looking at his watch. The end of the match? she wondered. And then – the watch, the referee's watch, some-thing about it. Something about the watch. She felt for her own, twisted the strap, held it up to the light from the TV, examined it.

Nothing.

Nothing, but something.

She knew it for sure. Something to do with a watch.

That was what she'd been thinking about when she fell asleep. A watch. But somehow it didn't have the resonance now that it had had before she'd dozed off. It had lost something. Which annoyed her. It would be harder now to make whatever connection there was to make.

Switching off the television, Marie-Ange uncurled herself from Monsieur Chabert's chair, stood up and stretched. She'd sleep on it, she thought.

But first, maybe, a breath of fresh air. A walk round the *place*. A *chocolat* at Mazzelli's.

64

It was a warm night, a half moon tethered to the wrought-iron cross on the church tower, wave after wave of silver-edged clouds sliding past it. As she stepped out on to the pavement Marie-Ange saw that the *place* was still busy, lights glinting and winking in the trees, cars parked outside the Fontaine Dorée, people out for a stroll. But before she closed the door behind her, she reached back to the peg for her shawl. There was a nip in the air that she hadn't expected and she was glad of her jeans and rollneck. Wrapping it round her shoulders she stepped away from the Fontaine des Fleurs and headed down to the Brieuc turning at the bottom of the *place*. From there she crossed in front of the *mairie* and followed the slope up to Mazzelli's.

Despite the chill Marie-Ange decided on a table on the terrace. She found one and made herself comfortable, pulling the wrap closer. From inside the bar she could hear a low buzz of voices – Lepantre, Frenot and Lanclos, by the sound of it – the jukebox too but, best of all, only a few metres away the comforting splash of the fountain.

She took a deep breath, held it, then let it go. As she did so, Tomas appeared with a tray bearing her *chocolat*. She'd ordered it so often, usually at this time of night, that there was now no need for her to say anything. As soon as Mazzelli or Tomas saw her coming across the *place*, they reached for the cacao.

298

'Where's your father tonight?' asked Marie-Ange, as Tomas put down the mug.

'Cinema, with my mother,' replied Tomas. 'In Cavaillon. Every other Friday they go. He hates it.'

Marie-Ange laughed, thanked him for the *chocolat* and watched him turn back to the bar. Which was when she saw old Dumé step out on to the terrace, take a look at the shifting sky, sniff the air. As Tomas passed him, he said something to the lad, then turned in her direction.

Of all the people in St Bédard, Dumé had been the hardest nut to crack. At first, all she'd managed to get from him were grunts and nods whenever he passed the shop on his way to the Brieuc turning, a wave of the stick perhaps to acknowledge her greeting. But gradually he'd softened, the grunts and nods replaced with an occasional '*Ça va, Mam'selle*', a pause sometimes to nod approvingly at her displays, then stopping by to say something: how his son was out at Chant-le-Neuf on a job, what the weather was up to, or had she seen Lepantre's new shell-suit – 'you wouldn't believe it!'

And now he was heading towards her, clearly intent on having a few words. He pulled over a chair from a neighbouring table without bothering to ask if it was free and sat himself down with a grimace, positioning his stick between his legs.

'So, the party's off then, here and at the château,' he began, as though he didn't need confirmation from her. 'They finished in the *mairie* an hour ago. It's decided.'

She nodded. 'The Comtesse told me this afternoon.'

Dumé gave her a sly, sideways look. 'She pay you yet for your trouble, you'll excuse my asking?'

Marie-Ange sipped her *chocolat*, shook her head. She'd meant to say something that afternoon, but sensing the Comtesse's grief – just back from identifying her husband's personal effects in Cavaillon – she'd put off bringing up the subject of money. Even if the old crow did have a bundle of cash in her bedside cupboard. At least she'd be able to use all the flowers she'd ordered and the trellising she'd put up in the ballroom for the Comte's funeral.

Dumé nodded, as though he'd suspected as much. 'Always been

mindful of money, that one,' he confided. 'Always on the look-out for extra cash. Like trying to hoist our rents. But she can't do it and she knows it.'

Over Dumé's shoulder, Marie-Ange saw Tomas coming back to their table. On his tray, balanced at shoulder height, was a small carafe of water and a glass of Granier for her companion.

'How come? The rents, I mean,' asked Marie-Ange.

'It was the old man. The old Comte. Edouard,' said Dumé, accepting the pastis from Tomas, dribbling some water into the glass and sipping it without stirring. 'Anyone living in the *place* at the end of the war, he gave 'em life terms, rent increases set at one per cent below the national rate, never more than two per cent increase per annum. Nothing she can do about it. Set in stone, it is. Till the day I dies.'

'How long have you lived here, Simon?'

'Born here,' replied Dumé, liking the sound of his name on her lips. 'Nineteen fifteen. Over there. *Chez nous*. On the second floor at the front. Where the children sleep. I'm at the back, now, first floor. But after I'm gone, the boy Patric's got to make his own arrangements. Stay put and pay, or move out. Same with the rest – the Héliards, Mazzelli, Lepantre, the Séguin girls, Madame Blanc. Next generation and it's all change. Then she can charge what she fancies. Or sell. There'd be enough takers, that's for sure.'

'I thought they had money.'

'Who? The de Vausignes?'

Marie-Ange nodded, took a sip of her *chocolat*.

'They've got a title sure enough, but money? No. Spent that. Or as good as. Enough to see them through, you asks me. If they watches theirselves. I mean, you just got to look at the place, the château. The last few years they've let things slip. The boy Patric went out there one time to give a quote. Wanted the work so bad he made a good offer. And still they said no. A place like that . . . you got to maintain it or you loses it. Would never have happened with the real de Vausignes.'

'The real de Vausignes?'

'The original family. Been there centuries, they had. This lot, they're not of the blood – you get my meaning. Married into it.

Took it over. The Comte, the one just gone, he's the step-son, right? Legally adopted, but nothing to do with the old boy.'

'Tell me,' said Marie-Ange, taking this in, thinking of the photo in the Comtesse's bedside table, 'do the initials "AV" mean anything to you?'

'AV?' repeated Dumé, looking up into the branches of the trees. 'Up at the château, you mean? Albert. Must be. Edouard's son. Albert de Vausigne.'

'And "PR"?'

Dumé gave her another sideways look. 'What's with all the initials?' he asked, tipping a drop more water into his Granier, swirling the mixture together.

'A photo I saw in the château. A photograph – in a frame in the library,' she added. 'Two men, one young, one older, but just initials. AV. PR. I wondered . . .' She let her words trail off.

'Large man? Red cheeks?' Dumé took a swig, pinched his lip with his fingers.

Marie-Ange nodded.

'Paul Rocsabin. Has to be. Her ladyship's father. He and Albert used to go hunting, out with the dogs. Old man Rocsabin was always getting the boy up there on one pretext or another. The major reason being that he wanted the young feller to notice his daughter.'

'And did he?' Judging by the photo Marie-Ange had seen – the fall of hair, the eyes, that devil-may-care grin – the Comtesse must certainly have noticed him.

'Not a chance. There was someone else. One of his gang.'

'Gang?'

Dumé put down his drink and felt for his pouch and pipe. He tamped down the tobacco and lit a match, held it over the bowl and looked at her over the top of his cupped hands.

'The Maquis, Mam'selle. The AAC. *Aux Armes, Citoyens*. That's what we called it in these parts. Back in the war.' He took a few puffs and the tobacco crackled, the smoke snatched away with the breeze. 'There was a lot of us in those days. Up in the hills, sleeping rough, cutting a power line or two. I was twenty-seven, twenty-eight when I started, but young de Vausigne, he was in it from the beginning. Soon as the Krauts came south.

'Me, I'll tell you the truth. I joined up 'cos I had to. Called up as a guest worker by the STO. It was either join the Maquis or help Herr Hitler. But Albert de Vausigne? Like I said. Right from the very start. Though not many knew it.'

'And this girl . . .' asked Marie-Ange, bringing him back to the point. 'The one . . .'

Dumé nodded. 'They was in the same team, see, Albert and this girl. Tight as ticks they were.'

'Did you ever meet her?'

'Once or twice. Joined forces for an action in, let's see now . . . Pertuis, I think. A rail line. Another time at Roussillon. Winter it was. The early hours. Dark as shit and cold as fuck, excuse my English. They was always up front, the two of them. In charge, you know. They really made a dent.' Evidently Dumé relished the memory.

'So what happened to them?' asked Marie-Ange.

'Him, he was shot. Caught by the Boches on the Brieuc road and put up against a wall. After they'd played around with him a little first. The way they did back then.'

'Is that the sign by the bridge?' asked Marie-Ange, knowing it had to be.

'The memorial? That's right. That's the one. That's where it happened,' replied Dumé, sucking at his pipe. 'You could hear the shooting from here. All hell breaking loose. Course, I wasn't in on that one or I might not be here now. A dozen or more *résistants* killed and six Krauts. There was reprisals, of course. As well as the four they executed, they took three men from Chant-le-Neuf, three from Rocsabin and two from here in St Bédard. Anatole Parmentier was one, Michel's grandfather, and the old Comte's groom the other. Arab fella, Houssaye was his name. Hung 'em up right there,' said Dumé, nodding at the trees across the road from the terrace. 'So's everyone got a good look. Two of us for each of the Krauts got killed. Some places they'd have traded ten for one. I suppose you could say we was lucky.'

Marie-Ange looked up at the trees, leaves shifting in the breeze, and remembered the sounds she'd heard during her first week in St Bédard – the creaking of branches, the stretched squeaking of a rope. So that was what it was, she thought, pulling the shawl round her, knowing now she'd never hear the sound again.

302

'And the girl?' she asked. 'Albert's friend? What happened to her?'

'Got away, so I heard. Never heard a thing more about her. But she must have been gutted. Close they were. The real item.' Dumé struck another match and set it to his pipe. Between puffs to get it going, he continued his story: 'The word was someone grassed 'em up. Told the Krauts what they was planning. That road there, you see, from Cavaillon to Brieuc, was a well-used secondary transport route for the Boches. Lot of traffic, there was. Usually nighttime. The plan was to ambush a load of arms. Albert de Vausigne had brought in some back-up, more than he usually had, that's for certain. Which was where some say the leak came from. Someone he'd wanted in, someone he'd approached but they couldn't make it. Or didn't show. I mean, you don't squeal to the Boches about an op you're taking part in, *hein*?'

Marie-Ange shook her head. No, that seemed unlikely.

'So far as I knows,' Dumé continued, clamping his teeth on his pipe, 'only the two got away. The woman, Albert's girl, and a young lad from Barjas. Name of Bonaire. Got flung off his ship in Toulon when the Germans took over. No more than a boy, he was, but a nice kid. Lives out round Apt, I'm told.'

'Could it have been him? The one who grassed?'

'Bonaire? Not a chance. Like I say, you don't drink the water you've . . . well, you know what I means.'

Marie-Ange smiled, nodded.

'And anyway he was straight as a cue, Bonaire. Hated the Krauts. The reason he joined up the moment he could was his old man had been sent off to Drancy.' Dumé laid down his pipe, reached for his glass and finished the liquor in a single gulp. 'And you know what that meant? Back in those days?'

Marie-Ange knew. You didn't live around the goods yards of Metz without knowing about Drancy.

'So who do you think blew the whistle?' she asked, watching him put down the empty glass and take up his pipe.

'*Pouff*,' said Dumé, tapping the pipe on the table leg, then rising painfully to his feet. 'Who knows? It was all a long time ago. People don't seem to be interested any more. And what difference would it make, eh?'

Quite a lot, thought Marie-Ange, not knowing why she should think it.

Quite a lot.

65

That last weekend in July a summer mistral hurtled down from the north.

Jacquot liked to think he could sense them coming – the strong neon sunsets; the clouds at night racing across a starry sky; that dry dustiness in the air; the lizards burrowing themselves out of harm's way and the *cigales* falling silent in the days preceding the blast.

People said how they hated this wind, how it drove them crazy, depressed them, made them ill-tempered and out of sorts. But Jacquot loved it – the power, the bluster, the complete self-confidence. Raw and delinquent, it swept down the Rhône valley like a bar-room brawler looking for a fight.

It was the wind that woke Jacquot on the day of Tatine's funeral – or, rather, a downstairs window that had been left unlatched the night before. By the time he got to it, gathering his night-shirt round him, one of the panes was cracked and a hinge had worked loose from the frame.

A few desultory pelts of rain slapped against the glass as he secured it. Outside, the sky was low on the hilltops and grey as granite, the spindly tops of the cypress trees whipping this way and that and the driveway filled with leaves from the olives, spinning and pirouetting across the gravel as though frantically searching out some place to shelter from the wind. But there was nowhere to hide. Even when they found some protected corner and huddled into steep drifts, the wind would search them out and scatter them sooner rather than later.

It was, thought Jacquot, making his way to the kitchen, as good a day as any for a funeral.

The service had been scheduled for four o'clock that Monday afternoon at the Abbaye de Laune, in its stone-flagged, stone-vaulted chapel. At a little after two Jacquot left the office to Brunet, went home and changed into a dark suit. Then, with Claudine beside him, he drove the forty kilometres to Laune, a longer journey than planned thanks to the wind buffeting the Peugeot, trying to shoulder it off the road. For a seven-kilometre stretch on the autoroute, Jacquot had to throw his cigarette out of the window, grip the wheel with both hands and, at Claudine's insistence, secure his seat-belt.

As if calling by to visit Sandrine, they parked in the abbey's gravelled forecourt, surprisingly full for a weekday afternoon, but instead of turning right through the cloisters to climb the stairs to her room, Jacquot and Claudine turned left and made their way to the chapel where the *abbesse* was waiting for them at the door.

Her hands were tightly clasped and she seemed relieved to see them. 'I tried to call, but there was no reply,' she began apologetically.

Claudine looked at her anxiously, thinking something had gone wrong.

'There was just the one caller, you see, *un vieux*, an old gentleman, asking about the arrangements. The time, you know. The day. So of course I told him. I didn't think to mention it to you. He must have passed it on,' she said, stepping forward and pushing open the door. 'It's just that the chapel is so small. There's so little room. And we never expected quite so many people.'

Claudine and Jacquot looked through the open door into the chapel and then at each other. If they'd expected to be alone, they were badly mistaken.

Instead of the small private ceremony they'd anticipated – the two of them, the *curé* from Salon, the *abbesse*, maybe a few of the sisters – every seat in the chapel was taken, the pews packed tight as a jar of Collioure anchovies, the side aisles crowded with wheelchairs and those who'd arrived too late for a seat. From the doorway where they stood it was almost impossible to see Sandrine's coffin, draped in a tasselled *tricolore* by the altar. Which also surprised them: they had made no arrangements for any decoration other than their wreath. As they made their way down the central aisle, accompanied by the low hum of an organ, and the odd cough and shuffling of feet, line after line of ancient faces turned in their direction.

'Who are all these people?' whispered Claudine, as they slid into the front pew, which had been kept free for them.

'How on earth should I know? Maybe it was that notice of yours in the papers.'

The day after Tatine's death Claudine had posted it in the local paper and in *Le Monde*. She'd had Jacquot read it before faxing it off. It was simple and to the point:

> On 22 July, at the Abbaye de Laune, Salon,
> Sandrine Eddé passed away in her sleep, aged 79.
> A patriot. A fighter for freedom.
> Our beloved Tatine.
> *On vive ensemble, on mort tout seul.*

'I'm not so sure about your take on Pascal,' Jacquot had remarked.

But Claudine had remained adamant, would not be swayed. 'Well, it's true, isn't it?'

And that was that.

Except, clearly, it wasn't. Within a week of that announcement, a crowd of people had turned up to show that you don't die alone. Or, at least, die forgotten.

The service was brief: a swift, whispered litany of prayers and benedictions from the *curé*, the formal responses from the congregation rising ragged but sincere from behind them, and a single psalm, which had every voice in the congregation a beat or two behind the organist.

As the *curé* gave the final blessing and the first notes of a Bach *Sanctus* that Tatine had loved filled the chapel, a half-dozen men, all in their seventies but still sprightly looking, stepped from their pews and gathered round the coffin, medals clinking, sagging from their suit lapels.

And in an instant Jacquot knew who the mourners were. The medals. The medals. Old soldiers to a man. All her old comrades. From the war. Come to see her off.

Taking their order from one of their number, a man with a wide shock of white hair and the ribbon of the Croix de Guerre in his buttonhole, they hoisted the coffin on to their shoulders and with a shuffle of feet, got into time and slow-marched out of the chapel.

So much, thought Jacquot, for the wheeled gurney the *abbesse* had promised when he'd asked about burial arrangements, and the abbey gardeners, who'd double as pallbearers.

As the coffin was borne away, he and Claudine followed it, acknowledging the sad smiles and nods of commiseration they received as they passed through the congregation. In the last pew Jacquot saw an old boy, in a corduroy suit he must have bought in the fifties, lift his hand and salute as the coffin passed, tears welling in his eyes.

Outside, the mistral was waiting for them. As the *cortège* filed like a black snake across the chapel courtyard, hands reached for hats as it bore down on them, tugging at trouser legs, coat-tails and the flag draped over the coffin, lifting its tasselled edge and slapping it against the wood panels. Jacquot expected to see it lift off and sail through the air at any moment, but as they passed beneath the archway leading to the graveyard he noticed that someone had had the forethought to tack the flag to the wood.

Much the same forethought had been employed at the graveside, where a pair of high trestles had been set beside the grave. The pallbearers had simply to walk either side and lower the coffin a few centimetres to take the weight off their shoulders.

In short order, the flag was removed, folded and presented to Claudine, canvas straps were looped through the coffin's handles and a dozen men stepped forward from the mourners to join the pallbearers and take the strain as the trestles were removed.

They've done this before, thought Jacquot as, gradually, the straps were played out and the coffin was lowered into the ground. Old soldiers burying their own.

Afterwards, when Jacquot and Claudine turned from the grave, a tall, distinguished-looking gentleman with a thin cover of grey hair scraped back over his head stepped forward, introduced himself.

'Colonel Hugo Rascousse,' he said, shaking their hands, extending his sympathies, his condolences.

Jacquot remembered the name from the citations in Sandrine's deed-box. Renard. Head of Network F2.

He fell into step beside them, the wind whipping around them, Claudine clutching at her skirt, and the three of them followed the other mourners from the cemetery.

'We never knew what happened to her,' the colonel explained. 'After the executions she just disappeared. No one knew where she'd come from and no one knew where she went. It was like that then. After the war. Liberation. So much confusion. All we had was the name of a lawyer in Avignon. But there was never any response from her. She never got in contact.' Rascousse spread his hands and sighed. 'Which, of course, we respected. Then, last week, Bonaire read the notice. Captain Henri Bonaire, the lead pallbearer. With the white hair? He fought with your aunt. As did I on many occasions. He called me and the others. The word was passed round. We should have got in touch, I know, to ask your permission. We didn't think the chapel would be so small.'

'It was so good of you to come. To do this. So many of you,' Claudine managed to say when they reached their car. 'Tatine would have been so . . . touched.'

'We could have filled your little chapel a dozen times over, Madame,' replied Rascousse, 'but many of us are old now and could not make the journey. I can assure you, though, that they will be thinking of her in their hearts today. Those who are left. In that terrible time when our country was taken from us, there were a few, like your aunt, who refused to give in, refused to accept, refused to compromise their honour or surrender their country. Without fear for her safety, she did everything in her power to turn the tide of war. And many of the men here today owe her their lives. Including me. She was a very, very courageous woman, Madame. One of the very bravest.'

By this time, tears were streaming down Claudine's face and she clung to Jacquot as though to a rock in a stormy sea.

'I think . . .' began Jacquot.

'*Mes pardons*, Monsieur, Madame. *Je m'excuse*,' said Rascousse, his hand reaching out to touch Claudine's arm. 'I am so sorry. I did not mean to . . . Please forgive me. It was just . . . after all this time . . . It is important for you to know the kind of woman Sandrine Eddé was. How she will never be forgotten.'

And with that he bowed his head and walked away.

'Dear God,' said Claudine, gulping for breath. 'Dear God . . .'

Dear God indeed, thought Jacquot as they watched the old soldier start his car and join the convoy of mourners leaving the abbey, heading back wherever they'd come from.

66

It had been a busy week for Marie-Ange. For the last five days she'd spent every evening in St Bédard's church, arranging the floral decorations for the Comte de Vausigne's funeral.

On Monday Picard had helped her bring the trellis-work from the château and by Tuesday night they'd secured it to the walls and the columns of the church, just as she'd done in the de Vausignes' ballroom. On Wednesday afternoon the blooms that she'd ordered for the de Vausignes' anniversary party had been delivered – lilies, jonquils, anemones, bucharica irises, white-wing peonies, marguerites, asters, trilliums, petunias, primulas, violas, saxifrage – all tightly budded creams, golds and whites whose stems she soaked overnight in buckets of water diluted with Indian ink. On Thursday evening, every petal veined with black, she and Tomas wheeled the flowers to the church and by Friday evening the job was done.

As far as Marie-Ange was concerned, working in the church had distinct advantages over the château. It was less than a hundred metres from her front door and there was little risk of bumping into Antoine de Vausigne. The church also seemed to be the only place in St Bédard where the wind was kept at bay.

She'd heard of this wind, the mistral. Who hadn't? But it was the first time she'd ever been in it. And she hated it from the very first

311

gusts. The way it caught at her hem and flicked her hair as she set out her racks at the Fontaine des Fleurs; the way it pushed at her displays, snapped at her awning and rattled her shutters; the way it tore around the *place*, snatching flyers from car windscreens and scattering them far and wide, whipping up the dust and thrashing through the branches of the trees.

Up until that last week in July, the Vaucluse countryside had captivated Marie-Ange – the warmth of its sun, the scents of its hedgerows, the distant hills and blue skies (blue as the Madonna's skirts, said Dumé), the meadows of sunflowers, fields of rustling maize, the olives, the eucalyptus, the *spear-tip* cypresses. In short, it was about the sweetest place she'd ever been.

Until now.

Now she had to sleep with her bedroom window closed, couldn't hear the fountain when she woke in the morning, couldn't hear the doves scratching on the tiles above her head, couldn't hear anything, save the endless groaning, moaning and breathless whistling of the wind as it howled round the *place*.

And the grit and the dust carried on this horrible wind found its way into everything: into her breakfast *brioche* from Doriane's, no matter how tightly she sealed the paper bag on the trip home; into Adéline's ginger and camomile tea; into her evening *chocolat* at Mazzelli's; into her eyes, nose, ears, prickling across her scalp, gathering at the corners of her mouth and grubbing between fingers and toes. When she let out the bathwater at night a line of it marked high tide, and making her deliveries in the Chabert van was nothing short of a nightmare of violent buffeting and stomach-churning shudders, a fight to keep control and stay on the road.

And, except the tourists, pretty well everyone in St Bédard remained inside, waiting it out.

Three weeks, a month, it could last, Caroline Parmentier told her when Marie-Ange called to replace the table decorations at the Fontaine Dorée.

Six weeks, I've known, said Agnès at the *pharmacie*.

You get used to it eventually, said Adéline, wearily, delivering another of her sister's terrines.

Spring's the worst, confided Mazzelli, over a mug of gritty *chocolat*. It's never so bad this time of year.

And so it went, day after hot, muggy, dusty, blustery day until Marie-Ange was just about ready to scream. Would it never stop? she thought. This . . . rampage. Would it never end? Had cloudless skies and sunshine gone from the earth for ever? How could people bear it?

It was still blowing on Saturday morning when St Bédard, but for Mazzelli's bar and the Parmentiers' *auberge*, closed down at midday. It was Gilles de Vausigne's funeral that afternoon, and customers were gently shooed from premises around the *place* as Clotilde Lepantre, the Bulots, Madame Héliard, André Ribaud and the Tesserats latched their shutters and rolled down their blinds as a mark of respect.

That morning the Fontaine des Fleurs had not opened at all and no one had seen Marie-Ange until, a little after midday, she crossed the *place* to the church, waving to Agnès Héliard as she passed in front of the *pharmacie*. Above the church she could see a slice of blue sky and though her black dress still sucked against her body she didn't need to tip forward into the wind to keep her balance. Maybe, she thought, maybe it was coming to an end.

Inside the church Marie-Ange made the final adjustments – spraying, pruning and dead-heading, crumbling aspirin into the iris and lily vases to either side of the altar and clipping back loose ties on the trellises. Then she sat down in one of the pews, resting her head right back so that she looked up into the distant heights of the church, and wondered if he would come.

The policeman. Jacquot.

She was certain he would. The Comte had been murdered, after all. It had been the talk of St Bédard all week. And a woman too, which had stirred some lurid speculation round Mazzelli's bar. Six murders in six months, in this tiny corner of Provence. Seven deaths in all, counting Monsieur Bartolomé's suicide.

He had to come. She was sure of it.

Marie-Ange had decided to confide in Jacquot after their meeting in the Martner hot-house, the evening she rode back to the Rocsabin stud. There was something strangely familiar about the man, as though the letters she'd been writing to him for the last four months had somehow drawn them together. As she brushed down Pierrot at the stables, forked some clean hay into his box and gave him the last of her sugar cubes, she decided the time had come to pool resources. She didn't need anyone to tell her that Jacquot was as uncomfortable with the Chabert case as she was.

Maybe her letters had done some good after all, she thought. Maybe between them they could get to the bottom of it, because she was getting nowhere by herself. Just a raft of mixed messages she couldn't for the life of her decipher – something to do with the war, she knew that for sure. Something to do with the memorial by the bridge.

Connections. Just make the connections, she kept saying to herself.

But time was getting short. Talk was, the trial was winding up. And despite the best efforts of Maître Messain in courtroom two in the Lyon Palais de Justice, things were not looking good for Eric Chabert.

That Jacquot was someone she could trust – had to trust – Marie-Ange was in no doubt. Their meeting in the hot-house had confirmed it. The fact that he was there at all. And the way his eyes cast about, as though he was looking for something, some clue, something he'd missed the first time round.

And the times she'd seen him across the *place* at Mazzelli's. Sitting in the sunshine. Thinking things through. Looking ill at ease.

She'd known who he was the first time she saw him, didn't need to have him pointed out. And she'd watched him – the way he lit his cigarette with cupped hands, the way he sipped his beer and brushed at his lips with his fingers, or pulled at that ponytail of his.

He wasn't at all what she'd expected. Which hadn't stopped her knowing who he was. It had just surprised her, that was all. The way he looked. The kind of man he was. The policeman in Metz had been thin as a stick of celery, bald, glasses, and that dreadful belted raincoat. But this was a different animal. This one looked . . . cool, handsome. And judging by the way she'd flustered him in the hot-house – all that playful, flirting flower stuff – he didn't seem to know it. Which made him seem even more attractive.

She liked a lot of things about him. The way he dressed – the boots, the linen jackets, the white T-shirts, though the jeans suited him better than the chinos. The way his eyes settled on her, gently, kindly, green as a peony petal, etched with a spray of laugh lines; the way he spoke – all rough and smoky; the way his words seemed to wrap round her; those big hands of his, holding out the note-book for her. And the ponytail. She even liked the ponytail. It was not the way a man of his age should wear his hair. But it suited him, that thick curling plume of hair lapping over his collar, clasped in a rubber band but not so tightly drawn that it stretched the skin at his temples. She wondered how old he was – late forties, maybe fifty. A good age. And in good condition too; the bulk of a Gérard Depardieu – with the same kind of tilting, busted nose and sleepy eyes – but the height to make it seem lean and slender. For a moment she felt a tiny bolt of envy for the woman he loved, the woman whose birthday it was, the one for whom he would buy an orchid.

That was something else that had impressed her. His honesty. Telling her there was a woman in his life with no thought to keep the information back. When men met Marie-Ange, the last thing they ever did, as she well knew, was volunteer information about wives or girlfriends. Contented, too, by the look of him. Which pleased her. And put her out a little as well.

She was thinking how nice it must be to have a man like that come home every night when she was roused, in the deep, stony silence of the church, by the click-clack of a door-latch. To the left of the altar, the Widow Blanc bustled out from the vestry with a pile of pressed Communion cloths. Marie-Ange glanced at her watch. In another fifteen minutes the service would begin. She watched the old lady lay out the cloths on the steps of the altar, genuflect, cross herself and hurry down the aisle, shoes ringing out on the stone flags.

'Why, Marie-Ange,' she said, stopping at her pew and looking around at the flowers, 'you've made it so beautiful. All the flowers. And black too. I'm not so sure the old devil deserves such a send-off.'

'Everyone deserves flowers,' replied Marie-Ange.

'Well, I suppose . . .' she conceded. Then, leaning forward and lowering her voice: 'But he was such an old goat, *chérie*. Terrible. You wouldn't believe . . .'

But before she could say more, the great door of the church

creaked open, a shaft of daylight split the shadows and the first of the mourners arrived.

'So, here they come,' said the Widow Blanc, 'the great and the good come to wish the old dog God speed,' and with a nod to Marie-Ange she bustled off.

Within minutes the pews started to fill and, surrendering her seat, Marie-Ange made her way to the back of the church, taking up position behind the christening font, watching the arrivals as they pushed aside the damask curtain inside the door and made their way down the aisle. A few dress uniforms, formal frock coats, an official civic sash or two, black suits and overcoats, top hats, veils and gloves.

But no ponytail. No Jacquot.

It was only when the bishop, attended by the Curé Foulard and a flock of prettily surpliced sacristans, had begun the mass that the great church door winced open once more. Marie-Ange peered through the gloom as the curtain switched aside and . . . there he was, slipping down the side aisle opposite.

Marie-Ange felt a stir of excitement.

It was beginning.

67

The mistral seemed to have lost some of its punch by the time
Jacquot arrived in St Bédard, the lamp-posts and balconies hung
with snapping black ribbon and the fountain wreathed with garlands
of rustling black taffeta, all of which, a day or two earlier, the wind
would have snatched away.

It was Jacquot's second funeral of the week. First Tatine at the
Abbaye de Laune, and now, five days later, Gilles, Comte de
Vausigne, released from the Cavaillon morgue for interment in the
family crypt.

Jacquot, sitting at a table on Mazzelli's terrace, had only just made
it. For the last three days he'd been in Aix, providing Claudine with
moral support as she made the final arrangements for the opening
of her summer exhibition. That morning, flushed with success at
the reception her work had received the evening before, she'd
delayed Jacquot longer than he'd intended in their room at the
Hôtel des Augustins. By the time they turned on to the autoroute
for the drive north, Jacquot was certain he'd never reach St Bédard
in time.

But he had and now he got to his feet, looking over the crowd
that had gathered in the *place*, as the plumed horses and glinting
glass-sided hearse bearing Gilles de Vausigne on his final journey
turned into the square from the Chant-le-Neuf road.

Gilles, Comte de Vausigne. Edouard's adopted son. Second in

line to the de Vausigne title. Was he the one who'd gone to the Germans all those years ago? Was he the one who'd set up his step-brother on the Brieuc road? Since his lunch at Chez Gaillard, Jacquot had thought of nothing else, playing it through, time and time again. Certainly, as a theory, it seemed to fit. Gilles goes to the *Kommandantur* and betrays his step-brother to secure the title and his future. Only Martner finds out about it. At the *Kommandantur* where he worked, or after the war in a cell in Aix-Luynes. And puts the screws on him all these years later. Pay me or else. Is that where the doctor's unexplained good fortune had come from? Cash provided by the Comte de Vausigne to keep his secret safe? Until finally the Comte grew tired of the blackmail, the drain on his finances, and decided to do something about it?

It would have been so easy to say yes. So satisfactory. Even if, with the Comte's hearse now clattering across the cobbles towards the church, it was too late for Jacquot to do anything about it. Just the tantalising possibility that there, through the etched-glass panels of the hearse, lay the Martners' killer. Certainly de Vausigne had had good reason to betray his step-brother. The château and the title would have been powerful spurs. And certainly he was tall enough to climb the Martner stairs two by two, tall enough to knock those pictures out of line.

But possibilities, tantalising as they were, were not the same as probabilities, and Jacquot doubted that the Comte was the Martner killer. Could a man in his seventies have recovered from that fall in the Martners' kitchen? Recovered enough to chase a young girl out of the house and up the drive? And would a man with a dozen guns in his cabinet be so clumsy with his weapon of choice? Jacquot didn't think so.

Metalled hoofs and bridles ringing, steel-rimmed wheels crunching over the cobbles, the Comte's hearse drew up at the steps to St Bédard's church. As the four black horses snorted and stamped, their purple plumes shivering in the wind, a rank of pallbearers in sashed top hats and tailcoats stepped forward to draw out the coffin, hoist it on to their shoulders and, step by slow step, carry it into the church.

And as they did so, one final car came to a halt at the church steps. It was the de Vausignes' Citroën Légère, Picard ramrod straight at the wheel, the bonnet strung with black ribbon. Jacquot squinted against the dust blown up from the *place* and watched as the new Comte helped his mother from the back seat.

Or could it be that Albert had been betrayed by the Comte's wife, Hélène de Vausigne? *Née* Rocsabin. The name Tatine had written a thousand times, page after page, in that old school note-book. Maybe it had been the Comtesse whose treachery Martner had witnessed all those years ago, treachery he had decided to make her pay for.

But if Albert had been the man she loved, as old man Gaillard had implied, how could she have countenanced betraying him to the Gestapo? As Jacquot watched the Comtesse climb the church steps, supported by her son, to be formally greeted by the Bishop of Cavaillon and the Curé Foulard, one thing was certain. Whatever the truth, there was no way the Comtesse could ever have been the Martners' killer. Too old now, too frail, for that terrible killing spree at Mas Taillard.

Finishing his beer and dropping some coins on the table, Jacquot left Mazzelli's terrace, squeezed through the crowd and made his way to the church, the wind snapping at his coat-tails. At the top of the steps he pulled open one of the doors, slipped into the church's cool, dark interior and made his way down one of the side aisles.

The first thing he noticed was the sense of space. Here, unlike the more intimate crowding at Tatine's funeral in the chapel at Laune, the droning voices of the bishop and the *curé* sounded distant, solitary, echoing upwards into the arched elevations above the congregation. And although the incense was thick, coiling up in wreaths of smoke from the thurifers attending the bishop, the second thing Jacquot noticed was the overwhelming scent of flowers. Roped through the Communion rail, wound round the stone pillars, set in floral chains on the pulpit and decorating the end of every pew, a mass of blooms seemed to cover every inch of the church. Even the Comte's portrait, standing on an easel at the altar steps, was framed with flowers.

And something else, Jacquot noticed. Every bloom, every petal he could see, was veined with black.

'Indian ink,' came a whisper from behind him. 'In case you were wondering.'

Jacquot looked round to find Marie-Ange Buhl standing at his shoulder. He'd wondered whether he'd bump into her again. The girl in the hot-house. The letter-writer. And for some unaccountable reason he'd known that he would.

'You're late, by the way,' she continued, looking past him, trying to get a glimpse of the coffin.

'Miss Buhl. You were expecting me?'

'Marie-Ange, please.' She turned back to him. 'I'd have been surprised if you hadn't made an appearance.' She pulled a bag of Tesserat's pastilles from her pocket and offered him one.

'And I you, Miss Buhl,' he replied, shaking his head at the pastilles. 'From Alsace, from Île de France, Brittany, Poitou-Charenter. And most recently, of course, Brieuc.'

'So you've found me out, Chief Inspector. Bravo. And I suppose now you want to have a few words with me?'

'I most certainly do,' replied Jacquot.

68

Ten minutes later Marie-Ange Buhl and Daniel Jacquot were sitting at a table in the back of Mazzelli's bar. The terrace had been packed, as though the Comte's funeral was some kind of tourist spectacle, so they'd come inside and found a table wedged in a far corner beside a one-armed bandit.

Marie-Ange watched him order for them, a beer and some white wine, saw the way he settled himself, made the best of his chair. And, for a moment, she wondered whether she'd been right to make a move. She knew they were on the same side. And she'd done nothing wrong. But would he understand what she was going to say to him?

As Tomas moved off to fetch their drinks, Jacquot turned to Marie-Ange and gave her a long, cool look, this woman who cared for the doctor's orchids, who lived in the Chaberts' house and worked in their shop. The one who'd been writing him letters for the last four months. He wasn't altogether sure where to start, had no idea what to expect. But somehow he knew it would make for an interesting exchange.

'So, Miss Buhl . . .' he began.

'Marie-Ange, Chief Inspector. After all, I feel I know you.'

Jacquot nodded. 'So, Marie-Ange. Tell me about Eric Chabert.'

'What's to tell?' she replied lightly. 'You have the wrong man.'

Jacquot scratched the side of his chin, nodded again as though they were both agreed on that. Then, quietly: 'You have proof? I

321

should remind you that withholding information from the police in the course of their investigations is a criminal offence.'

She shrugged, made a little *moue*, and immediately sensed that their meeting wasn't going to be quite as straightforward as she had hoped. She wondered if she'd underestimated him. He was a policeman after all.

She shifted in her seat, slipped a fall of hair behind her ear. 'It is all I have, Chief Inspector, but it's enough for me.'

Tomas brought their drinks and she reached for her wine, sipped it. Jacquot did the same with his beer, pinching the foam from his lip with thumb and forefinger.

They put their drinks down on the table, played with their glasses like gamblers fingering their chips. Neither seemed keen to proceed, but Jacquot broke the silence between them.

'You understand, Marie-Ange, we need more than . . . female intuition,' he began, with a gentle, patient smile. 'Next week the jury will be sent out to consider the evidence and reach a verdict. I'm sure you don't need me to tell you that it does not look good for Monsieur Chabert. So,' he continued, 'how do you know he's innocent? What makes you think he's innocent?'

Marie-Ange gave him a calculating look, knowing how he'd probably react when he heard what she had to say, but knowing she was going to say it anyway. 'I saw his picture in the paper. And I knew. Just like that. This man did not kill the Martners.'

'You saw his picture.'

'Sometimes that's all it takes, you know. A photograph. A name. A place. Without any warning, you know something. Absolutely. Without question. It's like a kind of . . . clarity. Which I guess,' she said, trying to lighten the mood, 'is why I never vote.'

Jacquot nodded. 'You said "sometimes".'

Which surprised her. He was taking it in, still reserving judgement. Which was why she continued, explaining things from the beginning. So there'd be no misunderstanding. About the marshalling yards of Metz. About the raised voices on that fourth-floor balcony in the street where the woman died, the scream that rushed through the air and ended with that dreadful, final thud. The only thing she didn't make any reference to was her monthly cycle, how the two things always seemed to coincide.

And all the time Jacquot sat there and watched her, sipped his beer, listened, didn't say a word.

'It's like echoes,' said Marie-Ange, anxious to make it as clear and comprehensible as she could. 'Things from the past that find their way into my present. And stay there until I acknowledge them, understand them. Sometimes these . . . echoes are loud and strong, sometimes they're just soft, distant. But however they present themselves, I know they mean something. That I hear these things for a reason. Like now. With Eric Chabert. Unfinished business.'

Behind them came a sudden snap of snooker balls and Marie-Ange started.

'I have to say—' began Jacquot, not really sure what he wanted to say.

'I know, I know . . . It all sounds crazy,' she interrupted, not wanting to hear what he had to say, knowing what it would be. 'If you don't believe me, call the policeman in Metz. Fayard was his name. Ask him about the letters he received. About the teacher. He'll tell you.'

But still Jacquot looked unconvinced, and now she was beginning to feel a little foolish. Which exasperated her. So she decided to go one step further and tell him about the girl she'd seen in the nursery in Metz, the one who'd been murdered.

'To be completely accurate,' she said quietly, 'it wasn't just the photo in the paper that started this.'

'Go on,' said Jacquot.

'It began with a girl.'

'A girl?'

'A young girl. The first time . . .' she took a breath '. . . the first time I've ever seen anything.'

'So now you see things,' said Jacquot, and immediately regretted saying it. He had seen her flinch, seen that he'd hurt her. To cover he said: 'And this was . . . ?'

For a while Marie-Ange said nothing, debating whether to go on, sliding a finger up and down the icy side of her glass.

'Please,' encouraged Jacquot, surprising himself.

'March,' she replied, relenting. 'In Metz. I was working at a nursery. There were four of us there, in one of the hot-houses,

323

sitting at stools along the bench, repotting seedlings, a few metres apart. Suddenly I felt someone beside me. Heard a voice.'

'The girl?'

Marie-Ange nodded.

'She just . . . appeared?'

She nodded again.

'A ghost?'

'I suppose . . .'

'And what did she say? This . . . girl,' said Jacquot quietly.

The way he asked the question, the way he leaned forward, speaking so softly, made Marie-Ange feel better. She'd said enough to scare off most people, but he was still there, still listening. She knew she'd been right about him.

'At first I could make no sense of it. She was speaking in German, which I don't understand too well. But there was one word I did get. '*Gärtner*'. She said 'gardener'. And then she switched to French. Not so good French, but I knew what she was saying. '*Pas lui. Pas lui.*' And though I understood the words, they meant nothing to me. Until the day I opened the paper and saw that picture. Read the story. That's when I knew who she'd been talking about. Eric Chabert. And I knew she was right. It wasn't him.'

'And what did she look like, this girl? Do you remember?'

Marie-Ange had known he was going to ask her this, and she knew she couldn't really answer. She'd never had any sense of what the girl looked like. Just that she was . . . there.

'Young. Blonde. Skinny. Not as tall as me. I seem to remember a dressing-gown, pyjamas . . .'

Jacquot nodded. Kippi. That was who it sounded like. The pyjamas. A dressing-gown. That was what she had been wearing when they found her on the Martners' driveway. But it was not conclusive. Marie-Ange could have read those details in a paper, guessed at them, seen a photo somewhere.

'The strange thing was,' Marie-Ange continued, 'she was wearing only one shoe. An espadrille.'

69

It was as if Tomas had tipped cold beer down the back of Jacquot's shirt. His scalp tightened, prickled, and he shivered. No one outside the investigation knew about the espadrille. There was no way Marie-Ange could have known that. No chance. Unless she'd been there. Or unless she was telling the truth.

'The granddaughter, Kippi,' Jacquot said at last.

Marie-Ange nodded, smiled. She'd seen how the shoe detail hit home. Knew she'd said something important, something that made him believe her. 'That's what I guessed.'

'So you started writing letters.'

'Yes.'

'And came here to St Bédard.'

'Yes.'

'To do what, exactly?'

'Well, if it wasn't Chabert who killed the Martners – and it wasn't – then who did?' she said. 'I thought, you know, being close to the scene, like that street in Metz, maybe something would happen. Maybe something would become clear.'

'And has it?'

'I don't know yet.'

'Yet?'

'I feel . . . near something. I mean, I know I'm in the right place.

That I'm close. But right now?' She shrugged, looked almost forlorn. 'I just cannot say.'

Then, for an instant, she remembered the Comtesse's bedroom, something catching her eye, something at the edge of her vision, something important. But the next instant it was gone. Out of reach.

Jacquot sighed, patted his pockets for his cigarettes.

Marie-Ange fell silent, leaned forward, elbows on the table, swirling the wine in her glass, shaking her head when he offered her a cigarette, watching as he lit one for himself, blew a stream of smoke above their heads.

'I'll tell you something I do know,' she continued. 'From what I've heard, they were not popular in St Bédard. The Martners. Not disliked enough for someone to want to kill them maybe, but they certainly didn't know how to make friends. And St Bédard's friendlier than most.'

Jacquot looked interested. Brunet had told him the same thing. He wondered if Marie-Ange had heard anything new. 'Go on,' he said.

'First they were bad payers. Never left a tip when they ate at the *auberge*, never paid their bill at Bulot's until Delphine had to phone them, remind them. And Kippi? According to Marc Tesserat she was a little light-fingered in the *tabac*.'

'And, of course, they were German,' added Jacquot, lightly.

'That too,' Marie-Ange replied, embarrassed that it should be so. 'And there are long memories hereabouts.'

Then, changing the subject, she said: 'Let me ask you something. You do believe me, don't you?'

'About your voices? Or about Chabert?'

'Both.'

'I don't necessarily disbelieve the first – your voices. But I certainly believe, like you, that Eric Chabert . . . may be innocent.'

There, he'd said it.

'And what makes you think that?'

Jacquot shrugged, not wanting to give too much away. 'Inconsistencies. Coincidences.'

Marie-Ange didn't need to ask. She just waited, held his eye, knew he'd tell her.

And he did.

'First – and you'll think this ridiculous – well . . . it's just that Eric isn't tall enough to be the killer.' Jacquot didn't bother to explain about the pictures on the staircase or the two-stair footprints – how he knew the killer was taller than Eric. So he was pleased to see her nod which encouraged him to go on.

'Second. Prints on the gun, but none on the shell-casings. It doesn't add up. What? He wears gloves to load, but not to shoot?'

She nodded again. She understood. 'Anything else?'

'Whoever killed the Martners was not comfortable with a gun.'

Marie-Ange frowned, as though she'd followed the logic so far, but this last supposition evaded her. 'How do you know that?'

Jacquot spread his hands. 'He was clumsy, wasn't used to it – hit a banister trying to take a shot, fired off another wild round in the kitchen. Eric Chabert wouldn't have done that.'

'He?'

Jacquot smiled. 'That's my guess. A man. No proof, just a feeling. Also, the killer knew his way around. Had been to the house before. Someone the Martners would have known. Or someone who knew them, knew where their bedroom was, knew to double back from the hot-house into the kitchen rather than follow round through the guest wing. Which was where he intercepted the granddaughter, only a chair got in the way. Which gave the girl time to get down the hall and outside. Where he did catch her. Trying to run with only one shoe on.'

Now it was Marie-Ange's turn to register surprise. So that was what the shoe was all about.

'But wouldn't Eric have known the lay-out too?' she asked, confident enough to play devil's advocate.

Jacquot shook his head. 'Says he never went inside the house. The garage, the tool shed, a store-room for the hot-house. That was it. Of course, there's no one to check that with now . . .' Jacquot paused, shot her a look. 'But I believe him.'

'Not even for a coffee? In the kitchen?'

'He says not. Brought his own flask usually. Sometimes Madame Martner came out with a drink half-way through his shift. Or sent Kippi when she was staying.'

'Which was how they got to know one another.'

'You'd make a good detective.'

'I am a good detective. What else?'

'The murder weapon,' said Jacquot. 'It was stolen in November, three months before the murders. But in November Eric had no reason to think about murder. He had no motive. He was in love with Kippi; and he hadn't yet been sacked, told to stay away from her, been rejected.'

'And?'

Jacquot paused. It was as if she knew there was more. Things he'd left unsaid. This would be more difficult. This was thinner ice. But no less thin, he decided, than Marie-Ange's voices and apparitions.

'You have to step back a bit for this,' began Jacquot. 'Take the long view. A bit of a leap.'

'Okay,' said Marie-Ange. 'I'm listening.'

Jacquot stubbed out his cigarette. 'In nineteen forty-two, Josef Martner was called up and posted to France. The Occupied Zone. And after serving in Toulouse he was transferred here, to Cavaillon, as a medical orderly with the Abwehr.'

'It's strange you should mention the war,' Marie-Ange put in.

'How so?'

'Just a feeling I have. Something I can't seem to shift. Something to do with the war.'

Jacquot took this in. 'Anyway, after the war Martner gets repatriated, marries well and lives well. Gives up work and travels all over. But the money doesn't last. He and his wife don't have the same financial freedom they once enjoyed, and after a few years in Hamburg and Paris, making ends meet, they move south. Here. After forty years, Martner comes back to Provence, buys a home near Cavaillon and starts to live well again. Money to spare.'

'So? What does all this mean?'

'Call it a theory,' replied Jacquot, eager now to test it out, putting into words what had filled his head since leaving the Brasserie Chez Gaillard the previous week. The temptation to gauge someone else's reaction, just as she must have gauged his. Sitting here, at a table in the back room of Mazzelli's, the chance to speak out was just . . . irresistible. Also, he felt right somehow in trusting her. He took a deep breath. 'I believe that Martner found something out when he worked here in Cavaillon, during the war. And then, much later, when things got a little difficult for him, he remembered what he'd seen or heard during the war and came back to put it into play.'

'"Put it into play"?'

'Blackmail. Someone he knew with something to hide. Someone who'd be prepared to pay for his . . . discretion. It's the only way to explain the money.'

'And that money is . . . ?'

'The money we can't account for. Like I said, when Martner moved down here with his wife they had enough to get by. Nothing more. Not the kind of money to cover the expenses he was running up. His hot-house. His equipment. The trips abroad. Everything paid for in cash. And nothing in the records to show where it came from.'

'And this is money that has nothing to do with Eric Chabert?'

Jacquot shook his head. 'Nothing whatever. Which is the main reason I believe the boy is innocent. There's someone else mixed up in this. Someone we don't yet know about. Someone who thinks they've got away with murder. And I believe it's got something to do with the war. And Albert de Vausigne.'

Marie-Ange nodded, as though agreeing with every word of Jacquot's theory. Particularly the bit about Albert. Something had nagged at her from the moment she'd set eyes on that photo of Albert with Hélène de Vausigne's father.

'You know about this? About de Vausigne?' asked Jacquot, noting her reaction.

'Simon Dumé. He lives here in St Bédard, next door to Fontaine des Fleurs. He told me about it. Back in the war there was some kind of ambush on the Brieuc road, near the bridge. He says someone told the Germans about it, betrayed de Vausigne.'

Jacquot was taken aback. She knew almost exactly what he knew. 'Did this Dumé know who?'

Marie-Ange shook her head.

'Well . . . it's my bet Martner knew. Either he saw someone at the *Kommandantur* or overheard something. Or maybe he found something out when he was held in prison after the war, before he was repatriated. And forty years later, when he needed some money, he got in touch, put on some pressure. Which is, I'm increasingly certain, how he ended up dead. His wife, daughter . . .' Jacquot shrugged '. . . they were just in the way. Peripheral. It was Dr Martner the killer was after.'

'You're saying the killer was the person Martner was black-mailing?'

Jacquot took a gulp of beer, wiped his lips. 'Not necessarily, but that's how it usually is.' He held a hand in front of his mouth, catching his breath, then continued. 'You hold someone to ransom, threaten them, make them part with money – lots of money – and you run a very real risk that one day they'll turn on you, try to do you damage. Either they'll do it themselves or they'll bring someone in. Usually the former. Just do it and be done with it, kind of thing. Almost . . . instinctive. To put an end to the blackmail – the cost, the anxiety; to rid themselves once and for all of the risk of expo-sure.' Jacquot paused. 'Especially if you're playing the kind of game that I suspect Dr Martner played.'

'Which was?'

Jacquot was silent for a moment, trying to gather his thoughts, working things out in his head as he went along. 'There are two kinds of blackmail,' he began. 'The one-off payment and . . . well, let's call it the pension plan. The first, the one-off payment, is usually made as part of an exchange. Incriminating evidence. Letters, photo-graphs, whatever. There's a handover. You pay the money, you get the goods. And usually – usually – that's the end of it. But if you're buying silence, which was what Martner was offering, there is no exchange. The blackmailer still has the evidence – the information, whatever it is – and he can keep you swinging as long as he likes.'

'Until, as you say, you decide to do something about it.'

'Correct. Now, I can't say for certain what arrangements Martner had in place, but it's my guess he was probably going for the fund option. Small amounts but regular. One hundred, two hundred thou-sand francs a year. Something like that. A fund the victim pays into. Nothing too arduous, nothing too demanding. A little here, a little there. Martner probably worked out what his victim could afford and that was what he asked for. A nice little earner.'

'So what went wrong?'

'Either Martner got greedy and upped the ante or, as I said, the killer decided enough was enough. If he couldn't buy Martner's silence, he'd get it another way.'

'So do you have a suspect?'

Jacquot side-stepped. 'I know someone who would certainly have benefited from Albert's death, someone who had motive, means and opportunity to betray him. But he could never have killed the Martners.'

'You're talking about the Comte, aren't you?' asked Marie-Ange, nodding over his shoulder towards the church.

'What makes you think that?'

'He was the step-son. If his step-brother had inherited the title, what was there left for him? What kind of future?'

Jacquot nodded.

'Anyone else? Any other suspects?' Marie-Ange lifted her glass and finished her wine. 'The Comtesse, for example?'

Jacquot frowned. 'Why do you ask that?'

'Because . . . there is another voice I've heard.'

'Another voice?'

Marie-Ange paused, suddenly uncertain again. 'A new one,' she began. 'I've heard it twice so far. Just this last week. Working in the church. A lovely, lonely, soft voice. Like a whisper. A woman's voice. Elegant. Elderly, I'd say.'

'And what does this new voice say?' asked Jacquot, feeling the hairs on the back of his neck start to rise.

Marie-Ange put down her glass.

'Just one word,' she replied. 'Over and over again. "Rocsabin".'

70

Sunday morning the *cigales* were out in force, a crackling hum of unseen activity. Lizards scuttled from their hiding-places in the rocks and the sky was bright and clear, a thin, watery blue. It had rained hard in the night but for the first time in a week the low ceiling of racing, pewter-coloured clouds had gone, the mistral barnstorming its way south, out into the ocean, all that was left of its passing a scatter of fallen leaves and a faint tracing of red dust on windowsills and car windscreens.

Jacquot drove east into the Luberon hills with all the windows down, the rush of air as fresh and clean as the sky above. It felt as though Provence had been washed, rinsed and hung out to dry in the sparkling sunshine. Which was the other thing Jacquot loved about the mistral. The way it rearranged everything, tidied the place up, blew away the cobwebs. A summer spring-clean.

The house he was looking for was easy to find, exactly where the old lady had said. To the left of a swallow-swooping twelfth-century church. At the end of a narrow cobbled path. A green door set in a high wall.

Jacquot parked his car in the village square, in the shadow of the church, and followed the path on foot. It was walled on both sides, a passage of flaky gold stone that rose above his head, tightening the further he went. When he came to the green door, where the alley ended, he didn't bother to knock, just opened it as he'd been instructed to do and stepped into their garden.

Jacquot had phoned the evening before, after calling Hugo Rascousse. When the colonel heard what he wanted, he'd given Jacquot the number.

The wife had answered, cautious at first, but after Jacquot mentioned Tatine's funeral and Rascousse's name, she had become more animated. Her husband was out just then, she told him, but they would be happy to see him. The following day? *Bien sûr*, Monsieur. We will have some lunch, *non*?

Closing the door behind him, Jacquot found himself in a flag-stoned courtyard bordered by terracotta pots – oranges and lemons alternating with great blooms of pink hibiscus and yellow mimosa. In front of him stood a low stone house with butter-yellow walls, ivy weaving around turquoise shutters and the buttress peaks of the Grand Luberon rising above the pantiles.

An old woman, kneeling on a stuffed sack, was weeding a flower-bed by the front door. When she heard the latch she turned, shaded her eyes and got painfully to her feet. She wore a straw hat trimmed with a blue band, thick gloves and a housecoat tied round the middle.

'Monsieur Jacquot?'

Jacquot walked across the courtyard, held out his hand.

'Madame Bonaire?'

She pulled off a glove. 'That's me,' she replied, and shook his hand, shiny berry eyes twinkling in the leathery folds of her tanned face, taking in Jacquot's ponytail, pointed boots and leather jacket with an easy smile.

She looked at her watch. 'Just in time for lunch,' she said, pulling off her second glove and dropping them both on to the sack. 'You'll find Henri out back with his bees. Tell him lunch will be ready in twenty minutes. No later, you hear?'

Leading him round the side of the house and down a chip-wood path shaded with hoops of heavily scented jasmine, she stopped at an open doorway and pointed ahead. '*Là-bas*,' she said, then patted his arm and disappeared into the kitchen.

Behind the house Jacquot crossed a gravel terrace set with chairs and a wooden table in the shade of an old olive tree, and stepped down on to a strip of sloping lawn edged with oleander bushes and linden trees. At the far end of the lawn, a wall of gold limestone rose clear out of the ground, a craggy face that must have stood twenty metres or more above a line of brightly-coloured bee hives. The lid of one had been removed, set against the rock, and an old man, in shorts and singlet, his head covered with a black netted hat, was bent over the open hive.

Ten metres away Jacquot heard the busy drone of bees and saw them swarming around the hive. He stopped where he was, not wishing to get too near, and coughed politely. The old man turned, waved and reached down for the lid. He replaced it carefully, then came up the slope towards him. Even from a distance Jacquot could see that a handful of bees still clung to the bare skin of his arms and legs but he seemed unconcerned. As he approached, he brushed them gently away.

'Monsieur Jacquot,' he said, rolling up the veil of netting and pulling off his hat. 'I didn't recognise the name but I remember you from the funeral.'

'And I you, Monsieur.' Which Jacquot did. The shock of white hair was unmistakable. The man who had led the pallbearers at Sandrine's funeral, the one who'd presented Claudine with the flag from the coffin.

They shook hands, and Jacquot ducked as a solitary bee dived between them.

'Don't worry,' said Bonaire. 'They won't sting.'

'Then if they don't sting, why the netting?' asked Jacquot, looking around apprehensively, still not convinced.

'Mouth, nostrils and ears,' replied Bonaire, releasing his hand. 'My bees love to burrow. It tickles. And I'm very ticklish.'

It was a wonderfully intimate admission and Jacquot smiled.

Bonaire looked around. 'But it's too hot to stand here chatting,' he said. 'Come. Let's get ourselves a drink.'

On the terrace, Madame Bonaire was setting out a jug of wine, a bottle of rum and three glasses. She pulled the cork from the rum and poured three tots.

'English sailors are right, you know,' said Bonaire, picking up his glass and raising it to his guest. 'A wonderful drink. Keeps Monsieur Mort from the door. And at our age you don't want him come knocking.'

Jacquot nodded his agreement and raised the glass to his lips, ready to sip.

'No, no, no,' said Bonaire, putting out a hand to stop him. 'The first you drink fast, like this,' he continued, and tipping back their heads, Madame and Monsieur swallowed their rum in one, as one.

'But the second you take more gently,' advised Madame Bonaire, dabbing the corners of her mouth and pouring another shot for each of them, taking hers and heading back inside. 'And one only, mind,' she said, turning at the door. 'Lunch will be out *à la seconde*. And put on your shirt, Henri, if not for your health, then at least out of good manners.'

When she was gone Bonaire did as he'd been told, with a grumble about old women, and the two men settled themselves at the table.

'I am sorry I did not have an opportunity to speak with you and your wife at the funeral,' he said, 'to say how sorry I was for your loss.' He shrugged, as though he couldn't have helped himself. 'So many old faces. And I knew Rascousse would speak for all of us. She was a fine, fine woman.' He raised his glass. 'To Sandrine.'

'Sandrine,' said Jacquot, not bothering to correct the old man with regard to Claudine.

They put their glasses down. 'So, Monsieur. What is it I can do for you?'

'Actually it's "Chief Inspector". I am a policeman.'

'Aha! Chief inspector no less. I should have known,' replied Bonaire, sizing up his guest, just as his wife had done. 'The boots, the ah . . . the hair. Signs of rank nowadays, *non*? So, how can I be of help, Monsieur Chief Inspector?'

Jacquot pulled out his cigarettes, offered one, but Bonaire shook his head. 'No, no. You go ahead, though. I gave up years ago but I still love the smell.'

Jacquot lit up and Bonaire leaned forward, taking in the scent of burning black tobacco.

'It's about Sandrine,' said Jacquot. 'I believe you worked with her in the Resistance?'

'For two years. Since they threw me off my ship in Toulon and told me to go home. We were surrendering. *Pah!*' The old man took a sip of his rum.

'You worked with her for two years? The whole time?' Jacquot had imagined them working together every now and again – not constantly. And certainly not for that length of time.

335

'*Mais oui. Certainement*. The whole time. Hid out together. Ten, twelve of us. Up there in the hills,' he said, pointing to the wall of stone at the foot of his garden. 'Of course I didn't know her real name then. Only afterwards. She was . . .' Bonaire looked to the sky. 'Rose. That was it. Rose. Me, I was Choufleur – cauliflower. Even then I had a white head.' The old man smiled, ruffled his hair playfully, making it stand on end for a moment before it collapsed back.

'There was one action I wanted to know about particularly,' said Jacquot. 'On the Brieuc road, near St Bédard?'

Bonaire grunted. 'I know the place. Of course. Not likely to forget it. Rose, Sandrine. We were the only two made it out. The rest. *Pffft*. Gone.'

From the kitchen came a rattle of plates and a moment later Madame Bonaire appeared on the terrace carrying a large tray. She laid it on the table and distributed a selection of thick faience plates: slices of sausage, a mound of home-made *rillettes*, a heap of scarlet radishes, a bowl of wrinkled black olives, a basket of bread cut into chunks, three red apples and a wedge of ashy goat's cheese. A Luberon lunch.

'So. Help yourself, Monsieur,' she said, sitting herself between the men. 'Before it gets cold,' she added, with a smile.

'And some wine, Monsieur,' continued Bonaire, flourishing the jug in front of Jacquot till he had to toss back the last of the rum and hold out his glass. 'From our own vines. Down the hill apace. You'll have passed them on your way here,' he said, splashing a pale rosé into Jacquot's glass, then his wife's, then his own.

'So. *Santé*.'

For the next thirty minutes they ate – the *rillettes*, the radishes, the bread, the cheese – talking about the season, the crops. When Madame Bonaire had cleared the dishes and gone inside for some coffee, Jacquot switched back to Sandrine. 'They say there was an informer. The action at St Bédard bridge?'

Bonaire shifted uncomfortably, spread his hands. 'That's what they said. That's what I heard. Two or three names.'

At that moment Madame Bonaire reappeared with the coffee, set out the cups, poured.

'Names?' she asked.

'The war, *ma chère*. Monsieur Jacquot wants to know about the war. *Collabos*. Collaborators. Informants.'

'Oh, they were everywhere,' she said, passing round the sugar.

Jacquot took one lump, Bonaire two, his bent fingers plopping them into the cup, picking up a spoon and stirring vigorously.

'Like I said,' continued Bonaire, 'two or three names at least. But in those days, you wanted to get someone into trouble, settle a grudge maybe, you gave any name you chose. Just to make mischief. It didn't have to be true.'

Bonaire caught his wife's questioning look. 'St Bédard. Monsieur Jacquot wanted to know about it.'

Jacquot noticed Madame Bonaire's lips tightening.

'It was her,' said Madame Bonaire. 'You know it as well as I.'

'Denise, we do not know that. We cannot be sure. There were many mistakes made after liberation. Many innocent people . . .'

'I tell you it was her. Jealous, she was. Everyone knew it. That's why she did it. To get rid of Sandrine. She and Albert . . . well . . .'

'And who exactly is "her"?' asked Jacquot, knowing the answer.

Madame Bonaire looked at her husband. He made to shake his head but seemed to know it would do no good. It didn't.

'Hélène Rocsabin,' she said. 'Still lives there, I hear. The nerve. Not that anyone would know. Not now. But back then? Oh, there was talk. But she was canny. Kept her head down.'

'But surely . . .' began Jacquot.

Madame Bonaire shook her head. She knew what Jacquot was going to say. 'A woman scorned, Monsieur. You know the saying. Believe me, there is nothing you men should be more afraid of.'

Later, after the coffee cups were cleared and Jacquot made his farewells, Bonaire saw him to the gate.

'You shouldn't listen too much to my wife. It's just rumour. About the lady. Who knows?'

'But there was an informer?'

'You ask me . . . there had to be. They were waiting for us. Right there by the bridge.'

The two men shook hands and Jacquot turned to leave.

'It's strange, you know . . .' called Bonaire after him. 'After all this time . . .'

337

'What's strange?'

'You're not the first to come round here asking about that night at the bridge.'

'I'm not?'

Bonaire shook his head. 'No, no. Just last week. A girl. Very . . . You know what I mean. *Pouff*. A real Marianne.'

71

When Jacquot arrived home a black Chevy jeep was parked in the drive. He knew it from somewhere but couldn't place it. He made the connection when he saw the dogs, tied to the shoe-scraper outside Claudine's front door, panting in the afternoon sun, leaping to their feet when they saw him, barking, straining at their leashes.

Weimaraners.

Benedict.

He was wondering how to get past them – and what could possibly have brought Max Benedict out here on a Sunday afternoon – when the front door opened and the man himself stepped out, shushing the dogs, untying them, pulling them into order. Behind him Claudine stood in the doorway.

'Chief Inspector, how good to see you again,' said Benedict, reaching over the dogs' heads to shake Jacquot's hand. Then, turning to Claudine, he said: 'Madame, a delight to meet you at last. And thank you so much for taking such good care of me.' He gave a small bow, then turned back to Jacquot, the sun flashing off his spectacles. 'I wondered, Chief Inspector, if I might have a word?'

Jacquot caught Claudine's eye. 'A moment. I'll be back.'

Claudine understood, closed the door.

The two men walked to the jeep. Benedict opened the hatchback and the dogs leaped in, flung themselves on to a blanket and lay there panting. As he swung the door closed one of the dogs lifted a leg and licked his balls.

'Useful trick, that,' said Benedict, with a grin. 'Solve so many of the world's problems if we could do the same, don't you agree?'

'A great talent,' replied Jacquot, not knowing what else to say. 'Most rewarding.' What he really wanted to do was be angry, give Benedict a piece of his mind. Coming here like this, uninvited. And at the weekend. But as usual he found himself gently charmed. And intrigued. Benedict was not the kind of man who paid house calls on the police unless he had something they wanted, or wanted something they had. The last time they'd met, in the olive groves beneath the Martner estate, Benedict had given them the murder weapon. Jacquot decided to play this one along.

'You have a fabulous place here,' said Benedict. 'I thought I knew the area but this is a true *bijou*. I must have driven past the bottom of the lane a thousand times but I never suspected there was anything up here.'

'The sign usually puts people off,' replied Jacquot, wondering how Benedict had got the address, but not surprised that he had. The man was a journalist, after all. Not much he couldn't find out if he put his mind to it.

Benedict nodded. 'I'm sure it does,' he replied, pulling up the collar of his coat as a gust of wind shivered through the olives. He looked back at the house. 'Do you still have the mill pond?'

Jacquot gestured to the side of the house.

'May I?' asked Benedict, and without waiting for an answer he set off to take a look.

Jacquot followed him down the path.

'No wheel,' said Benedict sadly, standing beside the mill race. Even in summer the water still flowed, tumbling over a mossy ledge into the pool.

'The place was a wreck when Claudine found it,' said Jacquot. 'The wheel was long gone.'

'But still a wonderful spot,' sighed Benedict, taking in the sloping lawn, the border of almond trees. 'Even if you have the same problem as me,' he continued, pointing to the leaves that the mistral had littered across the lawn and the surface of the pond. 'I had to get the pool man out from Cavaillon. Such a bother.'

With a final look round, Benedict zipped up his jacket and reset-tled his half-frame spectacles. 'Well, I mustn't be keeping you. So good of you to show me round, Chief Inspector.'

Which rather threw Jacquot. He'd been certain Benedict was there for a reason. The man had even said he wanted a word. And now it looked as if he really had just . . . dropped by.

'I read your piece on the Martners, by the way,' prompted Jacquot, as they walked back to Benedict's car. 'Not bad.'

Benedict looked surprised. 'I'm honoured. And? What did you think?'

'Pretty fair, on the whole. Nicely written . . .'

The story had appeared in the *Figaro* weekend section, syndi-cated by Benedict's American magazine. Brunet had brought it into the office around the time Chabert's trial started, and shown it to Jacquot. It began, of course, with Benedict's own role in the story, finding the murder weapon. After establishing his involvement he'd outlined the murder and described the police investigation and arrest with surprising accuracy, given that Jacquot had made sure that all Benedict's enquiries were rerouted to Public Affairs and his access limited to press calls only.

'But,' continued Jacquot, 'you didn't seem . . . convinced.'

'So you really did read it?' said Benedict, pulling out his car keys. 'My, my. And you're right. I *wasn't* convinced. Eric Chabert? Why on earth would he do such a thing? Because the girl drops him? Because he gets the sack? No, no, no. I don't think so. The boy may be a bit dim, if you know what I mean, but he's not stupid. No, there's something else going on here. Which reminds me . . .' said Benedict.

Aha, thought Jacquot.

'Do you know? I was enjoying myself so much I'd almost forgotten the reason I dropped by.'

'And that might be?'

'The Rocsabin fire. I think I might have something of interest.'

'Which is?'

'On the night of the fire I was on my way home from a dinner party in Barjas. The Rheingolds. Do you know them?'

Jacquot shook his head.

'Charming couple. American. Anyway, where was I? Oh, yes. I

was driving home, on the back road between Barjas and Lucat, must have been a little after midnight, when a car just hurtled round that hairpin – you know the one, by the chapel? – and hit my wing-mirror. Twenty minutes later, I'm sitting out on the terrace with a nightcap when I hear the first fire engines tearing up the valley road and see the sky above Rocsabin aglow.'

'Did you happen to notice what kind of car?' asked Jacquot.

'A Mercedes, I think.'

'And did you happen to see who was driving it, Monsieur?'

'Regrettably not. The headlights . . . The speed . . . It all happened so quickly.'

'Model?'

'Not new. A saloon. Blue.'

'You could see the colour?'

'I have a scrape of its paint on my mirror. Right there,' said Benedict, pointing to the wing mirror secured to the car door on chrome struts, one of which was slightly buckled. 'You can just see it,' he continued, as Jacquot bent down to look. 'A light blue. It seemed to me that a car racing away from Rocsabin like that, even if it wasn't on a direct route from the warehouse, might have some-thing to do with the fire. Which is why I took the liberty of calling by on a Sunday.'

Jacquot felt in his pockets, found some paper, folded it into a makeshift envelope and stooped down to scrape some flakes of paint into it. 'And the reason you didn't report this earlier?' he asked, closing the envelope and slipping it into his pocket. 'The Rocsabin fire was more than a week ago.'

'I called you from the airport first thing the morning after. Thought it might be important. Left a message but you never called back.'

Jacquot remembered. A message slip from Mougeon with Benedict's name and a mobile-phone number. There'd been no message, no sense of urgency, but he'd called back anyway, from Aldo Mazzelli's terrace, on his way out to Rocsabin. He hadn't been able to get through and, knowing it was Benedict, he hadn't both-ered to try again.

'Airport?' asked Jacquot, changing the subject.

'On my way to New York. Work. Arrived back late last night to discover it's not just a fire any more. It appears you have another murder on your hands. And the Comte de Vausigne no less.'

'A double murder. There was a woman too.'

'The Comtesse must be devastated,' said Benedict, opening the driver's door and climbing into the jeep. Pulling on his seat-belt, he gave Jacquot a look, but Jacquot knew better than to volunteer any more information.

'I'm grateful for your interest,' said Jacquot, closing the door on him.

'You'll let me know if I can be of any further assistance?' replied Benedict with a smile.

'Be sure of it.'

Jacquot watched as Benedict started the Chevy and turned out of the drive. One of the dogs appeared in the back window and barked silently. A hand appeared from the driver's window and waved.

Jacquot waved back.

He might have had trouble placing the black Chevy, but Jacquot had no trouble placing a blue Mercedes.

72

Picard opened the door.

Jacquot and Brunet stood on the château steps. It was first thing Monday morning.

'I'd like to see Antoine de Vausigne,' said Jacquot.

Picard stepped aside for them to enter, then showed them across the hallway to the garden terrace.

'The Comte is staying in the summer-house. By the pool. Just follow the path,' he said, pointing across the lawn to a stone archway set in a low wall at the edge of a stand of trees. 'I'll call through to let him know you're coming.'

Antoine, dressed in swimming shorts and shiny with sun-tan oil, was spread out on a lounger reading a manuscript when Jacquot and Brunet appeared through the trees. He pushed up his sunglasses as they skirted the pool, watched them for a moment then let the glasses drop back into place. Beside the lounger was a breakfast plate covered in flaky *croissant* crumbs, a half-filled cafetière and a large saucerless cup that had left a tangle of circular stains on the stone.

'Monsieur de Vausigne, *bonjour*,' said Jacquot, noting the mess beside Antoine's lounger. Inside the cottage he could hear a phone ringing. Picard.

Without looking up, Antoine flicked through the remaining pages of the screenplay as though seeing how much more he had to read, then let it drop to the flagstones. 'Comte, Monsieur. *Comte* de Vausigne.'

Jacquot spread his hands as if desolated by his forgetfulness.

'So what is it I can do for you, Chief Inspector?' asked Antoine, reaching for the packet of cigarettes between his legs, lighting one, then dropping lighter and packet on to the discarded screenplay.

'First of all, please accept our condolences on the death of your father.'

'Thank you, Chief Inspector. That's . . . very kind of you.' Antoine glanced away to the trees, distracted for a moment. Sniffing lightly and pulling at his nose with thumb and forefinger, he turned back to Jacquot. 'Unbelievable. Quite unbelievable. My mother is beside herself, of course.'

'Of course,' said Jacquot, as though there could be no other possible reaction.

'So, tell me,' Antoine continued, 'what is it I can do for you now that you have delivered your condolences?'

'I believe you are the owner of a blue Mercedes, Monsieur,' began Jacquot.

'That's right,' he replied sharply, noting the 'Monsieur'. 'What of it?'

'We believe it may have been involved in a traffic accident,' replied Jacquot.

'Believe what you wish, Chief Inspector,' said Antoine, reaching out with his cigarette and tapping ash on to his breakfast plate.

Jacquot considered this. And then: 'Is your car here, Monsieur?'

'It is.'

'If it's not too much trouble, perhaps you would be kind enough to show us.'

Antoine de Vausigne sighed deeply. Getting to his feet, he slid on slippers, snatched up a dressing-gown and, with no indication that they should follow him, set off round the side of the guest cottage down a narrow path to a stone-built garage. The Mercedes was parked outside it, beneath the trees, dappled with shade.

'*Voilà*, Chief Inspector. One blue Mercedes, although it doesn't look to me like it's been involved in any accident.' He dropped his cigarette and ground it out.

'Would you mind?' asked Brunet, starting forward, meaning to examine the vehicle and asking permission.

'Be my guest.'

Brunet walked round the car, taking his time, examining the bodywork from wheels up while Jacquot and Antoine stood in silence, side by side, observing his progress. As he came round the boot, he stopped by the back passenger door, ran his hand along the edge of the roof, then gave Jacquot a nod.

Jacquot joined him, followed by Antoine.

'And this, Monsieur?'

It was easy to miss but an inch above the Mercedes' back door the metal trim had been flattened and a long, thin scratch had removed a layer of paint.

The new Comte's face clouded. He leaned past Jacquot and ran his fingers over the damage. 'Christ, how did that get there?'

'How indeed, Monsieur?'

'Well, how the hell should I know?' he snapped, clearly exasperated.

'So you're saying you have no knowledge of this damage?' continued Jacquot, knowing that he didn't. The annoyance was just too good, too genuine. No one could act it that well. De Vausigne might be a spoilt, unbearable little *crapaud* thought Jacquot, but he wasn't lying. There was no way he could have driven the Mercedes and not felt the impact of Benedict's wing mirror, or remain unaware of the damage to his car. If, indeed, it had been Antoine's Mercedes involved. As far as Jacquot was concerned it seemed a near certainty, but they'd have to wait for the tests on Benedict's sample to confirm it. Even then there was no reason to suppose that the Mercedes and its driver, whoever it might turn out to be, had had anything to do with the fire or the murders. As Benedict had pointed out, the incident had taken place on the Lucat road and, with Guy Bartolomé's suicide and that incriminating can of petrol in the boot of his car, the case had already been closed. But still . . .

Stepping away from the car and wiping his fingers on his dressing-gown, Antoine shook his head. 'That's exactly what I'm saying. No idea at all. Must have been done in town. Some incompetent *salaud* getting too close. How on earth should I know?'

'Maybe. Maybe,' nodded Jacquot. 'But, then, maybe not. I wonder if you would mind telling me when you last used the car?'

'Couple of days ago.'

'And where were you on the evening the accident was reported?'

'Which was when?'

'Nearly two weeks ago, Monsieur. The night of the fire at Rocsabin.'

Antoine looked surprised. 'The night of the fire? Well, I was here the whole time. Here in the guest-house. With my mother. Having dinner.'

'Just the two of you?'

'That's right. I cooked. Picard and his wife had the night off. Visiting their brood somewhere.'

'And the dinner ended when?'

'My mother likes to get to bed early. I walked her back to the house about ten thirty, elevenish.'

'And the car was where?'

'I don't know. Up at the house, I think. In the courtyard. Picard had used it to . . .' And then a possibility dawned on him. '*Merde alors*, if it was that old . . .'

'And you remember seeing it there?'

'No, I don't. And I don't remember seeing it here either. I can't remember.'

'So you don't always park the car here, Monsieur?' asked Jacquot, indicating the garage.

'No. Not always. It depends.'

'Depends?'

Antoine brushed his hand through his hair. He was getting annoyed. 'Depends whether I'm going to the house, or coming here. Whether I use the front or the back drive. Sometimes I park it here. Sometimes I leave it at the house. It's not that long a walk, Chief Inspector. I mean, I do have legs.'

'And the evening of the dinner?' continued Jacquot. 'You saw your mother home and . . .'

'I saw her up the garden steps and left her at one of the terrace doors. I did not go round to the front. Which was why I didn't actually see my car in the courtyard. I just assumed it was there. Or here.'

'Well, apparently it was in neither place, Monsieur,' replied Jacquot. 'From what I can see, I should tell you it seems very probable that this is the car reported on the Lucat road a short time after you had dinner with your mother. And only a short time before the fire at Rocsabin.'

'Well, it's got nothing to do with me, Chief Inspector.'

'Could the car have been taken without your knowledge, Monsieur?' asked Brunet.

'Well, if you say it was involved in this accident, it must have been, mustn't it?'

'Would you hear the car from your cottage if someone was driving it away?'

'Depends where you're going. You'd need the engine to get up the front drive, but the back drive over there,' Antoine gestured through the trees, 'why, you could easily coast it.'

'And where do you normally keep your keys, Monsieur?' continued Brunet.

Antoine waved at the guest cottage through the trees. 'Jacket. Kitchen table. I don't know.' He paused, looked Brunet up and down. 'Where do you keep yours?' he asked. 'On a hook, I suppose.'

'With your permission,' said Jacquot. 'I'd like some of our boys to come up, take a look at the car? If that's all right?'

Antoine shrugged.

'Say this afternoon?'

'If you think it necessary.'

Jacquot thanked him, then paused, seemed to consider something. 'Tell me, you came back to the guest-house after seeing your mother home?'

'Correct.'

'And what then, if you don't mind my asking? After you got back?'

Antoine smiled but said nothing.

'Watched TV? Listened to some music? Went to bed?' prompted Jacquot.

'Not exactly, Chief Inspector.'

Jacquot saw the amused look. 'You had company?'

'Correct.'

'Would you mind telling me the name of your companion?'

'To make sure I'm telling the truth? You don't really imagine I'd kill my own father, surely?'

Jacquot demurred, said nothing.

'Her name is Frankie Alzon,' Antoine replied.

Beside him, Brunet cleared his throat.

'She's a nurse at the hospital in Cavaillon,' Antoine continued. 'Charming girl. She came out here after her shift. Round eleven. She loves films. Writes these little scenarios for me. Which she acts in.' He smiled. 'And you know something? She really is very good.'

73

After leaving Antoine by the pool, Jacquot and Brunet crossed the lawn and climbed the terrace steps to the château. Picard was waiting for them at the french windows. He looked perturbed. 'I'm so sorry, Monsieur,' he began. 'I tried to call the Comte but got no answer. Did you manage to find . . . ?'

'Yes, yes, no problem,' said Jacquot. 'But I wonder,' he continued, stepping past Picard into the hallway, 'since we're here, whether it might be possible to have a few words with the Comtesse?'

'If you'll wait here a moment, sir, I'll see if I can find her.'

Moments later he was back, shoes tapping over the stone floor. 'If you'd care to follow me, Messieurs, Madame la Comtesse will see you in the morning room.'

The Comtesse was standing by the fireplace. She was dressed in black. The outfit made her look thinner, taller. And, Jacquot was forced to concede, mighty elegant. Picard announced them and withdrew, closing the door behind him.

The last time they'd spoken, at Cavaillon Police Headquarters, Jacquot had watched Hélène de Vausigne fight back her emotions as she sifted through the plastic bags that held her husband's belongings. Nearly two weeks later she still looked shaken, her icy cool fractured, her movements and voice unsteady. Behind her, looming above the mantelpiece, a portrait of the Comte as a younger man,

350

hands elegantly pocketed, a gun held in the crook of his arm, had been framed in black silk.

'Chief Inspector. Inspector Brunet,' she said, nodding in their direction.

'Madame,' Jacquot began, 'I'm sorry to bother you again at this time but I would be most grateful if I could ask you a few questions.'

'I believe I have told you all I know,' she replied. 'What more can I say?'

'As far as the Rocsabin incident, and your husband, yes. But I'd like to speak to you about something else entirely. To do with the war.'

Hélène de Vausigne crossed to a sofa and sat down, sliding her legs to one side and folding her hands in her lap. She gestured for them to take a seat opposite and gave Jacquot an intrigued by-all-means-carry-on look as he made himself comfortable.

'Your maiden name is Rocsabin, is it not?'

'That is correct.'

'And during the war,' Jacquot continued, 'you lived at Rocsabin, I believe?'

'In the war? That is also correct. Until the very last days when the Germans requisitioned the château and moved us out.'

'I didn't know that,' said Jacquot.

Hélène de Vausigne nodded. 'The Allies had landed by then and the Germans were on the run. They needed a good defensive position. And Rocsabin was certainly that, had been for centuries. You can't move up the valley without passing Rocsabin. And the Germans knew it. They held the Allies there for ten days. Until the big guns were brought up. And that was that.'

She clasped her hands, looked round the room.

'We stayed here, my mother, my father and I. With Béatrice and Edouard. Close enough to hear it all. I remember going back with my parents, after the fighting was over. And the château was gone. Just rubble. Nothing left. And that was how it stayed, oh, for years . . . until we cleared the land and built the furniture warehouse. Exactly there.'

'So your family, the Rocsabins, and the de Vausignes were friends, as well as neighbours?'

'That is correct. It was always hoped that I would marry Gilles. The two families, you know . . .'

'Gilles? Not Albert?'

Hélène de Vausigne started. 'Certainly not Albert. At first, of course. When we were growing up, we saw a lot of each other. But later it became clear we had little in common, just that we were the children of friends and neighbours. You know how it is, I'm sure. And then Gilles arrived on the scene . . .' For a moment it looked as though the memory might bring on tears, but she steeled herself. '. . . after Albert's father remarried.'

Jacquot appeared to give this due consideration.

The Comtesse gathered herself. 'But I really can't see what this is about, Chief Inspector, where all this is going,' she said, managing a helpful smile.

Brunet shifted in his seat, also uncertain where all this was going. Thirty minutes earlier they'd been quizzing the son about his Mercedes, and now here they were discussing the war with his mother.

'Just trying to clear a few things up,' replied Jacquot.

'From fifty years ago? Really?'

'Did you know that Albert de Vausigne fought with the Resistance?'

Hélène de Vausigne sighed patiently. 'In those days, in this part of the world, almost every young man fought in the Resistance. Or, at least, that was what they liked to tell you. Still do, some of them.'

'And women too.'

The Comtesse looked down at her hands. 'I helped where I could,' she replied quietly.

'Women like Sandrine Eddé?'

The Comtesse gave the name some thought, trying to place it, then shook her head.

'You might have known her as Rose Valence?' said Jacquot, the name on the false papers in Sandrine's deed-box. 'Her *nom de guerre*, if you like.'

'No, no. I'm sorry. I do not recognise either name. But that means nothing. There were many groups then, many outfits.'

Jacquot nodded. Of course there were, of course there were, he seemed to be saying. What he actually said was: 'Sandrine Eddé worked with Albert de Vausigne. In the same group.'

There was silence for a moment, as Hélène de Vausigne considered. 'Maybe,' she replied. 'It's possible.'

Jacquot nodded again. Said nothing. If what old man Gaillard and the Bonaires had told him was true, and he had no reason to doubt them, then the Comtesse had to be lying. She must have known, or known of, Sandrine Eddé. Or Rose Valence.

Somewhere in the house a clock sounded the hour.

'You say you worked for the Resistance?' Jacquot continued.

'Now and then. Running messages. That sort of thing. I was young. A girl. Sixteen, seventeen. I had an easier time getting around. The Germans didn't pay me much attention.'

'But no action?'

Hélène de Vausigne looked at him sternly. 'No action, no. Nothing . . . direct.'

'In June nineteen forty-four there was an incident near here, on the Brieuc road. By the St Bédard bridge. Maybe you recall?'

'Of course I recall,' she replied sharply.

'Did you play any part in this action?'

'I did not.'

'But you knew about it?'

At first the Comtesse said nothing, then she nodded. 'Albert told me about it. I knew it was coming.'

'The when and where?'

'Correct. But I was not happy. I had a feeling about it. I tried to dissuade him.'

'Why was that? What feeling?'

'A couple of months earlier Albert's team had carried out a similar operation between Brieuc and Barjas on the same transport route. It had been successful. Very successful. They had . . . liberated . . . a substantial cache of arms and ammunition. As a result the Germans were on the lookout. It was too soon to repeat the operation.'

'And that was what you told Albert?'

'That's what I told Albert. But he wouldn't listen. He said the Germans would never expect a second strike in the same place. And, anyway, they'd made up their minds.'

'"They"?'

Hélène de Vausigne raised a hand to her mouth, cleared her

throat. 'The planners. Albert and the planners. He told me it was arranged. They wouldn't change it. Couldn't change it.'

Jacquot remembered the pencilled notation on the map. The date, the time. Sandrine had been on that operation. One of only two to escape, according to Rascousse.

'Does the name Rascousse mean anything to you? Hugo Rascousse?'

Hélène de Vausigne shook her head. 'Rascousse? No, the name is not familiar.'

'Colonel Hugo Rascousse was in overall charge of Resistance fighters here in the south. He was known by the code-name Renard. He told me that the operation at the St Bédard bridge failed because someone betrayed them.'

'I've heard that said. But I do not believe it,' said the Comtesse firmly, squeezing her hands together. 'They were pushing their luck, that's all. The Germans weren't stupid, you know.'

'Rascousse says it was a deliberate trap,' repeated Jacquot. 'Nothing to do with luck.'

'I really don't see where this is leading, Chief Inspector. I mean, this was fifty years ago. What possible—'

Jacquot cut her off. 'At the end of nineteen forty-three, a medical orderly called Josef Martner, a close neighbour of yours for the last ten years, was posted to Cavaillon.'

Hélène de Vausigne stiffened. Jacquot and Brunet both noticed.

Jacquot continued: 'Nearly forty years later Dr Martner returned, bought a house here, retired.'

'Many Germans do,' she replied, calmer now, patiently, as though speaking to someone who seemed not to grasp what was plainly obvious, widely known, regretfully accepted. 'As I'm sure you know. The climate here is a great attraction. We may not like it, this . . . invasion, but what can we do?'

'Now, Dr Martner was not a rich man,' continued Jacquot, as though he hadn't heard a word the Comtesse had said, 'but he lived a life he really could not afford. What I want to know is . . . how did he manage that trick?'

'And how do you suppose I can help you with that?' replied the Comtesse, crisply. 'I never knew the man. I told your colleague here when the murders were being investigated. And I seem to remember

I told you the very same thing. Dr Martner may have lived here, I may have passed his house dozens of times, but we never met.'

'And there, you see, is my problem, Madame,' said Jacquot, sitting back, crossing his legs. 'Because I believe you did know him. Maybe not that well during the war, but certainly in the years he lived here. In fact, I'd say you got to know him very well indeed.'

'Ridiculous! Quite preposterous! I really don't know what you're trying . . .' Hélène de Vausigne got to her feet and started for the door. 'I think, perhaps, it's time you left, Chief Inspector.'

'Not quite,' replied Jacquot, keeping his seat, certain now that he was on the right track, the scent stronger than ever. That his hunch, formulated on that walk from Gaillard's brasserie to his office and on the drive back from the Bonaires', was paying off. 'Unless, of course, you'd like to continue this conversation at Headquarters.'

The Comtesse gave him a withering look. 'Please don't threaten me, Chief Inspector.'

Jacquot spread his hands but said nothing.

'What is it you want to know?' she said quietly, returning to the sofa, settling herself.

'I want to know if Dr Martner was blackmailing you.'

The silence stretched away. Birds were trilling in the garden, the *cigales* hummed, somewhere a dog barked.

When the words came, they were soft, resigned. 'Yes, he was.'

'Because he knew what you did in the war? How you passed on certain information to the Germans? Collaboration?'

The word hit her like a slap. The word that made the blackmail possible.

'He knew, didn't he? Martner. Maybe he saw you at the *Kommandantur*. Maybe he overheard something. As a medical orderly he was hardly operational. But he found out, didn't he? He knew you were the one who gave the game away. The one who told the Germans about the action at the bridge.'

Hélène de Vausigne held his eye, then looked at her hands, twisting in her lap. For a moment or two she said nothing, then turned to the french windows as though the past was waiting for her on the terrace, waiting for her to acknowledge it.

'When I went to the Germans,' she began, 'I was shown into a colonel's office. I forget his name. He was having his teeth checked, of all things. At his desk, boots up on the table, a little white bib round his neck. He made no attempt to dismiss the orderly, just made me say everything in front of them both. As though to humiliate me. For someone else to witness my . . . treachery. The orderly was there the whole time. Forty years later he introduced himself.'

'And is that why you killed him?' asked Jacquot, knowing absolutely that she had not. She might have been able to fake the break-in at the château, but she certainly wasn't strong enough to handle that shotgun – not for twenty-odd shots' worth, she wasn't. And somehow he couldn't see her recovering too quickly from that fall in the kitchen, or chasing Kippi up the drive.

'No! I did not. Absolutely not. That is not true.' The Comtesse looked outraged. But then, slowly, the anger passed and a smile played across her lips. 'Although I can't deny, Chief Inspector, that it was welcome news.' She sighed. 'All that money.'

'How much did you pay him?'

'Over the years? A fortune,' she replied. 'Twice, three times a year. A hundred thousand here, fifty thousand there. Whatever he needed. For his holidays, I suppose, or his blessed plants.' She cast around the room. 'Paintings, silver, family things. Even land. I had to sell so much. But now I don't have to pay another *sou*. Thanks to someone else, to whom I shall always remain immensely grateful.'

Hélène de Vausigne had clearly regained her composure. She pinned Jacquot with a cool, implacable stare. 'And now, I think, you had better leave, Chief Inspector.'

The two men got to their feet and Jacquot followed Brunet to the door. As Brunet opened it, Jacquot turned to the Comtesse. She was standing by the sofa, her back to them, staring out of the window.

'What I can't understand,' said Jacquot, 'is why you betrayed the man you loved. Because it was Albert you loved, wasn't it? Not Gilles.'

Hélène de Vausigne turned to him, lifted her chin. Her voice, when she spoke, was calm, accepting. 'Yes. It was Albert I loved. I always had. He was so . . .' She shook her head as though she was unable to find the right word. 'But I never meant him to die. That was not the plan. It was the woman, the name you said. She was the one I wanted out of the way. Without her . . .' The Comtesse sighed at what might have been.

Jacquot said nothing. He sensed there was more to come.

'The night of the raid, Albert came to dinner. At Rocsabin. Later, when it was time for him to leave, after my parents had gone to bed, I . . . I made myself . . . available. I was certain I could get him to stay.' She smiled, and then the smile faded. 'But I couldn't. He wouldn't be . . . persuaded. He just . . . laughed. Gave me a hug. Told me I was his little sister. Which . . .' her face hardened '. . . Which. Made. Me. Hate. Him. Suddenly, right then, right there, I just didn't care any more.'

She felt for the sofa, lowered herself into it. 'I never saw him again.'

'Thank you, Madame.'

Outside the château, Jacquot strode ahead. He was strapping on his seat-belt by the time Brunet got into the car.

'Mind telling me, boss, what on earth all that was about?'

'An opening shot,' replied Jacquot, starting the engine, looking over his shoulder as he turned the car. 'Just an opening shot.'

74

Frankie Alzon lived in a small *atelier* overlooking a corner of the market square in Cavaillon. Even at four in the afternoon, long after the stalls that lined the square had been taken down, the sweet scent of melons still hung in the air, the gutters littered with their discarded sabre-shaped crescents.

'Maybe I should stay out of this,' suggested Brunet, as the two men climbed the stairs leading to the top floor of Alzon's building.

'Oh, I don't think so,' said Jacquot, savouring the prospect of seeing his assistant come face to face with an old acquaintance. Which was how Brunet had described Mademoiselle Alzon on their drive back to town. 'No, you should be there, you knowing her and all.'

When they reached her door, Jacquot held back so that Brunet had to knock. As they waited, Brunet straightened his tie, brushed back his hair. He looked distinctly unhappy, like a cat caught in a shower of rain.

When she opened the door Frankie Alzon was tugging on a silk dressing-gown. Her cheeks were flushed and a sheen of sweat covered her throat and brow. Over her shoulder, the doors to a tiny roof terrace were open. On the terrace was a towel, a wine glass and cassette player. A narrow square of sun slanted across the towel. Frankie Alzon had been sunbathing.

'Yes?' she said, pushing a wedge of blonde hair from her eyes.

358

It was clear she hadn't been expecting visitors and she seemed cross with herself that she'd answered the door.

Jacquot knew at once that Antoine hadn't phoned to warn her that the police might come calling. He was too cocky, too sure of himself – and the facts – to bother. He knew that Frankie Alzon would back up his story.

'Inspector Jean Brunet,' said Brunet, showing his badge, 'and Chief Inspector Jacquot. Cavaillon Police.'

The word 'police' seemed to make no impression. Instead she looked at Brunet's badge and back at his face.

'I know you, don't I?' she asked. Then grinned when she made the connection. 'Jean Brunet, that's right. But I don't recall you being a policeman. Lawyer, wasn't it?'

Already Brunet was squirming. Jacquot stepped forward, taking gleeful pity on his assistant. 'Mademoiselle Alzon? I wonder if we might come in. A few questions?'

She gave Jacquot a look, clearly liking what she saw. 'Sure,' she said, and stepped aside, closing the door behind them, squeezing past to show them through into a cramped little salon.

The place was a mess. A spilled stack of magazines on the floor, three empty mugs and a dirty ashtray on the coffee-table, a basket of washing set beside an ironing-board. After a week of mistral, the sun's reappearance had clearly taken precedence over housework.

But the apartment had a certain charm, Jacquot decided as he and Brunet settled themselves on a sofa covered with throws. It might be untidy but Frankie Alzon had made an effort: the cast-iron fireplace painted a deep gloss crimson and filled with a mass of sunflowers, a threadbare green carpet patched with rugs, and the walls hung with movie posters in clip frames wherever the bulging plaster allowed. He liked the smell of the place too: a warm pulse of garlic, perfume and cigarettes suspended in the kind of languid, ticking heat you get when you live in an attic and the sun's been hammering down all day. Snug and faintly naughty, he thought, a good place for long lovers' afternoons, the windows open, the muted calls of the market-sellers below and the drowsy cooing of pigeons. Yes, Jacquot liked it a lot. It was much like the apartment he'd moved into when he first arrived in Cavaillon, under the eaves on Cours Bournissac. The same kind of lay-out too. Bedroom to the right, an arched opening behind Mademoiselle Alzon leading to a small galley kitchen, and beyond that a bathroom with no window. When a bulb blew, it would be pitch black in there.

Curling up in the room's single armchair, gathering the edges of her dressing-gown to tuck round her legs, Frankie Alzon reached for a packet of cigarettes, lit up and gave them a mischievous 'Well?' look, her brown eyes switching between them, brows arching, leaving them to make the play.

'We're investigating a traffic accident, Mam'selle, on the road to—' Jacquot got no further.

'A traffic accident? A chief inspector investigating a traffic accident?' She blew out a stream of smoke, and laughed. 'Hey, I mean, I know Cavaillon's quiet, but—'

'A traffic accident involving a car that might have been used in the commission of a crime,' explained Jacquot.

'You mean, like a getaway car? That sort of thing?'

'That sort of thing, yes.'

'So? What's it got to do with me? I haven't been in any accidents.'

'We believe the car in question may belong to a friend of yours.'

'Oh, yeah? Who?'

'Perhaps I could start by asking, Mam'selle Alzon, what you were doing on July the twenty-first? A Tuesday. Around, say, ten o'clock?'

'Morning or evening?' she shot back.

'Evening,' replied Jacquot.

She gave it no thought. 'Working. At the hospital. Twelve till ten. Tuesday through Saturday. Never finish before ten-thirty, though. Not in Casualty, you don't.'

'And afterwards?'

'Afterwards . . .' She frowned. 'What day did you say?'

'Tuesday. The twenty-first.'

'Tuesday, let me see . . .' And then she smiled. 'That's right, I met up with a friend.'

'Friend?'

'Old friend. Bit of business. Bit of fun. You know?'

'And the friend's name, Mademoiselle?'

She reached forward for the ashtray, settled it on her lap, tapped in some ash. 'Antoine – Antoine de Vausigne. He lives the other side of St . . . Whatsit? Bédard,' she continued. 'Big old place. Beautiful.'

'And you arrived there at what time?'

'Say, a little after eleven? Around there. The time it takes from the hospital. I still had my uniform on . . .' She gave Jacquot a look.

He nodded. 'And you stayed how long?'

Frankie Alzon narrowed her eyes, snuggled deeper into the chair. 'Let's say the birds were singing when I left, Chief Inspector.'

Jacquot smiled. 'You said "old friend",' he continued, changing tack. 'Have you known Monsieur de Vausigne long?'

Frankie Alzon shrugged. 'Couple of years. Why? What's all this got to do with Antoine?'

'We believe the car involved in this incident may have belonged to him.'

'Oh, yeah? Well, I can tell you he wasn't doing any driving that night.'

'You're quite sure?'

'Believe it,' she said, stubbing out her cigarette, then leaning down to put the ashtray on the floor.

'And did you happen to see the Mercedes when you arrived at the house?'

There was silence for a moment while Frankie tried to remember. 'Not that I recall.'

'You used the front or back drive to the château?'

'The back drive. Didn't want to disturb the old lady, Antoine's mum.'

'Tell me,' asked Jacquot, after a brief pause, 'you mentioned business. You work for Monsieur de Vausigne?'

'You could say,' she replied, with a smile. 'I write him screen-plays. Scenarios. For his video company. Do a bit of acting too.'

'And how often do you see him?'

'Whenever he's down here. I don't know, four, five times a year. *Il est là* – he's cool.'

'And have you visited him in Paris?'

'No. Not yet,' she said, a trace of disappointment in her voice. But she gathered herself. 'I guess you could say I'm his Cavaillon branch. More use to him here.'

'And when he's here, does he stay with you? Or at his parents' house?'

'Both. It depends.'

'And how long does he stay, when he's with you?'

'Varies.'

'A week?'

'Never that long – a weekend, maybe. Overnight.' And then, suddenly, Frankie Alzon pursed her lips, glanced at her watch, and Jacquot knew in an instant he'd gone as far as he could, knew what she was thinking. Why was she bothering with all these questions when the sun was shining outside and her tan needed attention? He'd been waiting for it, the moment she clammed up. And this was it.

'Look,' she said, sharp and flinty now, 'I don't really see what all this has got to do with a car crash. I mean—'

'You're quite right, Mademoiselle. Quite right.' Jacquot clasped his knees and pushed himself to his feet. The springs in the sofa had sunk him lower than he'd been prepared for. 'All just routine stuff, really. But thank you for letting us take up so much of your time.'

'Mmmmhh,' was all she said, a little disapprovingly, then pulled herself out of the chair and showed them to the front door. 'Tell me,' she asked, turning the lock and opening the door for them, 'does Antoine know you're here?'

Jacquot turned in the doorway, holding up Brunet who was forced to stand only inches away from her: 'Of course, Mademoiselle. It was Monsieur de Vausigne who gave us your name and address. How else . . . ?'

'Okay, okay. It's just . . .'

'The sun is shining and time is short, *n'est-ce pas*?' said Jacquot.

'In one,' she replied, and smiled. Then, turning to Brunet, she let the smile fade as she looked him over: 'Always preferred doctors myself,' she said, and with that she stepped back and closed the door.

75

As Picard drove off, Antoine checked the name and address that Duc had given him. Panisse. He'd heard of it. A private club on Place Véran, a small square off Gambetta, just a couple of blocks away.

It was a little after ten and, thanks to Picard, he was late.

Picard and the police.

They'd phoned that afternoon, someone from Cavaillon Headquarters, asking if they could bring his car in for a paint match rather than do their tests at the château. They told him they'd bring it back the following day or he could pick it up himself, if he preferred. He told them he'd collect it in the morning, then left a message with Frankie saying he was coming into town later, and what about dinner?

An hour after he put down the phone, a couple of police mechanics turned up with a flat-bed truck and winched the Mercedes aboard. Antoine had supervised the whole operation, flying into a rage when it looked like the bumper was about to connect with the winch struts.

Without the Mercedes, and having drunk a little too much wine by the pool, Antoine had Picard drive him to Cavaillon. Which was why he was running late. Despite a clear road the old man had kept under eighty the whole way, easily enough to put Antoine in an even fouler mood had it not been for the Citroën.

There was something soothing and stately about its progress, Antoine had decided, something about sitting there in the back, with Picard up front, which made eighty k.p.h. seem just about the right speed. No wonder his father had liked it so much. It was a fabulous motor. The original grey-felt trim and roofing, the looped grips, the etched-glass reading lights, the spotless carpeting. And the leather upholstery – soft, shining, hardly a crack anywhere. Beeswax polish and saddle-soap, that was the secret. Once a week. A good buffing. You had to hand it to Picard, he knew how to keep the old jalopy in order.

Worth a bit too, Antoine reckoned. One of his father's better investments. And as Picard pulled up in Cours Gambetta, he wondered how much he'd be able to get for it. Classic car, excellent condition . . . Or maybe, just maybe, he could keep it, set something up with the new film company. Rent the car out as a prop. Top rate. There was easily enough room up front for a camera, lights . . . and, as he watched Picard glide away from the kerb, he thought of Frankie naked on the back seat. Or Louise. Or Zizi. Or . . . He'd have a talk with his accountant, see what they could come up with.

Five minutes later, turning into Place Véran, he spotted the sign he was looking for, a blue neon 'P' set above closed double doors on the far side of the square. He was just a few steps away when one of the doors opened and a large man in an evening suit stepped out. 'M'sieur?' he asked, blocking Antoine's path

'I'm not a member,' said Antoine, glancing up and down the pavement. 'I've come to see Christophe.'

'And you are?'

'Duc sent me.'

'Please go on down, M'sieur,' said the heavy, stepping aside. 'Your friend is at the bar.'

Antoine's 'friend' was no such thing. They'd never even met. Duc had given him Christophe's name and number in case supplies ran low, and Antoine had called to set up the meet. When Antoine mentioned Duc, Christophe had had no trouble in accommodating him. Just as Antoine had no problem identifying his man as he trotted down the stairs and into Panisse's bar. Sitting on the furthest stool, with his back against the wall, Christophe wore a sharp black suit and braided hair. He was playing with a lighter and looked as if he owned the place. Antoine recognised the type and walked over.

'Late's not nice,' said Christophe.

Antoine shrugged. 'Rude's not nice. That's what Duc told me.'

Once again Duc's name seemed to do the job.

'It's in the car,' said Christophe, finishing his drink and sliding off the stool. 'We'll take a drive.'

A few minutes later, in a throaty BMW Z3, Christophe pointed to the glove compartment as they pulled out of the *place* and headed out of town.

'Half an ounce. As requested.'

Antoine pulled an envelope from his pocket. 'Nine thousand francs. As requested.'

Which was exactly the moment that the two men became aware of a flashing blue light appearing from nowhere and the rising, heart-stopping wail of a siren.

'Shit,' said Antoine.

'I'll lose them,' said Christophe.

76

If she had driven without headlights Marie-Ange would still have found her way to Rocsabin. There was a full moon in a cloudless sky, so bright that the road she followed was as clear as a twisting white ribbon.

It was a little after ten when the hairpins straightened, the road levelled and she pulled into Rocsabin, parking the Chaberts' van in a side-street beside the church. As she climbed out from the driver's seat, she was suddenly glad of her wrap, tugging it round her shoulders. The village was only a hundred metres higher than St Bédard, but the nights were sharper here.

Marie-Ange wondered which direction she should take. She had no idea what she was looking for, and no idea what to expect. But she knew she was there for a reason. Forty minutes earlier, she'd been crossing the *place* from Mazzelli's, thinking about her bed, when without any warning she heard a voice whispering in her ear. Whispering a name. Over and over again so that it sounded like a single word – Rocsabinrocsabinrocsabinrocsabin. She'd spun round but there was no one there. Just the whispering. The old lady's voice again. Soft but urgent. She could almost feel the breath that came with it, tickling her ear, and she'd shivered from the top of her head to her toes. Ten minutes later, starting the Chaberts' van in the *mairie* car park and turning on to the Chant-le-Neuf road, the whispering stopped as suddenly as it had started.

She had known then for certain that she was headed in the right direction.

It wasn't the first time Marie-Ange had been to Rocsabin. She drove through the village every Wednesday afternoon on her way to the stables, and called there twice a week to deliver her table sets to the restaurant Ravigote. But tonight was the only time she'd been there after dark.

Marie-Ange decided to start in the *place*, drawn by the chatter of voices rising from the outside tables at Ravigote. Rocsabin was larger than St Bédard but not as pretty. Most of the buildings around the *place* had been built since the war and lacked the gentle elegance of St Bédard's crescent of townhouses. The only thing that Rocsabin had was its position, its elevation, one entire side of the *place*, bordered by a low wall, set above the length of the Brieuc valley. Which was where Marie-Ange headed, sitting on the wall and gazing across the valley at the twinkling lights of St Bédard and Chant-le-Neuf, the ridge above them smeared with a distant orange glow from Brieuc and Cavaillon.

It was there, sitting on the wall, that Marie-Ange became aware of a dark, cindery smell that reminded her of the scent in the Château de Vausigne the afternoon that Antoine had caught her snooping. Without knowing why, she returned to her car, started it and headed out of Rocsabin. Five minutes later, on the road leading to the stud, she pulled into the car park of the HacheGee furniture warehouse and switched off the engine.

For a minute or two she sat where she was, listening to the gentle ticking of the engine and the distant barking of a dog. Through the windscreen the blackened hulk of the warehouse with its scorched brick walls and twisted, lumpen interior rose up pale and ghostly grey in the moonlight, cross-hatched with shadows from the scaffolding that had been set up as supports until the authorities decided what to do with it. Around its perimeter a line of wire mesh fence panels set in blocks of concrete had been put in place to keep out the curious. On every third panel a notice with bold red letters on a white background prohibited entry, warning of danger from imminent collapse.

Marie-Ange got out of the car and walked towards the fence, gravel crunching underfoot, the dog still barking, unseen, somewhere beyond the line of trees that edged the far side of the car park. The scent of burning was stronger here, which struck her as strange. With the mistral storming its way through the previous week there should have been no smell at all.

It was at that precise moment, walking towards the warehouse with the moon casting her shadow directly ahead, that Marie-Ange felt an icy puckering across her skin and sensed a growing silence, a turning down of the ambient volume around her. She could still feel the gravel underfoot but she couldn't hear it so clearly now. Nor was the dog barking quite so loudly, as though it was being dragged away. Marie-Ange stopped and looked around her. Nothing moved. The moon still lit the scene like a photographic negative but the silence now was total.

She took a breath, waited, wrapping icy hands into the ends of her shawl, burrowing her shoulders into its warmth. And then, out of the silence, beyond the blackened hulk of the warehouse, came a distant boom-boom-boom-boom-boom, like a line of big guns firing, one after another, from somewhere far away in the valley. Followed, seconds later, by a whistling shriek of shells and a series of crashing, thunderous explosions, making her duck and crouch. It was as though a war had broken out around her. Yet everything she could see was still. Nothing moved. No shadows in the pearly moonlight but her own and that of the scaffolding. Nothing to explain the mayhem raging around her, the sound of falling rock and stone, the splintering of wood and the shattering of glass, the acrid scent of cordite and the bitter, dusty taste in her mouth.

Marie-Ange straightened, walked to the fence and looped her fingers through the mesh while the battle raged around her, staring into the warehouse's empty, charred interior. And as she did so, the sounds diminished and the silence came again, deep and muffling.

And then, behind her, breaking into the silence, she heard a vehicle pull into the car park and she turned, apprehensive, expecting to see a sweep of headlights. The security people come to check the property, she thought, wondering what she'd say, how she'd explain herself being there. But there was nothing. Nothing to see. Only the sound of a car door slamming shut, and footsteps on gravel, coming towards her, closing, brushing past, only inches away.

Marie-Ange shuddered, shut her eyes. Although she knew what was happening, knew there was nothing to fear, she realised she was scared, her heart beating wildly, body trembling. Clinging to the wire, she tipped back her head, opened her eyes and gazed at the stars as though to fix herself in the real world, tear herself away from the ruin in front of her.

It was then that the voices came – not words, just sounds – ringing out at her from the warehouse. A woman first – indignant, challenging, then pleading, low and desperate – cut short by a single gunshot. And then a man's voice – shocked, horrified – followed by a second shot.

In the silence that followed, Marie-Ange eased her fingers off the mesh and stepped away from the fence. Somewhere close at hand came the rising bark of a dog, the whistling call of a nightjar and the rich, honeyed scent of night-flowering jasmine.

Whatever it was, she knew it was over.

77

Jacquot felt a great contentment settle round him. Feet up on the sofa and ankles crossed, a joint between his fingers, a glass of Armagnac at his side and a lulling tenor sax from João Gilberto somewhere in the shadows. It couldn't get much better than this, he thought, his mind straying to Claudine's warm body one floor above.

Claudine had gone to bed an hour earlier, but he'd stayed on, pouring himself another drink, sliding another disk into the CD player and rolling himself a final spliff. It was the last of the previous year's crop and Jacquot knew that soon he'd be pruning off a few likely heads to keep himself going till harvest. He wondered if the new crop would be as good as the last. He'd raised them from seed, potted and repotted the growing stems and finally planted them out at the back of Claudine's garden, away from prying eyes but not from the sun. Seven full hours a day. He'd lost two plants in the mistral, uprooted, blown God knew where, but the half-dozen that remained were more than six feet high already, the tilting heads sticky and brown, the scent more and more pungent with every passing day. Jacquot took in a crackling lungful of his homegrown and blew a long, perfect cone of blue into the shadows.

Which was when the phone rang. He peered at his watch in the light from a single candle. A little after midnight. He reached out and picked it up.

It was Marie-Ange. 'I'm sorry to call you at home, Chief Inspector, but you said I could.' Her voice was low, troubled.

'If it was important,' he chided.

'I think it is. Very important.'

'And it couldn't wait till tomorrow?'

'Are you cross? That I called.'

'Well, it is quite late, Marie-Ange.'

'Don't be cross, please. And I did think about calling tomorrow but I just had to speak to you.'

Jacquot decided he didn't mind her calling at all. Even this late. Even at home. Even if it was work.

'So, what can I do for you?' he asked, wondering idly if it had anything to do with her visit to the Bonaires. What had she found out there that he might have missed? What had they told her that they might have kept from him? He fully intended to pull her up on that one before the call was through. The next thing, she'd be going out to the château to interrogate the Comtesse.

Instead she said: 'I believe the Martner murders and the Rocsabin fire are related.'

Which gave Jacquot pause. It was one of the reasons he'd stayed up after Claudine went to bed, rolling himself another joint, thinking it gently through: the Martner murders and the Rocsabin fire. Two apparently unrelated incidents. Four murders in the first, and two in the second.

Six murders in a ten-kilometre radius in only four months? If Chabert hadn't been in the dock, there'd have been hell to pay at Headquarters. And they'd certainly have started comparing the two crimes, searching for similarities.

Similarities, parallels, patterns, coincidences.

Coincidences. There were certainly enough of those. The gun used to kill the Martner family owned by the de Vausignes. The alleged killer a man who worked for both families as gardener. The Comtesse blackmailed by Martner. Her husband murdered in Rocsabin. In a warehouse the family co-owned. Built on the site of the Comtesse's childhood home. And now possibly – possibly – her son's Mercedes involved in a traffic accident on a road that led to Rocsabin, on the night of the fire. Not to mention the Sandrine angle – her long-ago affair with a man the Comtesse had loved and, by her own admission, betrayed. He could probably come up with a half-dozen more if he made an effort. And rolled another joint.

He'd also forgotten he was on the phone.

'Are you there, Chief Inspector? Hello?'

'How "related"? I see no similarity,' said Jacquot. 'You're just hoping that whoever killed the Martners, killed the Comte in the warehouse fire. Which would put Chabert in the clear.' Jacquot felt bad at being so tough with her.

But she didn't rise to it.

'It's difficult,' she said. 'Still not clear. But I do believe these deaths are related. Something to do with the de Vausignes.'

Jacquot shivered. After everything he'd pieced together during his break with Claudine in Aix, Marie-Ange's timing was uncanny; the way she matched her thoughts so closely to his findings.

'I told you, Marie-Ange. It's not enough to believe something. In my line of work I have to have proof. And please don't tell me "voices". Don't tell me "echoes".'

Which was all she had. As Jacquot suspected.

But it didn't stop her: 'Did you know that the Comtesse was in love with Albert de Vausigne?'

'Is that what Bonaire told you?' he asked, letting her know that he knew of her visit.

'Bonaire's wife.'

'It still doesn't prove anything,' he said.

'And the Comtesse knew Martner, didn't she? She was the one being blackmailed, wasn't she? Because she was the one who betrayed Albert.'

'Correct.'

'But she didn't kill them.'

'Also correct. The killer was a man, remember?'

'Did the Comtesse ever visit the Martner house?'

'I can't be certain. She told me she'd passed their home a dozen times, but—'

'And did Gilles know what was going on? About the blackmail?'

'If he did, it didn't appear to worry him, or stop him dipping into the family pot whenever he got the chance.'

'And the son? Antoine? What about him? Did he know about the blackmail?'

'Not so far as we know,' replied Jacquot.

'Did he know the Martners?'

'I don't have that information in front of me. It would be on file.'

But Jacquot knew it wouldn't be. Antoine de Vausigne would not have been interviewed after the Martner killing because he hadn't even been in St Bédard.

And then Jacquot heard a great burst of breath down the line. 'Of course . . .' he heard her cry. 'Oh, God, of course, of course.'

'I'm still listening.'

'It's something I saw,' she said in a rush. 'Proof. What you want. To do with the Martners,' she continued. 'I've been trying to work it out. And right now, just this minute . . .'

'And that is?'

'The wristwatch. The green stain on the strap. It's a pollen stain. Very distinctive and very hard to get rid of. The more you try to remove it, the greater the damage. It spreads, settles, works its way in. It starts out yellow, but when it comes into contact with salt it turns green.'

'Salt?'

'Sweat, for instance.'

'And?'

'The point is this particular pollen comes from only one flower. I'd bet my life on it. An orchid. *Epidendrum longifolium radicans*. It's a tropical epiphyte. It anchors itself to the branches of trees and sends down just masses of aerial roots.' Marie-Ange took a breath, let it out. 'And the only place I know where you'll find it outside Honduras, Guatemala and the Jardins des Plantes in Paris is Dr Martner's hot-house.'

A seed in Jacquot's joint exploded with a tiny crackle and a spray of hot crumbs fell on to his chest. He sat up, tossed the joint into the ashtray and brushed away the embers. But not quickly enough. Three pinprick holes had been singed into his new T-shirt. *Merde.*

Marie-Ange was still talking: 'Now the remarkable thing about the *longifolium* is that in the right conditions, with expert care, it flowers spectacularly. But only for a few weeks each year. No more than a month. In this part of the world, in the right conditions, that would be around February. And the pollen is only secreted a matter of days before the flowers die. So if you have that pollen on your clothes, or in this case on the strap of your watch, you must have been there, in Martner's hot-house, right at the time when that particular flower secretes its pollen. The last few days of February. And if you say you weren't there, then you're lying.'

'So who does this watch belong to, Marie-Ange?'

78

'You have a visitor,' said Brunet, when Jacquot arrived at the office the following morning, head still spinning from his conversation with Marie-Ange. 'An overnight guest, you might say. Brought in around midnight. Not a happy bunny.'

Jacquot took the charge sheet from Brunet and rocked back on his heels.

'Small world, or what?' said Brunet.

'Antoine de Vausigne?'

Jacquot went into his office and sat at his desk, skimmed through the charges – running a red light, resisting arrest, in possession of a so-far unidentified substance thought to be cocaine.

Brunet followed. '*Il y en a plus.*'

'Please. I like "more".'

'They've finished with the Mercedes.'

'Yes?'

'First, the paint matches.'

'And?'

'And there's gravel in the tyre treads.'

'From the warehouse car park?'

'Looks like it.'

'And?'

'Traces of petrol in the boot.'

'So?'

'The fire was started with petrol. That's what the fire investigators say.'

'And?'

'The Merc's a diesel.'

'Could be fuel for a lawn-mower, chain-saw?' Jacquot knew that any defence counsel worth his gown would argue the same point in court and sow the necessary seed of doubt. But this wasn't a courtroom. This was Jacquot's office, and after last night's call from Marie-Ange he knew for sure they were getting close. Everything seemed to be falling into place.

'Could be,' said Brunet

Jacquot knew his assistant wasn't finished. 'And?'

Brunet pulled out a chair and sat down. 'Well,' he said, studying his thumbnail, 'there's blood.'

'Blood?'

'One of Fournier's boys found what he thinks might be a spot of blood. On the door sill. Driver's side. They're doing tests right now to confirm it. If it is blood, I told them to run a match on Bartolomé and the Comte.'

Jacquot got to his feet. His stomach was turning cartwheels.

'Let's pay a call.'

79

There were two of them in the interview room. Antoine de Vausigne and his lawyer, Bernard Charron. The Comte, arms sprawled across the Formica table, was not at his best. He looked creased and needed a shave. In contrast to his client, Charron was snappily dressed in a double-breasted suit snug on the shoulders and hips, with a crisply ironed white shirt and shiny red tie.

'My client has nothing to say, Chief Inspector,' began Charron, when Jacquot and Brunet came into the room, getting to his feet as if the meeting was over before it had begun, buttoning his jacket. Charron and Jacquot had crossed swords on previous occasions and neither man had much regard for the other.

'And *bonjour* to you, too, Maître Charron,' said Jacquot, pulling out a chair and settling himself. 'Please, there's no formality here.' He pointed to a chair and Charron had no option but to unbutton his jacket and sit down again. Jacquot glanced at de Vausigne then opened the file and pored over the charge sheet as though refreshing his memory. Brunet stayed by the door, arms crossed, leaning against the wall.

'My client also categorically denies these ludicrous charges,' said Charron, tugging at the crease in his suit trousers, crossing his legs and tipping back in his chair.

'Of course he does,' replied Jacquot, looking up from the file and smiling. 'But, as I'm sure you'll appreciate, it is all rather out of our hands, I'm afraid. Wheels will turn. The usual thing. Although regarding last night's events your client is, of course, free to leave. Under your recognisance.'

Charron was taken aback. In the three years he'd been dealing with Jacquot he'd learned that these kinds of negotiation were usually more strenuous. He knew Jacquot. This wasn't his style. So he shouldn't have been too surprised a moment later when Jacquot continued: 'No, no. What I'd like to talk about this morning has nothing whatever to do with the possession of a class-A substance.'

Jacquot glanced at the test results, handed to him by Mougeon on their way down to the interview rooms, and now attached to the charge sheet. 'We've confirmed that by the way. Five half-ounce bags in all. Two in the glove compartment, the rest concealed in a door seal. Forty-eight per cent cocaine, twenty per cent lactose, eighteen per cent Psillionysetimol – that's a regulated amphetamine in case you're interested. And the rest, calcium silicate – the stuff you shake on to a wound. Antiseptic. You can get it in any *pharmacie*.' Jacquot smiled across the table at de Vausigne.

Who scowled back.

'And neither,' continued Jacquot, 'does it have anything to do with resisting arrest or—'

'I did not resist arrest,' snapped de Vausigne, making to rise. It was the first time he had spoken and his voice sounded hoarse and unsteady, his bottom lip as shiny as Charron's tie and trembling with indignation. Charron put a hand on his arm. De Vausigne shook it off and cleared his throat. 'I was having a drink. The man offered me a lift home. Because you had my car. It's not my fault he ran a light or had drugs on him. How was I to know?'

'Please, Monsieur Le Comte,' his lawyer interrupted.

'Ah, yes, your car. Which, funnily enough, is precisely what I would like to talk about.'

Charron turned to de Vausigne. 'Your car?'

'For your information, Maître Charron, information that your client may or may not yet have given you, our investigations have established that his car, a blue Mercedes, was involved in a motor incident, nearly two weeks ago now – the paint match confirms it, by the way – on the road between Lucat and Rocsabin. Less than twenty minutes before a fire was reported at the HacheGee furniture warehouse. A warehouse in which your client's father was murdered. Of course, Monsieur de Vausigne has denied driving his car at that time and has kindly provided us with the name of a witness to confirm it.'

De Vausigne nodded, stretched back in his seat, clasped his hands behind his head.

'But we are still left with a car that is "taken" without your client's permission and involved in an accident, a car that may also have been involved in the commission of an arson and murder. And, most astonishing of all, a stolen car that is returned to the place from where it was taken. Extraordinary, don't you think? Quite, quite extraordinary. The car thief who returns the car.'

Charron tried hard. Jacquot had to give him that. He might not have known what Jacquot was talking about, but there was always the formula to fall back on. Jacquot had heard it so many times.

'Quite so. Quite extraordinary,' said Charron, reaching for his briefcase, sliding away his notepad and pocketing his pen with a flourish. 'But if, as you say, Chief Inspector, you have established that my client was otherwise engaged,' Charron turned to de Vausigne, who nodded smugly, 'then it would seem to me . . . it would seem to me that—'

But Jacquot wasn't listening. 'Tell me, Monsieur,' he said, looking directly at de Vausigne, 'do you ever carry petrol in the boot of your car?'

'You are under no obligation to reply,' Charron interrupted, caught on the hop once again, 'whatever all this is about. And I advise you most strongly—'

'Of course I don't carry petrol in the car,' said de Vausigne, paying his lawyer no heed, evidently sure of his ground. After all, he'd spent the night of the fire with Frankie Alzon. 'And why should I? It's a diesel engine. Or maybe you hadn't noticed.'

Jacquot shuffled through the file as though searching for something. 'No lawn-mower? No chain-saw?'

'Hardly, Chief Inspector. In Paris I live in a flat. And down here Picard handles all that.'

'Which means,' said Jacquot, closing the file, 'that I regret to say we must keep your car a little longer than we expected. For further tests. I'm sure you understand, Monsieur.'

'This is simply—' began de Vausigne.

'And I am sure my client is only too happy to help the police in any way he can,' volunteered Charron, trying to smooth the waters.

'For which we are most grateful,' said Jacquot, getting to his feet. 'Most grateful.'

He went to the door and opened it. 'And now, Messieurs, if you'll follow me, we can sign all the relevant release papers and . . .' smiling at de Vausigne '. . . see about having your property returned to you.'

At the property room behind the front desk, Jacquot called up de Vausigne's belongings. They arrived in a large sealed manilla envelope, which Brunet tore open, tipping out the contents. Wallet, watch, small change, silver bracelet, lighter, cigarettes. A bundle of five-hundred-franc notes.

'You'll confirm all these are yours?' asked Brunet.

De Vausigne shot him a look and took possession of his belongings, distributing the lighter, cigarettes and change to various pockets, sliding the bracelet over his wrist, pushing the wad of notes into an inside pocket and strapping on the watch.

'If you'd be so kind as to sign for them, Monsieur,' said Brunet, offering him a pen.

De Vausigne took the pen and scrawled his name on the sheet.

'If that is all, Chief Inspector?' asked Charron.

Jacquot nodded and Antoine de Vausigne and his lawyer left the building.

80

A little more than three hours later, up on the fourth floor, Brunet came into Jacquot's office. Jacquot was on the phone, boots up on the windowsill, watching a flight of pigeons as they circled the belfried spire of Église St-Jean. The air crackled with heat and a breeze from the open window ruffled through some papers on his desk. Down in the street a car horn beep-beeped.

Whoever it was he'd been talking to, Jacquot said thanks, bade them *adieu* and spun round to replace the phone.

'Results are through, boss.'

Jacquot gestured for Brunet to take a seat.

'Fournier confirms it's blood on the Merc's door sill.'

Jacquot smiled.

'But it's not Bartolomé's, and nor is it the Comte's. Nor does it match the sample our police doctor took from de Vausigne last night.'

Jacquot knew where this was headed now. The puzzle was finally falling into place.

'Just out of interest they did a search.'

'Good,' said Jacquot.

'And found a match.'

Jacquot smiled, said just one word: 'Martner.'

Brunet looked astonished. 'Actually, the daughter. Ilse.'

81

Jacquot stepped from the lift into the underground garage at Cavaillon Police Headquarters. Everything was as it should have been. Strip-lights and a concrete floor, the casual revving of an engine, the clink of spanners and the hum of extractor fans.

Albert de Vausigne wouldn't recognise the place, thought Jacquot. Fifty years earlier Gestapo cells had occupied this lower level of the Cavaillon *gendarmerie*. Jacquot had seen the pictures, called them up from the planning-department archive after Claudine told him about the building's past. Black-and-white shots. Dark and chilling. Long stone corridors, a webbing of overhead pipes, a line of cells fitted with stout wooden doors, iron hinges and barred viewing slots. In the bottom of each door was a second, larger slot where food was passed in to the occupant. The cells were cramped and narrow, room for a bed, slop bucket and not much else. High on the outside wall of each cell, at ground level, a small, barred window gave on to the courtyard.

As well as pictures of the cells, there were other shots too: a shower room with a line of cubicles, a bunk-room, what looked like a small kitchen and a large, windowless room set with chairs and a table. On the back of this last photo someone had scribbled 'Interrogation Room'.

Today they'd call it an interview room.

Albert de Vausigne could have told them the difference.

But now the old cells had gone, the *gendarmerie*'s current 'holding rooms' relocated to the ground floor following a programme of renovation and refurbishment in the sixties. Sections of the original building had been torn down and rebuilt, the cobbled courtyard with the horseshoe-shaped doorway and caged bulb above it had been laid with Tarmac, while the high stone wall that separated the *gendarmerie* from the street had been replaced by iron railings and an electronically controlled sliding gate.

Below ground – where the old cells, shower room, kitchen and interrogation room had once been – a far-sighted planner had opened up the space and installed a garage and service facility for police vehicles. There were inspection pits, a fully equipped workbench along one wall and a glass-walled office in one corner – with a ramp sloping up to the new courtyard car park above.

It was here that Jacquot stood, one level below ground, taking it all in. No shadows here, thanks to the strip-lighting. No smell of sweat and fear, just petrol fumes and oil. For a moment he wondered what Marie-Ange would make of the place. Despite the clean-up, he had a feeling she wouldn't much like it. There'd be echoes here, alright. Lots of them. And none very pleasant.

Jacquot looked around. To his right was the ramp, leading up to the car park and a band of blue sky; straight ahead, a line of numbered parking spaces for squad cars awaiting service; and to his left the garage and maintenance area. In commercial premises the walls would be covered with pin-ups, a radio would be blaring out, and the grease-monkeys would be calling it a day by now, the place packed with owners waiting to pick up their vehicles, settle their bills. It wasn't like that here. A team of overalled mechanics was still at work, two stripping down an engine block, two others with a squad car over the inspection pit, and another leaning under the hood of a police van. Beyond, in the small glass-walled office, the chief mechanic, Plessis, was finishing his paperwork before the next shift clocked on. He saw Jacquot and waved. They'd already spoken on the phone and Plessis knew what was coming.

As well as servicing and maintenance, this underground area was also used as a 'clean' environment where suspect vehicles could be examined by Fournier and the forensic boys. Suspect vehicles like Antoine de Vausigne's blue Mercedes, standing on a thick white plastic sheet under an overhead light just a few steps aways from Jacquot.

He walked over to the car, its door handles and windows, boot latch and fuel cap still smeared with the grey carbon powder used to lift fingerprints. He stooped to peer through the open driver's window. Apart from more powdery smudges on the gear-lever, steering-wheel and rear-view mirror, the interior was as clean as a whistle, everything they'd found inside – scraps of paper, receipts, gum wrappers, empty drinks cans, an assortment of biros and pencils, cassette tapes, the contents of the ashtray, glove compartment, door side-pockets and boot – ranged along a trestled examination table set clear of the vehicle.

Jacquot was inspecting the flattened trim above the Mercedes' rear passenger door when a squeal of tyres turning down the metalled ramp signalled the first arrival.

Showtime, he thought.

82

Jacquot glanced at his watch. A little after six.

An hour earlier he'd sent Brunet, Mougeon and two squad cars to the Château de Vausigne – one team along the back drive to the guest cottage, one team to the main house. A couple of gendarmes had accompanied them as back-up. He'd told Brunet to come straight down to the garage when they returned rather than park in the yard outside. And here he was, with Antoine de Vausigne in the caged back seat.

Jacquot leaned back on the bonnet of the Mercedes and hooked the heel of his boot on to the bumper.

First out of the squad car was Brunet. He nodded to Jacquot and opened the back passenger door. Leaning in, he took hold of de Vausigne's arm and hauled him out. As Jacquot had requested, the Comte had been handcuffed.

'This is an outrage,' said de Vausigne, straightening up, rattling the cuffs. 'An absolute outrage.'

But Brunet paid not the slightest attention. It wasn't difficult to imagine how the journey into town must have been.

When de Vausigne saw Jacquot by the Mercedes, he tried to pull free but Brunet kept a firm grip on him. None of the mechanics paid the slightest attention.

'This is a disgrace, Chief Inspector. How dare you treat me like this? I demand to see my lawyer.'

'A disgrace indeed,' replied Jacquot. 'But please don't fret, Monsieur. Your lawyer is on his way. I took the liberty of calling him on your behalf. My guess is you'll be keeping him pretty busy.'

Jacquot had hardly finished speaking when another squeal of tyres announced the second squad car's arrival. It pulled up beside them and Mougeon got out of the front passenger seat, then came round to open the rear door. A black trouser leg appeared, followed by a tiny curled hand. Mougeon took it gallantly and helped Hélène de Vausigne out. With a courteous nod she thanked him, then started when she saw her son. 'Antoine?'

Antoine looked equally surprised. 'Maman?'

Her eyes settled on the handcuffs. 'What on earth is going on here?'

'Madame,' said Jacquot, with the kind of stiff bow that Dietering would have been proud of, 'so good of you to spare the time.'

The Comtesse turned towards him. Her eyes narrowed, and her chin rose. 'Whatever all this is about,' she said, gesturing to the handcuffs round her son's wrists, 'I'd appreciate an explanation, Chief Inspector. We have friends for dinner this evening and—'

Behind them the lift doors pinged and rolled open. Jacquot turned, smiled. 'Ah, Maître Charron. Perfect timing. Please be assured that you have missed nothing.'

'Monsieur Le Comte? Comtesse?' said Charron, setting down his briefcase. He, too, saw the handcuffs and turned to Jacquot. 'What exactly . . . ?' And then, recognising the Mercedes that Jacquot was leaning against: 'Isn't this your car, Monsieur Le Comte?'

'It certainly is,' said Jacquot. 'And a quite remarkable car, too,' he continued, smoothing his hand over the bonnet of the Mercedes. 'A 200D. Nineteen sixty-six.' He nodded in the direction of the mechanics. 'According to the boys, they're called Fintails. Lovely cars. Bit heavy on the corners but a very comfortable ride.'

'I trust we're not here to discuss motor-cars,' said the Comtesse, icily.

'Oh, but we are, Madame. Particularly this one. As I said, a quite remarkable car. With a quite remarkable past.'

'Chief Inspector—' began Charron.

'Yes, indeed,' continued Jacquot, ignoring the lawyer. 'Quite, quite remarkable. Used by not one but two killers. In the commission of not one, not two, but three separate crimes. Seven murders in all. Not many cars with that kind of background, wouldn't you agree, Maître Charron?'

Without waiting for an answer, Jacquot pushed himself off the Mercedes and walked over to de Vausigne.

'Monsieur de Vausigne, tell me, if you would, how many times a year do you visit your parents?'

De Vausigne shrugged. 'Every couple of months. Something like that?'

'So, let's say . . . six times a year?'

'I guess. Thereabouts.'

'In November last year?'

Antoine looked to his mother. 'November? I don't think so.'

His mother shook her head in agreement. 'But you were down for Christmas,' she said.

'And February?' asked Jacquot. 'How about February?'

De Vausigne shifted uncomfortably. 'February? I don't . . .' He turned to his mother.

Again she shook her head.

Jacquot seemed to give this some thought, then turned to the Comtesse. 'Madame, I am sure you will be delighted to hear that not only did we retrieve your shotgun, we have now apprehended the man who broke into your home last November and stole it.' He indicated de Vausigne with a sweep of his hand, as though he were making an introduction. 'Your own son, Madame. Hence the handcuffs. Hence Maître Charron.'

'Antoine? Why, that's ridiculous.'

'But that, Madame, is not all. Far, far from it.' Jacquot walked over to the evidence table and started sifting through the various bits of paper. He selected one, then turned back to the Comtesse. 'For several years your nearest neighbours were Dr and Madame Martner of Mas Taillard, is that not so, Madame?'

'That is correct, Chief Inspector. As well you know.'

Jacquot turned to Antoine. 'Did you ever meet the doctor, Monsieur?'

'Martner, you say? No, not that I recall.'

'Or any member of his family?'

Antoine shook his head.

'And you never visited their house?'

'If I didn't know them—'

'You'd have had no reason to visit them at home. Of course. But you did know them, Monsieur, didn't you? And you did know what the good doctor was up to. And you did kill him, didn't you?'

There was a gasp from the Comtesse. 'No, Antoine. It's not possible.'

Antoine ignored her, his eyes following Jacquot as he strolled back to the Mercedes.

'And the rest of his family. With the gun that you stole from your parents' house. Driving this rather fine piece of German engineering,' continued Jacquot, patting the car's roof, 'leaving it in a lay-by off the Brieuc road to make your way on foot up to the Martner house. Is that not so, Monsieur?'

At which point Antoine looked away, raised his eyes to the strip-lights above their heads in a lazy, distracted manner, as though what Jacquot was saying was of no interest to him whatsoever.

'Which means, Monsieur, that you are now under arrest for the murders in February this year of Dr Josef Martner, his wife, Jutta Martner –'

Hélène de Vausigne reached for her son, gripped his arm. 'This cannot be. Say it's not true, my darling. Tell me it's not true.'

'– their daughter Ilse, and granddaughter Kippi,' continued Jacquot.

'Why this is simply preposterous, Chief Inspector,' Charron began.

Jacquot turned to the lawyer and waved the piece of paper he'd taken from the evidence table. 'In which case, Monsieur Charron, your client will be able to explain this. A record from the traffic authority here in Cavaillon that a charge was levied on a car bearing this registration for failure to display a valid parking *permis* for Parc Boulevard Crillon. Dated last November. The day before the château break-in – a date, as we have established, that Monsieur de Vausigne can't seem to recall.

'Of course, there's also the small matter of blood on the door sill of Monsieur de Vausigne's car. Madame Brauer's blood, by the way. Oh, and animal blood too, on the accelerator pedal. Presumably the Martners' dachshunds.

'And then there's the pollen stain on Monsieur de Vausigne's watch-strap.' Jacquot pointed at his handcuffed wrists, the green stain on the watch-strap clearly visible. 'A stain from an orchid in Dr Martner's hot-house, an orchid that only blooms in February. Nor should we forget, *enfin*, the matching fibres from his car rug on the murder weapon, and a matching twenty-bore shell found beneath the spare wheel.'

These last two 'facts' were untrue. Jacquot used them simply to load his case, to stretch and unsettle his suspect.

He walked back to the evidence table, replaced the traffic-authority record slip where he'd found it and turned back to de Vausigne.

'On November the twenty-sixth last year, Monsieur de Vausigne, you stayed in Cavaillon with Mademoiselle Francine Alzon. She was working the late shift back then. At the hospital – midnight to ten. Which you knew about. After she went to work and left you alone in her apartment, you drove out to the château and broke in, removing a Beretta twenty-bore from your father's gun cabinet.

'Three months later you returned to Cavaillon, the last week in February, and this time you used the gun you'd stolen from the château to kill Dr Martner and his wife. Regrettably their daughter and granddaughter had arrived a few days earlier for Madame Martner's birthday. You might not have intended to kill them, but they saw you. You had to shoot them too.'

'And what possible motive—' began Charron.

'Motive?' repeated Jacquot, glancing across at Hélène de Vausigne, whose features were pinched with shock. 'Money, Maître Charron. Money. Watching his inheritance bleed away. Putting an end to a particularly unpleasant and costly blackmail. A most persuasive motive, wouldn't you agree?'

Jacquot walked back to the Mercedes and perched himself on the bonnet, stretching out his legs and crossing his ankles. 'What do you say, Madame? When did your son find out about Dr Martner?'

'I didn't know that he had,' replied the Comtesse.

'Monsieur?'

Antoine said nothing.

'I suppose it must have been obvious,' Jacquot continued. 'Paintings, family silver, things going missing. Maybe letters from your bank, Madame, left lying around. Concern at the state of your finances? Loans being called in? Maybe even pressure to sell the château. A title without a château, Madame. Like land without a title, no?'

83

There was silence in the underground garage, Jacquot's questions left unanswered, the mechanics over in the service area working on as though nothing was happening.

'But it wasn't just the good doctor dipping his fingers into the family pot, was it, Madame?' continued Jacquot, pushing himself away from the Mercedes and walking over to her.

Hélène de Vausigne lifted her chin, half turned her head from Jacquot, but kept her eyes on him.

'Plessis,' called Jacquot over his shoulder. 'A chair, *s'il vous plaît.*'

A moment later Plessis appeared with a chair, placed it beside the Comtesse and wiped the seat with a cloth. Without a word, she sat down, slid her knees to one side and crossed her ankles.

'Those trips your husband made to Aix,' Jacquot began again. 'Business? Property matters in Brittany? I don't think so, Madame.'

Standing beside Brunet, Antoine turned to his mother.

'How long had the *affaire* been going on?' asked Jacquot. 'The latest one, that is, with Madame Bartolomé.'

'I don't know what you think you're suggesting, Chief Inspector—'

'I'm suggesting, Madame, that your husband was not in the habit of visiting Aix alone. Indeed, so far as I have been able to ascertain, he was usually accompanied on his "business" trips. According to the reservations manager at the Hôtel Pigonnet, room seventeen

391

was reserved on a regular basis for the Comte and Comtesse de Vausigne.'

Hélène de Vausigne straightened her shoulders.

'A fine hotel, Le Pigonnet,' continued Jacquot, 'and not cheap. Take room seventeen. Even in low season it's only a few *sous* short of two thousand francs a night. My friend the reservations manager told me that. Nice fellow. And you know what?' said Jacquot, taking two photographs from his jacket pocket. 'When I showed him your photograph, Madame, he didn't recognise you. But when I showed him this one, of Madame Bartolomé, he identified her immediately as the Comtesse de Vausigne.'

'This is preposterous. Gilles was—'

'Gilles was spending your money, Madame. Money that was, thanks to Dr Martner, in short supply. A suite at the Hôtel Pigonnet every month or so, tables at Le Prieuré, at Hiely . . .' Jacquot walked back to the Mercedes and placed the two photos on the bonnet, felt around in an inside pocket, pulled out a notebook, flipped it open and found a page. 'Ah, yes. Here we are. The Auberge de Cassagne, the Ermitage Meissonnier, and Hostellerie Les Frênes. Some of the best tables in Provence, wouldn't you agree? And always tables for two. Several thousand francs in a matter of months. Quite the epicure, your husband.'

Hélène de Vausigne raised her brows disdainfully, studied her fingertips.

'And so generous too. Not just the size of the tips that the *maître d*'s remember, but all those small gifts for Madame Bartolomé as well.' Jacquot consulted his notebook once more. 'A Rolex from Temps Perdu, a bracelet from Joailliers des Paumes, clothes from Gago, on and on. There was hardly a shop in Aix that I visited where they didn't recognise your husband's photo. Or Madame Bartolomé's. His wife. The Comtesse. And everything he bought? Paid for in cash.'

Maître Charron's eyes were wide. He coughed, tried to collect himself. 'I think, Chief Inspector . . .'

But Jacquot was getting into his stride. The ball was in his hands and he was running for the line. He could feel his heart beating.

'So where did he get all that cash, I wonder? Certainly not from you, Madame. No, no. He got it from her, didn't he? From Grace

Bartolomé. From the tills at the HacheGee warehouse. No wonder it was always "sale day", "cash discounts".'

Jacquot slid the notebook back into his pocket. 'But let's go back to the night of the Rocsabin fire, shall we? You were having dinner with your son, is that not correct?'

The Comtesse made no reply.

'And after your son had seen you back to the house, instead of going to bed you borrowed his car, this fine old car, and drove out to the furniture warehouse for a showdown, taking the lower drive so that there was no need to start the engine and alert your son, who by then was entertaining Mademoiselle Alzon. And on your return, you used the front drive, coasting down into the château's forecourt. Never a sound.'

'You have proof, of course, to back up these ridiculous allegations?' asked Hélène de Vausigne, gathering herself.

'Yes, Madame, I do.'

The Comtesse made to say something, but Charron interrupted. 'Please, Madame la Comtesse, I do advise you—'

'What *proof*?' she asked, ignoring Charron, steel in her voice, feeling more certain of her ground. So far this was all conjecture. It would never stand up in a court of law and she knew it.

'Shortly before six o'clock, before joining your son for dinner at the guest-house, you made a telephone call. To the Hôtel Pigonnet. You left a message. My friend the concierge found it for me. I was lucky. They keep copies, you know, for a week, sometimes longer. I have it here.' Jacquot brought out his wallet and slipped a piece of paper from it, unfolded it. '"HacheGee Warehouse,"' he read out. '"Eleven. Be there."'

Jacquot took the message slip to the Comtesse, held it out for her to read if she wanted to. She didn't bother to look, simply turned away her head. Jacquot slipped it back into his wallet.

'Of course, there's no signature,' continued Jacquot, 'but phone companies also keep records, Madame. Which is what this is . . .'

Jacquot walked over to the evidence table and picked up a sheet of paper. He returned to the Mercedes and laid it on the bonnet beside the photos. A column of figures was visible, one of the entries highlighted in green. Jacquot pointed to it.

'July the twenty-first. Five thirty-seven p.m. 42 59 02 90. That's

Le Pigonnet's telephone number. "Duration of call, two minutes, fifty-two seconds." The time on your phone records and the time the message was received and noted at Le Pigonnet are the same.'

Hélène de Vausigne smiled, seemed relieved. 'You're quite right, Chief Inspector. I'd forgotten. I did call my husband at the hotel. But we spoke. I did not leave any . . . any message.'

'It must have been a very short conversation, Madame.'

'It was. I needed – I needed a telephone number.'

'But when Inspector Brunet and I came to see you about your husband's car, the day after the fire, you said you hadn't spoken to him.'

'I'm sure you must be mistaken, Chief Inspector.'

'You may be right, Madame, you may be right. But the fact remains that this message was handed to your husband shortly after that phone call. Apparently he and . . . the "Comtesse" were on their way out to dinner. Clos de la Violette, in case you were wondering. Probably the best restaurant in town. According to the concierge, they asked him to cancel the reservation and checked out soon after. Driving back to Rocsabin, it would appear. To the HacheGee warehouse. Where you met them, Madame.'

'I did no such thing.'

'And where you killed them. Using Madame Bartolomé's own gun, the gun she kept in her bag.'

'This is ridiculous, Chief Inspector. Really. How could I have known that Madame Bartolomé carried a gun?'

'The same way Joel Filbert, the warehouse manager, knew. He told me Madame Bartolomé always had it with her, never went anywhere without it, said she showed it to him on more than one occasion. Just as she probably showed it to you, Madame. Where and when I cannot say, but you knew . . .'

The Comtesse was shaking her head. 'You're dreaming, Chief Inspector. This is *absurde*.'

'Chief Inspector,' began Charron, 'I really must object in the strongest—'

But Jacquot held up a hand. He wasn't finished yet. Not by a long way.

'Now normally, in a situation like this, the killer would leave the gun at the scene of crime, maybe in the hand of one of the victims or on the floor . . . And he would do that to divert attention, hoping to persuade the police that what they were looking at was nothing more than a tragic lovers' quarrel – murder, then suicide. She shoots him, then shoots herself. Or the other way round. What the killer wouldn't do is start a fire. It may be a good way to cover tracks but . . .' Jacquot smiled '. . . the dead don't light fires. As my colleague, Inspector Brunet here, pointed out when we found the bodies.' Jacquot looked at Brunet for confirmation. He nodded. 'And when no murder weapon was found at the warehouse, it was clear that someone else had to have been involved.

'But then,' continued Jacquot, looking at the Comtesse, 'you never intended leaving the gun, did you? Much more convincing to implicate someone else. And who better than Guy Bartolomé? The retired *lycée* teacher, a wreck of a man, according to Dr Buisson who treated Bartolomé after his breakdown.

'So after you started the fire you left the warehouse and called in on Guy, didn't you? And what did you do when you got there, apart from planting the empty petrol can for good measure? Well, we'll probably never know for certain unless you choose to tell us. But what is certain is this. You sat Guy Bartolomé down at the kitchen table and you shot him with his wife's gun. Ensuring, you believed, that the murders would be blamed on him, the wronged husband, who'd come home and shot himself rather than face the music.'

There was silence again. A long drawn-out silence punctuated by the tapping of a hammer, the hum of extractor fans and the sound of a phone ringing – quickly snatched up – in Plessis's office. And all the while Hélène de Vausigne sat there, completely unmoved by Jacquot's conjectures. She was more resilient than he had given her credit for. Even the news about her son had failed to rock her.

Photographs, phone records, hotel messages, shop receipts . . . All of it, Jacquot knew, was circumstantial. It was nothing without a confession. Yet still she refused to give way, and he wondered if he'd have to play his final card. Tell the Comtesse where she was. Draw her attention to their surroundings. The underground car park. What it had once been. The place where she'd sent Albert all those years ago. Weaken her resolve. Break her down.

And then, quietly, she said: 'He was going to leave me.'

Hélène de Vausigne glanced up at them – Brunet, Jacquot, Charron, Mougeon and, finally, Antoine – as though seeking a kind of understanding, an acknowledgement that what she had done was the only thing she could have done. 'They'd been planning it for months,' she continued. 'Grace was going to leave her husband, and Gilles was going to leave me. He told me . . . he told me we'd have to sell the château. Said he didn't care. Said he hated the place. Always had. Told me he was going to live by the sea. Some place they'd seen near Théoule.' The Comtesse took a deep breath and then, in a level, reasoning voice, she continued: 'I simply couldn't countenance it. It was simply not . . . permissable.'

Hélène de Vausigne smiled sadly at her son, reached a hand towards him. 'My darling, you would have lost everything. There was nothing else I could do. Don't you see? I had no—'

But before she could say another word, Antoine had pushed her hand aside, lunged forward and snatched Mougeon's gun from its holster. Two shots rang out. The first had Mougeon crumpling to the ground, gripping his left leg, the second shattered the rear indicator light on the Mercedes. As the shots thundered round the underground car park, Antoine turned and sprinted up the ramp into the courtyard above.

84

Claudine Eddé stepped out of Déscharme's art-supply shop on to Place Lombard and felt a thrill of guilt course through her. She had spent far more money than she had intended. Usually she managed to restrain herself when she visited Déscharme but the success of her show in Aix had made her bold. The last painting sold. A sell-out. So she'd gone quite mad. In Déscharme's, of all places.

Old man Déscharme had called that morning to say that Madame's order for the series-seven cadmium reds and yellows had finally arrived from Sennelier's in Paris. At two hundred francs a tube that would have been bad enough, but then Claudine had spotted the Alizerin crimson and the viridian marked down, and then, wandering down a dusty side aisle that smelt of linseed oil and rabbit gum, she'd seen the brushes. The Rafael Mangouste 24s.

At first she'd dithered, walked on, but then come back. Making sure she couldn't be seen, she'd removed the cover from one of the brushes and run her thumb over the bristles, then smoothed them against her cheek. That was all it had taken. Now, nearly three thousand francs poorer, she stepped away from Déscharme's and felt both dizzy and delighted with her extravagance.

Back in her car, she placed her precious brushes and paints on the passenger seat, snapped on her seat-belt and pulled out of Faubourg du Cagnard, joining the evening traffic on Sadi Carnot.

She glanced at her watch. Nearly seven o'clock. She still hadn't told Daniel the news about Aix. He'd be so pleased for her. Maybe even take her to dinner. A celebration dinner. Gaillard or Scaramouche. He could choose. And he was so close, only a couple of blocks away. And she was heading in that direction anyway. She'd call at his office and surprise him.

85

Antoine raced into daylight, heart pumping, sweat already starting to slick through his hair. It wasn't easy running with handcuffs round your wrists and a gun in your hand. But he was doing fine, doing fine. Twenty metres clear. Half-way to the entrance gate. By the time they got their wits about them, he'd be long gone. Out of there.

There was just one problem, though. How far was he going to get with the handcuffs and the gun – running through the streets of Cavaillon? What he needed to do was put some space between him and the *flics*, hole up some place where he could get rid of the handcuffs and hide out a while. But where?

And then, turning in between the stone pillars of the entrance gate, bouncing over the ramp, came a blue Citroën, an estate, with a woman at the wheel. A car and a driver in one.

Antoine swerved away from the gates and headed for the Citroën. He saw the woman, the driver, look out through the passenger window as he ran towards her, then frown, not sure what was happening. And then she spotted the cuffs and the gun.

But it was too late for her to do anything. He was there, wrenching the door open and throwing himself into the front seat. He slammed the door shut, then swivelled round in the seat, feeling something snap beneath him, and raised the gun to her head, double-handed, the links between the cuffs swinging.

'Drive!' he screamed. 'Get going! Now! Now!'

86

After the strip-lights in the underground garage the sun caught Jacquot by surprise, blasting down from behind the belfried spire of St Jean. Staying close to the wall of the ramp, he slowed as the courtyard came into view, keeping low in case de Vausigne was waiting for him. Behind him he could hear the Comtesse calling out for her son, and the sound of running feet coming up the ramp behind him. He glanced round – Brunet and the gendarmes, with a couple of the mechanics a few metres further back.

Shading his eyes and squinting ahead, he spotted de Vausigne racing for the entrance gates, a long shadow chasing behind him. He was running in a kind of stoop, either trying to keep the gun and cuffs concealed for when he hit the street or because he found it difficult to run with his hands clasped in front of him.

It didn't matter, he was well ahead of Jacquot and in another few seconds he'd be out on the street.

And then Jacquot saw a car turn in through the gates. Oddly familiar. A blue Citroën. An estate. A woman driving.

Claudine.

Jacquot knew exactly what was going to happen next. Antoine changed direction and headed for the car. Seconds later he was there, hauling open the door and jumping in, pointing his gun at

Claudine's head, screaming at her to drive, then looking over his shoulder as Jacquot came to a halt a few metres short.

'Any closer and I'll shoot. I swear it.'

87

Two worlds. Jacquot was aware of two worlds. Out there, beyond the railings, cars passed by in a steady rush-hour stream, a mother pushed a buggy, two kids skateboarded past, a man in a bus read the evening paper.

Yet here, a few steps away, was another world. A car, a gun, a killer. And the woman he loved.

'You shoot her and you lose your ride,' said Jacquot.

'Then I'll shoot you,' Antoine replied, turning the gun in his direction.

'Stay away! I'm fine,' Claudine pleaded.

Off to his left, Jacquot caught a glimpse of Brunet, working the control box beside the gate. With a rattle the gate began to slide across the entrance.

Antoine saw it too. 'Keep it open. Or I swear . . .' He waved the gun between Jacquot and Claudine.

Jacquot turned, waved Brunet away from the controls. The gate stopped with a jerk.

Inside the car, Antoine dug Claudine in the leg with the gun. 'Drive, fuck it! Just drive – now!'

But the car was pointing in the wrong direction, away from the gate. Claudine tried to find reverse and the gears grated, the engine stalled.

'Go forward – go forward and turn!' he shouted, and as Claudine restarted the engine and wrestled with the gear stick, Jacquot thought about rushing the car, getting hold of the gun. But he knew he'd never make it.

And now the car was moving, swinging round in a tight circle, wheels screeching on the hot Tarmac, Antoine keeping the gun on Jacquot every inch of the way.

As they drew level, sunshine glancing off the windscreen, Claudine tried a smile for Jacquot, but it didn't work. She looked terrified. And then she saw him raise his right hand to his left shoulder and sweep it down across his chest. Claudine frowned. He did it again. And then she understood. And suddenly looked very scared.

'Let's go! Let's go!' screamed Antoine.

Gripping the steering-wheel, Claudine started forward, gradually increasing her speed, then pushed down hard on the accelerator. The car surged forward, heading for the open gates, but at the last moment she swung the wheel to the left and threw up her hands as the gatepost bore down on them.

It took only a second or two for Antoine to realise what was happening. Desperately he snatched at the wheel to correct their course. The bitch was—

But it was too late. The Citroën hit the pillar a little off-centre, hard enough to have the back wheels lift off the ground, hard enough for de Vausigne to lift off too, his chest slamming on to the dashboard, doubling him over, his head and shoulders splintering through the windscreen.

As Jacquot ran to the car, he could see that Antoine was no longer a threat, the top half of his body slammed up against the concertinaed bonnet as though embracing it, blood spilling from his face, the gun lying out of reach on the Tarmac.

But Claudine . . .

Held back by her seat-belt, her head drooped on to her chest, a fall of hair concealing her face. But she was alive. He could hear her moaning.

'Claudine!' Jacquot tried to pull open her door but it was stuck fast. He reached in, carefully lifted back her hair. Her eyes were clenched tight shut, her wrist lay at an odd angle in her lap, but she was talking, saying something.

Jacquot leaned closer.

'My brushes,' she cried. 'He's broken my brushes.'

88

Jacquot took the road for St Bédard, changing down for the first of the hairpins out of Rocsabin, playing the wheel through the turns that followed, tapping his fingers to a rousing Jackie Wilson number. It was a week since the de Vausignes' arrest and he had been out to see Max Benedict, to thank him for his help in the Martner killings and the Rocsabin fire – the gun and the scrape of paint – and to provide, off the record, of course, an account of the de Vausignes' involvement, in case Benedict was planning any further features. It seemed the very least that Jacquot could do.

The two of them had had lunch together on Benedict's terrace, an omelette, some salad and *chèvre*, a bottle of Bandol, with Mailer and Vidal lying on their sides, panting in the shade.

'Will he live? De Vausigne?' Benedict had asked.

'He'll live, but he won't be making any films for a while.'

'And Claudine?'

'She broke her wrist, cracked her collarbone.'

'I shall send her flowers.'

'She'd like that.'

Normally Jacquot would have driven back to Cavaillon the way he had come but after their lunch he'd decided to return via St Bédard. There was something he wanted to do. Someone else he wanted to see. It was the first chance he'd had since news of the de Vausignes' arrest had broken, seven days of bedlam after the

404

Chabert trial in Lyon was halted and the jury dismissed. On TV Jacquot had watched with quiet satisfaction as his old colleague Gastal, red-faced with fury, was mobbed by journalists outside the Palais de Justice, refusing to answer any questions, fighting his way down the steps to a waiting car.

In St Bédards, parking behind the *mairie*, Jacquot crossed the Brieuc road, passed into the shade of the plane trees and made his way across the *place* to the Fontaine des Fleurs. They'd spoken on the phone, of course, but he was looking forward to seeing her, thanking her in person. But as he drew closer, Jacquot saw the grille was down, the shop shut.

Wednesday. Half-day closing.

At the door he rang the bell, heard it sound somewhere inside. But there was no answer. He turned and looked round the square.

Maybe Mazzelli's, he thought.

Which was when André Ribaud walked by. 'The Chaberts will be back later today, Monsieur. If you're looking for Mademoiselle Buhl, then I am sorry to say she has gone. Closed the shop after lunch. Told me she'd write. Is there any message?'

89

Only old Dumé saw her leave.
From the cool, rustling shadows of the olives he watched the silvery spokes flash between the vines as she spun downhill, hair flying, shoulders thrust forward, legs held tense, feet on the pedals as the bike picked up speed on the long, cornering descent, cycling out of their lives and the life of St Bédard for ever.

We'll miss her, he thought sadly, and that's the truth. And he felt in his pockets for his pipe and tobacco.